SIMPLE THINGS OF LIFE
A Novel

SIMPLE THINGS OF LIFE
A Novel

DHARANIDHAR SAHU

ATLANTIC PUBLISHERS AND DISTRIBUTORS

Published by
ATLANTIC PUBLISHERS AND DISTRIBUTORS
B-2, Vishal Enclave, Opp. Rajouri Garden, New Delhi-27
Phones : 5413460, 5429987

Sales Office
4215/1, Ansari Road, Darya Ganj, New Delhi-110 002
Phones : 3273880, 3285873, 3280451
Fax : 91-11-3285873
e-mail : info@atlanticbooks.com
web : www.atlanticbooks.com

ISBN 81-269-0028-8

Typeset at
APD Computer Graphics, Delhi

Printed in India at
Mehra Offset Press, Delhi

Dedicated to My Children
PIKU, LIPI *and* LISA
with a cautionary request :
Do not find your Bapa in
Debasis or in Anjan da.
Needless to add, all characters
and events in this book are fictitious.

On lonely traveller, rest awhile, move on!
No need to stay put, no need to run.
You are on a strange planet, you know.
You will meet surprises wherever you go.
You have no idea, no maps, no guide.
If problems come, take them in your stride.
If you find something good and beautiful,
Smile from ear to ear and feel grateful.
If you get something ugly and bad,
Stop smiling, philosophise and feel sad.
The frenetic and the placid, the wild and the tame,
The bad and the beautiful, the hurricane and the flame
Have been playing this game of love and strife
Known otherwise as the Simple Things of Life
Since the time when the earth was young.
Lo, in the flicker of that flame, I write this song.

Anonyomus
(Translated from Oriya by the author)

CONTENTS

PART I

1. Mysteries, Disturbances 1
2. Infolimia 8
3. The Mumbo-Jumbo 18
4. A Case of Lynching 37
5. On the Top of A Mountain, A stream 47

PART II

6. An Apology, A visitor 49
7. At the Dinner Table 56

PART III

8. Down the Memory Lane 69
9. Rooming with Andy 77
10. Uri and the Tenants 82
11. Trivia and Trinkets 84
12. I Stand Confessed 89
13. Anjan da Meets Uri 94
14. The Upshot of Love 105
15. Anjan da's visit : A Romance 122
16. Terror on the Beach 125
17. The Snow White Cat 131
18. A Secret Proposal 135
19. A Love Story 144
20. Appearance and Change 147

21. Andy in Love 149
22. Blood and Thunder 156
23. Andy and Krishnā 166
24. Gulling the Rogue 170
25. The Soothsayer 177
26. The Fly in the Marmalade 179
27. A Dispute, A Digression 182
28. A Peculiar Sickness 187
29. Walking in Sleep 196
30. A Peculiar Sickness (Two) 201
31. The Pressure of Guilt 204
32. Revelation 212
33. Convalescence 224
34. Anjan da's Second Visit : A Bad Joke 227
35. An Accident 251

PART IV

36. A Pleasant Surprise : Andy and His Wife 256
37. An Expedition 265
38. The Woman and the Anchorite 282

PART I

1

MYSTERIES, DISTURBANCES

I was in the labyrinth of a dream. In a haze of what to do.

I clearly remember I was not a mute spectator. Not a passive dreamer.

I told them : "Dear Friends, have patience, show forebearance towards the snake. This is no ordinary snake. Have you ever seen a big snake as green as this one? For your own safety, let the extraordinary alone."

Now, the wild mob is hard at it. With crow-bars, plough-shares, hockey sticks, hatchets, sticks, sickles, portable rocks, muscular hands, bare bodies, grimaces of violence and oodles of frenzy.

The snake is dead, mutilated. It's so green, so big, so shining. Its tail shows the last flicker of animation, then it lies still.

The mob hates snakes. I've feeling these people's violence has something to do with the snake's greenness. I watch a burly man emerging from the crowd. He has strong hands. His face is disfigured with hate. He holds a long crow-bar. He walks onto the dead snake and strikes it repeatedly with all his brute force. He wants to make sure the snake is dead. He casts a villainous look at me. I avert my eyes from the sight.

I stand at a remove with a young woman : my sister, or my wife, or my mother when she was young. I look at the carcass of the snake, fascinated by its colour and its great size. The memory of the event makes me sick; I mull it over in my mind. How quickly these violent rogues reduced a magnificent, mobile and defenseless creature into a heap of cerulean meat!

That's done it. The crowd disperses in all directions. We two — I and the young woman of whose relationship with me I cannot be sure — stand riveted to the ground, gazing blinklessly at the dead snake. I've a hunch that my young companion has either co-operated with the crowd of snakehaters, or silently approved of its action; that, for me, it was a loss; for her, a good riddance.

As we watch it well-nigh hypnotised, the green heap begins to stir. Earlier it struck me as a common snake. Now the word "python" occurs to me : the great green python that slouches about slowly in the dense forests, bosky heaths and bracken-covered terraces of mountains.

Its tail wags, and slowly gathers a tuft of brown hair. Its smashed snake-head becomes the large head of a lion complete with mane and deep-set, feline eyes. Its colour changes from green to pale yellow. It stands on all fours, shaking off its mortality. I am filled with amazement and fear. I sweat.

My young companion trembles. She is primed for flight. "That means it was not truly dead," she whispers.

"Didn't I say it was extraordinary? Where on earth have you seen a green python? Didn't I tell those felons not to kill the snake?" I say.

"You gave them a good reason to kill it," she says, and then adds : "The snake's extraordinariness reduced its chance of survival."

"What do you mean?"

We both realise it's no time for argument.

The big beast glares around menacingly, letting out a muffled roar. Then it sees us, and walks towards us with slow stiff strides.

My young companion panics and hares off in the direction of the hutted camps and sloping-roofed, mud-walled houses. I take another road that runs parallel to the embankment of a canal. The lion quickens its pace. It chases the young woman first. I am worried about her safety, and wish anxiously she should get into a house and escape the beast. For some unknown reason, I am utterly unable to run. I, however, walk fast breaking into a jog fitfully, turning frequently backwards to see if the lion caught hold of the dear young woman. The lion loses the sight of her and gives up the chase. Now it approaches me. Its ferocious face, its shaggy mane shaking, its tongue flicking, is looming large before me. My legs get stiff. I stand stock still. The beast lumbers past me without attacking me.

A profound feeling of optimism seems to have possessed me : the lion chooses its prey. The behaviour of the lion reminds me of a dream about another performing beast I dreamt long ago. It seems that a dream which contains a message of sorts may become a folklore of the mind. "This is no ordinary beast," I keep persuading myself.

I watch the wood-cutter's charming daughter. She sits on a shaded rock, crooning a sad song, making a garland of pink fuchsia and scarlet flame-of-the-forest she has just gathered. A few yards from where she sits, a mountain stream with black waters flows by. She hears the roar of the lion, but she is not at all afraid. It is as if she is waiting for it and making a garland for it.

I know; I become aware of what has happened to her.

The bandits are rough, large and cruel. They love to kill defenseless travellers and villagers and to loot. They've killed her father two years ago. They pulled him out of the wooden cabin, called him an informer. "You grassed on us," they told him coldly, "and you must die." The man denied the charge, but they won't listen. They killed him in front of his twelve year old daughter. The bandit leader spared the girl. He declared to make her his moll when she would attain her puberty. The bandits have stuffed the girl's cottage with food grains, fruits and ornaments. The leader has told his mates to keep a strict watch over the girl. She is a captive. Like a tropical fruit, she is ripening to be devoured. She feels lonely, weeps for her father, befriends trees, stones, butterflies, birds and the mountain stream with black waters.

In the middle of the jungle, the bandits gather to relax. They see an old lion in a thicket, and shoot it with their guns — just for fun. They pump one hundred bullets into the massive body of the natural king of the forest. They have plenty of bullets to spare.

Now, they build a fire, roast a couple of mountain goats and a full-grown deer on barbecues, drink rum straight from the bottles, relax, stretching their limbs, joking, laughing insouciantly, shouting, singing, sniffing the flavour of roasted meat. Not far from where the bandits revel lies the carcass of the lion, its skin riddled with bullet holes, dark blood leaking out of each hole.

All of a sudden, as the thugs are busy making merry, the body of the lion begins to stir, stands up on all fours, shakes the dry leaves and inertia off and sends out a big roar to announce its unexpected return. They see the resurrected beast and are filled with apocryphal terror. Stunned and scared shit, the bandits — some drunk, some tipsy, some sober — run helter-skelter, bumping into one another. Some take to their heels, some clamber over rocks, some climb up the trees, some lurch drunkenly, some slip into the thicket and crevices, some simply stay put. The bandit leader, a mastodon of a man with walrus moustaches tries to reach for his gun. The lion pounces on him and tears him to pieces, tearing at his flesh with its teeth. After making an example of the leader of the gang, it makes short work of those who stood transfixed to the ground, of those who failed to make good their escape.

It pulls a burning brand and drops it on the big pile of boots, guns, looted property, bandits' clothes, daggers, cartridge-belts, etc. Cotton catches fire first, then leather, cartridges, guns — smoking, crackling, exploding.

The lion watches the bonfire standing on a rock, and then it lopes off into the forest guided by its unerring sense of smell, tracks down its quarries by shaking and even uprooting the trees on which they perch, by chasing them as they run for cover, by crouching into the thickets where they hide. It attacks one bandit at a time, sinks its teeth and claws into their bodies, skewering and tearing the limbs apart, smacking its lips with a lazy ferocity of purpose, watching them die slowly. It seems to be sure of its power, and so allows each bandit a chance to save himself if he could. But it doesn't happen. Their race for life turns out to be an extension of horror and trembling. It stalks one bandit after another, roaring, whimpering, its heavy mane drenched in blood, its body riddled with bullet-holes which, like the eyes of Argus, see everything, its tail raised aloft like a pennant of siege. It moves with bounding strides, stops short at the sight of a bandit, scowls at him, opens its jaws wide, then snaps them shut, and then attacks him physically. It locates six bandits who perch precariously on the branch of a big, gnarled tree. It clambers up the tree like a cat and shakes the branches with all its force. They drop to the ground like ripe mangoes — ripe for its maw.

Now the lion is scouting about the forest for the remaining bandits. As if it wants to scour the evil off. It heads for the hide-out of the bandits, a natural cave surrounded with trees. The remaining bandits have regrouped their forces to recoil on the lion. When they see the beast, they train their guns on it and shoot; they spray bullets on its already battered body, but, lo and behold, it advances undeterred towards the shooters, pounces on them and bites off their heads. It is as though the soul is determined to keep living in the ruins of the body. It is possessed with an anger that can never be placated, with a frenzied, diabolical force — unstoppable like the fury of a tornado. Words like terminator, incubus, scourge keep occurring to me as I watch the death-defying predator spreading real panic among the bandits who are used to spreading terror.

The wood-cutter's daughter seems to have grown considerably as I am watching the movements of the lion. Now, she is not a slip of a girl, but a full-blown stunningly beautiful ingenue, leggy, lissome and laid back. She kneels deliciously on a rock amidst flowers — magnolias, crimson rhododendrons, flame flowers, scarlet hibiscuses, arranged in small separate heaps — crooning a sad song and making a garland. She reminds me of my sister, my wife, and my mother when she was young, though she does not resemble any of them. Two bandits come running. They tell her to get into the cabin immediately : "A lion is hot on our trail. Hey wench! Get into the cabin or climb a tree, quick!" The young lady doesn't care.

"You thieves, you killed my father. Let the lion kill me." She mutters these words without looking up.

The bandits get into the wooden cabin and latch the door from within.

The lion walks with long majestic strides towards the cabin. The young lady, now decked out with flowers, looks up quietly and sees the beast. It sees her and sends out a mighty roar which sounds like a groan. The lion stands near the closed door of the cabin and tries to push it open. The cabin shakes, the door rattles. The two bandits apply their full force to the door. But the door soon yields. The lion enters the cabin and makes short work of them. The wooden floor is flooded with blood. The flower lady watches the lion. A brief smile blooms on her lips. A smile of grateful appreciation! She is not afraid of the beast. She finds in it a kindred spirit. It does what she wants to do herself.

The lion walks onto her. Now it does not roar. It purrs like a familiar cat. It looks at the standing young lady with tender eyes. Then it collapses to the ground. She kneels down in front of the carcass and places a garland on its head.

I wish with all my heart the dream ended there. But it goes on. The young woman goes back to her seat on the rock and busies herself in her work. Every now, and again she looks at the dead lion. The massive body lies a few yards away its face, mane and body plastered all over with the dried blood of the bandits, every part of its tawny, dirty-looking skin riddled with bullet-holes. Open wounds attract flies, large green flies. Now a million flies settle on the carcass which looks like a monstrous beehive.

Once again the carcass stirs. The pretty damsel sitting on her flowery perch notices it, and is surprised. All of a sudden, it stands up on all fours, raises its tail, opens its mouth wide, smacks its lips. In the gathering gloom of the evening, its eyes flicker like fireflies. It slews around and glares belligerantly at the kneeling woman. There's slaughter in its eyes. She stands up nervously. It tears off the garland with its paws. It moves towards the trembling woman and ravishes her.

The work done, it bounced out of the forest into the world of man. The night falls. The moon shines through the leaf-fringed branches. The mountain stream with pitch-black waters flows by. The re-resurrected beast, it occurs to me, does not discriminate. The Doomsday beast, sheathed in a blanket of flies, prefers the human world to the jungle. It kills beauty and innocence. The mauled body of the wood-cutter's daughter stretching full-length on the rock amidst flowers bears testimony to its utter lack of discrimination. In the human world, ten thousands bullets will be pumped into its already bullet-torn body, ten thousand swords will slice its body, ten thousand spears will pierce its sides, but this creature will not flinch and slacken its rage. The arsenals of the world cannot disturb the flies covering its body, let alone kill it.

It was a frightful dream. It made me feel sick. Still reeling under the impact of the dream, I decided not to entertain such dreams in future. "If the dream is bad and disturbing," I told my somnolent self, "it should not be dreamt in the first place." In the morning, while basking in the winter sunshine, I considered myself funny for taking such an improbable decision. "Dreams choose their dreamers, not dreamers their dreams," I corrected myself. What made me feel wretched and confused was that one bad dream could rake up the memories of a worse one of similar nature. That dream kept me preoccupied for weeks. It tempted me with an ambiguous symbolism. It begged of me an interpretation. One day while chitchatting with my friends I described the dream in a nutshell and asked them to interpret it for me. They didn't take it seriously. They all agreed that a dream was after all a dream and only the neurotic and superstitious people bothered about its significance. Tapas, one of my listeners, a morose-looking man of forty told me confidentially when we were alone : "Look, yaar, these dreams will make your life hell if you don't leave them alone. Do you know why my wife left me? I have not told you that. She saw me chasing, kissing, embracing even screwing other women, in the dream of course and went on interrogating me about it whenever we had a chance to talk to each other.

"She was such a fine woman before these blasted dreams poisoned her mind. She became a perfect shrew, a nagging detective. Honestly, yaar, it got on my nerves. I lost my temper. She had already lost hers. She went away with our four year old son to her father's house. She has not written me a single letter in these three months. I tell you frankly I've no affair with other women; so?"

Tapan's story gave me good cause to forget the dreams, particularly those unpleasant ones which had teasing undercurrents of meaning. But the mind loves to remember what it decides to forget. The more I remembered my dreams, the deeper I was drawn into the whirlpool of my self. Small events loomed large. Events that had nothing to do with me appeared very urgent and personal. Even when I thought I was walking on the beaten track of reason, I found myself wandering in the pathless woods.

2

INFOLIMIA

I found myself wandering in the labyrinth of news.

For people like me, news has always been something that other people do, or are made to do. So I had practically no trouble in dealing with the newspapers. Just as a vegetarian skims over the list of non-veg items in a menu out of casual curiosity. But after that dream about the lion, I felt a change within me.

Like photographic paper, my mind and heart became sensitive to light of day, to external events. I began to believe that in order to understand life and the world around me I should have to know, and reflect upon, what our most conscientious media served me with. They take so much of trouble to collect whatever is happening in our big, strange world, in the outer space, in the mind of man, in the animal kingdom — the tragedies that trouble mankind, the comedies, the farces, the vaude-villes, the antiques, the aberrations that entertain mankind, the mysteries, the miracles that surprise mankind, the human holocausts and the natural catastrophes that stalk mankind, the scientific and intellectual inventions that enrich and enlighten mankind, the absurdities which confound mankind and the beautiful perspectives that give a sense of euphoria and contentment.

The news reminds us of our middle state, of the inescapable paradoxes of our lives. It tells us we live timidly in a brave new world. It tells us that the modern man has feet of medieval clay; that we bring the skeletons out of our cupboards and display them proudly in our drawing rooms. The news tells us how man harnesses nature, fuses and diffuses atoms to acquire power; how people fox each other in thousand different ways, how Nature is outraged, how in retaliation Nature clamps curfew on the perverse humanity by releasing incurable epidemics.

The news has ravished me, intoxicated me. I have come to realize that the news is the thing. People are busy making it, breaking it and taking it. Sometimes the market fluctuates, and the makers of news outnumber the takers. A glut of news. Dime a dozen sort of situation. Then the media buy it cheap, deck it out, garnish it, varnish it till it glitters, and then broker it.

The space craft Galileo transmits photographs from the fifth planet Jupiter, dead men backslide to their old habit of living to tell us about their adventures to the beyond, poverty stalks the third world, an uncontrollable prosperity afflicts the first world and economic reforms push the second world to a lunatic fringe; money, power, religion and sex — the redoubtable foursome — play a round of golf on the golf-links of human mind using man's reason as a ball; prehistoric alchemy is staging a comeback; water is changed into petrol, brass is transmuted into gold and coal into diamonds; one superfast train rams into a herd of hundred buffaloes, skids off the rails and leaves ten thousand dead; one baby is miraculously saved when two jumbo jets dash against each other at a height of twenty five thousand feet; in the cities, the pavement dwellers breed like rabbits, and they will outnumber the house dwellers in a not so distant future; countries hedge their borders with long-range ballistic missiles fitted with nuclear warheads; cockroaches, the scientists predict, would survive a nuclear holocaust; at least one million planets in the universe support life; an overcrowded boat capsizes in the Brahamaputra, two hundred feared killed; mother drowns her children to please her lover; an American woman cuts her husband's sexual organ irritated by his amorous advances; poisonous gas leaks out in the midnight killing sixty thousand people in their sleep; balloons filled with germs float in the air; angry villagers lynch thirty one suspected witches; nine hundred fifty prisoners and under-trails have their eyes gouged out by the righteously indignant policemen; the Serbs, the Croats, the Chechenians, the Taliban, the Tamil Tigers, the Suicide Squads, the Ulfas, the Bodos, the Irish rebels, the terrorists in the Punjab and Kashmir, the Naxalites, the Skin Heads, the Hamas, the Ku Klux Klan, the Drug mafias, the Neo-Nazis and a dozen militant outfits — all armed with A K 47's, A K 56's, rocket launchers, dynamite, time bombs, idealisms and cyanide tablets — are fighting for their respective causes. Determined to be newsworthy for a day, to hug the limelight for an hour, people bitch, streak, run berserk, train their guns on humanity, contradict themselves, fulminate, and, if nothing works, buy the limelight.

"Not only now, but always, I tell you," says a wag, "Money has the last laugh. Virtue is its Man Friday, beauty its moll. And the world's grapevine has it all."

Once, when I was in a painful state of excess, fluttering like a fly caught in a cyberweb, or like a sparrow, trapped in an Internet, I casually enquired : "What news Puja?" I thought she'd take it easy and talk about the weather. I was much mistaken in that. Infected perhaps by my maniacal enthusiasm for news, she had taken great pains to arrange the headlines and scoops from a wodge of old newspapers in the shape of an awkwardly scribbled, a more awkwardly rhyming song. Inspired by a most impersonal passion, (if such a thing is humanly possible), she yacked away, she kept yacking on :

"A lot, darling, a slew, an epic of information :
A Libyan delegation comes on a three-day visit :
The inflation rate soars to a double digit.
It's politically incorrect to call women wo-men;
They've found the secrets of a dinosaur's brain.
Archaeologists have excavated the Noah's arc :
Scientists have discovered Top the sixth quark.
Ecologists are busy greening the Sahara desert,
Cows yield more milk after listening to Mozart,
The Beatles and the Punks are staging a comeback,
Economic reforms draw a lot of flak.
The brewers of Bavaria have concocted a beer
That'd make its grey takers green with desire.
Married couples proudly declare their adultery,
Cancer kills annually fewer people than dowry,
An ecological disaster is coming upon us
As trees are felled to give our writers a chance.
Psephologists say after the general elections,
The LS will be a rag-bag of sixty political factions.
And the President, using his constitutional authority,
Will give one month to each party to prove it's majority.
As a result, this country, in a span of just five years,
Will have sixty PMs and sixty councils of ministers.
In a world where hopes are cheap and fulfilments, dear
Let each aspirant be great at least for an hour.
Apocryphal stories are doing the rounds here
About the rake-offs, kick-backs, the misuse of power.

About woman who to carve out a career,
Have decided never to say no;
About men who, to acquire money and power,
Practice volte-face and quid pro quo.
Politics and subornation have secret links;
Some scams lie embalmed, but the Bofors stinks.
All's honky dory with the mafia and the vigilante.
The Judge calls the Parliament a fish market.
Ornithologists say, in so far as building skills go,
Man is not wiser than the New Caledonian Crow.
Genetic engineers work day and night
To turn swans black and crows white.
Technocrats, computer-nerds and business men
Try transcendence thro' TM, Bipasanā yoga and zen.
The epidemic that struck Surat was plague;
The Western leaders meet tomorrow at the Hague
To deliberate on the NPT, sanctions and aids;
The peacekeeping jawans mount four raids
On the militants' hideouts in Srinagar;
India will host many an international seminar
On American exceptionalism, on pisciculture,
On how to stem the depletion of the ozone layer.
On the lumpenization of politics, on the orchids,
On the issue of God's gender, on the giant sqids,
On the questions of equal status and rights
Of the lesbians, gays, eunuchs, hermaphrodites,
Of people possessing portmanteau souls,
Transvestites, drag queens, transsexuals,
Beggars, lepers, heterosexuals, freaks, scavengers,
The people suffering from AIDS and the whores...."

Puja might have gone on had I not implored her with folded hands to stop reciting her listings.

The Argus-eyed media, armed with most advanced technologies; super computers, geosynchronous satellites, audio-visual contraptions, have appropriated God's omniscience and omnipresence, and acquired the divine ability to scan the macro and the micro worlds at a single glance, taking note of a sparrow's fall and a leviathan's siege, the death of a quark and the birth of a star. And what do I do? Simple! I, like the most of my tribe, glut myself with the news items dexterously collected, deliciously cooked and attractively packaged by the media. Like that Egyptian femme fatale Cleopatra, news makes its takers hungry when most it satisfies because of its unfading charm and infinite variety.

As my restlessness increased, I tried to look at the situation differently. In other words, I felt a need to measure the extent to which my recent craze to acquire information has contributed to my feeling restless. When a man gets hungrier after eating, he may be suffering from a psychopathological disorder called bulimia. Just as men who suffer from satyriasis and women who suffer from nymphomania do not understand what it feels like to be sexually satisfied. Just as people who are possessed with an uncontrollable desire to make a fire, to set anything they see ablaze, are supposedly suffering from pyro-mania.

Such symptoms even if they appear in a majority of mankind cannot be called healthy ones, because these desires logically contradict the very function of their fulfilment. By refuting the possibility of fulfilment, the desires cease to be desires and become forms of illnsss.

One day I was visited by a friend who happened to be a doctor by profession and rationalist by choice. Witty, cantankerous and well-informed as he was, any conversation with him, however innocent the topic and self-effacing the other party may be, was sure to grow into an argument. Any simple idea I dropped would be a red rag to his bullish mind. To agree with another man, to support someone else's idea on any conceivable issue was an insult to his originality, which he would never own up. It seems, he had already thought seriously on all the ideas the human mind is capable of conceiving and formed his own opinions on them.

Least apprehending his belligerent disagreement, I introduced my findings on the nature of my illness.

"Dr Poak," said I, "When an appetite scorns cloying, we call it gluttony; in the case of food, it's bulimia, in the case of sex, it's nymphomania or satyriasis depending on the gender of the patient. I have, of late, suspected my unappeasable desire to know everything that is taking place everywhere without pausing to know what purpose my knowledge would serve; then I've dubbed it a form of illness, named it **Infolimia,** an upstart neologism which means an insatiable appetite for information. I've also found that this disease, which has assumed epidemic proportions in the contemporary world, has a bright future and little or no chance of being eradicated because both the patients suffering from it and the people who have not yet been contaminated by it consider it an auspicious and wholesome acquisition of the mind; that far from being a sickness, it is a sign of good health and advancement."

Dr. Poak was much peeved by my idea and its extended expostulation. He lifted his bushy eyebrows as a child lifts a dead cockroach by its whiskers.

"Hey, Debasis," said he, "if I understand what you mean your sickness lies in considering it a sickness. I'd rather you visited a psychiatrist who cures a number of imaginary ailments by prescribing placebos."

He looked around, saw Puja standing at the door, listening to our conversation, and requested her with cordial familiarity to make tea.

I could sense his intentions. He wanted to send her to the kitchen.

"First of all, Debasis," he said confidentially when he saw her gone, "the thing such as nymphomania and satyriasis, which you so piously brand as disorders, and which you find in people with hyperactive libidos, are actually blessings in disguise. When the sword and the scabbard love each other to distraction and cling to each other inextricably, struggle is the first casualty.

When there is no struggle, there can be no conflict. What does the Holy Bible say? "Put thy sword into his place : for all thee take the sword shall perish with the sword." Have you ever seen people fighting and killing and injuring each other with their sheathed swords? In order to help life maintain itself on this earth, Nature has made a few people wise, and she made a majority of people otherwise. And those who are made otherwise are endowed, for reasons best known to their creator, with a lot of life-denying, peace hating, malevolent energy which if not properly utilized, diverted and spent in less harmful activities would create real havoc, destroy life and defeat the very purpose of creation. I firmly believe, I'm sure you'll believe, that if the world's highest honours, awards, rewards, etc. would ever be given to the causes instead of their champions, they should be given to nymphomania, satyriasis, bulimia, etc. because these traits divert the dangerous and surplus energy to relatively less harmful preoccupation. Isn't love better than war? That's the butterfly of my point, man; try to catch it. I also advocate for bulimia on the grounds that when a man spends most of his waking hours in eating, he is left with little time for beating others. Again, a great eater would soon become fat, flabby, lazy and immobile, and spend most of his remaining time in bed, or in the loo or in the gym to shed his unmanageable blubber. So where is the time to be in a fret, to harm mankind?

I was getting impatient. "Doctor Poak, Doctor insect," I thought peevishly, "Would you never stop yammering!" but I said : "You see Dr. Poak, I can catch the butterfly or the gadfly of your point if I wish to, but I don't subscribe to your view of things. Nature cannot make people unnatural, nor can she be pleased with it. These excuses are like the drugs which...." "Yes drugs, the psychedelic drugs," Dr. Poak snatched my sentence; "I was just going to refer to the drugs." My position regarding the uses of drugs is well-known. The arguments I put forward for nymphomania and bulimia are also applicable to drug addiction.

"Look, Debasis. Try to think clearly. Drugs do more than the scriptures and law courts can, to restrict violence, to curb corruption. It rhymes, ha, ha. Now I'll tell you how. If you follow the line of my argument, you can guess; but I'll explain it nonetheless. A drug addict considers himself the monarch of his nut-shelled empire, and leaves the real world alone. Have you ever seen a man cocooned in such a paradisiacal contentment and blissful intoxication trying to colonize other's worlds? No, you won't. So, I'd rather suggest the conscientious government, instead of banning drug use, make drugs freely available at a subsidized rate."

"Now about your newly found sickness, what do you call it?"

"Infolimia," I said, and hastened to add "It's an acronym for information bulimia which stands for an uncontrollable desire to acquire information, without bothering to know what to do with it; a relentless curiosity bordering on frenzy."

"Didn't I say, Debasis, it's a sick mind which calls a perfectly healthy habit a sick syndrome. You question the very basis of knowledge. You glance at the question papers for recruitment tests for such jobs as Bank assistants, Junior typists and Administrative services. The candidates are required to know the plays of Kalidas, the heroine of Hamlet, who killed who in the Mahabharat battle, Quantum theory, Einstein's famous equation $E=MC^2$, Bill Gates, the Hawala scandal, Marcel Proust, Magic Johnson, Catch-22 situation, Michael Angelo, the Beatles, the director of Gone With the Wind and Glasnost. The list goes on and on. Why do they ask these questions? Because the candidate is supposed to know these things. Those who know more get the job."

I waved my hand desperately to restrain him. I feared he would never stop. After listening to Puja's long song on news, I was pathologically scared of the listings. As soon as he paused, I. blurted out : "That was not my point, far from it. Candidates, I know, are subjected to that sort of gruelling test. So they have every reason to know as much as they can to get a job. Their curiosity is perfectly understandable. Once they get jobs, they'll call it quits. I only mean these millions of people, and I've no hesitation to confess I am one of them, who are well in their middle ages and even old ages. And they have neither chance nor hope to make use of their mind-boggling store of information."

Dr. Poak cleared his throat. "I consider those people who have no chance or hope to capitalize on information, and yet never slacken their zeal in acquiring it, superior to those who use their acquired information to get jobs or seats. In the former case it's knowledge for its own sake. The modern world is an extended family, or we may call it our big little village. Is it not proper for a good villager to know what' s happening in his village? It is a sacred, hence important, responsibility which we ought not forsake, lest we should be called irresponsible, ignorant. Frankly, Debasis, you are doing the most proper thing by gathering information. Your fault, however, lies in finding fault with your correct enthusiasm. The world becomes a better place when it is peopled with cognoscenti and literati, than with ignoramuses and dunces. My motto is : Dear folks, get obsessed with something less dangerous, some good will come of it. At least, you'll be saved from doing something more dangerous, say from cognizable offence. How do you like my motto?"

I wished to contradict Dr. Poak with : You godless rogue, your crass rule of thumb rules out the very possibility of transcendence. As if man is born only to desist from evil. As if staying put is a sign of progress ! As if status quo is civilization! Why can't man get obsessed with higher aspirations? You show symptoms of an incurable, chronic confidence. I leave you at that stage."

But I said amicably to him instead : "Very well."

The world, I reflected gloomily, is peopled with the likes of Dr. Poak and their supporters. My problem was mine not theirs. They prescribe, even practise obsession. I feel utterly wretched by being obsessed. Our roads will never converge. So I offered Dr. Poak two cups of tea and led him to the gate. I strained my politeness by saying "Sure" when he insisted "We'll meet again and discuss about your 'Infolimia' at length."

I decided several times to ignore the events that didn't concern me, to break myself free from the clutch of information. But, alas, the more I tried to escape, the deeper grew my obsession. Then I threw off my hands and shrugged my shoulders and chuckled to myself, and realized : "If this disease called Infolimia is a modern one and it has attacked you, you've to suffer from it. You cannot cure it by being impatient. If anything can go wrong, it'll certainly go wrong, however, hard you try to set it right."

3

THE MUMBO-JUMBO

The rainy season passed without a downpour. Once or twice it drizzled. Several times black clouds reared, spread across the sky, darkened the day, crackled, rumbled, sparkled and finally dispersed into serrated specks of cotton wool. Clouds, when they rose higher, loafed and glittered, but became utterly waterless and detached. Height enucleated them. Distance rendered them impersonal. The earth was dry. The crops failed. Tanks, rivers and wells got dry. Essential commodities became scarce. Prices rose vertically. Dogs howled throughout the night. Houses were burgled; ornaments were snatched in broad day light; some godowns were looted by the desperate villagers. The ministers and lesser representatives of people announced : the government has enough foodgrains; drinking water will be supplied plentifully at the doorsteps; agriculture and other loans upto twenty thousand will be waived; inflation will be brought low; seeds and saplings will be supplied to the farmers free of cost; the Centre has sanctioned fifty one crores to fight the draught situation — and people are advised not to panick.

But the people knew better. They knew such promises were empty, dry like the high floating white clouds. They know that age-old truth : If you're poor, you're at the mercy of the weather.

Man cannot control the weather, only the gods can. The old men said they had never witnessed a rainy season without rain; that when the gods wanted to punish mankind, they sent down droughts, famines, floods, earth-quakes, cyclones, hurricanes and epidemics; that the gods had one hundred and one reasons to be angry with mankind, etc. etc.

After a gap of more than three months since the last drizzle, on the 19th of October, jet black clouds rose from the western horizon. People watched them rise higher and higher. It was midday. In less than two hours the entire sky was covered with the dark dense cloud mass. The world was plunged in darkness. People prayed hopefully.

Then it rained.

Full three days and two nights it rained continuously. Thousands of young men, women and children stood in the rain dancing and singing. Old men smiled, revealing their gums.

The weather cleared on the fourth day. The river, the tanks, the wells and the ponds were brimming with water. Frogs kept on croaking all through the night. Life returned to normal. But four days after it rained again, continuously and heavily, for six days and seven nights. Rumours floated like rooftops. Rain water washed away trees, electricity poles, thatched roofs, belongings, godowns, cattle, goats, sheep, dogs, cats, and thousands of human beings, turned land into sea. All rivers got mixed up — denuding the land, enriching the sea. People could not remember what the ministers and government officials had promised. They prayed and cried and panicked. Telephone and electricity connections were dislocated. Postal service was disrupted.

Rains stopped on the eighth day. The sun shone on the submerged land. Water receded slowly. Life returned to normal after a month, or so. Seeds were sown, plants were planted, new houses sprang up where old houses stood, buildings were whitewashed and gardens were again hedged. The old men said they had never witnessed such rain in all their lives. The gods figured prominently in their talks.

The winter was unusually cold that year. In January, mercury dropped to seven degree celsius, about five degrees lower than normal winter temperature. Old people died in thousands. Government and many charity organizations distributed blankets and woollen garments. Big trees were hacked down to warm the houses. In towns as well as villages, life came to a virtual standstill at the nightfall.

On the third day of February, an old woman, while worshipping the bronze idol of Lord Krishna when he was a cowherd boy, heard the sound of flute. She looked up suspiciously. Coming out of her prayer room, she looked around to locate the flutist. She found none. On reentering the prayer room, she heard the melodious tune of the flute. Unable to believe her own ears, she called out to her twenty eight years old son, a farmer and her daughter of eighteen.

"Do You hear the flute?" she asked them as soon as the entered the room.

They heard the flute. The sound was coming unmistakably from Lord Krishna's flute. They could not hear any sound when they came out of the room.

The news of Lord Krishna playing flute spread rapidly from mouth to mouth. Curious people gathered. People who entered the prayer room heard the flute, and while there. But they could not hear it when they crossed the threshold. Hundreds of people — men, women and children, boys and girls — vowed that they heard the sound of God's flute while in the puja room.

The local newspaper flashed the news on the first page of its morning edition. The day following, a famous English daily carried an equally puzzling news item. Certain Dr. Dev, a senior lecturer in Sanskrit in Benaras Hindu University heard the sound of Veena while worshipping in his prayer room in which there was a porcelain statue of goddess Saraswati. Dr. Dev and his young wife whose name, coincidentally, was Saraswati, not only heard the sound of Veena, but could see the movement of goddess's fingers. They called some of their neighbours who were thrilled to hear the divine sound of music. One of their neighbours, Mr. Saxena, an adept in classical music, told the reporters that it was raga Malkosh the goddess was playing on the Veena. What baffled Dr. and Mrs. Dev and their neighbours most was that they could not hear the sound as soon as they walked out of the puja room. The neighbours denied they had seen any movement of the goddess's fingers, but Dr. and Mrs. Dev claimed they saw what they saw and said what they saw so clearly.

It was only the beginning of an event. Next day, all the no-nonsense newspapers had no other news items to speak of.

Millions and millions of people — some of them well-known politicians, sports and celluloid personalities — listened to the divine maestros for free. Some people in the Western Maharashtra saw, with their own eyes, the metallic and stone snakes circling Lord Shiva's neck and arms swaying their hoods and flicking out their forked tongues and heard, with their own ears, the god's percussion instrument *damru* producing dum-dammat-dum dammatum-dum sound and his stony mount Nandi the bull bellowing like a rumble of thunder.

On the third day, the situation was beyond control. The Central and State ministers cancelled their foreign tours and hopped from temple to temple to listen to the divine performers beaming like street urchins watching their lanky matinee idols flooring a battalion of bare-bodied, muscle-flexing, shaven-headed, and armed marmydons by using their inalienable fists. Everybody who was anybody was interviewed by grave and important journalists; ordinary mortals were grilled by famous reporters; TV cameras were installed in the temples and private prayer rooms to telecast the cosmic orchestra or the solos, as the case might be, live for the non-believers of the whole world to see and to believe what they saw. From the remotest hamlet to the poshest city down towns, from a two inch miniscule image to the larger than life statue, through the length and breadth of the subcontinent the gods and goddesses decided to entertain their terrestrial devotees. Some film music buffs testified — looking as puzzled as rakish — before TV cameras that they had actually most truly unmistakably heard goddess Saraswati playing a Hindi film tune on her celestial Veena. On being asked about the reference of the song, they said it was from Guru Dutta film *Pyasa*. Or was it from *Jhanak Jhanak Payal Baje*? They, however, could not be sure. The connoisseurs and practitioners of classical music had a tough time identifying the ragas. It was not possible to know whether they visited so many temples on their own, or they had been dragged by some enthusiasts. They did not visit the Shiva temples for it was not possible to catch the ragas in the clatter of damrus and the bellowings of the bulls. The whole Hindustan was in a carnival mood. No one was neutral. Ordinary people were going gaga. The gods suddenly became as true and alive as their nextdoor neighbours. Important and intelligent people who thought they really heard the sound of music behaved with studied ambivalence. Fearing to be dubbed as foolishly gullible at a latter date should the whole heavenly music turn out to be absolutely human, they toned down their enthusiasm tempering their faith with a healthy dose of scepticism. Their observations can be summed up; If to see is to believe, if to hear is to believe, if circumstantial evidences were capable of guiding our sense of judgement, while holding the view that our senses can be duped, while maintaining that our sensory perceptions, however erratic or faulty may they be, are our only compass to give us a sense of direction as we sail on the vast oceans of terrifying uniformity, we had actually a wondrous strange encounter with a miracle. We'll, of course, be more surprised if we say we have not heard what we have truly heard. A lived miracle becomes a fact to reckon with. Mysteries are only a matter of time.

The miracle pushed its frontiers further. The Hindus living in England and America and Indonesia and many other countries drove to the temples of performing divinities in their glossy impalas and limousines praying, all the way, not to be deprived of the privilege of hearing the divine music because of their voluntary separation from the holy land of their ancestors. Being more secular minded than their counterparts in Hindustan, they dragged hundreds of Christians, Sikhs, Muslims and Jews — black, red, white, yellow — to the temples of Lord Krishna and Shiva. If it happens to us all, the non-resident Hindus thought, these worshippers of shapeless single god would no more call us antediluvian preglacial ritualistic believers in thirty three crores of heavenly beings; that while the very materiality of their gods was yet to be ascertained, our gods are not only the living preservers of their devotees, they are also very considerate. Otherwise, why should they leave the seven star luxuries of their celestial abodes and come down to the planet earth to entertain their devotees with sweet music? The idols of Lord Krishna listened to their prayers and played on their marble flutes the raga Malkosh or was it "Megha Malhara?" or was it more mundane raga "Desh?" One middle aged American Mr. Strong Hold, an ex-flutist in Zubin Mehta's Philharmonic Orchestra was simply overwhelmed to hear a solid marble flute, held in a most incorrect way, almost an inch away from the god's lips, producing such a melodious tune. "I was amazed and impressed," he announced. And added with a condescending chuckle before a Star TV crew : "The god may be a better flutist than me. No chance, yaar, when you compete with a divinity." An excessively corpulent man standing nearby told the TV crew. "As I know him, man, Strong can't lie. He's a man married to integrity."

The foreign feedback intensified the indigenous lust for belief. The fence-sitters who were swinging pendulum-fashion between Vedantic tradition and Western rationalism, between saree and haute couture, between bhang and scotch whisky, between mahaprasad and Kentucky fried chicken, between limbu sharbet and Coca Cola, between medieval obscurantism and enlightenment, between Ravi Varma and Pablo Picasso, between Shamanism and Yuppism jumped predictably to the safe side of umbilical tradition when they found Lord Krisrnna behaving like Hariprasad Chaurasia and Lord Shiva behaving like Alla Rakha, the Goddess of learning strumming the veena strings and the stoney Nandi bellowing like a maverick bull. And the so-called non-believers teetered to the top of the fence vacated by the fence-sitters. A handful of non-believers who, fearing to lose their belief in disbelief, had formed or joined the fraternity of rationalists in order to cloak their individual selves with an armour of ideological collectivity and derring-do scientism, came forward with clear-cut explanations on a platter. Some diehard rationalists flatly denied the possibility of any extra-natural occurance in a natural world. They considered it quite below their dignity as rational, enlightened homo sapiens living in a postmodernist, scientific time to explain a baseless superstition, a case of mass hysteria, an acute instance of schizopherenic paranoia. "A sick mind," they declared arrogantly "enables the man to see and hear what he wishes to see and hear, that's it." The more rational among the rationalists bothered to explain the phenomenon. Drawing references from the latest findings in the fields of psychology, science, etc., they, by making a liberal use of technical jargons and incontrovertible laws, explained the mind-matter relationship. The phenomenon, *i.e* the flutes, veenas and damrus producing sound, is nothing compared to the radios and televisions. They said. "People do not consider it a divine miracle when they buy a radio as tiny as cigarette packets, put an ordinary battery in it, and hear what's being said or sung in London, Colombo and New York. People do not call it a miracle when a pocket-size TV set beams a cricket match played in a field thirteen thousand miles away, live. A good mechanical engineer can tell you why, what, which, how."

They said many such things to explain all the miracles away, but there were not many takers. To intelligent believers, the pat shipshape explanation given by the rationalists was indeed confusion worst confounded, even far worse than belief. One resourceful rationalist travelled further afield and roped in Pythagoras, the celebrated philosopher-cum-mathematician of ancient Greece, and expostulated his theory of the music of the spheres. According to Pythagoras, he explained, "the celestial spheres, by moving in accordance with the natural laws of harmony, produce magnificent music which, ordinarily, is not audible to mortal ears. Now our scientists have proved beyond doubt that human ears can hear sounds of a particular frequency, and are deaf to sounds of higher and lower frequencies or wave lengths. The ultrasonic or supersonic sounds are not audible to mortal ears. Now the question arises, how could Pythagoras, being a mortal himself, hear the supersonic or ultrasonic music of the spheres he referred to? The answer is rather easy : The music of the celestial spheres could be fluctuating and varied in its wave-lengths from time to time, like the chance conjunctions of the planets and satellites of the solar system which cause the solar and lunar eclipses. At certain points of variation or fluctuation, the music of the spheres becomes suddenly audible to human ears, like the rare planetary conjunctions when the nine planets are arranged in a straight line once in a millennium, like the Haley's comet tranversing the solar system once in seventy nine years."

Miracles were not confined to music only. How to explain the animation of those bronze and granite king cobras circling Lord Shiva's neck? Again, by what stretch of imagination the tom-tom clatter of the damru and the bellowing of a bull could be called the melodious music of the spheres?

As though the musical proof was not enough, more and more gods came forward to confound their devotees with other proofs of their presence. Lord Ganesh, the pot-bellied and elephant-headed son of Shiva and his divine consort Parvati, violated the time-honoured practice of the heavenly beings to partake of the essence of fruits, milk and sweetmeats offered to them by their earth-bound worshippers and spare the gross, and started sipping milk. Nobody knew how it started, and who first tried to spoonfeed the god. For the rules of worship do not permit a devotee to take liberties with the idols. Anyway, people came to know about the lactic phenomenon when it was already a conflagration. People were so ashamed of not knowing the news earlier that they tried hard to streamline their exclamations of holy horror and puzzlement when they heard it for the first time. Without wasting time, they carried all the milk they had at home and rushed to the nearest image of Lord Ganesh. The more devout daily worshippers who had stone, wooden, clay, or metallic images of the rodent-riding god in their prayer rooms were spared the trouble of standing in the queues light years long. People stood in the queue carrying buckets, glasses, pitchers or even plastic jars filled with cow milk.

The milk phenomenon like the earlier musical one was not confined to Hindustan alone. New discoveries in the field of cybernetics — E-mail, Internet, information super highway, fax, and prehistoric telephone — has turned the whole globe into a cyclotron in which information moves at a terrific speed giving the motion an appearance of solid staticity. (A wag once said : this electronic media and information technology have changed the world into a big big bedroom where the young people strip, streak, make merry and love, and where the rest watch them with delicious embarrassment : this is the world of the doers and voyeurs.) The news of the miracle reached England and America. And the non-resident Hindus there, the Argus-eyed reporters of the elitist and tabloid newspapers besieged the Ganapati temples with cow milk and video cameras. The god seemed to be no discriminator of religions, for he sipped milk offered by the Muslims and the Christians. Almost all the British and American dailies gave this miracle frontpage coverage complete with photographs, scoops and eye-witness accounts given by a host of celebrities. The BBC TV showed it on the breakfast bulletin. A mass hysteria broke loose. The miracle became a talking point in the pubs, drawing rooms and offices. It was as if a contigent of Martians landed on the earth with their saucer-like spacecrafts simultaneously in Washington, London, and New Delhi.

Some senior citizens remembered a similar event which took place half a century or more ago when the regular programmes on the VOA were suddenly interrupted and an audibly shaken Orson Welles announced, with graphic details, the landing of the Martians in America and the devastation the war of the worlds had caused. The scare story spread widespread panic and people left their homes and ran for shelter. But, then, the terror was for a brief period of time when fact and fiction intercepted each other. Now the aliens seemed friendly and familiar. Only some proofs were given, about their materiality and visit. There was no cause for terror. By behaving like the earthlings, the gods seemed to be making a point : "As of the days of yore, we are again at your calling distance. This is for your information and, of course, necessary action."

"Seeing is believing" rent the air. A bewildered British researcher from BBC television telephoned an Indian journalist : "Can you find me a sceptical Hindu? Have you located a single Indian who has visited a temple and is not impressed by the miracle? Honestly, I myself have spoonfed a full litre to a six inch metal idol placing it on my lap, and, believe me, Sharma, my pants and shirt are dry. How on earth you explain that? Ants in my pants! Amazing!"

My wife Puja decided to manage a day with lemon tea and carried the whole pot of milk — one and half litres — to our neighbour's house which accommodated a bronze image of Lord Ganesh. "I am a facts person, you know," she pleaded, bursting with excitement, and said what everybody was saying : "Seeing is believing." And I offered resistance : "Look, Warship, I mean Puja, there is a piece of good advice given by one of our wisest and wiliest ancients, Chanakya : don't tell others if you think you have seen a slab of granite ferrying passangers across a brimming river, or if you've heard a black-faced monkey singing melodiously. People will call you nuts."

And she. "Then, husbandji, come and see with your own eyes. Who cares to hear it from you?"

She was correct. I stood on the threshold. A dozen or so woman have already sat in the prayer room of our neighbour surrounding a twelve-inch tall bronze image of Lord Ganesh. A barebodied, loinclothed priest with a couple of marigolds tied to his pigtail was kneeling before the idol ladling out milk from the bowls and tankards. The milk vanished as the rim of the ladle touched the lip of the god beneath the trunk. In less than two hours, all the containers were empty. The wooden pedestal on which the idol stood was dry. The milk did not dribble over the idol. The room might have been flooded had the milk been spilled. Some women sobbed out of excess of emotion. Men and children who stood thronging the door looked aghast. It was a moving scene. I thought I was watching a P.C. Sarkar magic show. What was miracle after all, if not magic with a pinch of religion! Legerdemain of a saffron-clad god-man! I thought, as I stood there watching the show, that a magician has to be an honest man, for had he so wished, with half of his conjuring tricks, he should have become the greatest god-man of his time, blessing the Presidents, Prime Ministers and the high and the mighty by placing his feet on their heads, cocking a snook at the laws of the land and enjoying such luxury and devotion, and having such power over the body and soul of his million devotees of both sexes as the Heads of States, the Arab Sheikhs, the Eastern potentates and the billionaires cannot dream of. I decided once for all that the magicians are noble men for not spiritualizing their capacity to surprise others; but that did not help matters. I was vis-a-vis a most incredible happening. By drinking so much of milk, by depriving this generally under-nourished Hindustan of one of its chiefest source of nutrition, what does Lord Ganesh want to prove? That he exists? That he suddenly suffered from malnutrition and some celestial doctor suggested he take a lake of cow-milk? Or, does mankind suffer from a mass hysteria ? Or, the gods, exercised about modern man's depletion of faith, have deputed Lord Ganesh now, Lord Krishna, Lord Shiva, Nandi and Goddess Saraswati a few months ago, to manifest themselves in order to remind the unbelieving and half-believing Hindus of their own physical existence? Then why don't these gods offer resistance and manifest themselves when the antic dealers and their accomplices steal hundreds of images from temples, pack them up like sardines and export and auction them? Why don't the gods lose their temper when hundreds of crooks, criminals and charlatons call themselves the deputies of the Gods, or even God Himself? Why shouldn't the gods tell their devotees to be less cruel and malevolent? Why don't the Chiefs of the gods —

the Hindu Trinity Brahma, Vishnu and Maheswar, Jehovah, Allah and the Father of Christ, etc. and their messiahs — hold a summit meeting and send mankind a signed agreement to prevent their gun-totting followers from commiting genocide, from making the earth a slaughter house in the names of different gods and their well-meaning messiahs? "Look, ye mortals," their agreement should state unambiguously, "Our aim was to arouse the divine qualities in you. They are kindness, love, a yearning for transcendence, mastering your temptations, and, above all, goodness. We live in perfect amity here in heaven. If you claim to be our true devotees, you ought to live in good amity on earth. Not a drop of blood should be shed in our name, for cruelty in any form is not approved by us. Be good, and live." Why don't they do that? How can a god guzzling milk, another performing on flute, and another strumming away at her string instrument, send the right message? To be alive is not enough, they should be morally alive. I was actually bursting at the seams with ideas, most perplexing ideas.

As I went on mulling over the music and milk phenomena, I found myself struggling in the intermediary space — between belief and dis-, between the terra firma and the interfering wizards from outer space, between the transience and permanence of human soul. I believed in everything, doubted everything; I was mobbed by the notions of most contrasting kind : angels wrestled with men, ghosts wrestled with rationalists, light wrestled with darkness, integrity with greed, love with hate, science with superstition in the twilight zone of my mind. I could not decide how to react to these events. Life struck me as wacky and contrapuntal. People who stigmatized life and called it a whacking lie sounded as convinving as those who celebrated it, glorified its materiality and possibility. I thought I had gone bust. I tried my best to know something for certain, some incontrovertible evidences. During such moments of inner turmoil, I envied the sheer simplicity of the believers and the hard — boiled scepticism of the rationalists.

The dogmatic deniers of the miracle, this time, used three cardinal principles from science and psychotherapy such as "surface tension" (due to which a thin layer of milk is formed over the spoon when it touches the idol; then, within seconds, the layer spreads to the torso of the idol and starts trickling down.), "the capillary action" ("the milk in this case is sucked in because of the psychomotor movement of the muscles of the hand holding the spoon, a movement which tilts the spoon to such an angle that the viscocity of the fluid adds to the gravitational pull, causing the milk to go down Ganesh's bulging tummy"), and "the mass hysteria" caused by a sudden outburst of chronic repressions bottled up in the collective unconscious of people of a particular community, which momentarily disrupts the normal functioning of the mind, obliterates all vestiges of rationality and makes the mind utterly vulnerable to suggestion. As a result of this, the auditory and ocular organs, the nerves connecting them to the brain and the discriminating faculties of the mind function erratically, persuaded and overwhelmed by a psychic afflatus generated by an excess of intention.

Needless to say, these explanations had as many loose ends as one would like to find. When the guardians of modernity, rationality and scientific temper desperate to dispute a claim to which million people world over bear witness, use such convoluted language to dress up certain rudimentary rules of science and psychology in order to keep their own sanity in-tact and to satisfy the demands of their fraternity, who should I turn to? It beat me completely why these rules — surface tension, capillary action, siphoning, viscosity, collective hysteria, mass paranoia, etc., — should start functioning simultaneously on a particular god's idols on a particular day? Why such mass psychosis affected the enlightened, sceptical non-Hindus in the USA and the UK? Then, what happened to the vast amount of milk — several million litres by a modest estimate — which was lapped up by the elephant-headed idols? The temples and the private prayer rooms might have been deluged with milk in that case.

I could not be convinced by the scientific explanations. Then again, I couldn't be certain about the miracles either. Both strained my individual ways of reasoning, even though I had a first hand experience with the milk miracle. "By not believing in what you had seen," Puja put in effectively, "you behave much like a diehard rationalist whose sole aim is to discredit all evidences of the senses." "No," said I with disarming naivete, "I don't give a damn to those determined debunkers of all miracles."

"Then," whispered Puja the warship, "You should consult a psychotherapist. He will tell you your problem." She did not know Dr. Poak had already advised me to do the same.

"You needn't bother about that," I said patiently; "I know my condition myself."

"I'd be enlightened," she mocked.

"Between the two cloud-kissing mountains of belief and disbelief," said I firmly, "lies the fertile valley of confusion, the ideal site for all civilizations of the world."

Then Puja with her acerbic wit : "Between two cliffs of extremes — belief and disbelief — lies the chasm of utter confusion, a mentality that hangs suspended in space unable to belong to this side or that side, always afraid of falling down."

I accorded her the benefit of doubt. I realised that a person choosing to colonize the valley of confusion should not chase after certitudes, should not try to logically convince others and his own self about the justness of his choice. That'd be a contradiction in terms. Any attempt on my part to convince someone about the concreteness of confusion would be a self-defeating enterprise. So I thought it quite the thing to back out from all arguments with an uncharacteristic haste and enter my utopia of uncertainties.

As though my acquiescence was not enough to satisfy her, she returned to the subject with an impish smile, and said : "Between the two spread-eagled legs of a woman lies the valley of your confusion, the artesian well of your imagination. And between the two cliffs (she pointed at her bosom) lie the beds of your civilizations, ancient as well as modern, — Indus valley, Grecian, Egyptian, Mayan and American. I don't know, husbandji, if you mean that."

I was not amused. "I mean exactly that," I said icily and moved out.

Once settled in the unsettling utopia, I resigned myself to the ambiguity called life, allowing myself the quixotic luxury of indecision. I decided to be indecisive about the miracles that had just taken place around me. I quaffed a nip of actual, undiluted gin along with a mental cocktail of a layman's understanding of the sciences of the small and the big — the nano and the mega, the electrons and the super nova, the neutrinos and the black-holes, the atomic structure and the billion to the power trillion galaxies littering the universe, the yet invisible organisms causing AIDS and the sperm whales and the fossilized Jurassic lizards. After some time, sobered up by a huge excess of excitement, I fell asleep.

The very next day, as I was taking my lonely walk, I was accosted by the postman and given a registered envelope.

It was a letter from Andy (a name as relevant to the condition I was passing through as Newton and Einstein to any discussion on general Physics). How on earth did Andy get my present address? I tried to recollect. Then I remembered my meeting with him in the train. A chance meeting that was, but how shrewdly it set off a chain reaction! How nicely it revealed an order of things which might have remained a secret for ever! I had promised to write to him about the expedition I was about to undertake. I had failed in my promise.

I was really afraid of reading the letter. The picture of an egregious Andy, unpredictable and devilish, loomed up before me. I carried the unopened letter in my pocket for two days. Then I opened it in a fit of sudden courage, and read :

Dear Debasis,

Your silence could be interpreted as support. At least I read it that way. But tell me was it not impolite and unfair on your part to keep me in the dark about your encounter with the holy man and his mountain? I don't mind that because I have more portentous things to mind.

For the last one and half years, I've been doing a research sort of thing on the apocalypse and its related areas. Let's call them celestial sciences. You know it has always been a subject after my heart and now it has become a subject of my soul, my whole being.

I can well imagine you're smiling condescendingly as you read these lines. The same old stuff — morbid, arcane, kinky stuff — you'd say. It has already become a habit with you to mock my serious findings, to make light of my sufferings, to trivialize my preoccupation with the hereafter. But this time I am not alone.

After reading the twelve volumes of the Encylopedia of Occult Sciences, The Prophesies of Nostradamus, the strange-but-true, stranger-than-fiction books of Swedenberg, Mme Blavatsky, Blake, W.B.Yeats, Colin Wilson, Yogananda and our Achyutananda, I've come to believe scientifically what I have always believed intuitively — that every square inch of space surrounding us is crowded with the spirits, gods, gremlins, angels, extraterrestrials of all kinds, who peek at us from behind the clouds of unknowing; that our planet earth, this motorized dungball bristling with life, is hurtling with a suicidal speed to crash against a blazing meteor or to blunder into a black-hole. The end of the second millennium of the Christian era is the terminal point of our humankind. Then of what avail human pursuits of pleasure, permanence and excellence? Of what avail is it to bother about love, friendship, glory, riches, power, research, writing, acting, singing, reform?

You may ask me why I am writing this to you. Just to give you this morbid, millenaristic information? Yes, but I'll tell you presently. One result of all my reading all this is that I am feeling wonderfully relaxed. What's life given me which I should be afraid of losing? Krishna has deserted me. Or is it too premature to say so? She had gone to her parents. In these four months, I have written her thirty letters — once in a week. But so far she has not replied not even once. You may not be knowing my mother died soon after I left the Wave Crest.

Three months ago, one night as I was preparing to eat my supper my cook-cum-servant Santosh, a middleaged grass widower like me, came running to me with. "An old woman in the kitchen, babu! How could she get there?"

I ran to the kitchen and there was no old or young woman there. Santosh vowed he had seen her. Two days later, the same old woman in a white black-bordered cotton saree was seen entering the kitchen by both of us. It was ten O' clock night. We left our food and rushed to the kitchen. There was no one in the kitchen. How could a woman pass through a grilled window ? Santosh wanted to quit. I persuaded him to stay. He told me about a tantrik, and we set out to consult him. The tantrik, a rawboned small man with two wives and six small children, listened to our story and meditated for half an hour. On emerging from his trance, he told me that my mother was visiting me and it would not be proper to exorcise the ghost of the mother. He taught me how to call spirits on a planchette. From that day on, I've been calling my mother before going to bed. She not only moves pencil on the planchette board, she also speaks to me. She warns me, upbraids me, chitchats with me. Believe me or not, we sometimes share jokes. She told me, once, how I used to dance in the rain naked with my tiny genitals jumping up and down when I was a child, and on one such occasion I sneezed two hundred and thirty times nonstop just after receiving two slaps from my father. She recounted with vivid details how my father grew terribly nervous thinking that his slaps caused my sneezing, that I'd sneeze to death and prayed God to be spared of the sin of murdering his own child. We had a hearty laughter together. When I asked her about unfortunate French woman who was raped and killed by some local hooligans, she said she had not met her yet. She told me that it was possible for the spirits to take any shape they wanted to.

I tell you, Debasis, henceforward when you see a totally black or a totally white cat snuggling up to you, eyeing you knowingly and miaowing, when an unknown dog follows you and rubs its body against your legs and produces some un-canine sound, when a bird — a crow, a pigeon, a drongo, a linnet, a sparrow, a weaver bird, a dove, a golden oriole or a minnow-eating cattle egret, a moorhen, a black stilt — visits your courtyard or window sill regularly watching you silently or chirping or clucking and crowing, when you find human shapes — clad in all black or all white — moving alone in the dark — be sure you are visited by some known or friendly people from the other world.

I have written a lot. I shall write more if you show interest and write back.

Yours Andy

Andy added in a post script :

Believe me, Debasis, the tantrik struk me as ominiscient. When I asked him who I was in my previous birth, he sat in a yogic posture, closed his eyes for ten minutes or more and came out finally with a knowing smile. I persisted, and he muttered like a man in deep trance. "Twenty six hundred years ago, white cake, gray flowing beard, relatively ugly, geometry class, name rhyming with ass." Then he came out of his trance and said he didn't remember a word he had just said when I requested him to explain the riddle. Back home I meditated on that riddle. Still trying to solve it.

If you are still disbeleiving me, I'll tell you what Narasingh (whom you called Man Lion) has said. You can hear the story from the horse's mouth. I usually visit the Wave Crest Lodge whenever I visit the town on business, and spend a few minutes in the old house reliving the past. During one such visit, Narasingh and his wife told me what has happend to them. It will chill your spine and curdle your blood and make you barmy. One evening, at about 7, she was washing utensils in the courtyard and he (Narasingh) was standing on the verandah overlooking the sea. In the flimsy darkness, he saw a woman entering the courtyard from the Northern end. Curious to see the woman, he came closer and discovered her. It was Uri. Her bangles were jingling and her face was veiled. He asked her when she had come, but she ignored him and walked on. She was moving towards the direction of his wife. Then he heard his wife shriek. She felt a touch on her back, looked behind, saw no one there and shrieked. He told her about Uri, but she said she had not seen her. Then they searched the place, but could not locate her. He, then, ran to Uri's home, and found it locked. Her parents and brother had gone out. Next morning, when Narasingh visited Uri's house, he saw them crying. He was told that Uri had passed away two days ago. Believe me, Debasis, Narasingh was sobbing when he told me that story. I went to meet Anjan da, but he was not home. I also couldn't meet Javed and Subramaniam. Narasingh couldn't tell me where they had gone.

Now tell me wouldn't you have believed a weeping Man Lion had you heard it from him? I am covered with goose-pimples as I write this.

Yours again,
Andy

I thought I'd explode. I hated Andy for stoking my wretchedness by harping on the esoteric. Had I not a vast excess of it already?

I consigned Andy to hell and his letter to the waste paper basket, and heaved a sigh of relief. To a mind married to confusion, the gathering gloom of a breeze-less, smog-covered winter evening could well give a snug feeling of wellbeing. Coiled foetus-like under the blanket of confusion, I had temporarily forgotten the world enclosing me. But, alas, I couldn't blank the world out by simply closing my eyes.

4

A CASE OF LYNCHING

The other day when I was waiting at the town bus-stop, the world scowled at me. It called me aside and bared its teeth. I was filled with horror.

There I stood waiting for the bus, with a mixed group of thirty odd people. A boy of thirteen or fourteen years old joined us. He stood near me, looking anxiously around, his teeth sunk into his lower lip, his body primed for flight. I looked at him casually. He was wearing worn-out, ill-fitting trousers, a dirty striped shirt tucked in carelessly, so that certain portions of the shirt were hanging out. His eyes flitted nervously from face to face. He saw two persons — one a dhoti-clad old man, the other a stout short young man — standing at a little remove engaged in a heated argument.

The old man was holding out two twenty-rupee notes to his companion who seemed to be unwilling to accept the money. The boy bolted out from where he stood, snatched the notes from the hand of the old man and ran away at full speed. The old man cried out Thief! Thief! and the young short man and six or seven persons from the group ran after the boy. After running a hundred yards the boy looked behind, saw the chasers and dropped the money and kept on running at full tilt. But the chasers ignored the money and continued their chase to catch the culprit. Very soon, they caught hold of him. I could see from the distance that all of these people were slapping and kicking and punching the boy with all their might. There was no police man around. The prostrate body of the boy was dragged to the old man. The money was returned to the owner. The boy was struggling to stand up. His nose and mouth were bleeding profusely. He was, now, surrounded by the whole mob of commuters about ten people kept kicking and pummelling the boy. Most people were swearing and loudly baying for his blood. I tried ineffectively to reason with people who were kicking and stomping and trampling on the boy who held his two palms on his head pleading for mercy. "Isn't that enough? Isn't that enough? Spare the boy. Are you human-beings or what?" I kept on shouting at the top of my voice. The old man was shouting, "Stop it! Stop it. He snatched my money, not your money. I don't mind why do you?" But the mob was past all caring. Then a state transport bus arrived. Some people who were busy beating the boy, left the spot and got into the bus still cursing and fuming. A police man materialized there. What happened? What's the matter? He shouted, pushing his way into the crowd. The crowd dispersed as quickly as it condensed. The short young man stood up on the chest of the boy, and raising one leg as high as he could dealt a kick on the bare rib of the fallen lump. Before the full view of the police constable, the old man and me, the ribs broke and his foot sunk into the boy's heart. Still cursing, the short stout young man merged in the crowd. The police man leaned over the boy, touched the boy's nose, felt his pulse and declared that the boy was dead. The old man broke down and cried out, "Bastards, murderers! Bastards, murderers! God sees everything you won't escape."

Then another bus came and left. Almost all commuters had left. I and the old man and the police man remained there. Then the police man advised us to get lost. "A murder in the broad day light!" he exclaimed. The old man walked a few steps, then sat down. He was not cursing now. His wrinkled cheeks were wet with his tears. The police man walked up to him : "What's the boy to you, baba?"

"He was nothing to me half an hour ago, son, he said stifling a sob, but now he is my grand son. He was nothing to me then. Now he is my everything."

"But he's dead, baba," intoned the police man with a sigh.

I left the place. I had almost forgotten what business brought me to the bus stop. I didn't try to recollect it. No work seemed important. The nervous face of the boy — I was cursed to have had the last glimpse of it — loomed large in my mind and obliterated all other images.

Left to myself, I found myself in the inner chamber of confusion, where miracles were intermeshed with human nature. Violence, I thought has become a clearly articulated art form inseparable from life. Only, there's a slight shift of focus.

Only sentimental people cry wolf : Mere anarchy is loosed upon the world, the Apocalypse is now, the ultimate *fin* de *siecle* marking the end of the second millennium of the Christian era, etc., etc. That's hogwash. These sentimental people would not bother to remember what history taught and life demonstrated — that senseless violence has always been the theme and timber of human construction. The boy had a premonition of what he was about to do, of what would come to pass. Otherwise, why did he look so frightened before the actual event?

I bumped into the dhoti-clad old gentleman on a sidewalk a month or so later, and greeted him with a knowing Hello. "I don't know you," he said curtly and brushed past me. I dogged him. "But I know you, baba", I said, deliberately stressing "baba" in order to remind him of the police constable. He stopped short and peered into my eyes suspiciously. "What do you want?" he asked impatiently.

I began : "I never thought I'd meet you. I wanted to ask you something very unimportant."

"What's that?"

"Was the boy your own grandson? I mean the boy who...."

"Please! Please!", he snatched my sentence and threw it overboard. "For God's sake, son, don't ask me that, don't please don't remind me of that. I'm past seventy. Had two strokes already. Please leave me alone."

I stood facing him. He looked away. All the wrinkles on his face seemed to be swollen with anger, hate and disgust. "I said leave me alone, didn't you hear? I don't know you."

He turned round, but I stood blocking his path. Our eyes met. The old man's anger infected me.

"You think the sky will fall if you have a third stroke and you die?" I put in quietly. "In a world where a fourteenyear old boy is beaten to death for snatching twenty or forty rupees from an old man's hand, it is scandalous to be seventy plus and still living. Besides, I asked a simple question. Just out of curiosity. You might have said yes or no, and passed on. Tell me honestly, didn't you break down? Didn't you curse those people who took law into their own hands and pummelled the defenseless boy to death? Didn't you tell the police constable that the boy was your own grandson?"

My angry words, like an effective homoeopathic dose, cooled down the old man's anger. He peered into me face, looked around anxiously to make certain no one was listening to our talk, and said *sotto voce :* "I had a grandson, my daughter' s son, who used to play such tricks on me. He used to run past me snatching away whatever I held in my hand, just to tease me. He used to drop whatever he snatched away when I ran after him shouting Thief! Thief! The child died almost ten years ago. Drowned in a boat mishap."

"Had the child survived", I said, "he could have been as old as that boy." "Yes," he replied.

"Now," I pushed on, "have you seen the dead body of your grandson? Try to recollect."

"No," he said thoughtfully, and asked; "Why you ask me that? Why are you so interested in my affairs?"

I, myself, didn't know why I was troubling the old gentleman with my queries. At that point of our conversation, I began to be increasingly certain about what visited me as a hunch and a wild guess.

Are you a plain-clothes detective or what? What do you extract? Make yourself plain, please. I'm wretched already. Don't make me feel worse." The old gentleman was trembling with some unknown fear.

"I'm just an ordinary person," I told him simply. "Both of us were affected by that incident. We share a guilty secret, don't we?"

"I don't get you, man," he flared up. "I feel guilty because my money was snatched. Why should you feel guilty? You were not one of those brutes who killed the boy."

"Both of us are guilty. I've a feeling we're worse than those violent people who did that. Don't ask me why. We're guilty, because we didn't care..."

"Either a liar or a madcap," shouted the old gentleman, staring at me with scorn.

"Shut up!" I shot back, peeved by his impatience to hear me out. "Mind your language, old man. You lied in the first place, didn't you? Now you lose your temper and your mind as well."

We eyed each other with defiance.

"You say I didn't care," he muttered angrily.

"I said we didn't care," I said in a tone of hurt pride. "And I've reasons to say so. Now tell me had your own grandson been subjected to such a mob fury, had my own brother been lynched or tortured in front of me, should we have behaved the way we behaved there? Say yes or no, and get lost. Our impulsive lies, I mean the lies we tell on the spur of the moment, often turn out to be truer than our much polished truths. That boy was your own grandson. You have to own it up. I, too behaved like a coward, like a spine-less pig. We both wanted to keep our turfs clean, that's all."

The old man looked aghast. His mouth opened to accommodate horror. Shame was a creepy-crawly centipede in my pants. I felt funny. I left the man in a huff to find a lonely place to get undressed to get rid of the centipede. Back home, I found Puja in the kitchen. Ranju was disporting himself with dolls and doll-like twenty-day-old kittens; a fresh-faced TV news reader was announcing an impending nuclear holocaust, demonstrating for effect a doomsday clock whose hand was inching towards the midnight and her lively face had no trace of mortality in it; then I found people going about their business, monkeys chewing guavas and a snail sitting on a thorn. I saw them all, and I believed that all's right with the world.

But I couldn't fit my conversation with the dhoti-clad old man into the go of reality. I broke the rhythm. Consonance without, dissonance within.

What was that consonance without? Or did that consonance cry out to be called by some other name? Name-it-and it-is-there sort of thing? Lovers wenching around, women selling themselves to buy ornaments, friends betraying each other, business men hoarding goods and manipulating the market to cause inflation, people shouting, shambling, cursing, pushing, fighting at the stock exchange, politicians vampirizing on those who voted them to power and becoming shamelessly unparliamentary within the parliament itself, religious locusts feasting on their respective scriptures trying to depopulate the planet by spreading discord, liars, lumpens, hermaphrodites, lesbians, homosexuals, burglars, pimps, sons and daughters of bachelors, pickpockets, hired assassins, pathological killers, beggars, bootleggers and werewolves are forming world-wide associations, holding annual meetings, drafting their constitutions, claiming equal rights, touting their charter of demands : streakers demanding for the right to streak, hookers to hook, wedded couples to cheat on each other. Parents have a right to engage their daughters not yet twelve in the flourishing business of flesh; each individual should have the right to marry another from either sex and to change his or her married partners at every new phase of the moon; the makers of the law should have right to break it; the police should have the right to kill and pillage and gouge out the eyes of the undertrials; the judges should have the right to accept gifts; the political leaders should have the right to surpass all others in all departments of crime. There are people who pre-empt the right to sermonize on peace and nonproliferation of nuclear weapons after acquiring or manufacturing thousands of atomic and hydrogen bombs sufficient to blow up this planet. There are people who think they should have the right to get the highest honours and prizes for peace while holding the humankind to ransom through the brinkmanship of war.

All these sounds seemed well-orchestrated. Each member knew the instrument he was playing on. What emerged was harmony of the highest order. I thought the whole world — man, nature, divinity — guided as it is by a higher destiny had always been like this; that each sound, even though considered discordant in isolation, had always contributed to general harmony. Judging from what the world always held to be well in order, I started to have misgivings about my own ability to understand. My activity (*i.e.,* to bully a well-adjusted old man) and my inactivity (*i.e.,* to see a poor boy lynched by a righteously excited mob) began to appear like new additions to that orchestra. "Quaff mugs of cocktail prepared so carefully by life itself," I told myself, "and dance like mad in the Dionysiac carnival, screaming, gyrating, grimacing, swinging, shucking the body till you get at the soul. By being like the rest, you fool, you'll lose your insularity in motion, find symmetry in confusion and achieve, simultaneously, a spiritual and political correctness."

I was well advised by my own better judgement, and did accordingly. Soon I found myself embracing and being embraced by, my confusion; got good vibes from what were previously a slew of problems. Warmth was overflowing. Wounds got healed without leaving any scar.

"Finally!" cooed a passionate feminine voice into my ear; "Finally, dear! So nice a feeling to have been imprisoned by your well being."

"Yes, Puja," I returned with equal ardor, "You're true. So nice it is to be imprisoned by the white arms of a woman, to be warmed up by your heat. But I was just mistaking you for confusion. I was only inattentive."

"'For what?'", she enquired charmingly.

"Confusion."

She was too eager to be offended by my confession. But after some time, she remembered it, and beefed me about the harmfulness of confusion.

"It's bad," she said, "to stay too long on an event or an issue, however important it may be. If you fail to make sense of something, if you believe two events are so disparate as not to exist or take place in one place, if you fail to connect one thing to another, then allow your mind to switch over to some other topic. What do we do when we see someone coming and we do not wish to meet him? We sheer away from him. Look at me. I don't suffer from confusion, because I sheer away from it."

I appreciated Puja's clarity. She didn't care a damn for anything that struck her as mystifying and came between her simple explanation and herself. I realised I was different. I loved to relish what baffled me. Not only I felt baffled by so many events, persons, etc., I also went ahead yacking on about them, as though by doing that I was trying to make some point. People I talked to, a majority of them, of course, soon lost interest in my topic. That meant that most people loved peace, not war. I also loved — and still love — peace as much as they do, but, unlike them, I discovered my peace in confusion. I am neither proud, nor ashamed, of my peculiar inclination. It is only a hard fact which I'm trying to cope with, and make sense of.

One fine morning, I woke up remembering a dream as confusing as the facts that pervaded my reality. In my dream I was transformed into a large bird — a kite or an eagle. I floated in space, now shooting up vertically higher than the clouds, now going gladly into a sudden nosedive, stopping short just a few feet above the ground, alighting on a cliff that rose sheer from the hard ground, stalling leisurely over the mango trees that had plenty of golden mangoes on them, now speeding across vast stretches of water — a few feet above the floating crocs — realising all the time that I was capable of defying the law of gravity. I was also wondering about my newly acquired power to fly. That dream continued for a pretty long time. Once or twice, I came close to waking but I tried my best to fall asleep again in order to prolong the dream. It was as though I was vaguely aware of my two states of being while dreaming, and was not willing to exchange my dream for my earth-bound reality.

Light and sound heralded the morning, and I woke up. But the clear memory of my flying dream buoyed me up and my mind began to bounce up and down.

While we were taking our morning tea, Puja asked : "Why were you flapping your hands so frequently in the night?"

"I don't remember that," I said, surprised by the information. "But I had a strange dream. I was a bird in my dream. I was flying all the time."

"I'd read somewhere," said Puja gravely, "that the soaring dreams are caused by flatulence. When gas accumulates in the alimentary canal, the body behaves like a balloon filled with hydrogen. Or was it those Batman and Phantom comics?"

I knew Puja was not mocking, but her explanation did not satisfy me. Again, that was Puja. All solutions stood just a slap away from her. At least, at a calling distance.

"Well, Puja," I began reflectively, earnestly, "We know that a man cannot change into a bird while still retaining his human mind. Such strange mutations take place in comics, mythologies, folktales, science fiction, etc. But of late, Puja, I've begun to believe whatever had happened in mythologies, scriptures, folktales, science fictions, dreams, imaginations, etc., might happen in real life; that the events taking place at one stage of time or one state of being could well percolate into another stage; that when we hear that Ravana owned a chariot that could fly; that Hanuman jumped from India to Lanka at one go, that the gods had close relationship with the humans, sexual and otherwise; that the inanimate idols of the gods and goddesses are capable performing on their musical instruments and sipping milk, we ought to accord these incidents a benefit of belief or benefit of doubt though they defy our customary logic. These incidents, as I see, do not actually defy the time-honoured laws of realism, they only broaden them and make them more accommodative. Haven't you yourself told me that some of your dreams came true? You know, what was science fiction in the eighties is scientific fact now."

Puja was a picture of patience. She took the last sip from the cup, and asked me to come to the point straightaway. "Tell me what have all these things to do with your dream. Context, please!"

Without wasting words, I told her that I had felt what it was to be an eagle in my dreams, and that I had begun to think it was humanly possible to be metamorphosed into a bird while wide awake.

Puja had never heard me talking such funny things at such length. She feared I was on the neurotic fringe, or something. So, instead of telling me her honest opinions about the topic, she tried to make light of it. She was amused by my apprehensions.

"God help!" chortled she, "Your worst fears should come true. The world is changing so fast that anything is possible. But you'll remember my request. Should you ever be transformed into some creature and be given an option in choosing your new shape, please get changed into a snow-white flying horse, so that we'd have a fabulous time together visiting all the lovely places of the world without spending a single rupee on transport. You'll be my Pegasus, I your Bellerophon."

"For God' s sake, stop mocking! Do you want to send me the message that I shouldn't take you into confidence? Ok then, I got the message." I was in sulks. I was offended; I was angry.

But Puja went on : "The divine powers that be may grant you your wish to become a flying horse with a sober human brain controlling his movements. Together we'll make impossible possible. The globe-trotting billionaires will envy us. Ranju will be absolutely delighted. We'll ride you in tandem. I assure you I'll hold him tightly, lest the poor thing be blown away. Well".... She brought her mouth close to my ear, looked around to make sure the child was not nearby, and added, beaming : "Well, hubbyji, this time I won't mind visiting Anjan da aka the holy man busy intoning Om Om on the flat top of the mountains. You know I hate trekking mountains. Have you ever seen a saree-clad woman doing such a cumbersome exercise? Now, I shall descend on your meditating anchorite. He may take me to be an *apsara* sent down by the gods to tempt him, to disturb his meditation. Please, request the powers that be to keep your vocal cord intact. Otherwise, you'll neigh when you say something and we cannot understand you. We shouldn't take Ranju to the ashram. Don't worry, I'll take care of that. We'll leave the child at the temple below. How do you like my idea? Is it not fabulous?"

Her banter humiliated me and clinched our conversation. "Don't believe it, you mocking bird," I wanted to tell her : "I would rather be a peregrine eagle if given a choice." I realised I shouldn't have shared my secret with a churl. Then I wondered what was my secret after all? All secrets as far as I knew had weight and density and some amount of guilt. My secret had none of these qualities.

Dr. Poak and Puja and the likes of them wouldn't be impressed by the causes of my inner perturbation. "They forget their dreams," I told myself : "and even if they remember them, they take them easy."

5

ON THE TOP OF A MOUNTAIN, A STREAM

One person, I believe, who would understand my inner perturbation and offer some solace is the man living on the top of a mountain. Then what prevents me from visiting him once again, or even several times when the going is heavy? Maybe, I don't want to bother him, to disturb his quiet quest for truth; may be, I am too lazy and slothful to take the journey and trek the mountain terrains.

"Thou art a soul in bliss, But I'm bound upon the wheel of fire...."

These words occur to me as I remember the man on the top of the mountain and compare my state with his. Whenever I remember him and the new world he inhabits now, I, instead of feeling wretched, feel very curiously restored and composed. The sheer magic of an alternative reality increases my ability to endure my own reality. I've always been, and still am, a man of the world, lacking the courage to back away from the temptations of life. My love for life is a river, broad and deep, dressed with a desert, decked out with the dunes of fitful despair and casual resignation. When I dig a few feet, or even scratch the surface, the water gushes out, quenches my thirst and buoys me up. Then, what good reason do I have to complain and grouse about? Isn't this life with all its tenderness and abrasiveness just the right risole for my eager self?

Now I've to decide how my present condition relates to the intimate stranger living on the flat top of the mountain in particular and to a small group of friends I roomed with in the sea-side lodge called The Wave Crest a few years before my marriage.

Sometimes, the world appears to be a terrifyingly vast wilderness in which it is difficult for people to meet each other once they part company compelled by circumstances. A few years ago, when I left the Wave Crest Lodge and bidded farewell to Anjan da and my inmates, we assured each other warmly that we'd meet again. But in our hearts we knew it was an empty assurance. I remember I broke down when I called on him just on the eve of my departure.

"It's unthinkable, Anjan da," I said holding his hand in mine, "that we'll never meet again."

"Don't say that," Anjan da said reassuringly. "We'll certainly meet again. You cannot escape a peripatetic loafer like me. Well, even if we do not plan our meeting, we'll bump into each other accidentally."

Anjan da's word proved prophetic. About three years later, I had the unexpected goodluck of dining with him in my home. He visited me twice. His visits and his presence, apart from reviving the memories of the Wave Crest Lodge, had a singular and far-reaching effect on me.

PART II

6

AN APOLOGY, A VISITOR

One fine morning an intuition visited me like an idle and intrusive acquaintance, and suggested I write the story of my life highlighting the moments of inner and outer confusion. I considered the idea utterly ridiculous and told my visitor so.

Look, dear, said I beaming with humility, a person who is prominent has a moral right or reason to tell his own story. People, generally, are interested to know more about those selected few whom they know already. Well, I gushed, a person can be prominent or egregious in a thousand ways. And the more prominent the writer, the greater and the prompter is the popular interest in what he writes. Association, you know, generates interest. Even when these celebrities do not tell or write about their own selves either out of modesty or out of laziness, there are Watsons and Boswells galore to do the needful. But, alas, I am nowhere near the lime-light, let alone hogging it. A modest sixty watts bulb, hanging perilously from a peg on the wall, lights up my world abridged into a hundred-and-twenty square feet room where I sleep, study and do many other things. Now tell me, my unwanted well-wisher, I remonstrated with my intuition, who on earth will be interested to know what happens to an unknown nondescript like me? Only when I, along with ten or twenty of my tribe, die en messe in an accident, or by consuming poisonous country hooch, or by fighting among ourselves, or in a natural catastrophe, some newspapers may publish the names of the deceased or the grievously injured. Tell me, if a taxi driver tells you unasked that he dreamt a funny dream, that his wife is afraid of cockroaches and a maker of the tastiest pickles of the world, etc., etc., wouldn't you wish the fellow should shut up and mind his wheel. In fine, I declared, I should learn to shut up and mind my own business.

True, persisted my morning visitor, you have neither the good-luck to be born great, nor the resourcefulness to achieve greatness, nor the daring to pre-empt eminence by denigrating what other people honour and idolize, and by making a fetish of the weird. You're a meek marvel for not having all that. Maybe, for that reason, the inscrutable powers of the universe touched you on the raw and tented you to the quick by making you watch their mystical antics, by making you a butt of their divine jokes. You had never asked for it, yes, but it's not your fault either if the extraordinary decided to manifest themselves through a most ordinary person like you.

Let them do what they like, countered I, let this world smile at me in public and bare its seamy jaws in private. But why should I tell what happens to me? To distribute my miseries, my discomfort? To market my confusion in order to confound humanity? There is so much suffering in the world! But people take it all in their stride, strengthen their minds by worshipping their gods, listening to religious discourses, reading scriptures. That's why I tell myself, and I tell others : If you've anything beautiful to say, say it; if not shut mp. No keening, please. No shaggy-dog stories, please.

What you call confusion, the obstinate visitor explained to me, is a certainty of a kind. Whenever a confusion is shared by a majority of mankind, it becomes a fact to reckon with. Confusion, in a sense, is the mother-lode of religions.

I think it's just the reverse, I said.

No, said the morning visitor; you have not looked at the situation closely. All religions use miracles as their original and ultimate sources of reference : incarnations of Vishnu, Angel

Gabriel becoming a courier between Allah and the Prophet, immaculate conception of mother Mary, resurrection of Jesus, etc., etc. They were all miracles which subverted the time-honoured laws of nature and unleashed torrents of confusion on humanity. Those confusions, in course of time, crystallized into faiths when their takers outnumbered the non-takers. So, concluded my visitor, release your pent-up confusions. They will get their local habitation and names in due course of events.

Finally, the visitor gained upon me, and I decided to write down those experiences and encounters which have been baffling me, troubling me and, paradoxically, enabling me to cope with my own confusions and troubles.

Left to myself, I found another good reason to write about my confusion. As I was taking my evening stroll alone, I bumped into one of my good friends. This time, it was my reason. You must write off a detailed description of your confusions, and by writing, allay them, coaxed my good friend, smiling omnisciently.

I could mark coercion in my friend's candour. How is it so? I inquired.

His arguments were as follows :

Once upon a time, he began ponderously, two thousand and four hundred years ago to be precise, there lived in Greece an exceptionally eclectic philosopher who, while canonizing tragedy, (or was he trying to rescind his mentor Plato's uncharitable indictment on tragedy as a politically incorrect artform which nurtured passions, enfeebled manliness, exalted emotions over reason and lionized the lower faculties of the mind?), observed that the emotionally charged mimetic spectacle of tragic suffering helped the spectators flush out from their minds the excess emotions of pity and fear by arousing the kindred emotions in them. Aristotle's therapeutic-cum-psychological-cum-aesthetic-cum-literary theory of catharsis — like is cured by like-appeared far-fetched, even bizarre to me — a placebo masquerading as a cure-all — until I discovered an empirical evidence of its genuineness in my contemporary society which is characterized by its universal and ubiquitous voyeurism. Nowadays, I find my contemporaries — of all ages, genders, castes and creeds — getting themselves cured, not only the excess but the whole, of such sterling qualities as virtue, heroism, love, simplicity, forgiveness, marital fidelity, desire to excel and tolerance by watching day and night, with total emotional involvement and immortal interest, films and television soaps which are at pains to inculcate all these virtues in their spectators. The more they watch great action, the quicker they pass out their ability to act from their system. If a man suffering from chronic constipation takes a purgative — more than what is prescribed —, he may excrete not simply the excess, but the whole of his inner substance and become dangerously empty. How do you find my idea?

My good friend left me abruptly. I thanked him for giving me some food for thought. After a lot of thinking, I decided to apply that time-tested, super-duper formula on my own mind which has an excess of confusion, information, traumas and nightmares. I thought that, by recollecting and reifying the bewildering train of events, by regurgitating the morsels of the past, by raking over old ashes and silted memories, I would be able to ease them out of my system and streamline my thinking process.

Encouraged by my intuition and reason, I delved deep into my subconscious mind — a big store-house of what I have felt, thought, experienced, dreamt, done, imagined and thought of experiencing and doing.

Since my early childhood till date, life, like a garrulous grand mother, had ceaselessly been engaging, entertaining, traumatizing and educating me with its inexhaustible ocean of stories, always keeping me on the tenterhook of anticipation. It tells me how patience pays ultimately, hate attenuates life, love stabilizes life, things may go bump in the night, fantasy is merely an alternative reality, God is all merciful, He hears what we say, sees what we do, knows what we think, fulfils all sincere wishes, preserves the meek, punishes the arrogant, distributes poetic justice, all things can change for better or worse, a frog may become a princess, a young man may be metamorphosed into an insect, each human heart is an Eden containing an upturned peepal tree laden with forbidden fruits of knowledge, its leaves touching the earth, its roots touching the heavens, and a golden serpent nestling down among the branches of that tree, any system that can be improved will be improved, any system that can rot will rot, the nature and quality of things people do or hope of doing depend on how they end them and how they themselves get ended, the human mind, by learning to fly, can soar above the clouds of unknowing, etc., etc.

As though these baffling dream encounters and real life experiences were not enough, I sometimes borrowed a great deal of confusion from some books and multiplied my own problems. One such writer was Franz Kafka who had enough confusion to spare. He fictionalized the twilight zone where the predictable laws of nature and society got inseparably mixed up with the mysterious laws of an elusive elsewhere. Even fiction, I wondered, could be a strategy to fox the unsuspecting readers.

It is years ago now when I left the Wave Crest Lodge and the town. I accepted the way of the world and went the way of all flesh, married to Puja, turned a new leaf and tried to make a clean break with the past. But.... but that was not easy. The mind, like the temple walls, preserved memory in a state of frozen animation. It was revived when Anjan da paid his visit to my home for the first time about three and half years ago, and once again six months later.

One evening Puja returned home looking agitated, sporting a cryptic smile. She was a swirl of excitement. She paced the room impatient to be implored about the mystery she was carrying. She thinks that important news loses a great deal of its importance when it is divulged without persuasion to disinterested hearers. On my part, however, I had developed a sort of mental resistance to her compulsive mode of exaggerating the importance of her washy news items in order to justify her delayed home-coming. That apart, I had come to a stage of believing that no news was worth bothering about unless it was flashed in the newspapers and broadcasted by radio and telly; that if any news items didn't interest the paparazzi, it would not interest me. I pretended to be seriously preoccupied with my papers. I was fully aware of the surface symptoms of her internal combustion. At one stage, I was about to ask Any news, Puja? or trenchantly what exactly prevented you from coming home two hours earlier? But I checked my curiosity. I still remembered how she exasperated me, a few days ago, with her "epic of information."

"It seems," she came out finally, "the gentleman has a glad eye for me."

Her words had the desired effect on me, and perked me up.

"Who? What gentleman, Puja?" I asked quickly. My heart missed a beat.

"You know I went to attend the annual function of our sorority, don't you?"

I nodded in agreement.

"There," she said animatedly, I listened to a very good speaker. He has the gift of the gab, and a mind to match his skills. He didn't harangue, didn't raise his voice, didn't use any of his limbs but the lips. His words were delivered slowly, coolly, loaded with unassuming emphasis and power of conviction. Other speakers hummed and hawed, roared and blustered, using all their limbs like trained mime artists to make their points, but this speaker carried the day. His name is Anjan Das Gupta. Is he known to you? Has he anything to do with Anjan da you talk about? Whoever he may be, I bet he took a special interest in me. Before the meeting, he was taking his tea with us. Four or five ladies were present in the room, giving him company. We introduced ourselves. When I said my name, he asked if I'd mind telling my husband's name. Then I told your name, he smiled gorgeously, saying I see, I see, and came forward with a most unexpected proposal : Well Puja, I'll dine with you tonight whether you invite me or not.

Then it was my turn to feel excited. I told Puja to prove her culinary skills that night, for he was the very man we had been talking about.

"Where have your organizers put him? When should I go to bring him here? By the way, what was the theme of his lecture?"

"You needn't bother about his transportation," said Puja slowly. She seemed to have recovered her composure after enthusing me and making me lose mine. "As regards the topic," she resumed, "there was no topic as such. You know in such meetings the invited speakers are supposed to speak ex tempore on any topic. Mr. Das Gupta spoke on the theme of reservation in general and the job reservation for women in particular. The president of our sorority, Mrs. Saxena, while reading her report, demanded that there should be job and seat reservations for women candidates, which, she thought, would enable women to get on par with men."

"It was a red-rag to the bull, if I am not mistaken," exclaimed I.

"You're much mistaken," said Puja with a smile. It was not a red-rag, but a bundle of grass to the bull, for he ate it up and chewed the cud. Quietly and confidently, he demolished the structure and the basis of reservation. He called it an official violation of human rights, a stigma on individual dignity; in its irrationality and cold-blooded cruelty it is as bad as the Jew slaughter of the Nazis, though not worse. He gave most convincing reasons why it is so. He warned that if law of the land enshrined and perpetuated discord in the name of social justice, a bloody revolution will set it right.

"He said that the beneficiaries of the quota system have greater reason than the non-beneficiaries to condemn it, for the man whose honour is slurred has greater reason to protest than the man who is materially disadvantaged."

"Yes, Yes, Puja," I blurted out, "that is he; that incorrigibly correct Anjan da, moving around with his inexhaustible arsenal of ideas and invectives."

"Believe me," said Puja, "he converted most of us. Mrs. Saxena, a fiery champion of reservation, told him after the meeting that she'd drop that demand because she was edified about its dehumanizing aspect."

7

AT THE DINNER TABLE

Anjan da had greyed slightly. His facial expression was calm. His naturally large eyes were calm, too, expressing a mind at peace. But a couple of deep, horizontal lines etched on his forehead were a silent testimony of the struggle that his soul had passed through to achieve that calm, that peace. He felt totally relaxed in our company.

Puja, as a rule, does not like to cook for my friends if she does not like them. But on this occasion, she cooked well because she grew very fond of Anjan da at first sight.

Anjan da took his meal silently, but cleared his throat while eating the rice pudding which Puja had prepared with special care. He was taking one spoonful of the pudding, keeping it in his mouth for sometime before gulping it, allowing his taste buds to get full flavour of it, like a connoisseur tasting wines. I thought he would admire Puja's culinary skill.

"Don't you think, Debasis," he said holding the plate containing the pudding aloft, "our food habits determine, and are determined by, our vision of life."

"How?" asked Puja.

Anjan da looked at me.

"I had not given any serious thought to such a point," confessed I.

"Maybe," said he gravely, "but you can do that now. Look, in our epics and dramas and scriptures we come across characters who suffer bitterly throughout their life, but somehow they all come to a happy end. Dushyanta and Sakuntala are finally united, Harishchandra ascends to heaven on a divine chariot after being subjected to most inhuman and undeserved suffering; Ravana, the king of Lanka, it is known finally, abducted Sita only to get himself killed by her divine husband Rama so that he would escape from the recurring cycles of birth and death. Our epics are chock-a-block with such instances. Such a world view has something to do with our custom of serving a sweet, nourishing dessert after feeding the guest with hot and spicy curries. Tasty simplicity after mind-boggling, palate-burning, tear-jerking complications! The karmic shower settling the dusts raised by the hurricane of living!"

Puja was impressed.

I told Anjan da that the comparison was a bit too far fetched.

"You see, Puja," he said turning to my wife, "Well I think you don't mind if I call you by your first name, would you?" (Puja shook her head implying that she won't). "Now you see, a potter wasp, a tiny golden creature with a sting, traverses vast countrysides, surveys jungles and mountains to get the right type of caterpillars to stuff her cubicles of clay where she puts her unhatched eggs. She knows what kind of food would be just right for her off-spring when they come out of the eggs. If a wasp can take so much of trouble to make the correct selection, why should we shy away from a far-fetched comparison? Tell me that."

Anjan da, however, didn't wait for an answer and continued : "Look at the literary scene of the state, of the country. No dearth of creative writers. They 're as prolific and stinging as the mother wasp, but not as selective and active. They scorn enterprise, do not give their imagination full scope to range the hills, worlds, universe and the mind, tie it down to their petty concerns. I tell you a writer has no right to be lazy when it comes to imagination, when it comes to choosing the right language to express it. A lazy writer manages whatever stuff is available nearby."

"Please take another helping," coaxed Puja offering another plate of rice pudding. Anjan da accepted it inattentively.

By the way, Anjan da, I began, "have they introduced creative thinking in the school curriculum?"

"Not yet," replied he, and added after a brief pause, "but I have not given it up yet. I have talked with some sensible educationists and politicians. They were all convinced, or should I say, pretended to be so, and assured me that they would give a serious thought to my suggestion. These people, you know, are more or less hamstrung by their own upbringing. They have never been given a chance to think independently. They have never wished to be other than what they are congenitally. More than three thousand years ago the Chinese emperor listened to Confucius and gave him a small kingdom to prove the efficacy of his theories on people. I am no Confucius, and there are no emperors now-a-days."

Puja looked askance at Anjan da. She didn't know what we were talking about.

"Have you given some suggestions for the school curriculum?", she asked.

"Yes, Puja. But they have fallen on deaf ears," said Anjan da, smiling at his own ineffectiveness.

"If they are good suggestions, I do not understand why should the authorities should not implement them," observed she, and then asked : "By the way, what are your suggestions?"

"First listen to me, then tell me if they are good or not," Anjan da began looking at Puja full in the face : "Our young students, both in the primary and secondary schools, are being trained to mug up informations and parrot formulas and are kept away from ideas, concepts and thoughts. On one hand we exaggerate their abilities to store information, on the other hand we underestimate their ability to think. I am not against the stuffing of the child's head with informations, and grammatical, scientific or mathematical formulas, for such training has its uses. But I maintain that a child doesn't become enlightened by memorizing facts and formulas just as the library building does not become enlightened for containing books, a hard disc for containing the complete set of Encyclopaedia Britannica. What's irreducibly human is man's ability to think, and to think anew, afresh. But where is the scope? So I suggest that Philosophy and Creative Thinking should be incorporated in the school syllabus as a compulsory subject, so that our children will imbibe a tendency for reasoning, for taking pleasure trips to the heart of the matter and to depths of the mind. They should be encouraged to activate their mental faculties. Shouldn't we pity the man who possesses the Magic Lamp but uses it to lighten his own mean room? Shouldn't we tell him you foolish man! You've Alladin's Wonderful Lamp, and you can lighten up the whole world by making proper use of it?'"

"But," interrupted Puja, "do you think, Anjan da, our children will understand philosophical ideas? Won't it make their burdens heavier?"

"I've given a serious thought to it, Puja," said Anjan da coolly. Even milk given to a child in undiluted form would cause diarrohea. I know that. Noble and profound issues and ideas found in vedantic, Greek and Western philosophies would be made to look like Barbie dolls and other playthings, and be given to the children to play with. No need to use any force. They'll be attracted to these ideas if they are put before the children in attractive, simple and recognizable shape and colour. Our country is not lacking in experts who can make the arcane simple, the philosophical lucid, the unfamiliar familiar. When our students imbibe ideas, their teachers instead of asking them to write essays on such crude themes as Pets, Parents, Best Friend, Cow and Rainy Season will ask them to compose on why Losing a Dear One is painful, Why a Thing of beauty pleases us, Why people are afraid of being Different, For What reason Someone Else's suffering makes us sad Can Good be relative, Why men fear Poverty, Death and Old Age, Can there be Different Gods for Different Religions, etc. etc. You know, when questions are like this, there can be no road-charts to guide the students to ship-shape answers. They will have to think deeply, consistently, differently and continuously to answer these questions.

"The questions will be so fashioned as to persuade the young minds to contemplate, to count on their own resources. Then the brown cells in the brain will stir, sit up, toddle about, stand up, first totteringly, then steadily, on their legs, run about, frisk, jump, acquire muscle and mobility — and finally enable the mind to perform incredible aerobics and trapeze feats. Students thus trained and timbered may become doctors, engineers, technocrats, scientists, teachers, managers, civil servants, police men, clerks, politicians, taxi drivers and entrepreneurs, but a sublime depth of understanding, and a systematic, original approach to all the problems will inform their life-style and mode of operation. Don't you see, Puja, there is something dangerously wrong with the society, with our society?"

Puja was not ready to face a question. She was all ears. "Well, well," she faltered, "I do not think the society is very bad. There are some bad people, yes; but that has always been the case. Problems will be always there, but our society is relatively smooth."

Anjan da shook his head. "This smoothness is deceptive, he said sadly. The smooth surface of a bomb, the smooth surface of the Loch Ness which hides a million monsters! Do you know why? We all are a part of the mob, the rabble; we are all mobbish; we are governed by a mobocracy. A rabble-rousing speech can make us insane. Haven't you known how the peace-loving people of this smooth society have behaved when there is a communal flare-up : neighbours kill each other, rape each other's wives, daughters and mothers, slit the throats of children, burn and loot houses and shops, burn human beings of another community alive. Remember the riots in Calcutta, in Bombay, remember how thousands of Sikhs were butchered in broad day light in Delhi, look at Bosnia the ultimate example of barbarism. I only quote a few instances. Tell me why such things happen! I know, such things happen because most of the people constituting the society are mobsters, they are utterly devoid of individuality and independent thinking. When there is a communal cause, people quickly forget their friends, their human-ness and behave like a pack of trained blood-hounds of their respective Gods and dons and go on tearing, torturing and killing one another. You call such a society smooth? You call human beings naturally peace-loving? You were not born yesterday. We cannot blame it on the leaders and the causes. The blame squarely lies with us, in our rabble-mentality, in our mobbish nature. My point is we can get rid of this rabble-mentality by an independent exercise of will, by thinking creatively."

Anjan da took a pause. He looked fresh and full of energy when he was speaking. But when he stopped talking, I could mark a deep melancholy descend on him. It was as though he were a victim of world's cruelty. I wanted to make him talk.

"Anjan da," said I with the eagerness of a neophyte, "do you think your creative or philosophical thinking can stem the tide of the communal riots in our country?"

"I'll exaggerate its power if I say it would," said Anjan da, and added : "Hindu-Muslim riots have their roots in the deeper layers of the mind. Immediate causes only accelerate them. Most of our young learners, much before they realise they are social animals, are made to realize they are religious animals. Rituals and commandments come foremost to their minds. They imbibe a truncated notion about their respective religions, and a pathological spite for or total ignorance about other religions. The seeds of discord are sown early in life. A month or so ago I shared the platform with the Education Minister, a cultivated and unassuming man. The meeting was delayed for some reasons, and we chatted about two hours together in a room. He told me that he was fed up with the comments of every body about faulty education system. I told him that the system was not exactly faulty, but the diet was certainly wrong. He wanted to learn my point. I offered an example : By teaching our Muslim children the wisdom inherent in the Upanishads and Bhagavadgita, the essential humanistic universal aspects of Hinduism, and by allowing our Hindu children to read Thomas Carlyle's essay on

Mahomet, 'The Hero as Prophet,' we will be able to inculcate in them mutual respect for each other's religion when they grow up. Peaceful co-existence is possible when the people in a multi-cultural, multi-religious society understand one another's cultures and religions. We discussed many other issues, but this issue figured prominently in our conversation."

"Was he convinced?" I asked.

"Convinced?" Anjan da smiled wryly. "Who can convince a minister? I told him in brief what Carlyle said about Islam, but he wanted to know about the man's nationality and time. On hearing that the author in question was an English man and lived when England was ruling over India, he was miffed, and fulminated against every thing British. As a Health Minister, he announced, I eradicated malaria and small pox, and as Education Minister, I deem it as my patriotic duty to eradicate English. That unfortunately clinched our conversation. But the bottom line is the man was talking in English, getting angry in English too."

Anjan da concluded his long discourse. Puja and I were almost hypnotised by his eloquence. Words and ideas come so naturally to him.

"I talked a lot, I suppose," he muttered softly; "Now it is your turn to tell me if my suggestions are feasible."

He looked at Puja for an answer.

She took time to emerge from her trance-like state.

"You're great, Anjan da," she exclaimed; "You're the most persuasive speaker I've ever heard. Amazing ideas, for sure, but I am afraid they may not find their takers. Our young students may find Creative Thinking classes more interesting or less galling than their Maths or Science or Grammar classes, who knows? I'm sure, such training in simplified philosophy and creative thinking will give depth to their personality and enrich the contents of their conversation when they grow up. It is also practicable."

"I don't think it's practicable," I chipped in, and began explaining it : "Anjan da, I told you before, and I still tell you it is a grand idea, a novel idea. But the hide-bound mobocrats who regulate our lives and education will find it too exotic for their palate. Again, even if they execute your idea and introduce creative thinking and philosophy lessons in the schools, things will not improve. Don't you know, Anjan da, most of the grand ideas begin with aplomb and promise, but are trivialized and misused both by those who impart them and those who receive them, in course of time. If I remember you had told me once about your disappointment in locating a serious-minded girl in your Philosophy department. As a senior teacher of Philosophy you must have come in contact with many teachers of your department both in the colleges and Universities. Tell me if you have discovered in them those sterling qualities. Do you find them less crazy and more enlightened than their colleagues in other departments? I maintain that those born with frivolous nature will complete a full circle, even score a century, and will go to the grave with their own nature in tact, howsoever, you try to initiate them into higher things. Instead of refining or reforming their inborn nature, a training in creative thinking and philosophy may make these people more clever and conceited. I've seen people quoting very apt lines from the holy scriptures to justify their devilish deeds. You will be horrified to hear noble ideas being distorted and vulgarized beyond recognition, and mouthed churlishly by mindless youngsters and their cocksure teachers. Don't you think a lecture on the Special Theory of Relativity will be wasted on a group of students who find Linear Equation mind-boggling?"

Anjan da smiled indulgently as if he had already anticipated such a counter argument, and he knew better. Puja was as much convinced by my argument as she was by Anjan da's.

"That's also true," said she innocently, tacitly admitting her confusion, and admiring my ability to contest Anjan da's suggestion which appeared to her unassailable·

"In the first place, Debasis," said Anjan da, "you needn't quote one of my juvenile experiences to refute my idea. I may have exaggerated ideas about my own self. Maybe, I was searching for a Helen who could talk like Socrates. I also do not claim that any philosophical orientation or creative thinking will be an antidote to evil. Religions and ethical brain-stormings have failed to make people better. Most of the traditional texts which try to improve human condition are being eased out in the modern societies. I only believe that an orientation in larger issues of life and creative thinking may enable men to think differently, originally, rationally. A mind so trained may look into itself and turn to itself at the time of stress in order to find a solution. Philosophy and creative thinking may also offer us consolations of philosophy which are superior to religious consolations; they may enable us to perfect the strategies of survival."

"You call them strategies," I countered energetically, "but, Anjan da, I call them tricks."

"Yes, why not? Call them what you will, but they're inescapable modes of adjustment and terms of truce with life," Anjan da said.

And I : "Then why do you differentiate between how people do it — religiously or philosophically? I also do not understand why you find one form of consolation superior to that of another."

"Because," said Anjan da effortlessly, "religious consolation is passive and has a touch of acceptance, whereas consolation that derives from philosophy is active and has a touch of transcendence. Religious consolation draws on the Law of Karma. Both the Law of Karma and Religious Consolation are based on an assumption which cannot be explained in factual, rationalistic language; both are based on a faith which scorns the evidences of experience and the logic of the quotidian. Religious consolation turns suffering into punishment, life into a prolonged imprisonment and moments of happiness into parole. On the other hand, consolations of philosophy which we find in the Stoic philosophy, in the Bhagavadgita and in the meditations of Marcus Aurelius are firmly based on gumption, on tolerance and on the pragmatism of life. Their building blocks, are fortitude, lucidity, renunciation, equanimity and full faith in the ultimate validity of all our actions, choices and sufferings."

Anjan da continued and said : "Haven't you felt it yourself that consolations of religion founded on the karmic laws make the sufferer glum, depressed and constricted? If you, like Job's comforter, tell A, whose wife B has run away with his friend C, that he is punished in this life for the crime he had committed in his previous life in which he had ditched his friend C and eloped away with C's wife D, don't you think A will feel terribly wretched? His present misery will be compounded with an unremembered act of guilt. The arm of the karmic law several births long has finally nabbed the culprit and condemned him. He will pay for his guilt because that is the rule, whether he recollects it or not. But, if his faith wavers, he may consider the law Draconian and the Judge a martinet and himself a victim. On the other hand, consolations of philosophy liberate and broaden the mind of the sufferer."

I was about to ask Anjan da to be more explicit on the nature of philosophical consolations, when Puja announced, smiling charmingly : "Honestly, Anjan da, I feel amused and intrigued. I am more or less convinced by both the arguments. It seems your point (she turned to Anjan da) is optimistic, and your point (this time she turned to me) is a bit too pessimistic. My common sense tells me that each is as good as the other." She was referring to our arguments on the Creative Thinking.

"You mean to say...." I began, but Anjan da overtook my speech.

"Well, Puja," said he, "you put it clearly, but you've failed to note that optimism has an edge over pessimism, particularly in this context."

"How?" Puja asked.

"By being optimistic," Anjan da said smiling confidently, "you take initiative and introduce a new system hoping for the good results. The present system has been tested. It has proved to be a workable system. I do not deny that. It discourages original thinking. It celebrates the status quo. We're all accustomed to this system. Human nature is so accommodative and elastic that it can get used to cannibalism. A workable system can be a bad one. A government by crooks may succeed in imposing discipline on the society, but in the final analysis such discipline proves to be far warse than anarchy. Now, if we introduce a new system, and if it proves equally bad or worse than the previous one, we can learn from our experience and revert to the old system. But if you take a pessimistic stand, mind you, you decide not to take any chances and allow the present system to continue. I think you got my point, didn't you?"

I agreed with him. I felt as if I had exaggerated the bad effects of creative or philosophical thinking to help Anjan da to be his usual self. I wanted to get the feel of his old eloquence.

Puja, inspired by Anjan da's ideas,observed perceptively : "I totally agree with you. I want to add that both optimists and pessimists err in considering a part to be the whole and exaggerate the quality of their wares. But whereas the optimist wishes with all his heart to prove right, the pessimist wishes in his heart of hearts to be proved wrong. That's why I have decided to be an optimist."

"An excellent reason, very fine," said Anjan da. He smiled contentedly as if by convincing us about the genuineness and viability of his ideas, he succeeded in getting them implemented. There was a touch of child-like satisfaction in his smile.

Puja removed the utensils and plates from the table, and scrubbed the table top clean.

For ten minutes or so, no one spoke anything. Then I began reflectively : "Anjan da, what about our friends? Are they still staying in the Wave Crest? Do you meet them often? What about Andy?"

"Javed and Subramaniam," said Anjan da, "are still living there. I visited them about seven months ago. Narasingh is still cooking for them."

"What about Andy?' I repeated my question.

"Ah, Andy!" chortled he : "By the way, Puja, have you met Andy yet?"

"No," replied Puja' "I've only heard about him from Debasis. Must be an interesting person."

"Interesting? Yes. Quite. I'd say a little more than interesting. A living sphinx, a human cross-word puzzle with a printer's devil, jovial now, maniacal next minute, now frivolous, next moment highserious. Oh, you have to meet him in order to know him. Debasis," he said looking at me, "I am afraid his condition has gone from bad to worse."

"How?" I asked anxiously.

And Anjan da : "He wrote a six-page letter to me a year ago. Six pages! He sent it by the registered post, enclosing a stamped and self-addressed envelope for a prompt reply."

"Was it very urgent?" I inquired apprehensively.

"What can be so urgent about an essay on women? I have not yet written back."

"Come on, Anjan da," I said accusingly, "you can't be so cruel. Would he send an essay for your comment? You should have…."

"Is he a writer, Anjan da?" Puja chipped in.

"Yes, why not? Has written quite a number of love songs and devotional songs. I found them good. He has set some of them to music. He has given up these habits; he is no more interested in writing, composing and singing."

"Oh," exclaimed Puja. "That means he is a singer too? Why should he give them up?"

"If your ulterior motives control your creativity," said Anjan da, "you'll create little, expect much. Like an angler, he used his lyrics and singing as baits, but the fishes turned out to be smarter than him. They nibbled all the meat away without getting hooked."

"That's a universal tragedy!" observed Puja somberly.

"What did he write in that letter?" I asked anxiously.

"You know him, Debasis," said Anjan da; "and you know his usual weakness for beauty. It has become an obsession with him of late. He seems to have a crush on every pretty woman he meets in real life or on the screen. Has proposed to seven women in one calender year, most of them are his students and colleagues. Some have politely refused to be his wife, but one or two were not so polite. He scraped up an acquaintance with a pretty colleague of his, and without knowing that the lady was already married, proposed to her. She shouted at him, cried loudly and made his life a hell. He informed me that he had written love-letters to some film heroines too."

PART III

8

DOWN THE MEMORY LANE

Anjan da might have said something more about Andy, but it was late already. Two elderly ladies came with a vehicle to take Anjan da to a hotel where they had arranged accommodation for him. He thanked us for the nice dinner, bade us good night and got into the car. Most of my questions about the inmates of the Wave Crest Lodge remained unanswered.

The Wave Crest Lodge!

The place has become a folklore of my mind. I had spent two and half years in that house. It was a wonderland where anything could happen. Like the Witches' Cauldron, it was always boiling, bubbling and cooking up most curious items and events.

Andy, the weirdest of the lot, maintained the white cat that crossed his road and snuggled up to him on bed was the reincarnated spirit of a bikini-clad French tart who was gangraped and murdered on the beach. Javed, the delicate, was tormented by an awful feeling of claustrophobia and suffered vicariously for Salman Rushdie who was under the Iranian fatwa for writing a novel and for making his protagonist Gabriel Farista dream politically incorrect dreams. Uri, the fisherman's young daughter, a dusky, full-bosomed, curvaceous and inscrutable ingenue, was the chief agent of an emotional catalysis, as well as the litmus test of our integrity. She slipped into the roles of a steamy temptness and a virtuous wife with effortless ease. Subramanian, a gawky bag of bones and principles, found a mosquito inside his bed curtains and spent the livelong night debating with his alter ego whether humans were ethically justified to kill other God-made creatures for their physical comfort. Sudhakar, the Yuppie, fell in love with long distances and an alluring limousine, and decided to be an entrepreneur and relinquished his job. Nityanand, a forty-year old practical-minded married man had a glad eye for Uri, desired to taste the exotic flavour of adultery at all costs, splurged quite a sum on her clothes and cosmetics, and, alas, when nothing came of it, dropped his pants out of exasperation. Narasingh, our errand boy whom we called Man Lion, outwardly obsequious, inwardly calumnious, cooked for us, slaved for us greasing our wheels and his palms in the process. And finally, Anjan Dasgupta aka Anjan da, a well-known public speaker, a maverick and an old friend of Andy's, was an occasional visitor to the Wave Crest Lodge. Hugely well-read, unassuming, eccentric in spite of himself, alternately compassionate and indifferent, cordial and remote, reasonable and opinionated, quietly flamboyant, popular and philosophical, socialistic and other-worldly, that man contains a wodge of contradictions without appearing brazen or shocking or contrarious. That polychromatic and polyphonic man was a bachelor when I first met him, but he soon succumbed to the way of the world and took a wife. He said he married under duress, but I thought he needed an experience of terra firma after staying too long in the rarified biosphere of ideas and abstractions. The life of that extraordinary man and my association with him, I suppose, may serve as a thread to string together the scattered events and characters, helping, thereby, the crazy contents of this story to cohere.

As my luck would have it, I met up with such friends when I was emotionally involved in Gregor Samsa's problems after reading Franz Kafka's story "The Metamorphosis" for the first time, and was trying to cover up my internal tumult caused by my fear of change.

Andy affected me more than any one else. I had known him earlier as a senior when both of us were students in the University.

Then, Andy had impressed me as a man with a highly volatile disposition possessing a fine frenzy long associated with great artists. He had many whims, but most of them were innocent. A lovable wag full of facile wit, a ready stock of amusing practical jokes and gimmicks, he was in great demand in merry company. While in a musical mood, he used to hum and whistle, sing and yodel, tap with his feet and fingers, and trill to entertain the company.

But as I watched him, he was transformed into a different person. He became a veritable spitfire, offended people without much provocation, took a keen interest in the supernatural and considered it more natural than what met his eyes. He firmly believed that he was being watched over by an army of invisible sleuths. The cat that rubbed its body against his leg, the dogs that barked at him, the linnet that stared at him sitting on the wainscot, the snake that slithered off into the undergrowth in front of him, the purring and spooning pigeons on the roof-top and the ravens that crowed near his window in the morning to wake him up were invested with the souls of the departed, his dead friends and dead enemies. He read arcane meanings into every ordinary thing he saw, heard, smelt, and dreamed.

Worse still, he was troubled by the fears of his own transformation, and shared his uncanny troubles with me. I met my feared familiar in Andy. I didn't tell him how I had been feeling and what I was thinking after reading Kafka's tale. I thought that might have aggravated his condition. What miffed me more was his eagerness to convince me and others that what he thought, feared and believed was true. Andy's extreme and pathological condition exorcised, to some extent, my feeling of panic. Some people, I concluded after meeting Andy at the Wave Crest Lodge, are fond of interlarding our most familiar, Humpty-Dumpty world, our proud reality founded on the natural laws of probability and certitude, with out-landish references and galling non-sequiturs to derive some pleasure by baffling others, by problematising the world. Look, Andy, I told him bluntly one day, if the Cassandras like I and you have a premonition that something cataclysmic, something incredible is going to befall mankind or to befall us and that is inevitable, we should keep our portentous secrets to ourselves and suffer with the rest. But Andy said he'd rather raise the roof. If a secret is heavy, said he, man cannot carry it alone.

It'd be quite the thing on my part to tell under what circumstances I was sort of forced to put up with Andy. Human destiny is more or less linked with official decisions on the terrestrial level. An official circular informed me that I was transferred to S. College in a coastal town. It was morning at ten when the train I was travelling in touched the station. I was new to the place. I found a hotel adjacent to the platform and checked in; then took my snacks there, put my luggage in a room and went to the college, my place of work.

I was loitering on the college corridor facing the portico when Andy chanced upon me, flicked out his hand through a grilled window on the first floor and hailed me boisterously. His stocky figure was impaled upon the window grill. He kept on chanting my first name and yodelled in a shrill artificial voice craning his compact neck. His pleasure of seeing me made him forget his surroundings. Arteries and veins stood out tout like brass spikes on his front neck propping up his ditched, square chin — a sight which suddenly reminded me of his shape while he used to sing in a pitch he could hardly master.

Two friends meeting in a new place after a gap of about four years, we beamed like two mercury bulbs scattering particles of happiness and light, reviewing each another with amused incredulity.

"So you're here already, Andy," I exclaimed; "By the way, did, you know I'd be here?"

And Andy : "So you're here finally, you rogue."

It was nice meeting an old friend at a place where all were strangers. I recollected and re-lived the vintage college times — long afternoon walks in general company with so many interesting topics to talk about. Andy was now the sole representative of that happy choir of care-free and perky birds. What a great time it was! Stale jokes tasted fresher than pure honey. Laughter, full-throated and belly-aching, was too impatient to wait till the jokes and repartees were completed. A glorious period, indeed, when a most casual glance from a beauty was love, and a smile of formal recognition was a blissful consummation! Aphrodite was our familiar, our guardian angel. I remembered Andy, the only good singer in the group, telling once : Boys, I feel a good voice is a catalyst when you're in love, and a great solace when you are in utter despair. That controversial statement engaged the whole pack of idlers for the whole evening till we realized it was already late for dinner. Our good friend Amzad maintained till the end, even while gobbling up his cold dinner, that money only deserved such praises because money is the king, and love and talents are its clumsy country cousins. Sumit the poet observed passionately that the great feelings are mute by nature, that it was ultimate vulgarity of our age, particularly of the Indian cinema, to express love and despair through songs. Brother Andy, he said with a nasal twang, if you can sing when you're in despair, I would say you have not yet experienced true sadness. Jagadish was rather abrasive. Look Andy, he said, if you look like a goat and sing like Rafi Sahib, your lady love would choose to mate with your song. Have you read Come to my parlour said the spider to the fly? Honestly, Andy, when I'm in love I would feel really randy. And when in despair, I would reach for a bottle of brandy.

Andy flew into a rage and called Jagdish a mindless rascal. What else can you do, you crow?, he rasped. Jagdish used to grin with great satisfaction whenever he succeeded in annoying others.

Finally, it was Sadashiv, famous for his laziness, pomposity and pout, who summed up the issue trying to please both parties.

"Take it from me," he began ponderously stressing almost all the words, "that any good thing and attractive quality a pair of lovers possess would serve as an efficacious catalyst or an excellent anodyne to these two emotional and violent states of the mind afflicted with love or tormented by frustration. But true love, as well as true disappointment, is beyond all addition, multiplication and reduction. When intense desire and intense despair possess you, you hardly remember your own endowments."

"Shut up, you fool," shouted Jagadish the bully; "you contradict your own statement. Don't try to mediate in a dispute because your head is muddled."

Sadashiv didn't take offense, and smiled disarmingly. He had a generous, self-effacing disposition. We often took liberties with him without any fear of reappraisal. We had never seen him losing his temper. When words became two hurtful, he would pout and sulk. I learnt later that it was he who coined the name Andy for Dhananjoy Purohit, about one year before I joined the group, peeved and amused by the latter's peculiar mannerisms while speaking.

Andy is certainly a funny name in this Sanskritized country where the only identification of a Hindu is his nomenclature and the only signifier of his caste and social hierarchy is his surname. His Hindu Brahmin parents would choose perdition rather than give their begotten son a name which sounds so sacrilegiously Christian. (Andy in fact had three sets of sacred threads : one set he wore across his torso not because, he told me one day, he wanted to declare his caste, but because he could not attend to the calls of nature without tying those threads to his ear, thanks to the power of conditioning. He preserved the other two sets for emergency when the first set was lost while bathing in the river or the sea or got musty and looked blacker than his hair.)

Andy, in fact, is the acquired nickname of a person who, while communicating in English, uses the tedious conjunction "and" too often, and never permits his sentence to meet its terminal punctuation, the period. As soon as he begins a sentence, he begins to identify with it with such an intense passion that the ending of that sentence reminds him of his own mortality, of his own end. He has the dithers of a half-hearted suicide. This Tithonus-complex works both ways, and he keeps on extending the life of his verbal alter ego by a liberal sprinkling of conjunctions, particularly "and."

If I get him right, Andy relished his new name and contributed largely to its perpetuation and promotion. One evening while we were taking a stroll, he explained his ideological position to us.

"You see, friends," he began earnestly, "we humans are living in a murderous world and we live and flourish and nourish ourselves by killing others, and by gobbling up any flora and fauna we lay our hands on, uprooting plants, breaking eggs, boiling seeds and leaves, slitting the throats of goats, sheep, deer, hares, pigs, stags, all types of birds, fishes and reptiles, and what is worse, we do not spare the cows, buffaloes, horses, frogs and snakes, beetles, termites and roaches and if you read the menu in a big hotel, you will have to believe that God almighty has created all the animals and plants to flatter the omnivorous palate of man, and you must be knowing how we get our clothes and good sleep, and I tell you we get that by fleecing poor sheep, by skinning plants and animals, by pulling out soft feathers from birds to stuff our eiderdowns, by swatting mosquitoes, by poisoning vermin, by pressing cute little bed-bugs to death, and when our self-interest or physical comfort is threatened we do not hesitate to kill our fellow men with homicidal or cannibalistic fury, and you may discover, now as we are sitting or walking here on the green carpet of our mother earth, we are crushing many insects and blades of grass, and for all these reasons I sincerely maintain that the nobler the man, the fewer lives he takes to satisfy his own needs and to keep his body and soul together, and the fewer sentences he terminates to express himself, to communicate his messages, and...."

He might have gone on, and on had Jagadish the bully not thrown a small, stinking beetle into his mouth out of sheer exasperation.

Andy spat out the insect and lighted a cigarette to fumigate his mouth.

We knew Andy well. He was very fond of fish and chicken. His impassioned filibuster on non-violence generated only distrust and mock-serious sympathy. He preempted all good reasons of the world for whatever he did, thought or even dreamt, and used to stick to his reasons with the holy zeal of a medieval inquisitor.

That aspect of his personality didn't endear himself to his friends, particularly when the issues were ideological. His obsession with "and" made him an oddball. In course of time, he tried to shorten his sentences, but he loved to preserve his exotic-sounding nickname. "I'm Dhananjoy Purohit, but they call me Andy", he'd always inform other people while introducing himself. The nickname was rather handy, and it drove his original as well as cumbersome, name out of circulation, thanks to the effectiveness of the Gresham's law.

Andy also had (and still has) a peculiar method to counter and neutrialise general disagreement. Some thought it was his natural disposition, some thought it was his strategy to cope with adverse criticism. When cornered in an argument, he would smile wisely and patiently to suggest that he knew better. He was wily enough to know that he who smiles last, smiles best. But his friends found his smiles clumsy and supercilious.

Andy had an ego out of proportion to what caused it. As a result, he was often found sulking about being neglected by his friends. He had a feeling that he had never been accorded the popular admiration which he deserved as a genius, as a man of many parts. Our friendship in the University was based not on my admiration of his parts, not on my commiseration on his misfortune for not getting the kudos and clapping for whatever he performed to impress others, but on a discrete truce between his profound concerns and my total dislike for the tongue-in-cheek praises people doled out to their entertainers as a matter of habit or courtesy. It seemed as if we didn't take our differences seriously. Nevertheless a sort of awkwardness, an undercurrent of antagonism persisted, and that perhaps prevented us from getting too close to each other even when the going was good. Our differences notwithstanding, we chummed up with each other. The uncomfortable gaps were filled up by my smiling monosyllables and his relentless tongue-wagging, by my stolid forbearance and his sentimental binge. My patience pleased Andy, and his enthusiasm made me patient.

As we hugged each other warmly on the college corridor, we persuaded our own selves to believe that there had never been great gaps in our friendship, that even if there were any, such gaps were bound to occur when the minds met, that we had been missing each other all these years.

"Come with me," said Andy, excitedly. He pulled me by hand and led me into a large oblong hall cluttered up with long wooden benches, chairs and tables. "This is our staff room," he informed me pointing at the mess. There he introduced me to some of his colleagues, decking me out with fine attributes which I never knew I had. The common room for staff was overflowing with sound and activity. Teachers — some young, some middle-aged, some slender like sticks, some unmanageably obese, some aggressively skulking, some male, some female — walking out, barging in like victorious captains, collecting in clusters round small round tables, some sipping tea from tiny paper cups, some huffing and puffing after long lectures, some playing cards, some arguing with one another desiring to be heard by the rest. One thing, however, was common to those sixty-odd grocers of knowledge present there : each of them was contributing his or her share of sound to the general commotion which was enough to confound any unfamiliar ear. Talkative Andy, I thought, must be occupying an egregious status in this boisterous hall of learning as a many-in-one entertainer, particularly as a theme and a raconteur of jokes.

9

ROOMING WITH ANDY

I suggested that we move to a good restaurant nearby and take our lunch together. He accepted my invitation readily and we shook hands vigorously. It has always been his practice to keep on holding the other man's hand after the hand-shake. This time he imprisoned my poor limp palm in his firm grip, and his thickset, stubby fingers kept on wringing it with apparent unconcern and cordial violence. The more my sore palm tried to wriggle out of his grip, the firmer it grew. Finally I allowed it to stay put until his grip was fully relaxed.

Violence has always been a part of Andy's personality, unredeemed and unredeemable. In the college days, I remember vividly, we were afraid of sitting or standing near him while gossiping and cracking jokes. Whenever he listened to, or told, something outrageously interesting, he would simultaneously shake in a paroxysm of laughter and strike the person next to him with all his brute force out of an excess of joy. The man who received such blows would be baffled by the unprovoked assault, and then quietly withdraw to a safer place. If this were pointed out, Andy would appear as apologetic and horrified as a serious man when he is informed that he was muttering obscenities in his sleep. Jagadish the bully always returned the blows with compound interest. On one occasion, Andy took several steps before falling down under one affectionate whack of Jagadish's. When Andy charged him for the blow, he declared earnestly that he was not aware of it. He cursed Jagadish with a broad-minded smile.

It was late afternoon when we finished our lunch. We hailed a rickshaw and Andy advised the rickshaw driver to take us to the beach.

"Where are you staying, Andy?" I inquired.

"I am staying in the Wave Crest House," Andy informed me, and added casually : "If you like you can stay with me. It is on the beach. You can watch the sea sitting on the balcony."

I felt relieved and thanked Andy profusely. "You came to me as God's good angel," I said smiling gratefully and added :

"Is it very expensive? Is it furnished? You see I have not brought all of my luggage."

"Don't worry about that, Debasis," Andy assured me, laughing at my concern. "You will share my room. There is an extra bed in my room. Bath and latrine attached. Twenty four hour water supply, a servant to cook for us and run our errands. And it is fully furnished. It was a hotel previously. I am occupying the whole hotel alone, ha, ha, ha."

I stared at him incredulously. I could not believe so many good things should come my way. My joy made me forget the pain in my palm, and I extended the same mauled hand for another shake. Andy held my hand in his vice-like grip and crushed it with all his force once again.

"Hey, Andy." I blurted out groaning in pain, "One should get one's palm insured before shaking hands with you. I think you have disjointed my fingers, you rattle-snake."

He released my palm and guffawed.

"Ha, ha, your hand is so soft. Like a woman's, ho! ho!"

Thank you for the compliment, "I said half-heartedly, looking at the sea." Andy had another fit of full-throated laughter.

"The sea surprises me whenever I see it," I said.

"When did you see the sea last time?" Andy asked. I did not reply.

The sun was about to set. The cool breeze blew over us. The rickshaw was moving on the sea-side road when a cat crossed the road in front of us. Andy ordered the rickshaw driver to stop and push back the vehicle a few yards. The man obeyed smilingly.

I was not surprised by Andy's behaviour. There are many people who consider the cat crossing the road as an omen and a warning. Andy narrated one of his experiences when he ignored the cat's warning while going on a bicycle and dashed against a standing bull and fell into a ditch.

"That does not prove your point, Andy," I told him jocularly; "Why couldn't you see a standing bull?"

"You don't mean to say I dashed against the bull knowingly?"

Andy retorted. "No one meets an accident knowingly."

"Maybe, carelessness," I quipped.

Andy was not prepared to accept it.

"You become careless when you're fated to meet an accident," he said, trying to prove that his not seeing a bull was preordained.

"In that case, Andy, your ignoring the cat's warning was also predestined," I extended the argument idly. "You could have ignored the cat's presence any way."

Andy took some time to comprehend my line of argument.

"I understand it like this," he said thoughtfully : "If you take the cat's crossing the street in front of you as a premonition, a warning, you can always exercise your option whether to avoid the catastrophe by stopping abruptly and retracing, or to take a risk by not stopping. You can avoid the catastrophe by becoming more cautious."

"You have put it cleverly," I observed; "But can one avoid an accident by becoming cautious? If you say yes, then what's the role of fate. You mean to say you will not meet any accident even if you drive most recklessly if you observe certain rituals when you see a cat? You acquire personal immunity by doing such a thing? Is Fate such a kind and considerate goddess that she sends cats to the drivers in order to warn them against the impending dangers?"

Andy looked at me, annoyed by my mocking tone and teasing inferences, and then averted his look.

"If you don't believe, nothing is important for you." He said in a tone of finality. He was in the sulks, and did not speak a single word until we reached the Wave Crest House.

Left to myself, I relapsed into a brown study. My palm was still aching. I knew that adjustment with Andy would not be easy. I met him after a long time. He seemed to have changed a lot for the worse. His handshake struck me as savage, and his ideas antediluvian. "I have to room and cope with Andy," I thought sadly, "for I have little option in this matter."

"No, not that," I debated with myself. "I could still exercise my option and tell Andy to help me find a house near my place of work." I did not do that because ennui most often got the better of good sense. There were many such circumstances in my life when my own activity surprised me and put me in difficult situations.

As soon as he entered his room, he broke his silence with a bang, shouting "Narasingh! Narasingh!" in an unnaturally loud voice. He called out a number of times but no one responded.

"He must have gone out," he drew the obvious conclusion. Then he looked at me full in the face, and said in a high-serious tone : "If you don't believe in anything, nothing is important for you."

"You've already said that," I reminded him.

"Yes, I said that," he said smiling murkily, and added after a pause : "Then, how can you explain this? My father died when I was twenty three. On the ninth day of his death, the priest spread a thick layer of fine sand in a wooden box, leveled the sand, locked the box and put the box in my room. He advised me to keep the door and windows shut throughout the night and recite holy mantras if I heard any sound and saw any shape. I was really afraid. The castor oil lamp was burning with a steady flame. The priest had warned me not to switch on electric lights. I fell asleep. I woke up hearing the muffled mewings of a cat. The lamp was already extinguished. I covered my face and lay still till the morning. I discovered in the morning, that the lamp had plenty of oil and wick left. The priest asked me if I heard any sound in the night. I told him what I heard. He smiled knowingly, and opened the box...."

He was about to reveal the inexplicable mystery when a commotion distracted us. A boy came rushing and informed Andy : "They are at it again." We came out of the room and saw an ebony-coloured, wild-looking man chasing a woman with a stick. "Go wherever you want to," the man barked, "to your parents or to hell, but don't come to this house again. If you do, this stick'll take care of you." The woman was crying loudly, and protesting : "You're a drunken dog, you'll drown in the sea tonight." "Their children — a grown up girl and a small boy — were pleading with their father to spare their mother, and not to driver her out.

I felt outraged and wanted to interfere, but Andy asked me to wait and see.

"Hey, Narasingh, where had you been; I was calling you," Andy said looking at the boy who stood watching the road-side show sporting a happy grin. He seemed to be hugely enjoying the show. He could not hear Andy's words, and kept on gazing at the spectacle.

"Shouldn't we enquire what's the matter?" I persisted.

"No," Andy said categorically and pulled me into the room. Then he said : "Last month there was such a nasty scene. I requested the drunken man to spare the woman. He glared at me villainously and told me to keep the woman if I so wished. A drunkard can be brusque, you know!"

10

URI AND THE TENANTS

Three days after my stay in the Wave Crest House, Andy recounted to me his dream in which he walked on all fours, he possessed great wings and his fingers turned into talons. "I've never dreamt such a dream in my life," he said. "What can be the meaning of such a dream?" "Nothing," I said, assuring him. Neither Andy, nor I was prepared to believe that dreams such as that one had no meaning and significance, for had we deigned to give this dream its due and interchanged it with reality, Andy's being metamorphosed into a four footed bird of prey might have assumed symbolic proportions, and appeared important to both of us.

Gregor Samsa was as ordinary a man as any of his colleagues when he drew his curtains and slept. But how extraordinary he became! That he was dreaming of his physical transformation and of his lingering death, could be a controversial proposition. It stands to reason that the relationship between man and his reality has to be based on trust, and that the reality as man takes it to be should not be very protean and slippery. Does the man who somnambulates know he's in a fugue?

Both Gregor and Andy would not wish the world *per se* to be beyond their expectations. Transformations of such magnitude, whether they occur in reality, dream or imagination, are a violation of the sacred covenant between man and his reality. Man suddenly becomes the victim of betrayal.

I assured Andy, banking upon my understanding of Freud's views, that dreams were a sort of surfacing of the subconscious and there was nothing uncanny about them. I spoke at length to make my (or some one else's) point, but he was not at all convinced.

As we were heatedly engaged in our arguments regarding dreams and their possible connections to the subconscious and the supernatural, Naransingh, stood giggling before us holding two glasses of tea. "Narasingh is a good boy, but a bad cook," announced Andy in a tone of sudden recognition. The boy stretched his smile from ear to ear and slunk away.

"Mysterious things are going on in this place," growled out Andy in a casual manner. "You've got to wait and see. And mind you, Debasis, you should be mentally prepared to face them. I am used to such things, you are not."

"What are these mysteries, by the way?"

"Forget that. I decided not to tell you anything. You'll know everything for yourself presently," Andy put in enigmatically.

"You intend to increase my curiosity," I told him quietly, "but you won't succeed. I simply do not bother."

"Alright then," Andy revealed finally, "the first floor is not occupied. But I have heard foot-steps, muffled conversations, sound of bangles several times, particularly in the midnight. Now we are two. I am no more afraid. I have a selfish interest when I ask you to stay with me, ha, ha, ha."

Andy went on slurping his tea grabbing the hot glass after bandaging it with his handkerchief. I followed his example. "We don't have cups and saucers here" confessed he with an apologetic chuckle. "Uri makes better tea and serves it in cups."

"Who is Uri?" I asked, placing the glass on the table, allowing it to cool down.

"You'll know her presently," observed Andy.

Uri turned out to be just another girl in her late teens, swarthy, vivacious and practical. Her fisherman father stayed the whole day at the sea, catching fish and turtles; her mother worked as a scullery maid in two houses; and her seven year old brother Buna spent his waking hours on the beach helping his father. Uri did the cooking, and, when the adjacent Wave Crest House was occupied, she made an income by supplying tea, potato chips and fish chops.

Uri, as a rule, never put on any under-garment. Her loosely hanging saree revealed the full contours of her body. Her breasts stood out defiantly, hard and fairer than the rest of her body, like two big pomegranates. Her jet-black hair was rarely plaited, but often hung freely. Her agility and carelessness had a child-like quality. If her customers refused any of her wares, she did not give up. "You have to take this," She'd command, and refuse to budge an inch from where she stood until the customer accepted her offers. She never liked bargains. "You give and I accept. No talk on money," she'd cajole, knowing well that she'd always get more than the market price.

11

TRIVIA AND TRINKETS

Two months later, four new tenants occupied the remaining three ground-floor rooms of the Wave Crest House. Six of us ate together and strolled together on the beach. One young member of our team, Sudhakar a tall young man with a boyish face, developed a crush on Uri in the first week of his stay. It was natural for all of us to entertain sexual thoughts about a full-grown, buxom, half-naked wench who literally touched our bodies and beds almost everyday. She didn't object when Andy pinched her arm, Sudhakar slapped her buttocks and Nityananda tugged her hair — on some pretext or the other.

One afternoon Sudhakar, the tall young man with a boyish face, was all alone in the building. His mind was busy devising some amorous strategies to lay Uri. As his good luck would have it, she materialized with a steaming cup of tea, and a plate of fried-chips.

Sudhakar confided to me later, that all strategies and good sense deserted him as soon as he saw her before him, and be began to tremble like a guilty child.

"Uri," he babbled, "How did you know I am alone? You brought only one cup of tea."

Uri smiled naturally and told him that she had only two hands and both of them were full. Her answer slightly daunted his purpose and removed his misconception about her availability. Sudhakar forgot all his successes with women, and remembered his failures and their attendant humiliations.

Uri sat on his bed confidently, her hands folded between her two thick things. Her hair was loose and her two breasts were covered half-heartedly by a calico print saree. A hot debate was going on in the mind of the young man. Each moment was precious and unrecoverable.

He slurped tea. The cup was quaking on the saucer. He deposited the cup on the table, and, finally deciding to take the chance, he sat down on the bed touching her warm body. She didn't stand up, nor did she budge.

Sudhakar wanted to engage her in a passionate conversation, and confess his desire. But he could not find any subtle quality in Uri, and feared that such serious talk would probably terrify the girl. He put his hand on her shoulder softly, caressingly. His body was wet with perspiration, his desire was uncontrollable and his mind drew a blank, refusing to deliberate. He was out of his depth.

Then, abruptly he planted a kiss on Uril's full cheek, and waited with the trepidation of a hunter who fired his last bullet at the tigress. Momentarily the catastrophe was averted, because nothing unpleasant or pleasant happened.

Neither she embraced him, nor did she rebuke him, nor did she shout for help.

Encouraged by his first sign of success, he pressed her palm with grateful cordiality and kissed on her other cheek. She stood up quietly, and said in a coy, sulky tone : "You haven't taken your tea yet. Take some chips; I've prepared it. Tell me if it is good." She offered the cup of tea to him without much ado. "I tell you I am not leaving you until you eat these chips and finish my tea. I sit here."

"What'd you do if I eat you, only you and nothing else," said Sudhakar, slowly recovering his natural poise and power of speech.

"Hey, Babu, am I food?" she wondered aloud.

Sudhakar thought he got the message. He stuffed his mouth with some chips and washed them down with a draught of tepid tea. He moved close to her, ran his fingers through her hair, sniffed it, and then, feeling greatly provoked, he tugged it with some force. She fell on her back on the bed. They snuggled up together. Her legs parted a little and the carelessly draped saree slipped from one of her breasts. She didn't offer any physical resistance, only muttered nonchallantly : "No, Babu, no. Mother must have come back. Leave me alone. Two rupees for tea and chips."

Sudhakar didn't pay any heed to her mild protest, but he noticed the open door and windows and, leaving the girl in that position, hastened to them. Returning after closing the door and two windows, he found the bed empty. He wondered where she could have possibly gone in less than a minute. He looked around, briefly baffled. The door leading to the bathroom was wide open. Hoping to find her there, he walked steathily into it. He was not in a position to give up. The violence, the sheer ferocity of his desire could have made him run ten miles, swim a river in spate and scale a ten-foot boundary wall to meet the object which aroused it, and was capable of slaking it.

Uri, who had just slipped under the bed, emerged with the deft agility of a cheetah, took the cup and saucer opened the door and closed it from outside — all she did in less time than the man took to check the bathroom which contained a latrine with a separate door.

Sudhakar raced out of the bathroom, knelt down and peered under the bed, checked the other side of the life-size dressing-table mirror, the book shelf. He looked at the door and soon discovered that the door was bolted outside.

Andy and I were taking a stroll on the beach where we met our other mates. I stayed with them and Andy left us with his own old pretext : Call of nature. He heard whispers in the semi-dark room, and peered through the open window. That was the time when Sudhakar was planting his first kiss on Uri's cheek. Andy watched the proceedings standing in the dark corridor, and when Sudhakar pulled her hair, Andy stole a glimpse of her forbidden zone and ran full speed to us. By the time we reached the window, thrilled by the prospect of seeing an act of love live, the door adjacent to the window was already bolted from outside. We maintained silence and avoided the closed window which would open at any time.

Sudhakar was at his wit's end. He felt as if he'd go mad at once. He cursed himself for not checking under the bed first. He opened the window cautiously and said in low tone : "Uri, please open the door, please. Take this fifty-rupee note for your tea and chips : you needn't return any change. I'll give you this note, I promise, if you simply open the door. Only open the door, and you get fifty rupees. You can buy a saree by it. If you don't believe come to the window, I'll give it to you in good trust."

The fifty-rupee note was snatched through the window and the door was opened simultaneously.

Sudhakar confused, ashamed, stretched himself on the bed trying desperately to cover up his erection. He was charged by us for trying to rape Uri, which he violently denied, saying that there was sufficient provocation from her side, that she didn't resist his advances when he kissed her cheeks and squeezed her breast. "Can you imagine, chaps," he spluttered, "she even did not hide her private parts as she lay supine on this bed, here." He pointed to the exact spot, and wanted to convince his most incredulous accusers of his being driven to such a situation.

Andy looked indignant and solemn. He announced with the authority of the most experienced occupant of the Wave Crest House that Uri was not that type of girl. "I'm afraid, we may have to find some other place in a week. The owner will certainly ask us to vacate once he learns about such things from Uri." Andy sounded ominous and unnaturally formal. And Sudhakar looked like a perfect thug, though he tried to brazen it out by maintaining a cavalier attitude. "Take it easy, friend," he told Andy, "She is a cheap sort of wench. She won't tell it to any one. I bet one hundred bucks on it. Besides, why should the owner ask all of us to vacate. I can go alone should such an exigency arise. Don't worry!"

Andy looked away and snorted malevolently : "You don't know the history of the house, do you? The owner is a man of crores and principles — very very orthodox. He entrusted the house to an unscrupulous manager who turned it into a regular brothel, and minted money. When the owner knew of it, he sacked the manager and locked up the rooms and employed Narasingh to take care of the building. He had advised him to keep only respectable people — particularly college teachers, bank officers and doctors."

"Keep that history to yourself, Mr. Andy," flared up Sudhakar, staring him in the face. "I am not interested in your information. I can stay anywhere I please, and lay as many girls as I can get. That's it. Now call it quits."

Andy cast a nasty look at Sudhakar and was just preparing to retaliate, when Nityanand came out with a palatable suggestion. He whispered something in Andy's ear. Then, sporting the fifty-rupee bank note as a trophy, he began : "Sudha, I believe, was offering it to some one who would open the door. Now, we opened the door and as a result earned it. We'll buy two kilogrammes of prawns and have a good feast. Is it accepted?"

His proposal was heartily accepted. Sudhakar said that it was the only money he had but no one listened to him. Andy chuckled with strange satisfaction. Narasingh who we had nicknamed the Man-Lion was called in. The menace was diffused.

The most incredible part of the incident was its finale. Uri not only assisted the boy in the preparation of prawn curry and setting the table, she served and shared the food with us, as well. However, Sudhakar could not look her in the face and maintained a glum silence throughout. Because of her presence, no one dared broach the topic directly during the dining time. Subramaniam the vegan announced carelessly that he'd pray God almighty to make it possible for His humble devotees at the Wave Crest Lodge to have more such feasts without giving subscriptions. Sudhakar cast a villainous look at him, and the rest of us swallowed our smiles with our food.

12

I STAND CONFESSED

"You're alone, yet smiling, What's the matter, by the way?" Puja barged into my weird world of recollection, with that question. I was off my guard. My smile blossomed into a crazily coloured flower of laughter.

"Oh it's nothing—" I fumbled trying to control my laughter. "I only recollected a serious situation which ended comically."

Puja, after hearing out the brief account, concluded that the wench in question was a past master in the trade, though young.

I fully subscribed to her view, but just before the topic was about to be given up, I said, "You must admit, Puja, she was more mature and resourceful than any of us there."

"Why so? I don't know her, but I can say her resources are cheap and she was blase." Puja, like the rest of her tribe, had no other choice, but to condemn such behaviour in the strongest terms. Such uncompromising attitude noticeable among the wives and beloveds of the world, serves both as a vindication of their own virtue and as a warning against male philandering.

"You're uncontestable I know," I put in politely, but dear, what happened in that lodge during the next few months confused all of us, and may, if I am not gravely mistaken, confuse your highness too. Five of us believed privately and collectively that Uri was a "cheap sort of wench" as Sudhakar described her, and behaved with her in a way similar to how a lascivious boss behaves with his coy and comely personal stenographer. Andy, of course, was not a participant in that passionate game of hide-and-seek. He had many other things to worry about, too many irons on the fire.

Each of us found some occasions to be with Uri alone. Each one of us realized the weakness of the other, but we feared to declare what we knew or suspected owing to our own guilty feelings. Uri received rave notices. Precious garments and cosmetics were thrust into her eager hands. Nityanand, a forty year old man with three children, a skin-flint, spent quite a sum on Uri. He bought for her expensive cosmetics and saree. It was a gesture of love, he confessed later, which he had never extended to his devoted wife even once on their twelve anniversaries of marriage. I realized then that the more amorphous the desire, the greater was its attraction and irresistibility; that a woman's vulnerability much more than her beauty, caused passionate tornadoes, generated vibrations and aroused centripetal tendencies in men. Uri was not at all charming. Her face was round, her eyes nondescript and her nose flat. Her jet black hair was wiry and grossly dense like a tropical jungle, and she had the habit of chewing tobacco.

But she had some redeeming features apart from her apparent vulnerability. Her body was richly endowed with shapely breasts and buttocks, full cheeks, regular teeth and sensual lips. She was like a large whole-meal plain loaf, baked brown, which didn't have any taste in itself, but acquired a taste by getting mingled with the eater's ptyalin induced by his appetite and mastication. Sudhakar, who looked disarmingly jovial and asexual, refused to accompany us to the beach on several occasions on pretexts of indisposition and personal work, and preferred to stay put in the room hoping to have another tryst with Uri. I myself was the most interesting case. Notorious for my introverted nature, I managed with as few words as necessary to keep conversation going. I as well as my friends, knew that I was impregnable to any temptation of flesh.

One Sunday I paid a courtesy visit to a friend's house. returned towards noon and found the whole house empty. I went to the kitchen and found neither food nor our boy there. I was hungry but I didn't feel like walking a mile for food. I bought some biscuits and cakes.

I was just going to eat my humble lunch, when Uri knocked gently on the door. She was dressed like a bride. The room was filled with musk perfume. Her hair was shampooed and organized, her lips were red like ripe pomegranates seeds and her eyes were blazing. I was at a loss for words. She smiled like a witch who had just eaten a living hen. Scarlet lipstick was lavishly applied without skill and taste. Her semi-transparent cotton saree revealed her body in a more flattering light. Her body was shining as if she had bathed in a pool of clarified butter.

It was my moment of reckoning. She entered the room in her usual way and sat on my bed to my chagrin and surprise.

"Why do you sit there when there is a chair here?" I said smilingly.

She occupied the chair, but abruptly stood up and sat on the bed again almost touching my body. The impudent courage of the wench annoyed me. It never occurred to me that she was flirting and trying to include me in her list of lovers.

Without much wasting time I put my hand on her shoulder, my right palm resting on her left breast. She kept on chattering like a bird, totally unresponsive to my advances. She talked about her ability in cooking and making tea, her ill-tempered father who had driven out her mother four times after thrashing her, and about her dear little brother Buna. Like a meek lamb she yielded to my caresses, kisses and squeezing, and kept on talking of totally different things all the time. When my unsteady fingers crawled into her armpit, she started giggling.

"Please don't do that I am very sensitive to tickling," she spoke pleadingly through her coy giggling. I did not pay any attention to her words. My avid and inexperienced hands groped blindly-touching the untouchable areas of her body. She was not trying to free herself, nor was she attentive to my caresses. She was only speaking and giggling, writhing deliciously and complaining about my touching her loins and armpits.

My hands explored her body, felt the recondite landscape of her full body. My whole being was transmogrified into a tactual sensation, as if nothing existed beyond the sense of touch. Like a piece of metal in the baptism of fire, I glowed red hot and felt a curious sensation of melting. Terminal ecstasy, I felt, was as excruciating as a prolonged electric shock. Like a pet poodle, like a Barbie doll, she yielded to my caresses without being involved in the act.

As soon as I relaxed my hold, she stood up, arranged her clothes and hair, and asked me in a casual tone of voice if I'd like to have some potato chips and tea. I could not articulate a word, however, hard I tried. Stretched out on my ruffled bed, face upward, I felt as if life was ebbing out of me. I was hungry, exhausted and apprehensive and guilty — all at the same time. It was my first, and I assure you it was my last attempt on her.

Staring at the ceiling fan I remembered the definition of catalyst which I had learnt in my school days. "It is a substance that speeds up a chemical reaction without itself changing." Ten minutes later the human catalyst returned with chips and tea, and insisted that I must eat the whole plate of her "home made chips."

After narrating the episode with the lurid details, I feared the worst. Puja, as a rule, does not take such overturnes easy. But this time the salacious details of the story aroused sexual fantasies in her mind. I tried to cheer her up with some facetious remarks, but she preferred to hide her reactions.

Several days later when I believed she had forgotten the story, she broached the topic. "Tell me honestly if it was actually the last time. You know I don It mind such things. I simply want to know."

She was satisfied, or seemed satisfied, when I invoked a whole pantheon of gods and goddesses to be my witness. But she agreed with me that the girl called Uri or Furi was an unusual creature and an excellent promoter of her home-made products.

"Then what gifts did you give her, by the way?" She continued her query.

"Only a bottle of essence. I bought it for myself. She saw it, sniffed it, fondled it and sprayed her whole body with it. Just a week after that incident, she repeatedly said she liked the smell very much. Asked me what I would do if she stole it, or took it by force. I smiled at her, and asked her to take it. She grabbed it and walked away, without ceremony. She was gross, no doubt about it."

Puja appreciated my saying so; but she had only one thorn in her flesh which could not be removed. It was that she was deprived of the first touch, the first kiss and the first caresses of her dearest husband, and that such a despicable and dime-a-dozen type of hussy was the fortunate receiver of that privilege.

Just after narrating the Uri-episode and my not-so-dignified involvement in it, I realized my folly for saying it. Puja tried to put up an appearance as though she was too magnanimous to mind such an insignificant event which took place much before we knew each other. But I could see her face cloud as she listened to my salacious account. A fortnight following my revelation, I had to put up with her sulks, innuendos and formal monosyllables. One day I told her frankly that she was not as magnanimous as she pretended to be.

You should remember, Puia, I said impatiently, "it was I who told you about all that. You didn't find out that secret, did you? Now you behave as if I betrayed you."

"Not that, not that." she protested tearfully; "I am only trying my best to forget that feeling of loss. But it seems the malignant thorn will go on hurting me till my dying day. I feel cheated, that's all."

"But you were no where around then," I protested.

"So what?", retorted she; "I'm not blaming it on you. I feel cheated not because you chugged on me knowingly. I am only cheated out of my right to get your first contact."

13

ANJAN DA MEETS URI

It was a Sunday. The morning was at ten. We, the inmates of the Wave Crest Lodge, were sitting together in a room listening to Nityanand's litany of conjugal problems. He had a clear edge over the rest insofar as marriage and its attendant problems were concerned.

"Boys," he began avuncularly, "I'll give you a crash course on conjugal life provided you energize me with tea and your keen interest."

Sudhakar pulled his chair close to the experienced man and sat astride on it facing the speaker. Don't bother about censorship, Nityanandaji, he said; tell us frankly what happened on the first night.

He was hoping to hear a pornographic account, but Nityanand disappointed him.

"What I wanted to tell you, boys," he began, "is a piece of advice as well as a warning. The first night is the most crucial night. How you'll take your wife and how she'll take you, and what type of married life you'll have — all these questions are set and answered in that night, on that bed. As chance would have it, the newly-weds are eager to shed their clothes and their secrets. Their testosterone surges. They forget the world around them and the future coming to meet them. You'll be one up on your women if you manage to keep your cool and make her lose hers and remember that you are closeted with the woman not for a love-game, but for a power-game. If you have the advantage of her in the first encounter, you lord it over her rest of your life."

"You mean, Nityanandaji," I asked, "the married partners should not be frank to each other? Again, what sort of relationship will it be if the newly-weds try to dominate each other? Can there be any room for love if both the parties keep fighting?"

Andy joined his force with me. "According to our Professor of Conjugal Relations," he bantered, "the marriage bed should be an arena of struggle or a cockpit : the bull pitted against the toreador, the wrestler against a rival, the cock against a cock, two battering rams locking their horns. I bet I was much edified by the crash course."

Nityanand flashed a smile of noble tolerance. "Hard-boiled romantics," he muttered. "I sympathise with you. I'd have been surprised had you agreed with me. There ought to be some difference between people who know and people who don't."

"As far as I know, Nityanandaji," said Javed innocently, "there can never, I mean love and true friendship are not possible without frankness just as a person cannot make a picture without talent. Once I drew, I mean I wanted to draw a cow, and believe me it looked like a dog. Not a correct dog either. I mean its face looked much like a dog's."

Nityanand cast a disapproving look at Javed. His all too practical intelligence perhaps found Javed's analogy a bit tenuous.

He was about to explain his empirical position when there occurred a temporary interruption.

Anjan Das Gupta, whom we fondly addressed as Anjan da, knocked on the open door and entered the room. The Public speaker in him beamed at us with satisfaction by seeing so many persons gathered in one place. He was offered an upholstered chair near the table. Narasingh was called and asked to prepare tea. During the past few months Anjan da had visited us twice or thrice and endeared himself to all inmates of the lodge. Narasingh was excessively fond of Anjan da. He used to express the speciality of his favours in a variety of ways : by running his errands with greater promptness and devotion. Though Nityanand and Anjan da belonged to the same age-group, and though Anjan da, who was yet unmarried was not as wise as Nityanand, we all knew his views on marital relations would be more edifying than the latter's.

Nityanand who, a few minutes ago, was bursting with homilies and tips on marriage fell silent. We, on our part, were so preoccupied with our listening that we took time to broach a new topic. The silence was oppressive.

"Why don't you continue your conversation?," Anjan da said, sprawling on the chair.

"Anjan da," began Nityanand haltingly, "I was just going to instruct these green and callow acolytes about marriage management, I mean wife management."

"Please go on, Nityanandaji," said Anjan da, and added graciously : "I think I shall learn something from your practical experiences."

"How will you apply that knowledge?" I asked. Andy added : "What do you say? You think he can't have a wife if he wants to? Theories on marriage may force him into it, who knows? You know Abhay? The fellow took a one-month crash course in computer operation by paying five hundred rupees; then mortgaged his wife's gold ornaments in the bank and bought a computer. He needed the machine for practice." Andy laughed heartily. We all laughed.

Anjan da smiled precisely.

Nityanand was getting more impatient. His knowledge was troubling him.

"These green, callow would-be husbands," he said addressing Anjan da in particular, "are trying to counter my hard-earned wisdom with a card-board sword of romantic idealism."

"I see!" observed Anjan da half-seriously; "It is a battle between innocence and experience."

Exactly!" said Nityanand.

"I believe, Anjan da," put in Javed quietly, "innocence if it's truly innocent should survive the onslaught of experience. But according to Nityanandaji, experience can be obtained at the expense of innocence. He says the husband-wife relationship should be based on un-truth, I mean on lies. How can that be?"

"Yes," Nityanand crowed : "I maintain that in conjugal, as well as in all other relationships, truth plays the villain, complicates matters, raises hurricanes, unhouses hornets and torments the truth buff to no end. It's sheer simplicity of some die-hard truth tellers to believe in the ultimate victory of truth over un-truth, love over need-based relationships, frankness over deception and intrigue. For this reason, simplicity is weak and naive. If you have it, you'll be always defeated, you'll be the most wretched man on earth. Call me what you may, I'll maintain that conjugal truth-telling is the saddest thing a man can ever do. It's a type of masochism. It is like giving a whip to your partner and asking her to keep on flogging you with it."

Sudhakar, at this stage, caught up with Nityanand. "You're right, Nityanandaji," he said animatedly; "no man should give a woman so much of leeway and some good reasons to blackmail him. Drinkers of conjugal pleasure should be advised to drink their favourite tipple as much as they want but should be warned not to spoil the party by vomiting."

Anjan da reacted sharply to what he bluntly called rubbish and baby-talk. His frown silenced both Nityanand and Sudhakar.

"Nityanandaji," he said gravely, "your diatribe against truth seems to be an outcome of your unpleasant experience. Am I right?" (Nityanand nodded meekly.) Sudhakar, if I am not much mistaken, your tippling allusion reeks of your own unpleasant experience.(Sudhakar averted his eyes, blushing guiltily.) Now both of you are up in arms against truth for purely subjective reasons. I don't see your enemy. You're only fighting with your own shadows. Truth, as I am given to understand, has nothing to do with innocence, experience, belief or disbelief in God. In a sense, truth as a term of popular usage is a euphemism for the personalised prejudice, which one man uses to counter another man's prejudice. Truth is dependent on un-truth in order to be what it is. It is a form of oneupmanship people practise to get the advantage over other people.

Andy knitted his brows and observed sarcastically that Anjan da was speaking with a determination not to be understood by others. "Debasis," he asked, "could you get him?" "Frankly, Anjan da," I said, "I cannot make out your point. I know you're disapproving of the popular notions or usages of the word 'truth,' but how can it be dependent on lies? Our ancient sages, you know, searched for the Truth, and..."

"I understand what you mean," Anjan da snatched away my sentence, and said : "But I am not referring to that transcendental Truth which our sages sought to realize, to that Holy Grail which our wise men wanted to possess. I am only speaking about its identical country cousin, the popular, terminological exactitude which is an antonym of falsehood. Let's take a pause and cancel our predilections for a moment. If you train a child to be its natural self, if you expose it to a surrounding where people speak out what actually happen to them, what they actually do and think, without any fear or shame, because there is no other way to express themselves, then, when that child attains maturation, he or she will speak the truth without being aware of the implications of the term 'truth.' Imagine a situation such as that, think of the prelapsarian state of human society and tell me if such expressions as 'speaking' the truth, 'the whole truth' and 'nothing but the truth' would be comprehensible to the citizens of that society. What I want to say is that our natural tendency to respond to events and to give an exact expression to what we think, feel, see and hear has always been influenced by surround mind-set and contaminated notions."

Andy disagreed : "You mean man is born true and it's the society that turns him into a liar?"

"Of course!" said Anjan da.

"Anjan da," I said fervently, "your point sounds romantic, I should say. The question of lying leads to the question of evil. If you allow me to formulate your philosophical position a little differently, you seem to suggest that man is born good, inherently noble, and the society has turned him evil and ignoble; that should a child be brought up in a natural way, the words like lie, deception, truth, falsehood, etc. would not be found in his dictionary. It's true had such a possibility prevailed these expressions might have sounded redundant; but such a possibility did not prevail, and such value-specific expressions had not only been coined but also had occupied the centre-stage of transcultural communication system. So it proves the fact that things could never have been otherwise. That's to say amoeba and evil, life and microbes evolved almost simultaneously and assumed their multi-celled complexity in the process of evolution, and contributed to the formation of homo sapiens."

"Now if we'll look through a dictionary, we find more than sixty per cent of words in it virused with value-judgment. If we remove ethically-charged words and phrases from human memory by conducting frontal lobotomies, all our orators would suffer from aphasia."

Anjan da was amused by my vehemence. Like Plato's caveman (who saw the sun for the first time), he blinked quizzically, and peered into my eyes to study their depth.

"Debasis," he said trenchantly, "your stream, unfortunately, is seen to its silt. Your self-punishing ecstasy intoxicates you. Whatsoever happened to humanity, I soberly feel, was not the best of happenings. The validity of an act does not and should not come from the fact of its performance. Those who maintain that an act is valid simply because it happens commit an error of judgment. That's why an empiricist is a fatalist in the philosopher's mask."

'My point is," Anjan da continued, "if we allow ourselves to be guided by such anthropological inferences, we'll step into the mud swamp of logical fallacy. Then we'll be tempted to draw the conclusion that what has already happened were bound to happen; that, given the inexorability and structure of human nature, the world we live in could never have been otherwise. What do we do then? We justify everything in the name of necessity : the good deeds that men do become a gimmick, the bad deeds that men do become a game. That's why, I tell you, Debasis, do not find fault with human nature when the reports of evil perturb you; do not draw consolation from circular arguments. To be natural is to be true. Your belief in the naturalness of action and of speech will cancel out all hesitation. Man is good in the state of Nature. It is not a philosophical posturing. It is my testament of faith. And my faith is supported by reason and circumstantial evidences. The human society we have today has survived a thousand holocausts, a million instances of evil. That's because man contains in him an indestructible seed of transcendence."

Nityanand looked on timidly as his favourite topic was snatched away from his grasp and changed into some high-serious stuff in which he had little interest.

"What do you suggest, then?" he asked Anjan da, reminding him of the original question. "Would you say we should hide nothing from our wives? If you say yes, then I tell you frankly that your book reading has not made you practically wise. If I tell you how much I suffered by being frank, these would-be husbands would never commit the same mistakes."

Anjan da was preparing to speak something, when I, unmindful of what Nityanand said, asked zealously :

"Anjan da, if man is inherently good, and if the society is a collection of inherently good men, then why there is so much evil in it?"

Nityanand glared at me belligerently for queering his pitch for the second time.

Anjan da was about to speak when a most unexpected and unfortunate event diverted our attention.

The backyard of the Wave Crest Lodge was surrounded by a six-foot high boundary. The brick boundary had a narrow door which opened directly to the sea. That door was partially visible to us. On hearing a screaming sound, we looked out and saw Uri running into the backyard through the open boundary door in full steam, screaming on the top of her voice holding a bundle of wet clothes. She ran into the room, undeterred by the presence of several males in it, and slipped under the table and sat huddled up, covering her face with her saree.

Anjan da, who saw her for the first time, looked aghast at her, and exclaimed.

"What's the matter, girl? What's the matter?"

Uri was shaking nervously and muttering : "monkey! monkey!" We thought she was being chased by some one who wanted to beat her. We were much mistaken in that, for no human being came chasing her.

Before we could realize what she meant by "Monkey" (which we took to be a term of abuse), a large black-faced monkey, its tail held aloft, galloped into the backyard, headed towards the room where we were sitting, and stopped short at the door when he saw us.

Instead of backing away, the oaf bared his teeth at us as a gesture of combat, and sat down on his haunches on the door step blocking our exit, and flaunting his erotically-inspired, flesh-coloured member. We were, indeed deeply offended by the brute's conduct. Our human instinct prompted us, as it had prompted our anthropoid forefathers to find out some weapons to fight against other creatures. Andy hoisted the complete works of

Shakespeare to threaten the monkey; I raised a plastic torch like a stick; Nityanand raised a wooden ashtray over his head tipping its contents over his carefully combed head in his haste; and Subramaniam found a wooden scale nearby and raised it like a sword. Our threatening gestures were wasted on the monkey who refused to budge, and returned our threats with chattering, and a gnashing and baring of his teeth. We realized that we were not a match for the formidable trespasser. The monkey was in a truly attacking mood. His uncontrollable desire, perhaps, made him recklessly brave. It stood on all fours, his dark eyes burning under his peaked forehead, his teeth flashing like a piece of lightning, its tail raised like a tentacle. The sight transfixed us. Uri was watching the monkey with terror-striken eyes.

Fearing we'd all desert her, she clutched Anjan da's legs. Anjan da was sitting on a chair adjacent to the table. He told her harshly to calm down and release his legs. In an abrupt, unexpected movement, he stood up bolt upright, held the two sides of the wooden table with his hands and hoisted it to his chest level and made at the simian bully at the door.

The monkey saw what was coming, quickly turned around and, galloped away. Uri stood watching the retreat of her aggressor. She was still trembling. Her nerves, like her hair and saree, were all in a mess. She smoothed her hair, wiped her face with the bundle of wet clothes she was carrying and heaved a sigh of relief. But however hard she tried to cover up her body, her physical virtues bared themselves. Her wet cotton voile saree was so sheer it might not be there. She cast a timid look around her, but didn't take her eyes off the standing figure of Anjan da's. He stood holding the table even after the monkey had left the arena. He perhaps feared the monkey would return. Subramaniam and Javed took the table from his hand and brought it to its original place. Peace returned. We occupied our respective seats. But we all felt as if something was wrong. Uri stood leaning against the door, in as awkward a position as one could imagine-, but kept devouring Anjan da with her blinkless gaze. Her great admiration and gratitude for her saviour made her

preached love, kindness and forgiveness. Given absolute power over humanity, such inspired vegetarians would construct Auswitzes in every village and exterminate two thirds of the human population, and would not feel guilty even for a moment for their action.

Andy abruptly excused himself, raising his little finger as soon as Anjan da completed his last sentence. Raising the little finger was not only a gesture of protest, but also an innocent and urgent desire to make water in the open. I knew he wouldn't show up again. Poor Andy was horrified by the speech. I too felt uneasy, because I said those words admiring Andy only to arouse amicable spirits.

I didn't speak and waited for his passion to subside. Uri, like God's good angel, came to our rescue. She was holding two cups of tea. When her eyes met Anjan da's, she smiled and blushed like a wife four days after marriage.

"Who asked you to bring tea, girl" Anjan da charged her.

"Nobody!" replied Uri.

"Then who will pay for the tea, please?" This time his tone was bantering and brusque.

"Nobody!"

"I see!" Anjan da said; "So you supply tea free of cost?"

I interfered, and assured Anjan da not to bother about the payment. He, after all, was our guest. He gestured at me to be silent.

"I asked you if you supply tea free of cost, did you hear?"

"Not to all", she answered, still continuing her cherubic smile.

"Why should I give tea free of cost to everybody?"

"Then what've I done to deserve your favour?"

"You know better. Mother sent tea for you. She forbade me to accept any money from you. That's all."

"But why?," Anjan da barked at her.

Andy reentered the room, smiling at Anjan da's puzzlement.

Uri shook her head. She pretended ignorance. She was only obeying her mother who knew the answer.

Anjan da looked puzzled, shrugged his shoulders and expanded. I explained the situation : "Don't you remember that monkey incident. She likes you because you saved her that day. You know none but the brave deserves the fair. When you hoisted this four-legged table and advanced towards the aggressive beast, you reminded me of Hercules with his club facing the Nimean lion, and of many great heroes of the past. No wonder Uri felt that way and had a crush on you."

Anjan da's laughter continued full five minutes. I had never seen him laugh like that.

Uri stood watching him, as if mesmerized. She handed over the cup to Anjan da who accepted it, still laughing.

She left when Anjan da told her that he won't take a sip unless he was left alone. He felt the pressure of her doting attention, and considered it unusual, ridiculous and bit too sticky.

"What type of girl?" Anjan da asked, leaning forward, whispering.

"Sprightly! Energy full to the brim and spilling over. That's she. Springy, light and sprightly."

"That's good!", observed he, looking steadily into my face.

I was surprised by Anjan da's sudden opinion.

"Do you know why that sort of energy is good?" asked Anjan da, and continued : "I'll tell you why. Energy in any form is a boon, a gift of nature. It keeps the world going. But it hates to be misused or trifled with. That's why you get a nasty shock when you touch a live wire. If you ask me I'll tell I like energetic persons."

"But the girl in question is utterly gross," chipped in Andy and added with a wry smile : "She has a lot of raw energy. You don't know her yet."

Others present there neither contradicted nor supported Andy.

"To begin with, Andy," said Anjan da peevishly, "your yard-sticks, your weights and measures are faulty. Don't trust them."

"We always measure with our own yard-sticks only, don't we?" retorted Andy.

"True," said Anjan da, but they can be wrong, they can be defective. You call a girl gross, because she does not rise to your level of refinement. But you are forgetting the discrepancies in your and her surroundings in which you both are brought up. Why you alone; all of us present here are born and brought up in a particular type of household and a particular type of society. Life has treated us with familiarity and amiable leniency. Our parents treated us with love and care, even might have splurged on our clothes and fancy items. A more or less strict moral code whether felt or not, informs our upbringing. Politeness, etiquette, good manners, mutual dependence and things of that sort have been fed to us along with food. But look at people around us who have none or little of these trainings. Life is a scowling, hard-task master to the children born in unhappy and poverty-stricken families. They get a raw deal. They are forced to work under horrendous working conditions for a pittance when they should be dandled in their fathers' or mothers' arms. The adults — in their own families and outside — beat them, brutalize them, laugh at their complaints, flog them mercilessly when they find any childlike trait or irresponsibility in them and use most obscene and rude words for them casually.

"What sort of people they will be when they emerge from such ordeals and torture chambers?"

"You've admirably defended Uri," quipped Andy smiling skeptically.

"Come on, Andy," said Anjan da in a tone of vexation; "I defended no individual. I only interpreted a general event. I tell you, don't use your yard-stick as a stick to clobber other people with."

Andy was not in a mood to take Anjan da seriously. A skeptical smile stuck to his face. He perhaps pitied Anjan da for not knowing what he knew.

15

ANJAN DA'S VISIT : A ROMANCE

A fortnight after Anjan da dropped in on us to tea. He spoke nothing and sprawled on Andy's neat bed with his shoes on. It was a marvellous evening — breezy, bracing and cool. The setting sun had coloured the white clouds and the whole sky. Andy and I were just preparing to go out. Anjan da declared that he was indisposed and would like to have a nap. "Arrange a cup of tea for me and leave me alone," he commanded.

Andy said : "Very well! Moths were once worms and caterpillars. You should stay inside your cocoon for a reasonably long time to add wings to your yellow, sticky, creepy ideas. Good bye, Anjan da."

Anjan da didn't look at him. We left him alone. On our way, we advised Uri to fetch our guest tea and her home-made potato chips.

"Amma!" she exclaimed, and ran into her house like a boy. We returned after two hours, and found Uri sitting on the floor cross-legged facing Anjan da. Both of them started when they saw us, and stopped their conversation. Uri stood up, collected the cup and saucer, and slithered away like a serpent. Anjan da started leafing through an old journal and behaved as if he was searching for some important information.

Andy talked in riddles.

"You know Anjan da when it rains?"

"No. When?"

"When the water vapour collects in large measure in the sky. It's the hot sunshine that does the work, what else?"

"Who doesn't know that? Did you discover this great truth today, while strolling?"

"Natural laws are akin to the laws of human nature. That's why we sneeze," said Andy.

"You talk in riddles, Andy," said Anjan da, without looking up. "Come to the point straightaway. What do you want to say?"

"Sneeze is a tornado in the wind-pipe, what speed, what violence! By the way, we saw black clouds surging up menacingly at the north-east corner of the sky, and we soon realized that they were caused by the hot sun."

"Andy, you are aiming at something. No beating about the bush, please. There is no tiger in the bush. Don't be fussy!" Anjan da was losing patience.

"The long and short of my speech is it is going to rain cats and dogs. I bet my soul on it. But who can tell me what message the falling rain transmits to the rising vapours?" Andy ended his playfulness, when Anjan da looked at him indignantly. He perhaps remembered how Anjan da reacted last time when he provoked him with his teasing hints concerning Uri.

"What was she talking about?," I asked Anjan da. I was apprehensive of another cloudburst of words.

"Oh, nothing." He evaded my query with a wave of his hand. But he soon realized that such an answer could convince others about his hiding something and make them more curious.

"She was speaking about her unhappy family. The girl has some funny ideas."

"What're they?," Andy inquired formally.

"She holds the view that the country liquor has something to do with wife-beating; that some women are addicted to thrashing and quarreling, and they are unhappy if they are not thrashed regularly and quarrel almost everyday," Anjan da told gravely.

"I know why she does entertain such ideas," said Andy, and added, "Do you know, Anjan da, her mother is regularly beaten and driven out, but she always comes back after a week or a day? What other conclusions could Uri draw from such actions?"

"It's necessity, cruel, cold, calculated necessity, Andy, that brings the unhappy woman back to her hell and children, not addiction. You should understand that. Your multi- faceted genius does not enable you to understand this simple truth, that's a pity."

"Does your Uri understand her own mother that way?," Andy retorted. "We should believe she knows her mother more than we do."

Andy's dig visibly troubled Anjan da. He guessed, though vaguely, that Andy was referring to his relationship with Uri, and romanticising it deliberately in order to enjoy his passionate outbursts.

"It's high time I should leave," he announced, standing up. "I dropped in to relax, not to argue on inanities." Then turning to me, he said, "Mother is not keeping well. She complains a lot nowadays."

When Anjan da was gone, I told Andy that his ostentatious show of familiarity didn't always mean intimacy with his friends, that it was time he stopped being a mocking bird. Andy, however, didn't care.

Inmates of the Wave Crest Lodge slowly, but reluctantly, got used to the new incarnation of the fisher man's daughter. She carried herself with such dignity as to force us to accept her present state to be her real self and her former self a sham. She fetched us tea and snacks when asked and stated the price in a slow definitive tone of voice, turned a deaf ear to our jokes, and barbed or veiled bons mots. While serving us tea, she pulled a long face and assumed a posture of stoical resignation as if she was bludgeoned into doing such work.

Her relationship with Subramaniam and Javed showed some posthumous animation like the severed tail of a lizard. She ceased to be her former self the day the monkey smelt her menstrual blood and chased her almost a furlong from the backwater where she was bathing, to our room. In our innocence, we attributed the cause to her trauma of being so indiscriminately desired by men and monkeys. She flirted with men no doubt, but she couldn't have done the same with the brute. "Had she fallen down on the snaky deserted road!" Nityanand surmised aloud with anxious relish, "Oh, let me not think on it! The impudent creature should be shot."

All our reflections were more or less like Nityanand's in the beginning. As an eye-witness to the incident, I had a hunch that there could be just another reason for the transformation : her first experiencing love for the hero of the occasion, Anjan Das Gupta. My guess, I felt, bordered on fantasy, and I never dared to share it with any one.

Andy, however, had an original, though abstruse, opinion as regard Uri's sudden change of behaviour. "A clever woman," he said, "employs different strategies to captivate different men, and she considered you fellows a lecherous, greedy bunch of crows fighting over raw flesh, and when she encountered a man of courage, who treated her as an ordinary wench much below his interest, she tried to get his attention which she prized, and modelled herself accordingly to ingratiate herself to him. You never understand women, you ravens; I do."

16

TERROR ON THE BEACH

Andy appropriated some power to himself by not getting involved in the Uri affair, and kept on calling us ravens, and using many such highly derogatory terms denoting lechery, greed and lack of discipline. As he mingled freely with the embittered, diminished and disaffected lovers of the Lodge, he had already known all the shameful details of each person's affair with the stormy petrel, and exploited, even blackmailed, us in a mean way. His acerbic wit cut into our honour and privacy, but we kept our calm. He considered himself an ascetic surrounded by lumpens, and minced no words to declare his feelings.

The hurt received is never forgotten; it is only glossed over by considerations of courtesy and peace. Such a hurt secretly snowballing in the heart's interior can erupt when the pressure increases and an opening is found.

One day Subramaniam requested Andy to give him a loan of fifty rupees. He was really hard-pressed. Andy didn't oblige him and instead told him with a vicious smile whether he wanted money to buy some gifts for some other wenches. Subramaniam felt outraged and wept. He spent the whole day on bed burying his face into his pillow. He spoke to us after a lot of persuasion. "I've lost honour for good," he lamented, after describing the incident, and added : "I blame no one, not even fate. I am to blame, I've gone down in my own estimation."

Nityanand's consoling words — that she was a shrewd bitch who seduced us all, that ninety nine per cent of men could have done exactly what we five did, given such circumstances — had no impact on Subramaniam, because he had always believed to have belonged to that remaining one per cent of men, who would triumph over all temptations of flesh.

We left poor Subramaniam to his private sorrow, but could not forgive Andy for his crude unfriendly cavils. We knew he could have used the same words for any of us, had we approached him for a loan.

We collectively decided to bide our time and do well by him as if nothing has happened. I faced the ordeal of sharing the room with Mr. Unspeakable (a new sobriquet was conferred on him) and I considered myself singularly unfortunate for such proximity.

Two days after insulting Subramaniam, Andy asked me to accompany him to the beach for an evening walk. I declined his invitation saying I was expecting some friends. He, however, persisted and assured me that he'd sing some of my favourite songs on the beach.

"You never sing, Andy," I said, "you only introduce your songs. I am not interested to know the history of your songs. Thank You."

He was in the habit of listing the known and unknown personages who admired that particular song which he was about to sing : how many prizes, kudos and embraces that historic song had already fetched him. Then after the song, he would not be at all satisfied if his listener praised it; he'd rather appreciate it if the listener told him that no living singer could sing better than him. If his listener was sensitive enough to tell him that, his name would be added to the preface of the song; if not, he would be a philistine without any taste or knowledge of music. Such a person would be rightly despised by the singer. Andy, fortunately, never remembered such hurts for long.

I accompanied him to the beach when he assured me he won't bother me with such details.

The sea looked grim under the crescent moon. The waves danced like drunken maffickers. While watching the sea, I felt a nausea. My head swam — rising and falling like the waves. The world, the whole creation, everything in it, were engaged in a wild dance. A tribal celebration, a Dionysiac revelry. The planets, the stars, the Milky Way, this earth, the protons, electrons, neutrons, photons, mezons — all danced and moved in terrific speed. "This is malignant speed," I thought, "the violent speed of the chaser and the chased. Its aim is destruction. What a sorry figure man cuts before this consuming vastness of nature! Does the host nature offer man a smile and a chair, when he calls on her?"

I was in no mood for a song. But Andy sang looking at the sea. A holy song in the honour of Lord Jagannath was followed by a love song. That love song described a mood which came over the poet when he espied a doe-eyed damsel of most voluptuous beauty going to the river with a pitcher. The damsel looked back and their eyes met, and the cupid's arrows of desire pierced the poet's heart. Then the poet quickly realized the impossibility of possessing her, and concluded his lyric with a Karmic consolation : Only the man who had worshipped Lord Shiva a million times and meditated on the bank of the holy Ganges would be worthy of such a woman.

Andy kept on singing the last four lines of the song several times.

"You like that part of the song?" I asked. He nodded in answer. He paused after reciting the last stanza a few more times, and asked me if I knew what it meant.

"Nothing can be simpler," I told him. "The wound in the desiring heart was healed up by an invocation of the Karmic laws. The poet didn't get the woman he desired because he had not acquired and accumulated enough virtue to be so happy, so rich in possession."

"It is so, exactly," Andy said shaking my hand, "But there is more to it than what meets the eyes and that's more important than the surface meaning of the song, and I may tell you what is that secret meaning if you express your eagerness to know."

I said I was prepared to listen, and added that the words were so transparent that there could not be any other meaning to these lines.

Andy pitied my ignorance.

"These lines, I tell you, Debasis, contain a code secret which, when unravelled, would make you understand everything Indian : our culture, the shaping norms and thinking process of our people, and whatever we can be proud of having and teaching the world at large." Andy cleared his throat, spat out and began ponderously. His right hand moved up and down like the composer's baton to stress his point.

"Do you know," he said, "these lines are written by a prince who was the heir apparent to the throne? He abdicated his throne in order to become the emperor of the poets. Considering the powers and privileges of the royalty of the early eighteenth century in India he could have possessed the beautiful woman he chanced upon for the asking. Then why such admission of his helplessness? That's because man must deserve what he hopes of getting. The good and happy things of the human world are not given at random to men who have them. There is nothing erratic, capricious and indiscriminate in the system controlled by God. The price of living is not negotiable. We all have learnt the rules of the celestial banking system by rote : you must draw according to your deposit. If you overdraw, if you acquire money, power, woman or anything by force or by unfair means, you're blacklisted as a sinner. Your good works are your twenty four carat gold deposits. Otherwise how can you explain these diversities and discrepancies of the world? The birth of a prince is celebrated by all citizens of the kingdom, and another child born to a beggar is taken no note of. But for such faith in the karmic laws and infallible ability of God at book-keeping, the suffering soul would soon succumb to despair or to barbarism. I have long been trying to deliver a talk on this issue at a public meeting. I, unfortunately, have not yet been invited to any such meeting."

"This is a fine observation," I observed, and added : "This line of thinking has long been in vogue. It has been used and abused by the vested interest groups to silence all protest, and to exploit others with impunity. This karmic law, as far as I understand as a layman, is a labyrinth which contains a dangerous beast. Again, suppose you are now addressing a big gathering, how'd you conclude your speech?"

"Just like that." Andy promptly answered. "I've already said everything."

"No, brother," I contradicted him with an ironic smile.

"You may conclude more or less like this : Brothers and sisters, if you are miserable, you ought to be so, you deserve such misery. Unhappiness comes from the sins or the crimes committed in this life or in your previous lives. Those who are rich, healthy and happy, they have a right to be so."

"This sounds too crude and sarcastic," commented Andy, laughing.

"Such sentences are not only crude and sarcastic, they are ugly and bald as well," I said. "You have dressed them with finery, cosmetics and wigs, to make them presentable. You add to people's actual present misery a vague sense of guilt. You arrest and try them without informing them about the nature of their crime, and finally sentence them to death or life-long torture. Simply because these moth-eaten heirlooms have a market, that cannot be sufficient justification for their continuation and their correctness."

Andy, I knew, would never give up his point. So, I tried to dilute our mutual enthusiasm. "I do well understand this prince-poet's state of mind, Andy," I put in amicably. "It's just like mine when I see a lovely girl whom I cannot get; it's like a hungry man's when he watches the diners in a posh hotel surrounded by delicacies which he can never afford. How diligently you try to refine or poeticise such a passing phase of hopelessness, it still remains as crude and primitive as ever."

Andy guffawed insouciantly.

We wended our way to the lodge. It was late evening. The wind was still. The moon hung in the crepuscular skyline like the sword of Democles or a slice of an orange. Some hiqh-floating clouds were still receiving the light from the sun. We reached our familiar sand bank which rose vertically about twelve feet and stretched more than a furlong close to the sea. Walking on that part of the beach during daytime could be an interesting experience, but to be there in the night when the beach was deserted and nature was still, could give one traumatic feelings of vertigo and confinement.

"Let's run," suggested Andy. I walked faster. A supernatural terror gripped both of us. Dark waters stretched to the horizon, and some big waves rose to our knees. The sand wall, unsurmountably steep and high, seemed to push us to the sea. A high-rising wave could have swept us to the dark depth and drowned us. We also could not see each other. I had to stretch my left hand to touch the sandbank, lest I should blunder into the sea. Sand trickled on my head and into my wet boots.

I kept on walking as fast as I could. It seemed unending. Finally, I reached the level surface. Andy was panting, lying full length on the raised slope. Sweat and sea water had drenched us completely. Some sand particles had gone into my eyes. My glasses had collected moisture. I could not see anything.

Andy, I discovered, was in a more wretched condition. He had stumbled twice and was almost swept into the sea twice. He escaped, he told me a few minutes later, by the skin of his teeth, because his fate had so ordained it. Luckily for both of us, the waves were very mild that afternoon. We agreed that had the waves risen a little higher, say to our waist level, we might have been washed into the sea.

An extreme form of fatigue seized us. We rested in that reclining posture for some time watching the sea which looked like a prehistoric monster crouching and slouching there, but chained down by a mightier force.

"What will happen, brother," I whispered reflectively, "if the sea breaks loose or God lets go the halter?"

Andy was too tired to speak.

We decided to take a short-cut to the lodge because the usual road was roundabout. We were too tired to walk steadily. The short-cut we chose passed through a burial ground full of bosks, boulders, old ruins and some casuarina trees. Light coming from the crescent moon and halogen bulbs on the main road revealed the paved path which moved zigzag through the murky stretch of land.

17

THE SNOW WHITE CAT

We met no mishap on the way, excepting a minor one. A white creature crossed the road in front of us. Andy clasped my hand and blurted out. "Hey, what is that?"

"Maybe, a cat or a hare," I said casually. "Have you ever seen any creature as white as that? It was shining in the dark," Andy persisted.

"Don't worry, Andy," I whispered; "Let's push on. We haven't seen all the white creatures of the world?"

But Andy was not satisfied. He started muttering some sacred mantras to keep the goblins off his body.

As we entered the lodge, Andy caught hold of my hand to detain me. "Wait," he said ominously. "Do you know who that white creature was? No, you don't know. How can you know? Last year, a French woman was gangraped and murdered on the beach, precisely where we sat. I knew her, I talked to her. She could speak English, though in a funny way with a French twang. All she used to put on, were a bikini and a bra, and she had no inhibitions. She had come all the way from France to see India and interact with her people. She avoided the educated and civilized people, and made friends with the local wastrels and college dropouts and the fishermen. But these people exploited her in many ways. Some one took her expensive camera for a day, and never returned it. Another ran away with her binoculars. They exchanged gutter slangs in vernacular in front of her and laughed like mad. When she showed some interest to learn the local expressions of a greeting, they taught her certain slangs which could offend anybody. I knew that when she greeted me with words which meant You're a buffoon and a rogue. How are you? One thing I couldn't approve of : her nudity. She was actually an angel, but her dress didn't confirm her nobility of nature. She had no sex appeal. Her chest was flat. Her brunnet hair was coarse. Her skin was covered in scarlet blotches. Only her sweet voice and beardless comely face proved her gender. But lust, you know, has no eyesight. They behaved with her as you people behaved with that fish-smelling coquet, Uri."

"Stop your nasty tongue from prating further," I almost shouted at him. "You'll repent for this harsh comparison, mind you. What has that French woman got to do with your seeing a white creature? I've enough of your good company, thank you." I refused to listen to his bleak story.

Andy giggled awkwardly, sheepishly. "I was only joking. I'm sorry," he said. "What I was going to say, that white creature could be the ghost of that woman, who knows?"

Intent on avoiding him, I muttered "may be," and walked away.

A couple of days later...

My sleep was disturbed in the midnight. I heard a groaning sound which continued for a long time. Then a violent shriek. I sat up, bewildered and afraid. The incredible pitch of that noise tore the night's silence into tatters. It came from Andy's bed, though it didn't sound like his voice. That shriek was repeated. I jumped out of the bed and switched on the light. A snow-white cat emerged from Andy's bed and sauntered out of the open window adjacent to his bed.

I inquired about the matter. He removed his hands from his eyes, and looked around cautiously. "Is she gone?" he asked. He heaved a sigh of relief when he learnt that the cat had left.

"Are you quite sure it was a cat?," he asked nervously.

I said that there was no doubt about that. Andy smiled scornfully at my ignorance.

"Then this is my small question : what's so special about my bed that a cat would be attracted to it. The world is open and vast, and there must be more then ten thousand houses in the town, isn't it?"

These questions were interesting. Why should a cat prefer a particular bed in a particular house? Ordinarily, a stray cat gets into the house while chasing mice, or searching for fried fish, and runs away at the sight of men. In this case, the cat got into Andy's mosquito curtain and slept with him -that too voluntarily. He went on finding reasons for his calling the cat the spectre of the French woman whose name he didn't remember, and shored up his arguments by multiplying miraculous coincidences.

I, of course, had my qualms, but I nodded my head like a marionette only to evade a heated argument in the midnight. When I found him getting more and more excited, encouraged by my silent agreement, I told him bluntly that it was an actual, flesh-and-blood cat, and nothing else; that if a ghost had a crush on a man like him, it should have assumed the shape of the loveliest woman of France, instead of being a cat, in order to win him over. "The cat could have found some other warm bed had you arranged your curtain properly. What's the use of a mosquito-net when cats can get through it."

In less than ten minutes, he was fast asleep and snoring. He usually snored when he lay on his back. I could not sleep. My sleep was violently jolted by the loud noise; then I was forced to listen to his banalities about the cat; and now his inescapable snoring sound would continue until the morning.

I felt terribly sleepy, but couldn't sleep, and kept on tossing on bed. I nourished a strong resentment for my room mate. I had not forgotten his malicious cavils at five of us, and his comparing us with the rapists. His tendency to connect ordinary events to supernatural motifs, his midnight shrieks, his snoring, his duplicitously apologetic manners after offending someone, his ponderous accents and supercilious look -all combined had started to affect my nerves. Though I did not hate him exactly, I found his presence disturbing. It's always so with me, that when I get annoyed with a person, I exaggerate his unpleasant qualities. His eccentricities become detestable vices. However, I sincerely wished that the cat should not come again to his bed, for that might further confirm his belief in the ghost and inspire his midnight rigmaroles and wild shrieks.

Other inmates, when they heard of this weird episode concerning Andy, considered it a purely pathological situation. They deputed Subramaniam, the meek one, to ask Andy if he actually had an affair with the French beauty. Andy, instead of losing his temper, thanked his interrogator generously for his frankness. "I understand," he told him, "It is natural to suspect my liaison with a woman who considered the sexual act a pleasure trip to the mysterious landscape of the body, but you've done a handsome thing by me by asking me that question and getting your doubts clarified. Honestly, I had no physical relationship with that unfortunate victim of male lust."

But Subramaniam was not convinced. "Then why do you associate the cat with that woman?" he asked innocently.

"First of all," Andy explained patiently, "both the cat and the woman are white; second, my first intuition, you may call it hunch, when I saw the creature, told me that. So far my intuitions have never proved wrong."

Either Subramaniam found the situation utterly ridiculous, spooky and hopeless or he was truly satisfied, he left him abruptly with a pretext. He was disappointed in his mission because Andy, instead of being offended by his questions, thanked him for his frankness.

18

A SECRET PROPOSAL

Two weeks later, when a spick and span Anjan da announced his marriage to some woman we all knew, we refused to take him seriously. I said : "We have the luck of seeing the century palm blooming in our lifetime." Andy teased; "The Devil never leaves mankind alone, he always leaves behind his progeny." Javed inquired humorously whether it was his first marriage or third. Sudhakar the silly said : "I bet the girl whoever she may be is a goner. She'd marry a library." Nityanand, the only married man amongst us, smiled as an old bandit smiles disapprovingly and condescendingly at a shop-lifter or a pick-pocket. Subramaniam had no words to express his anguish and horror at the news, because he had invested Anjan da with some ideal and holy qualities, and marriage with carnal and juvenile qualities. He blushed and squirmed like a virgin as if it was his own marriage Anjan da was talking about. He clasped Anjan da's hand and asked whether marriage was inevitable for a person like him.

After the monkey-incident, Anjan da used to visit the lodge at regular intervals. He made us all feel comfortable in his presence. He mixed freely with each of us — both separately and in groups, listened patiently to our arguments and personal problems. His tendency to universalize and philosophize small events of life, his compassionate and cordial disposition, his personal approach and his wide learning had endeared him to the inmates of the lodge. Andy's pre-emptive attitude produced no effect on Anjan da. Initially, Andy was sulky because his friend cultivated friendship with others, and offered a psychological resistance.

"Are they worthy of your company? Or are you a candidate in the forthcoming elections?" He'd insinuate, wearing a mean, disapproving smile. "Come on, Andy," Anjan da would say, "You flatter me too much. I've never considered myself so worthy as to alienate myself from my fellow men. I've acquired some notoriety as a public speaker, but you'd never find me at the hustings, never".

The day preceeding his announcement of marriage, or the declaration of his slavery, as Nityanand put it, Anjan da invited us to tea at a beach-side open-air restaurant. Seven of us sat round a rectangular table. A fat turkey was moving on the grassy lawn inspecting the eaters. The afternoon beach was festive and moderately crowded. Andy informed us that Anjan da had assured him he would reveal the name of his bride that very day. Though he had hinted about our familiarity with the lady, we could not make use of that clue. We remembered some important public figures who happened to be women and unmarried — their age, their caste, their connections with Anjan da, etc. — and arrived at unlikely conclusions.

Anjan da put the half-finished cup of tea on the saucer, lit a cigarette and declared that the name of his would-be wife was Uri. Javed dropped his cup on his thigh and screamed. The tea was steaming hot. Our bewilderment was visible. Our eyes refused to look up and our tongues stuck to our dry palates. I tried to remember the spelling of pneumatic tyres, fjords and rendezvous. Andy fidgetted as if he had some ants in his pants. Subramaniam felt a strong desire to belch and weep, and covered his mouth. Anjan da was beating time to some unheard music with his fingers, reviewing our reactions with a bemused relaxed look.

"I thought you, boys, would take the wind out of my sails by guessing correctly her name," Anjan da said, "but you all proved nitwits. Why're you so horrified?"

"Have you your heart in the right place. Anjan da or it's gone out to collect nuts," Nityanand ventured finally, still looking down.

"Happily," replied Anjan da, "it's still there. It'll stay there always. You need not worry about that, Nityanandaji. I find I am not getting the type of reaction I wished to get."

Sudhakar the ardent was more upset than the rest of us. He sat on the edge of his chair, poured tea on the saucer and slurped it. His hands were trembling.

Our condition was not much different from that of a bunch of hoodlums who suddenly discovered to their consternation that the woman they took for a slut and outraged turned out to be the princess herself. Anjan da admittedly had nothing royal about him. With his loose curdroy garments, unshaven face, bald front, straggling moustaches, peripheral hairs on his ear-lobes, slightly stooping and gawky gait, his old bicycle and a sun-tanned skin, he looked much like a trade union activist or a peripatetic philosopher. He had told us one of his funny experiences, when he was stopped at the gate, and was repeatedly asked to leave the gathering of the pre-meeting eaters by some organizers of a meeting to which he had been invited to be the chief speaker. "They took me for a scrounger," he said finally, "and they weren't greatly mistaken in that. I told them so when they pestered me with apologies."

Anjan da's natural eminence lay in his mind and eloquence. His presence in a group of strangers would not be felt until he was provoked to take part in a debate or a conversation. Once he began to speak in a soft, piquant and sure accent, people present there would feel a remarkable difference. Ideas would roll out trippingly like finished products. His idealism, soaked, as it were, with passionate references to reality and decked out with pungent irony, would generate an instant interest in others. After some time, a more-equal-than-equals status would be accorded to him, though tacitly, even by his peers and detractors. Once people got familiar with his inner resources, his outlandish outfit and ordinary appearance would acquire a peculiar distinction and associational identity.

If his declaration of Uri's name as his prospective bride took all the inmates of the Wave Crest Lodge by storm and affected our central nervous systems, that was what was precisely expected given the distinction of Anjan da as a highly regarded personal friend to each of us. He was not just another highbrow intellectual who befriended us condescendingly whom we could ignore and take easy. He had already occupied a prominent place in our heart's sanctuary, and we had learnt to take his views on us seriously as if they were matters of greatest importance to us. I remember an occasion when he expressed his desire for coffee, and we were ready to brave rain and cycle a mile to get a bottle of instant coffee; and of all persons, it was Nityanand, known for his sensitiveness to cold, who volunteered to run errands and returned after twenty minutes, all drenched, with a bottle of coffee. We all knew we might not have shown such readiness in that situation had our respective bosses desired coffee. It was a silent testimony of our love and esteem. Fortunately for everybody, Anjan da's inamorata was not present there to notice our wretchedness, to preside over our moments of reckoning. Each of us played out, in his own way, his role of a secret sinner in mime.

"The marriage would be solemnized in the court," declared Anjan da, breaking the uneasy silence; "and only twenty friends, including you six, are supposed to be present there. The Mermaid's Wing hotel has already been asked to prepare dinner for twenty two. Andy will contact the photographer, and you'd contact a florist." He pointed his finger at me.

Subramaniam said : "Anjan da, my congratulations. Will you mind if I ask a question?"

"Go on," encouraged Anjan da.

"What was the urgency which forced you to take this decision?," he asked with an ill-concealed disapproval.

The orator fumbled. He perhaps was not prepared to face such an invidious question from a meek one.

"Well," he said defensively, "I didn't tell you everything about home. Mother is old and sick. But she is never weak when it comes to nagging me about marriage. I know she needs a daughter-in-law more than I need a wife. She cries and squabbles with me when she finds me cooking and washing the dishes. The maid servant does not come regularly."

"In that case," persisted Subramaniam, "you need a nurse-cum-cook, not a wife. She might have worked in that capacity."

Subramaniam made us feel that it was his love and admiration for Anjan da which forced him to be so abrasive. I thought he was fretting himself too much.

"Look, Subramaniam," snapped Anjan da in a tone of controlled vexation, "I did not want a cook-cum-nurse. wanted a wife. Mother wanted a daughter-in-law and more than that, a grand son. Are you satisfied?"

"No I am not satisfied," Subramaniam rapped out his discontent.

"How can I be? You're a high caste Hindu....."

He faltered, looked timidly around. But his righteousness made him brave. And he resumed : "You're a high caste Hindu, and what is she? A fisherman's daughter, isn't it? She even cannot enter a temple. Besides ...."

"You should rather shut up," yelled Nityanand beside himself in indignation and added : "You talk appalling nonsense, you talk shit. Raising caste issues, and feeling no compunction. You talk what your obscurantist grand parents had taught you."

Subramaniam looked crest-fallen. He didn't anticipate that sort of reaction from his co-sufferers.

Andy reacted sharply, "Subramaniam perhaps meant she won't be a good match for Anjan da," he rasped, "You needn't get so worked up. Who, by the way, employed you as Anjan da's advocate?"

Nityanand frowned at Andy and shrugged his shoulders, but didn't retaliate. The situation was too tense to permit such petty bickerings. Each of us sincerely desired that the plan should misfire because it was the worst mismatch we had ever known. We did not have a good opinion of Uri even after her sudden transformation. She made herself cheaply available to us like a common flirt either to get gifts or to promote her wares. She became an ungrateful wretch after the monkey episode, and her consequent change-over. It was not possible for us, the jilted lovers, to admire Uri for anything. Our defeat had warped our judgment and delimited our power of seeing broadly. What we failed to see and judge accurately, was her eccentric power to control her emotions during most trying circumstances. We, however, ironed out our bafflement by deliberately misinterpreting her peculiar behaviour as an instance of the blase professionalism of an unlicensed sex worker.

Anjan da stood up with an abrupt jerk and suggested that we should leave the suffocating meanness of the cloistered open-air parlour and walk on the beach. "We'll settle our accounts there while inhaling the breeze fragrant with centuries and continents, while partaking of the boundless blue of the sky?," Anjan da said, looking at the sea.

Nityanand said casually that the only thing he could never tolerate in others was their intolerance, and added : "Look Anjan da, I've seen the world for four decades, what do I know about it? Yes, I can say, of all the influences that have gone into shaping, framing and constituting our consciousness, nothing is more wasted on us than the humanistic virtues of civilization. If we verify the finished, packed and certified products which roll out of our highest citadels of learning, we'd find them as gross and stiff as the ores from which they were once extracted. That's why our worst fanatics are our most learned intellectuals, and vice versa. My gorge rises at them."

It seemed the sea breeze and the blue sky had no impact on Nityanand. His language was brusque and angry, though partially redeemed by his passionateness. It was malicious, too, because it prodded poor Subramaniam in an unfriendly manner, and injured him.

Anjan da stopped him by grabbing his hand, and looked into his face, "I tell you Nityanandaji, don' fritter away your energy like this. Rummage into your own subconscious and find out how much of dross is there in the superfine finished product. Can't we talk of something else? Had I known that my revelation of the bride's name would be received this way, I might not have taken you people into confidence." Anjan da sulked. When we realized that Anjan da had already made up his mind and our collective resistance would not influence him, we felt ashamed and congratulated him.

"You'll be a happier man after marriage." I prophesied. "She won't attack you with broom-sticks and sauce-pans when you return late. Born and brought up in a household where the mother is regularly thrashed and thrown out by a drunken father, where total and unconditional surrender to every whim of the husband is the first rule of the conjugal relationship, she would prove an asset to an otherworldly husband like you."

"I am not thinking that way, Anjan da," put in Javed who had not opened his mouth so far; "I am thinking of a glorious future."

"Really? What glorious future? Whose?" Anjan da encouraged him. Javed's pretty face reddened.

"I mean," he fumbled, "What I wanted to say your progeny will be a more balanced lot, combining your intellect and her earthiness. My stratified country is in need of professional boxers who'd excel in pole vault, or greengrocers who'd read Plato's *Republic* when they find time.

"Don't think, Anjan da, I am ignorant about your Hindu scriptures. I know Vyasa was born when a great sage married a fisher man's daughter. Is he not your wisest seer and the most prolific epic writer? Scientists say great energy can be produced when matter and anti-matter meet, when mind and matter are conjoint. Once I held two big magnets, when I held the positive end of one magnet, close to the negative end of the other they pulled or were drawn to, each other. Then I concluded that nature approves of the marriage of the opposites. Socrates was given a Xantippe; Anjan da got a Uri. I hope a time will come when beauty and genius will be born out of the synergy of contraries."

Javed was, indeed a swirl of nervous energy himself. Anjan da patted his back, trying to restrain him.

Javed's shy and sentimental talkativeness surprised me. I'd never heard him talking like that. Equally surprising was Subramaniam's attempt to grill Anjan da whom he always regarded with high reverence. I and Nityanand also rasped at him. We were truly out of our depth. It seemed the utter strangeness of the situation had overwhelmed the five of us and made us feel nervous and stodgy.

Like the first-time takers of a heady cocktail, we felt assaulted from within and behaved unnaturally, awkwardly. Initially, I was trying to play it cool. I was reviewing the situation with a critical humour. But soon after, I felt a desire to drop a comment. The comment was only a comparison. I realized later that the comparison was utterly ridiculous. But my desire to say it was irresistible. And it was as apt as the desire was irresistible.

"Anjan da," I observed profoundly, "I think it's a good thing to get married."

My grave observation attracted everybody's attention. Anjan da looked at me helplessly. He was curious to know out of politeness.

"Why is it so, Debasis?," he enquired.

"Because," I put in philosophically, "Gregor Samsa was a bachelor. That was the cause of his undoing. I've a feeling that he might have averted the sad fate that befell him if he were married."

Anjan da looked puzzled, intrigued.

"By the way, who is that man? I don't think I know him," he said.

"Remember your Kafka, Anjan da," I said; "Don't say you don't know him. You've already told me that you know that story."

"O-ho!" Anjan da exclaimed; "You're referring to a character? Debasis, don't be ridiculous."

"No," I protested. "I am not joking. Marriage, you know, is a contract, a sacred contract in which two willing individuals, preferably a male and a female, mortgage their own bodies and souls, too, to each other to get pleasure and offspring. In my opinion, the bodies and souls which lie fallow and un-mortgaged may be pre-empted by the Devil who, after taking legal possession of them, may sow the seeds of discord on them and change them into odd shapes. That's why Gregor Samsa, a bachelor was fransformed into an insect. The Devil, we all know, is an eccentric conjurer. Another good reason to marry is that human nature, when left to itself, is like a rough-edged, spiky rock. The fret and fume of the married life hone it smooth and change it into a cuddly *salagram.*"

"For the sake of sense, Debasis, for God's sake!" cried out Anjan da impatiently, "stop such talk! Such banality can drive me mad. I am yet to understand why the news, of my marriage sticks in your craw. As far as I know, she is a good-looking and good-natured girl. Instead of congratulating me, you fellows behave strangely, and prate and blab idly. I am really intrigued!"

At that point, Andy jumped into the fray. "Anjan da," he protested vehemently, "do not say she is good-looking. True, we cannot see her nature and quality. So we give her the benefit of doubt. But we can see her and judge her physical features. If you give me a bribe of ten thousand rupees, I'll still refuse to call her a good-looking girl."

We silently hated Andy for being so blunt. Anjan da was offended.

"I see, I see," he muttered evasively, and remained tight-lipped.

The mood was spoilt irreparably.

19

A LOVE STORY

A few days later on, we managed to piece together the love story from some sketchy, reluctant accounts revealed to us by Narasingh and Anjan da himself. Though Anjan da maintained it was a simple marriage story, we had our own interpretations of the event.

One afternoon when none of the inmates was in, Anjan da came to the lodge. Narasingh the man-lion offered him a chair and offered to make tea for him. Just at that moment, Uri breezed in with a cheery smile and a plate of potato chips. "I saw you coming," she told him artlessly, "and brought this plate. I'll take it back if you don't want to eat. Mother is making tea for you."

She placed her plate on the floor and squatted on the steps. Anjan da took up the plate, gave some chips to Narasingh and started nibbling the chips. She was pleased to see him eat her chips. Then she ran to her home to fetch tea. She returned with three cups, offered one to Anjan da, one to Narasingh and the third cup was for herself. Anjan da sat in a wobbly chair, the other two sat on the steps. No one spoke anything. The tea-session over, Narasingh got up and wandered out of the gate. Uri sat on silently. She perhaps wanted to speak a lot of things, and as all she wanted to speak could not be spoken, she had decided to speak nothing. Anjan da could guess that.

Then he asked her if she'd walk down to the beach with him. "Me? with you?," she exclaimed incredulously.

"What's wrong?," he said nonchallantly,

Uri collected her cups and plate, and ran away without answering his question. Anjan da walked to the beach alone, and stood leaning against the large old hull of a boat that sat on a sandbank a few yards from the sea.

Was he trying to recover from a shock of embarrassment for saying what he should not have said?

Were his words fortuitous like his meeting with Uri?

Perhaps not. A man of his age should know what he was doing or saying. He was casual no doubt, but not at all insincere. Uri stood near him noiselessly. Her heavy breathing however, betrayed her.

"Uri!," said Anjan da without looking at her, "do you like me?"

Uri giggled, blushed, squirmed, but said nothing in reply.

Anjan da repeated his question.

Uri said yes and nodded vigorously to stress it.

"Will you keep it secret, if I tell you something very important?," Anjan da asked, turning his look at the girl.

"I promise," said Uri promptly.

Anjan da cleared his throat and said staring into the eyes of the nervous girl : "I want to marry you, I know I'm about twice of your age. I don't insist on it. You're free to say anything."

Uri expressed her surprise through her tears. She hung her head, pressed her fists to her chin and broke down into a sobbing fit.

"I am not a good girl, babu," she babbled; "I am not a good girl at all."

Anjan da lifted her face tenderly, wiped her face with his handkerchief and planted a kiss on her full cheek.

"Do not cry," he said softly; "you're free to say no I told you that."

Uri stopped sobbing and looked at Anjan da timidly, wonderingly as though she was seeing him for the first time.

"Your family won't accept me," she ventured; "I am a low caste girl. My father is a fisher man, you know."

Anjan da sported an avuncular smile.

"I've thought over that aspect," said he, "before I proposed to you. I've no family as such. Mother is past eighty and extremely enfeebled. Nothing bothers her excepting my singleness. Any girl I choose would be acceptable to her. Besides, she was a follower of Ram Mohan Roy and an ardent member of the Brahmo Samaj in her young days. Do you know anything about the Brahmo Samaj?"

Uri shook her head. "I've never heard of it," she said.

"All right," said Anjan da, "I assure you, you won't face any questions about your caste and past. Mother wants a caring daughter-in-law, that's all. Now it's up to you to decide, tell me straightaway a yes or a no."

Uri listened to what Anjan da said, and stood transfixed for some time. Instead of expressing her consent in words — for words seemed to have deserted her — she squatted down, touched his feet and caressed them with the tenderness of a mother nursing her newborn baby.

The beach was lonely. Anjan da raised her from the ground and made her stand facing him. "Does it mean yes?", he inquired to make sure. Uri nodded her head.

The day following that event Anjan da met and talked to her parents. They refused to take him seriously, but when he stated bluntly that it was a marriage of convenience because he wanted a women who'd nurse his ailing mother and cook for him, they believed him and readily consented.

The day before his marriage in the court, Anjan da dropped in early in the morning. The sky was overcast with dark clouds, and the wind was stormy. Uri's parents saw him on the road and followed him to the lodge. They sat on the floor and expressed their unwillingness to attend the marriage at the court. "We are not used to that sort of thing," her father said. "You and your friends will eat in our humble hut when you return from the court."

"That's not possible," said Anjan da, smiling benignly. "We'll eat in a hotel. That's more convenient. Well, if you don't mind, will you send Uri here?"

Half an hour later Uri came with seven cups of tea and snacks on a platter. Those still asleep were woken up by a wildly enthusiastic Man Lion who had already known the event. Uri refused to sit on a chair. She sat on the steps.

Uri the changeling cast a furtive look at the gathering of men and looked down. Her change of personality was complete. Her half-opened drowsy eyes, her face freshened by a good night's sleep and her becoming print cotton taffeta covering half of her head and upper portion of the body, presented her in a different light. She was an altogether different person.

20

APPEARANCE AND CHANGE

She was not beautiful, but none of her features were noticeably bad-looking. Now, her sober manners revealed the less noticeable, yet attractive, features of her body. Youth, good health and a feeling of contentment so effectively transformed her general disposition that our sceptical eyes were enthralled by her charm. Anjan da perhaps noticed that charm which we had missed. A wench who flaunts her charms and bares her fleshy assets, with coy and suggestive hints about her easy availability, I thought, arouses superficial desires in men, but a woman who does not try to impress others and conceals her assets from the common glare, inspires tender poetic feelings which slowly mature into an emotional appreciation. It was Uri who shamed us into realizing that eternal secret.

"Then what was her real self, tell me?" observed Nityanand when we were sitting on the beach that evening deciding the presentation we would give to the newly-weds, at the reception.

Subramaniam the impressionable who had already fallen to Uri's innocent charms came up with a lengthy answer.

"Nityanandaji," he said, "It is a Vedantic question concerning appearance and reality, real self and pseudo self, etc., etc. Our eyes and minds are not attuned to accept the real self and reality without make-up, just as our ears cannot receive supersonic music of the spheres. Show the skull beneath the skin to your cruellest realists, and they show you a clean pair of heels.

"I've felt it. Last year I paid a visit to my niece who is a famous actress in Tamil films with my father. Her beauty has secured her many admirers and if you tell her fans that there are women more beautiful than Sulekha, the common queen of all their hearts, they'd beat you up after calling you a liar. She rushed into the drawing room shouting something at some errant servant, and was horrified to find us there. She entertained us most against her will. She had oiled her hair and her face had no make-up. Believe me, she looked like a medieval witch, uglier than any woman I had ever seen. There was not a single item on her God-given body, which without cosmetics and rouges could deserve a second glance. You think I am exaggerating? May be, you are right. But you can guess the intensity of my disillusionment."

"But what has that to do with my most direct question, you gangling Southern clown?" blurted our Nityanand.

"A lot, a lot," persisted Subramaniam. "Since time's beginning men have been falling in for the cosmetic charms of women. Fifty per cent of the nation's wealth is invested in the industries to beautify women, so that the ardent males would happily and proudly succumb to their fatal charms; so that they'd never be at rest, scribbling poems on them, painting their pictures, languishing in love, coining fresh metaphors, celebrating passion in holy jargons. This time-tested fashion will continue till the doomsday. So, Nityanandaji, Uri's present self is her cosmetic self. This is the universal similitude which has been accepted, is accepted and will be accepted as real."

Andy kept on smiling enigmatically while Subramaniam was talking eloquently. His smile perhaps denoted that he knew better. But he did not speak anything and kept his superior knowledge to himself. He had already become a victim of love by then.

21

ANDY IN LOVE

When I concentrated on Andy's personality, an act which was forced on my as I shared the room with him, I felt that to understand him was to understand India. Five thousand kilometres were compressed into the five-foot frame of his body. Everything about him was ponderous, dense and contrapuntal. The way he carried himself (the tortoise its shell, Atlas, the earth, Hanuman, the Gandhamardan mountain) and talked, reminded me of an ascetic dropped in a den of bandits. Only thing that disturbed him and enfeebled him, was feminine beauty.

The white cat, he always maintained, was no ordinary animal; it was the ghost of that unfortunate French woman who, for some time, aroused his libidinal desire. But he was too ashamed to admit it even to himself. He had told me many of his one-sided affairs with women of great beauty. They had always fallen in love with him, often madly, but he had always succeeded in keeping them off from his body. These women were married, with doting husbands, but their irresistible passion for him made them forget their duties and responsibilities. He described several such situations when those beautiful women had tried to seduce him, always adding at the end that no other male in his position could have resisted the temptation. All his parables or anecdotes ended with the eulogies of himself and pious platitudes on virtue. After narrating his stories in detail, he would wonder at his ability to captivate middle-aged women in particular and all women in general.

On one such occasion when Andy was prating about his many love encounters, Javed asked : "Then, Andyji, your body is a prude, and your soul seems to be a profligate. I mean you are not so chaste emotionally."

And Nityanand : "Ha! Not so chaste? I think his soul is a depraved philanderer, a reckless Don Juan, a loose fish, a skirt chaser."

Andy did not deny the charges. He only reminded Javed and Nityanand that they were misusing the term 'soul.'

"You fellows," he said patiently, "you don't perhaps know the meaning of soul. You equate it with mind and emotion? Soul, for your information, is immortal, detached, transparent and stainless. It only wears a garment called body. Your shirt is not called Javed. Your coat is not called Nityanandaji, is it?"

Sudhakar was pruning his moustache with scissors standing near the wall mirror. He rushed to the spot, and said : "Well, Andy sab, if that's so, Javed won't mind if I make a hole in his socks, a very small hole, of course. Will your noble soul mind if I make a small hole on any part of his garment. I'll begin with its nose. Should I proceed?"

Andy was highly amused, and laughed heartily. That session ended happily. The issues were diverted.

Andy was not generally talkative. But his eloquence rose to a feverish pitch and became drunken babble when he talked about other people's vices and his own virtues. These two streams merged in each other. He had the ability to exasperate any patient listener while believing that he was only entertaining him. Another fault, almost child-like, was that he'd read only the surface meaning of an irony or an innuendo, and refuse to take offence when gulled. He thought that any one who listened to him, believed in whatever he said. Again, when on several occasions, I contradicted him or pointed out his own contradictions he used to agree with me with a sort of gorgeous catholoicity of spirit. These facile agreements, I thought, were mere strategies to engage my attention. By his baby talk and sentimental buffoonery, he had unwittingly granted me some power over himself, a discrete superiority. He used to be puzzled when I interrupted his passionate rigmaroles with light-hearted statements on some totally different issues. He'd be at a loss about what to say on those strange, out of context topics to which he had not given any thought previously, and decide finally to agree with me only to clinch them and cut short the period of interruption. My needles would not puncture and deflate his rotund vanity. I never took him into confidence, never talked serious things with him. Whenever I talked to him, my tone was ironic, bantering, admonishing or perverse. Either he had not felt it, or he had decided not to speak out his feelings.

A week after Anjan da's marriage, Andy confided to me his love for some one I knew.

"Come on, Andy," I said; "You talk like Anjan da. You ape him a bit clumsily. Don't you remember, he spoke exactly the same thing?" Andy grinned like a skull, and didn't oblige me by informing me about the girl.

Two days later, he ordered Narasingh, to prepare a lot of prawn fry and seven or fourteen or twenty one cups of tea for the next day. He offered him one hundred rupees to make the purchase.

"What's the big idea, Andyji?" asked Sudhakar who had just overheard him.

"Sudhakar!," Andy whispered conspiratorially, "I am going to tell you some of my interesting experiences. I feel like saying it out right now. Just wait till tomorrow. You'll find my experiences tasting better than prawns."

In the afternoon a platter full of fried prawns, richly spiced, oiled and brown, was kept on a small teapoy. It was a sight which made us feel like cats. Six of us sat on two cots, waiting for Andy to start talking and eating.

"I haven't told you some of my interesting experiences with women," Andy began, casting an apologetic look at me, requesting me to bear with repetition.

"That's most welcome, Andy sab. But what inspired you to tell them now?" Javed asked. We rallied our support for Javed by nodding or uttering yes, yes.

"Okay, Okay! I'll tell that at the end, not now," he assured us.

He told us about a dozen of beautiful girls who had pilfered his heart during the last several years. He not only remembered their names and qualifications, but also their parents' names, their present conditions, the names of their husbands and their professions, and the dramatic situations which brought them together. He also vowed in the name of God that his love was purely spiritual and aesthetic in nature and he had never entertained carnal ideas about them.

It was again Sudhakar the intrepid who interrupted.

"Then you're like that ace pickpocket who travelled in the Chennai-Howrah Mail with a wad of banknotes," he observed teasingly.

"What do you mean?", queried Andy anxiously.

"It's like this," explained Sudhakar. The ace pickpocket travelled like a common passenger. Twelve pickpockets picked his pocket twelve times. When these twelve thieves, belonging to the same light-fingered fraternity met at Howrah, they discovered that they had stolen the same bundle of bank notes which miraculously returned to the owner all the time. "The fellow could have stolen our balls without our knowing it," commented their leader. "Now, those girls who stole your precious heart must have felt like those pickpockets."

Andy laughed full-throatedly for a few minutes, then said :

"Thanks for the compliment. Those petty pickpockets must have realized who was the master."

We all knew that Andy won't host an expensive tea party unless he had an axe to grind. We requested him to come to the point without wasting more time.

"I am in love once again." He revealed the secret with a bang. "I do not remember if I ever loved any one as sincerely as I love this one. I am happy for losing my heart to a worthy thief."

Andy answered affirmatively when I inquired if there were degrees of sincerity, and maintained that he'd never love any woman in all his life with greater sincerity. "Goddess Venus has sculpted her in Elgin marble after her own image, and handed her over to Goddess of learning, Saraswati to train her in all the arts," Andy rhapsodised.

"Such a girl, I bet, must be a professional thief with a licence to loot and a keeper of stolen goods," said Sudhakar gravely.

"What do you mean?" asked Andy.

"You see, Andyji," replied he. "Human heart, I mean a man's heart is a precious object, and such an accomplished and pretty girl must have stolen a thousand hearts like that of yours."

Andy admired Sudhakar for his wit.

Later investigation corroborated Andy's description of Krishna, the daughter of the town's richest baker. This seventeen year doll-like girl was the most famous student of the Government College where Andy was a teacher. Music brought them together. She was a singer, an actress and the literary champion of the college. She also knew Odissi dance and could play on the harmonium and electric guitar. That apart, she was a bright and well-behaved student, as many senior teachers had testified. To put it briefly, she had more or less most of the qualities that usually go in making a film heroine, a type abounding in celluloid fantasy, but rarely seen in real life.

Given God the Maker's reluctance to endow a single mortal creature with so many sterling qualities, it could be assumed that some of this girl's moderate or ordinary talents had been elevated to great heights of excellence by chiefly three factors : One, her uncontestable excellence as a danseuse, as a cute beauty who had a puckish charm and classic good-looks, and as a singer of traditional songs; two, her being a topper in the State level examinations; three, her unassuming and charming behaviour with her teachers and admirers. Her rich and doting father, enthused by her natural gifts, surrounded her with local maestros and musical instruments.

Andy adored her from a safe distance. What changed him into a crazy lover was her role of Alma in the Oriya version of Williams' *Summer and Smoke.* She played that unconvincing character so convincingly, with such an uninhibited flourish that many young men changed their opinion of her for the better overnight. The raw, uninitiated slip of a girl was transformed into a full-blooded, liberated, and amoral woman, which added to her actual beauty, electrified the youthful imagination, and caused many an onanistic implosion of desire. Andy, however, had an advantage over others by being her teacher both in the class-room and the music hall.

He was the first person to congratulate her and praise her acting talent in poetic language as soon as she returned to the green room after her superb performance on the stage. She was beside herself with joy for being admired by a teacher. She was impressionable as was expected of a girl of her age, and her outrageous role of a nymphomaniac had left its traces on her. She was full of the joys of spring. As a result, she blessed him with a special smile, winked and looked at him like a coquet to express her gratitude. Andy's poor heart throbbed as if afflicted by Parkinson's disease. He was so overwhelmed by the newness of the experience that he cycled back four kilometres smiling like a picture all the way. On the way, he bumped into a sleeping cow, fell down from the cycle, and resumed his journey still smiling.

He hosted the tea-party next day, but had nothing else to announce except her reciprocation and his mortification. During the session of his proud confessions, which lasted several hours, he dropped Anjan da's name on four occasions, or may be five times, and always with sly understatements and guarded aspersions. At first we didn't take any note of his digs, but when he said let Anjan da admit he had half of such romantic encounters, and what a sight Anjan da's wife and Krishna would make if they posed for a photograph! We took a mental note that the fellow was jealous of Anjan da. I had to tell him rather bluntly, to leave the absent man alone when he brought him up for the fifth time with "The poor man will not believe his ears and be scalded by envy to see me mated with the most accomplished girl of the whole world." "Andy is randy, it rhymes, ain't it?" whispered Sudhakar into my ear, leaning over the desk.

Using the girl's first coy smile and sidelong glance as an impregnable cuirass, Andy took long strides on the path of love, and knocked on her door a week after. Her father ushered him in after he introduced himself. Krishna's middle aged father Mr.Chatterjee turned out to be an affable man and a great talker. He found in Andy a patient listener and a multi-faceted genius, but was disconcerted by Andy's ignorance about Bengali literature. Andy, on his part, found in Mr. Chatterjee a worthy father of an equally worthy daughter.

Next day Andy visited many small and big book shops of the town and bought as many Bengali books as he could lay his hands on, and a slate. He sat late through the night scribbling Bengali alphabets on the slate and on paper.

"Returning to your school days, Andyji?", observed Subramaniam. "It's too late to learn the mother tongue, ain't it?" Andy looked at him indignantly and told him to mind his own business. When Subramaniam went away, fully convinced that Andy was learning his mother tongue, Andy turned to me and commented wryly on him.

"Look at that Southern fool, he doesn't care to know what language I'm learning. He thinks I am learning my mother tongue. I am yet to see a greater fool. Ha, ha!"

"Carry on your work, Andy," I told him casually. "How do you bother what he thinks? Are you learning some new language?"

He left his slate and sat on my bed cross-legged. He was debating within himself whether to take his room-mate into confidence or not. Finally he decided in my favour.

"I'll tell you something, Debasis," he said. "Promise me, you'll keep it to yourself."

I assured him. "Have you other secrets? I thought you told all your secrets that afternoon. All right, I'll keep it secret."

"I have a bet with Krishna's father — that I can learn Bengali and read at least two novels of Sarat Chandra in less than a fortnight. He also promised to read two novels of Surendra Mohanty during that time. One who fails, will host the other at the Chinese hotel."

22

BLOOD AND THUNDER

Anjan da remarked after observing Andy for sometime that he was stand-offish and remarkably highserious. Andy smiled bloodlessly and said he was not keeping well. "How is life after marriage?" he asked Anjan da.

"Nothing different, of course. Why, haven't you seen any married man before, Andy?"

"One thing I know about friends who get married," said Andy, averting his eyes from Anjan da's look. "They shave regularly, live horizon-tally, buy vegetables and forget their old friends." His repartee was directed at Anjan da's clear-shaven appearance and long absence.

Nityanand the married entered the room, his face covered with lather. "Andy is right," he explained. "You see, Anjan da, I stay away from my wife, yet I shave regularly. Just habit."

Andy bolted from his bed and pushed Nityanand out of the room. "I never meant you, be sure. I didn't know you're married. All I know you're a loutish, irregular old man. You should be ashamed of declaring your marital status in public."

Andy's abrupt violence surprised every one present there. Nityanand pretended to take it as a joke, but when Andy didn't mellow down and smile, and applied physical force to drive him out of his room, he looked at him with anger and disdain, but spoke nothing.

"The old rogue thinks he's married!," mumbled Andy, looking around haughtily, as if he did an admirable piece of work.

The atmosphere, which had been quite friendly and normal a moment ago, was surcharged with an occulted guilt. Barring Anjan da, we all knew that Andy was scratching an old wound, for there could not be any other reason for such obnoxious behaviour. We felt sorry for Nityanand, the eldest amongst us, because he was as culpable as any of us. I remembered his harsh comparison a few days ago — he put us on the same level with the rapists of that amorphous French slut. Anjan da's presence prevented an unpleasant situation, or at least delayed it.

Anjan da, who was not used to that sort of scene, and was apparently ignorant of the historical background of Andy's outburst, walked up to Andy.

"Look, Andy," he said, placing his hand on him, "You behaved like a bully. Why are you so rough, why so short-tempered? Lost your sense of humour, or what?"

Andy the villain of the piece refused to speak anything. Anjan da repeated his questions, but when he didn't get any answer, he felt offended.

"I believe, you've lost your peace of mind, and now you're determined to spread discord. All right, I ain't coming again to your place until the peace is restored. O.K.?"

"Who asks you to come?" muttered Andy, viciously.

Those last words of Andy's produced a totally unexpected effect on Anjan da. He realized that something had gone seriously awry, otherwise Andy could not be so brusque with him. Anjan da, as was his habit, ordered for coffee. "Andy, I suppose, is frozen stiff. Tea won't be an effective remedy." He asked me to call Narasingh the coffee-maker.

Others slithered out noiselessly. I, Anjan da and Andy the Sphinx were in the room. Considering Andy's distracted behaviour, I apprehended the worst. "Is he going to disclose the terrible secrets concerning Uri?" I thought. "Nothing is impossible for him; nothing can be predicted about him." That was my only bug-bear. I didn't like to take chances. I asked :

"Anjan da, do you recollect what Envy said to Doctor Faustus?"

"No."

"It's something like I am sick to see others healthy; I am unhappy to see others happy; I am full of hate to see others in love."

Anjan da chuckled.

Andy placed his coffee glass on the table and said; "Do you recollect what Mr. Lust said to Faustus? No. You don't. He simply said he would prefer an ounce of raw flesh to a mountain of cooked meat. Didn't he say that, Debasis?"

"Why bothering so much about the deadly sins?" Anjan da said.

"You won't understand that, Anjan da," Andy replied promptly, peremptorily.

"I shall try to understand that later. Now I have to go. Thank you for good coffee."

Anjan da left. I felt he won't be visiting us for a long, long time.

Andy didn't apologize to Nityanand, and Nityanand was not mentally prepared to forget and forgive Andy. We spoke to him formally, and avoided his presence. Andy took his alienation easy. But he singled me out of the group, and talked with me as if nothing had happened, as if I were not one of those victims whom he antagonized by blackmailing. He spoke to me when others were absent or asleep.

"Do you know what'd happen if you tell everything to Anjan da?" I asked him. I was bitter. I was afraid.

"Oh, that bothers you?," he rasped. I could see the Devil smirking in him.

"You think I'm a fool? Are you people afraid of that? I know what I should do, and what I should not. Don't try to warn me. But I tell you, and you can intimate it to your accomplices, that if you boycott me and provoke me, no one would be worse than me."

That warning actually frightened us, and we decided to keep our hostility at a low key, and rub along with the perverse black-mailer. The more we tried to curry favour with him, the more intense was our spite, the more severe was the cold war.

Anjan da visited us after ten days. I was much relieved when Man Lion announced his visit. I feared he'd never come. It was about ten thirty morning when he entered through the gate. School students, mostly girls, were walking down the road dressed in magenta skirts and white shirts, loaded with heavy bags. It was the time when Man Lion would stand leaning over the portico column, and whistling a tune of some old film song pretending to be casual. The boy had developed a crush on a school-going girl simply because she had returned his look and smile. As the caretaker of the Lodge, he had also became inflicted with the love-sickness.

Anjan da surprised him with a thwack and he ran into the building loudly announcing Anjan da's arrival. The nervous alacrity with which he trumpeted the guest's arrival created a genial effect on all the inmates who were indoors due to the public holiday. It was a Muslim holiday, Id-ul-feter, but the Convent School was open.

Javed, Subramaniam and Nityanand greeted Anjan da on the corridor and escorted him to my room. Andy was in the bathroom, singing and farting flamboyantly.

Anjan da sat surrounded by four of us. Our Man Lion stood giggling on the threshold waiting for an order for tea.

"Andy sab loves solitude for a splendid reason," said Nityanand with an impish smile. His malice for Andy was public knowledge, albeit his great effort to appear humorous and objective. Ten days ago he was grossly insulted by Andy.

"What's that?," inquired Javed.

"It enables him to fart to his heart's content without feeling queasy," quipped Nityanand gravely. "His bowels, not his mind, feel much relaxed when he's alone in a lonely place far from the sniffing and listening crowd. Believe me, Andy has confided it to me."

We all agreed that Andy was a poet of sorts and such a pungent piece of originality could come from a fop who wore his ass in his sleeve. Anjan da felt outraged.

He felt more outraged because Andy, who in all probability was in the latrine, was singing a bhajan at a high pitch.

"Whistling a tune in the toilet is one thing," observed he indignantly, "but singing a full song there is another. The fellow doesn't distinguish between a latrine and a prayer room."

"But Andy sab does not think so," Nityanand announced. "He has told me that, honestly. The wind in the belly, he said, is like ideas in the head and feelings in the heart. They should be allowed to express themselves, fat-a-fat, the way they like. They may purr like a pigeon, whistle like a train, mew like a cat. He also added, I say it honestly, what're these flutes, drums, saxophones or mridangas, or for that matter all these music-making instruments, aren't they only different ways through which sound expresses itself so eloquently? He is a human saxophone, I bet."

Anjan da was not amused. We didn't laugh because we had already heard it from Nityanand more than once. Besides, we doubted if Andy said it at all.

Nityanand was trying to extend his yarn when Anjan da restrained him. "Is it quite the thing to stay so long in a latrine? Come out of it, please."

"You mean Andy, don't you?" Nityanand asked.

"No, Nityanandaji, I mean you," returned Anjan da rather bluntly. Nityanand looked grave in an affected way, sulking and liplocked.

Andy emerged from the bathroom muttering Sanskrit slokas, which was his wont and, ignoring us completely, stood before the picture of Lord Rama in a stiff gesture of meditation. He recited the slokas with great rapidity; his tongue wagged like the wings of a humming bird. Human beings were not supposed to make sense of these words, as they were meant for the ear of the gods. The more arcane these incantations, the more effective they were supposed to be. Andy forced us to listen to his pious inanities for ten minutes.

Then he turned round and recognized the ordinary mortals crowding his room and invading his bed.

"When did you come, Anjan da?," he queried half-heartedly.

Sudhakar the free-thinker with a scabrous tongue had stolen into the room already. Before Anjan da could reply to Andy's query, Sudhakar observed trenchantly; "We Hindus have framed our gods and goddesses, hung them on the walls of our bed rooms, drawing rooms and even kitchens and forced them to watch our sixty four ways of love-making, to listen to our petty gossips and consecrate our kitchen sinks, ha, ha, ha, ha."

Andy eyed him murderously and barked out : "Stop it."

"Don't feel offended, Big Brother," Sudhakar resumed his tirade. "Tell me honestly, what is so elevating about your incarnations that makes you people go nuts over them? A stunt beggar swindling and destroying a generous king, a desperate Brahmin axe-wielder determined to exterminate the whole race of Kashtriyas, a prince who kills a king who stole his wife not out of lust but to avenge his sister's loss of nose, and then throws the retrieved wife in a jungle because some citizens of his kingdom doubted her chastity. Now tell me you ascetic Hindu, what is so divine about these people and their works? Some of them are unfit to be heroes in our Hindi films, let alone the idols of our hearts."

"You blasphemous bully, you scoundrel, you rogue, you... : You!" Andy shouted at the top of his voice and advanced like a provoked gladiator. Before we could realize the gravity of the situation, Sudhakar and Andy were rolling on the floor, grabbing each other's throats. It was Andy who caught Sudhakar's throat rather too roughly. Sudhakar, who little apprehended such physical assault, tried to remove Andy's grip, but when he failed in that attempt he tried to strangle the thickset neck of his attacker. The room was not an ideal place for a wrestling match. It was crammed with furniture.

Andy, who proved to be the stronger party, pushed the enemy to the window where an earthen pitcher full of water was kept on a wooden stool. Before I could do something to prevent any serious damage, they knocked down the pitcher. It broke into pieces, drenching the fighters and flooding the room.

Anjan da, flabbergasted, was just preparing to interfere when a happy incident brought the battle to an abrupt ceasefire.

Andy was wearing a dry towel. When drenched it became heavy and slipped of his waist and dropped. Before it was too late he released Sudhakar's throat and tried to retie the towel.

"It is an instance of shame overwhelming anger," quipped a vastly amused Nityanand.

As soon as Andy loosened his grip, Sudhakar extricated himself and walked a few steps backwards and stood at a safe distance.

Andy was panting and trembling in an uncontrollable anger. Sudhakar had always the dubious reputation of being a bully who didn't give a damn for principles, religion and things of that sort. It was perhaps his first experience of being bullied, of receiving more insult than he could inflict on others. That realization, paradoxically made him patient, for he quickly felt that the sympathy of the spectators was tilting towards him. It pleased him secretly, and he concealed his wrath behind the veil of an exasperated politeness.

"I wonder," he put in placidly, "why you get so worked up over a trifle." Then looking at us he added, smiling miserably : "Andy wants to put a muzzle on my throat to prevent free speech. Why such over-reaction? Why such intolerance?"

"Shut up, you loafer," shouted Andy beside himself in anger and hate. His eyes glared wildly. He was opening and tightening his fists. His teeth were gnashing.

This outburst and behaviour blew off the veil of politeness from Sudhakar. "What do you think of yourself, you fat rogue?," he shouted at the top of his voice. "I've the right to speak whatever I want. You behave like a bigoted goon, the meanest lumpen I've ever come across. Look friends, the rustic wanted to throttle me! What do you think of me?"

At this point Andy remembered a farrago of foul words and expressions and exploded like a stink-pot :

"Do you ask me what I think of you? You are a knave, a rascal, a stinkard, as eater of broken meats, a base, proud shallow, beggarly, three-suited, hundred-pound, filthy, worsted-stocking knave, a lily-livered, action-taking whoreson, glass-gazing, super serviceable, finical rogue, one-trunk-inheriting slave, one that wouldst be a bawd in way of good service and art nothing but the composition of a knave, beggar, coward, pander and the son and heir of a mongrel bitch, one whom I will beat into clamorous whining, if thou deny'st the least syllable of thy addition. You brazen-faced varlet, you whoreson cullionly barber-monger, I'll carbonado your shanks!"

Sudhakar was mortified and astounded. Some of the words he heard for the first time and the indistinct, rapid manner those words were mouthed further complicated them. From a few words he could make out, he realized that a bucket of excrement was poured on him.

"What do you mean? What do you say?" asked a thoroughly puzzled Sudhakar. We were impressed by his oratorical skill. We were surprised by his great vocabulary of filthy words. But like poor Sudhakar, we could not understand many of the coinages and words.

Sudhakar, as he confessed afterwards, had never felt so wretched before. He was physically assaulted and verbally "carbonadoed." His face looked innocent; it showed a horrified innocence which came out of his humiliation.

"Don't think, Andy," he said, "my level of vocabulary is less. But my problem is decency. I am restrained from using them because people I respect are present here. I shall return your dirty words with interest, be assured."

Andy didn't open his mouth after his speech. He changed his clothes, combed his hair and inspected the scratch-marks on his neck in the wall mirror. Others were silent. The situation was tense but under control. Suddenly Sudhakar erupted again : "I'll kill you one day. I'll kill you."

"But you cannot kill my soul," observed Andy who has cooled down by now. "My soul you know is immortal. You cannot kill my soul."

"Had I a pistol, I could have killed your body, your soul, your everything with one shot. He thinks he has a soul! What an illusion!" Sudhakar mocked, laughing loudly, trembling like an epileptic.

Anjan da thought it proper to interfere at that stage. There was a lot of unredeemed, unspent violence in both of them — the believer and the non-believer. He asked Andy and Sudhakar to stop quarreling and shake hands. Sudkhakar slunk out of the room, and Andy averted his eyes.

"This is a sickening state of affairs," he observed sadly. "Fighting over issues you don't believe in. That's the shameful fact. It's useless to blame any party. Each party succumbs to its own reasons. It's happening in this room, it's happening everywhere."

"What a paltry reason to fight with a friend!", observed Javed morosely.

"He has no right to insult my gods," Andy rapped out; "Am I superior to your spiritual leader who declared a holy war, that fatwa thing, on a writer who made derogatory remarks on your Prophet? That's how the cookie crumbles. Don't ask further questions, OK?" Andy chortled, chucking Javed under the chin.

Javed blushed like a virgin, spoke nothing.

Andy resumed his tirade. "I am much better than your spiritual leader. I fought with my enemy, endangered my own self. But he sentenced his enemy to death which was a ridiculous act, because he had no legal right to give such a sentence. Then he set a heavy reward on his enemy's head, which was, in fact, an open invitation to all terrorist and hired assassins to kill the man and get the reward. You Javed, have no right to find fault with me."

Javed stood up and slowly walked out of the room. Subramaniam followed him. Nityanand was about to spit out some unprintable compliments, but his good sense and Anja da prevailed upon him. Andy was in a vicious, no-holds-barred state of mind, and could easily offend everybody.

I cast a nasty look at Andy and escorted Anjan da out of the room. Nityanand spat loudly on the floor and followed us.

Andy caught hold of Anjan da's hand and pulled him inside. "You can't go away like this," he entreated him, still looking down. "I'm to blame for all this, but was there not sufficient provocation? Tell me. I admit, the other day I was too harsh to Nityanand, but still then, you do not know everything. You'll never know."

Anjan da mellowed. He returned to his seat, and stared at the wretched face of the culprit.

"How long should we go on like this fighting tooth and nail over religion which we have reduced to an apple of discord?"

After a long pause, he advised Andy to make peace with Sudhakar. "Andy," he said in an ordering tone, "shake off this mind-set, come unstuck. Our gods ate strong enough to defend their honour and prove their existence. I tell you a good number of sensitive people choose to be unbelievers simply because they hate to belong to the fraternity of so-called believers who more often than not cheat themselves into believing. These Job's comforters speak without understanding and believing. Don't get angry if I tell it. Your defence of divinity is a posturing. Otherwise how can you switch over from a prayer to such physical and verbal atrocities?"

Andy looked repentant, but I knew he was only ashamed of the situation he dragged himself to. He wrestled with an upstart crow many years his junior in front of a hated group of lookers-on. He avoided Anjan da's look, and asked : "You cannot know who's a believer and who is not, can you?"

"Of course," retorted Anjan da; "Of course I can, you can, everybody can! The changing circumstances that beset man, his prosperity and affliction, are the litmus-tests of integrity. The acids and alkalis would affect litmus in predictable ways. It can't be otherwise."

Fifteen minutes later, Andy returned to the room with Sudhakar. "It is high time Sudhakar," I said emphatically, "You realized that you're a quarrelsome bully. You have greater reason to apologize to Andy." Anjan da nodded approvingly. Sudhakar shook hands with Andy. "I'm extremely sorry," he muttered looking at Andy. Two smiling faces lit up the room.

23

ANDY AND KRISHNĀ

A writer gets a crick in his fingers when he attempts to talk on love. It is so capricious a passion as to discourage any shipshape interpretation. It is an escalator connecting earth with heaven and hell, a proverbial carrot to the donkey, a drug to the addict, a thorn in the flesh of humankind, a sickness that mounts a multi-pronged attack on the heart, nerves, mind, soul and genitalia of the victim all at the same time.... He has to stop rather abruptly, lest he should be accused of cribbing.

A fortnight after, Andy informed me with a sigh that he had lost the bet because the two novels he was supposed to read, were very lengthy ones, and Mr. Chatterjee was an unusually fast reader. A few minutes after, he smiled like a crook and said : "Honestly Debasis, I'm a much happier man by losing."

"How come?", I asked coldly.

"When we were just getting into his air-conditioned Contessa to go to the Chinese Restaurant, I suggested why not bringing Krishnā with us, and he readily agreed. Had he lost the bet, he might not have brought his daughter with him, because he had to table the bill, in that case."

"Is he such a miser?"

"Oh no!" Andy contradicted me. "But who'd like to spend so much if that could be avoided."

"Did you propose to her?"

"Not exactly. But something like that. We sat, I mean Krishnā and I, on one side of the oblong table, and Mr. Chatterjee on the other. He took some whisky, and went on chattering from beginning to end. She laughed to all my jokes. She looked down shyly when I praised her. In the car, we both shared the back seat and Mr. Chatterjee was driving. Her long pleated hair studded with champak flowers fell on my lap. I removed a flower and went on sniffing at it. She saw it, and blushed. What does that signify?"

"Then why didn't you kiss her? That might have proved something?"

"No thanks. You know I am not your type. You people do not understand that woman is not all body, she has a soul. I'm all for soul." He spoke in a tone of bantering arrogance. I reacted sharply.

"So what, you prude? Does the soul of a woman hate to be kissed by a male? Again, what'll you do to her body if you marry her?"

Andy whimpered, fumed, fidgetted. "You bawdy fellows won't understand love. You worship the body, dote upon the body of a woman as the vultures fight over a carcass. You people are not much different from that monkey who chased Uri."

His voice was hatefully loud. I also heard the rustles of steps outside the closed door. Other inmates, I knew, were listening to the proceedings. I maintained my calm.

"You may wax as eloquent and righteously vociferous as you please," I said ominously, "but you cannot exorcise the rumours that surround you. I know such pious platitudes and holy anger can only come from a guilty man. You're only getting angry with your own criminal self."

"What rumours? What do you want to say?", Andy asked, troubled by my reference.

"At first we disbelieved the rumours,"I said bluntly. "But so many people could not be wrong. Even Uri told that to us. That was why she never ventured to go near you. You are one of those who raped and killed that unfortunate French lady. Believe me, had I been in your position, I could have gone to the police station and surrendered. I know an exposed guilt and the punishment meted out by the court are more tolerable than the secret suffering."

"You are one hundred per cent crazy," trilled Andy, laughing like mad.

"Yes, I'd choose to be crazy rather than a criminal, a cunning criminal."

"You believe in those baseless canards? I have never heard such an allegation before. Tell me who are the persons who told you that."

"I started believing in them after that cat episode," I explained; "Only a guilty mind can be so troubled by a white cat, and connect it to a murdered woman. Do you think people who actually told that to us would tell that to you? I think your naivety is a disguise, a mask. You pretend to be innocent." I rose up, and announced firmly : "I'm looking for some accommodation elsewhere. I am leaving this damned room shortly."

"Who cares?" retorted Andy. "You think I'll kneel down before you and pray you to continue here?"

"I also don't care to share a room with a crackpot and a criminal," I hit back.

"Well, now you're the right person to say who amongst us has an upper hand," Andy said smiling roguishly.

"You're cornered. The truth will be known, sooner or later. And you are a goner," I persisted.

"Look, Debasis, you aren't half so clever as I thought you would be and you perhaps don't know the culprits of that rape and murder case have long been apprehended, judged and sentenced. That's a closed chapter now. You extemporized that charge only to retaliate in a mean way. Now, let's call it quits, and begin where I had left."

"I am not at all interested in your story," I told him bluntly. I acknowledged defeat silently. I certainly underestimated his intelligence. "It is past midnight; I must sleep," I said, switching off the light.

Two days later, when Andy was absent, Nityanand came to my room and congratulated me for my presence of mind and resourcefulness. I gathered from his talk that they had not overheard the last part of our talk. Nityanand looked crestfallen when I informed him how I was outplayed.

"That means he'd go on tormenting us like that for ever, and we'd go on eating the humble pie," Nityanand lamented. He got the worst treatment from Andy because he, by being elderly and married, had sinned more grievously than others who were young and unattached.

"It seems, he is not as stupid as he seems," I said wryly. And added thoughtfully : "We've to locate his weak point and hammer the nail home there. I won't have sound sleep unless and until I make him miserable."

Nityanand shook hands with me heartily thinking I was doing him a favour. His grateful look fired my imagination and made me brave.

Finally, I came out with a stratagem which was applauded by Nityanand. Details were sorted out. The other three were intimated, because, should the plot materialize and prove effective no one may be deprived of the ecstasy of seeing the villain in the trap. Some errors and *faux pases* in the first draft were identified and new suggestions were incorporated, and the revised scheme was unanimously endorsed.

24

GULLING THE ROGUE

In the chirpy and crowded girls' common room of the college, a comely girl called Krishnā lost one of her note books. She inquired about it, searched for it, and finally gave up the search.

Andy returned to the lodge late, and our devoted servant Narasingh handed a bound notebook over to him. "A girl came, waited for you more than an hour and gave this note book," he informed an ecstatic Andy. He had no doubt about the owner of that blessed notebook. He looked suspiciously around, and found me totally engrossed in reading.

"Was she alone?," he began his interrogation.

"Yes."

"Did she leave any message with you?"

"She sat there. She was reading something. But she gave me only this notebook." Man Lion looked quite grave. "I offered to prepare tea for her, but she declined."

"How was she?" Andy went on inquiring as if he'd never stop, as if he got some satisfaction by extending the enquiry.

"Uglier than Uri's mother, blacker than me; she had a mole on her nose." Man Lion giggled and bit his nail.

Andy was shocked. He cancelled the enquiry forthwith and sat down holding his head. Now that his fond illusion was shattered, he looked at my direction with questioning eyes. Determined to avoid him, I rose with a sudden jerk and walked out of the room.

Andy leafed through the notebook which was unmistakably Krishnā's. He shook it holding upside down, and to his amazement a sealed letter and a withered champak flower dropped down. The note book had the owner's name on it, and its first few pages were filled with hastily scribbled lecture notes.

Two pairs of eyes were watching his every gesture through window chinks. He put the withered flower under his pillow after kissing it several times. Then he looked around to make sure that no one was around, and opened the sealed letter. He gloated over that brief letter. He tried to get the letter by heart.

Although all care had been taken to make the letter look natural we had misgivings about its exact impact on Andy. He had given us as many proofs of his naivety as of his cunning. Nityanand emulated the hand to a happy extent, but a keen eye could detect the difference. What the letter lacked in accuracy was compensated by the reader's beliefs and the rising adrenalin level in his blood.

It was about nine P.M. when Andy walked to the wash-basin with his razor, soap and brush. Javed was washing his face there. He looked at Andy with dilated eyes.

"Shaving now!" he exclaimed. Andy said only "Whoon!" "Are you going out?" Javed persisted. "Why,. does your law forbid shaving in the night? Mind your own business." Andy snubbed him recalcitrantly.

It was our first ray of hope.

Next morning Andy was very affable with me, which reminded me of his old self, and our cordial days at the university. He sat on my bed, touched my back and told me that it was time I woke up and did some reading. He informed me that morning was the ideal time for study, and he had already asked Narasingh to prepare tea for both of us.

"What's the matter, Andy? Why did you disturb my good sleep?" I feigned sleepiness.

"I had a horrible time in the class yesterday," he informed me.

"Why?", I asked.

"A student demanded I should explain the meanings or implications of some expressions or terms which she came across in some novels. Can you imagine, she challenged me?" Andy pretended as if he was speaking nothing but the truth.

"Believe me, Debasis, I had not a wink of sleep last night. I was thinking deeply on those terms. By the way, you read science magazines and science fiction. Is the black hole called divine hole?"

"Most unlikely," I contradicted him slowly, and added :

"You see, "Divine" is not a scientific term at all."

"That I know." Andy agreed, but requested me to ransack the shelves of my memory, for his honour depended on it. Honour of the teaching community was also at stake. "Teachers are supposed to know more than their students," he added.

"What're the other terms? I thought you had a good vocabulary," I goaded him.

"Slom. Slom. It sounds familiar. Have you come across such a word?"

"If it is an actual word, honestly I don't know," I said. "But if it's a teasing abbreviation it may mean S(he) Lo(ves) M(e)".

Andy shook his head. "Unfortunately it is a word, not an acronym. I don't think small dictionaries have that word. I am afraid, this 'slom' thing has some links with slum. Do you think so? Or is it sloom?"

"I have to think it over. I admit they are unusual words or technical expressions. You know, Andy, there are so many uneasy coinages, neologisms nowadays. As soon as a new expression sprouts up in the hide-outs of scientists, critics or city lumpens or in college campuses our lexicographers quickly collect it and consecrate it, and our word-merchants start hawking it. But what is game to those word-promoters is misery to the poor teachers like you. You face students, not they." I spoke earnestly. Andy was listening to me, but his mind was busy otherwise. He didn't mention the other terms. He had perhaps forgotten them, and was afraid of consulting the letter in my presence.

His restlessness and trepidation increased with the day. He had little time to collect big data. "How can I show my face to her and impudently admit my ignorance to her? What a sorry figure I'd cut? What will be her reaction? Will she be satisfied if I tell her that these words and expressions are not found in the dictionary? There is another way of lying. I'll simply attribute some arbitrary meanings to these terms. In that case I shall forfeit my face for ever, if she comes to know their true meanings." He packed off all those unknown novelists to the Devil, because they used such off-the-track expressions.

"Tell me, Debasis," he finally erupted like a volcano, "do these writers write to be understood or to baffle their poor readers. If I, given my exposure to literature and my word power, cannot make sense of any one of the five terms, who else can?"

"None," I assured him. He smiled in his misery. He kept on pacing the corridor, up and down, clasping his hands at his back, biting his lips, staring at the floor in fierce concentration.

Nityanand, who was watching him across the door, suddenly burst out into a peal of laughter. I came out of the room hearing his laughter and threw at him a warning glance. Andy woke up from his trance and walked up to the merry man, and stood facing him belligerently.

"Why're you such a mocking bird, Nityanandaji?", he demanded ferociously.

"Who, I?", Nityanand fumbled, stood up fearing physical assault.

"May I know what tickles you?", Andy demanded.

"It's nothing. I only remembered a humorous situation while watching you walk like this. My wife was in the labour room for twenty hours when our first child was born. I walked like this for full twenty hours. It could have been less traumatic had I practised and rehearsed such walking exercise before. That made me laugh. I am sorry if I offended you."

Andy ignored Nityanad's explanation and apology.

He walked up to me beaming with Eureka. The first expression, though funny, makes some sense to me. "Brassierization of udders" seems to me a veterinary term implying humanization of animals, or special care taken to protect the udders of milch cows as women shore up their mammary glands with brassieres. What's your opinion?

"May be," I said; "If cattle had brains and language, the bulls and even bullocks might have written and sung a million love lyrics on the succulent females of their species, and the cows, on their turn, might have put on wonderbras for special effects."

Andy was too worried to entertain any digression.

From me he walked to the kitchen where Man Lion was busy cooking. Standing on the entrance he shouted, "Narasingh, come here!" A few minutes later, the jovial Man Lion followed him to our room. Andy handed a ten-rupee note onto him and asked him to buy a packet of cigarettes. "You can keep change," he added magnanimously. Narasingh accepted the money and prepared to leave, when Andy called him back. "By the way," he inquired with a studied casualness of tone, "do you remember the girl who brought this notebook?" Andy was worrying who could be the messenger. The letter stated that he knew her well.

"Yes she was black, blacker than me, fatter than you."

"And a mole on the tip of her nose."

"Yes, babu. It was actually a wart sprouting a couple of hairs."

"What more?"

"She is bandy-legged, has big big ears, thick thick lips. Her hair (giggles, then hides his two large incisors) was crawling with ten thousand lice. I saw that. She'd put on a yellow saree with black stripes; her blouse was black, so I thought she was not covered; she was chewing tobacco, was frequently spitting out through the window without bothering to see who was outside.

She had an extra finger on left hand, but it had no nail. Her eyes were very very small and squinty. So when she was talking to me, she was looking at something else."

"How tall?", Andy asked.

"Very short, Sab. Very heavy. She has a good sense of humour. She called me near and asked does Andy Sir break wind?"

Andy looked puzzled.

"What did you say?", he asked anxiously.

"I said, Mem Sahib, Andy Sir may not be knowing what that thing means, let alone do it."

"Thank you, Sābash! You deserve a promotion, but, alas, there's only one post, and you are not educated. Otherwise, I would have recommended you to the house owner to make you a manager. Nonetheless, I will request the owner to give you a higher salary, don't worry. Now, fetch me a packet of Capstan and keep change."

Man Lion giggled gratefully and ran off briskly.

Flabbergasted, I looked at his receding figure. How coolly he extemporized! How quickly the rogue conjured up an image of feminine ugliness! How dexterously he fleshed out the details! So fictitious, yet so convincing!

As I listened to his grotesque yarn and watched him sprint away into the distance, I was filled with most disturbing thoughts. He was transmogrified into a diabolical djinni. Poor circumstances have bottled him; his condition as our servant has restricted his portentous power to range over a wider circumference, Ariel-like. This apparently innocuous imp whom we unceremoniously treat as a cook-cum-errand boy has enough native wit and resourcefulness to equal, if not outshine, the shrewdest of our authors. If given the charge of a flock of our so called wise men — the cognoscenti, literati, glitterati, *et al.*, he will lead them to the market place, sell them to half a dozen of prospectors there, and buy them back, too, while our complacent, commodified wise men think they are doing a handsome thing by him by giving him the pleasure of their illustrious company. Many such untutored, ill-nurtured offspring of dinosaurs abound in the back of beyond villages disguised as common lizards and chameleons! Many such chunks of dynamite litter the countryside disguised as ordinary rubble. Given a chance to realize their full potential, those parvenus may do more harm than good to humanity, at least do enough magic to surprise others. My contemporaries will bear me out. Our CBI sleuths have just discovered that certain ex-minister who was a cook-cum-dishwasher, much like our Man Lion turned out to be the richest politician of India, having about four crore rupees at home for his domestic expenses, owning twelve swank palaces in different cities of the country. We should not be surprised if our errand boy, by trying his hand in politics, becomes the wealthiest citizen of the country in less than a decade.

I was afraid he might overplay his part and spoil our scheme, but he also knew where to stop. I heaved a sigh of relief when he ran off to fetch a packet of cigarettes for Andy.

Andy rummaged through his memory, but could not remember to have seen any woman of that description. He sat brooding for some time; then he looked at me amicably.

"Really, Debasis," he said, "I have not seen such a woman. She must be a frightful and unforgettable apparition. I am sure, had you been present when she came, you might not have ventured to talk to her. I wonder in what way this ogress is related to the princess of my heart. What a horrible contrast!"

"Ask her when you meet her," I suggested casually. Then added : "May be, your princess is using the ogress as a backdrop to heighten the contrast, to appear more attractive. You'll never know the gimmicks of this fair and foul sex."

Andy scowled at me. "What?" he challenged, "Did you call her foul? Don't use the type of women you interact with as the touchstone. I admit that the woman was not only ugly, she was also very gross. Otherwise, why should she inquire about my personal habits?"

"May be, the princess had asked her to collect that information," I said cynically.

"Shut up!" he snapped at me. "You're embittered, I know. Those ugly women and jilted lovers have botchy cores, you open them and they stink."

I maintained a stubborn silence. Andy walked to the beach all alone.

25

THE SOOTHSAYER

Javed the ruddy-cheeked boy of the Lodge packed his large suitcase which meant he would stay a long time at home. "Thirty six hours on the train," said Javed, folding his bedsheet, "and if I stay less than fifteen days at home, there is no point in taking such strain."

We four went to the railway station to see Javed off. The train was running late by two hours. We walked to a bearded old man, sitting in a lotus posture at the fag-end of the platform. From what we saw in front of him, we concluded that he was a soothsayer.

"How much you charge for reading a palm or a horoscope?" Subramaniam asked.

The man looked at us calmly, then he smiled. His long white flowing beard, his thick black hair with streaks of white, his ochre-coloured loin cloth, his *rudraksha*-beads garland and three horizontal lines of sandal paste on his forehead, and, above all, his tranquil eyes reminded us of the *rishis* in some mythological television serials. We squatted down in front of him.

"Won't you charge any money for reading our palms?" Subramaniam repeated his question.

"Whatever you give," his rich bass voice rang out. "I accept money only to keep my body and soul together without begging.

If you don't give anything, someone else would. It does not matter."

I suddenly stood up and walked away. When I returned after half an hour, my friends had already become wiser about their past and future. Nityanand suggested eagerly that I should also show my palm.

"Nothing can be known about the future. Those who say it can be known, are charlatans and frauds." I wanted to hurt the soothsayer. But he, to my chagrin, was not at all hurt.

"He is right," he said, smiling kindly, looking at me while addressing my mates. "There are many such ignorant people around, I know. You show them the palm-print of an illiterate tribal and jingle your purse, and they predict about the promotion of the man to the highest office. If you inform him that the man so fortunate is a hunter of squirrels, a tribal, he would not be abashed. Then the man, he'd add bravely, is soon becoming the chief of his tribe." We all laughed. I was dragged to him. He looked at my palms and moved his little finger on my fate line. "Rise is steady. These islands on the line may pull you down, but you know how to overcome an adverse fate. You won't be marooned on those islands in vain; you'd transform that space into the beds of civilization. Needn't worry."

"Would you please show me your right palm?" I asked with mocking reverence. He stretched his big palm and brought it close to my face. His fate line rose from the base of his palm like the shoot of a vine and pierced the lowest phallanx of his middle finger. I had a stint in palmistry in my college days, but soon lost faith and interest in it. I had never seen a fate line bifurcating the palm so sharply.

"Now," I said gravely, "would you please tell us why you are not so lucky? Your fate line is very steady, isn't it?"

A cryptic smile played on his face. He withdrew his palm, fixed his compassionate gaze on my face.

"What do you know about me?", he asked.

"As much as I see," I retorted.

"Oh, let's not talk about it anymore. Now, what do you want to know about your future?"

"When will he get married?", my friends demanded in a chorus.

"No, he must tell me what he wants to know?"

"Yes, I want to know when exactly I am getting married," I said.

He took my hand again, drew some diagrams on a slate with a chalk, closed his eyes for sometime and announced the date and year without batting his eyelids. Javed, Subramaniam and Nityanand wrote down the date and year in their pocket notebooks.

"How can I be sure?"

"If you don't get married on the 19th of February next year, I would earn my living by polishing and cobbling shoes and never read a palm in the rest of my life. But I tell you, you must come soon after your marriage, or not at all. I won't be here if you are late."

It was the first week of April when he said that, We saw off Javed and returned to the Lodge late, after taking our dinner in a restaurant. Man Lion beamed like a piece of burning coal when we advised him not to cook dinner, but he soon paled when Andy, returning from his rendezvous, insisted on dinner. He muttered a curse on Andy and entered the kitchen.

26

THE FLY IN THE MARMALADE

Andy tried to conceal his misery under a muslin smile. His face was weather-beaten and sunburnt, but his curly hair had a good number of tell-tale pine needles. He was stalking with heavy steps as if he was burdened with the inexplicable. Yet he tried to keep up a cheerful, sugary expression. "Why on earth do you smile without feeling like smiling and who forces you to do that?" I thought of asking him, but waited for him to broach the topic. Any false move on our part would not only spoil the sport by queering the pitch, but might land the schemers in a dangerous swamp of trouble given the obsessive and phlegmatic nature of our butt.

When he thought that all the prying rogues in the other two rooms were asleep, Andy walked up to me with a questioning attitude.

"I had a miserable time, Debasis;" he began, "Yes, a most terribble time!"

"What happened? Where had you been, Andy?" My enquiries were as solicitous and inquisitive as I could manage to contrive.

"I didn't tell you everything," he said, "because I think you belong to the Devil's party."

"You are drifting away, not I," I protested. "Besides, who's a devil, who is an angel? We're neither, simply human."

Andy mellowed a little and then said in a confidential tone : "Krishnā wrote me a letter asking me to wait for her somewhere near the Light House."

"Really?", I exclaimed. "I bet, it's a filmi style tryst. Is she so romantic, so forward?"

"It was my damnation," he corrected me with a sardonic smile. "There cannot be any place more stinking in the whole universe than that spot. It is the open-air latrine of those fisher men. She must have seen the grove from a distance, and thought it an ideal meeting place. The odorless air smelt like cologne when I came out of that accursed spot. I spent full four hours there, but, to my great surprise and misfortune, she didn't turn up." He heaved a sigh and ran his fingers through his tangled hair.

"I am speechless with amazement," I said. "It was quite unbecoming of her to break tryst with her lover after fixing an appointment with him."

"Don't be so amazed, Debasis," Andy exclaimed with admirable calm. "Sex is easy, but love is difficult."

"What do you mean?"

"You know what I mean," he insinuated impishly.

"Andy, please forgive me for saying it. You're a pious rogue, a paranoid; you can exasperate any one, any one!", I told him point blank, and added after a pause :

"Why do you harp on the same old topic? Why're you so eager to make enemies? What purpose does that serve? You're blackmailing us."

"I was only joking," announced a guilty, apologetic Andy.

"Joking!" I said indignantly; "You deserve a six-month imprisonment in your hell-hole for being such a mocking bird. Your jokes are cruel taunts, mean, motivated stabs in the back."

"Why are you taking my jokes so seriously, I don't understand. All right, I won't crack them again," he said conditionally, "if you tell me the meanings of "Pantheraphile," "novercabhoya."

"I have never seen or heard of these woods," I said helplessly.

"Nor have I", Andy said in a conciliatory tone, and added :

"I wont's speak those things again. But you must admit we are arrant fools."

Andy spent several hours in the library next day, poring through dictionaries and encyclopeadias and reference books, but he could not meet any of these verbal conundrums anywhere. He opened each volume with hope, and closed it with despair. He consulted a dozen knowledgeable persons, but they pleaded ignorance. He strongly abnegated himself, and his regards for the knowledge-seeking beloved snowballed into reverence. In his wretchedness, he considered himself unworthy of her in knowledge, let alone in beauty and wealth. He even decided not to visit that stinking rendezvous and meet her there. But later he changed his mind. "That'd be worse," he told himself; "and I may lose her for ever."

27

A DISPUTE, A DIGRESSION

I was in the thick of my story. I was thrilled to find the discord-spreading fly in our home-made marmalade. And suddenly there was an interruption. Puja, holding a letter which she had just finished reading, swished into the room, and announced; "Marriage are made in heaven!"

I took some time to comprehend what she said. I looked askance at her.

"Now I am certain," she repeated excitedly, "Marriages are made in heaven."

"What about the marriages made in India? Are they worse or better?" I teased her.

She had no patience for jokes. She briefed me about the contents of the letter which her bosom friend Sunita wrote from Bombay.

The bridegroom's greedy uncle demanded twenty five thousand in ready cash at the time of marriage. His retired bureaucrat father tacitly approved the demand. The groom was a bumbling idiot, for he kept humming and hawing without openly contradicting his uncle. It was not possible for Sunita's school teacher father to arrange that sum at short notice. The happy occasion turned into a tragic fiasco. All persuasions failed. The groom and his party prepared to leave. Sunita's father wept, her mother fainted and her brother threatened to murder the greedy uncle. They were just minutes away from a catastrophe when a young man of the groom's contingent came forward with a proposal to marry Sunita without dowry. The handsome, strapping young man, an assistant in the Reserve Bank, was slightly younger than the bride. The marriage, was solemnized without much ado. Sunita described with great relish how the despicable, proud extortionists cut sorry figures and vanished from the scene.

Soon after marriage, Sunita's husband was transferred to Bombay where she was living now.

"Most objectively speaking," added Sunita in a post-script, "we're made for each other. It gives me the creeps to think that I might have married someone else. Sanjay gets goose-pimples when he imagines to have married some other woman. Puja darling, you'll be surprised to know under what circumstances he came with that bumbling idiot who might have become my husband. His father was ailing, and he himself was running a high temperature. But the bumbling idiot (now I call him my benefactor) insisted on Sanjay's accompanying him. Do you know what Sanjay thought when he stole a glance at me for the first time through an open window? Though we had not seen each other before, he thought he had known me for ages. It was like seeing an old beloved after a long gap of time. It was love at first sight. Believe me, Puja, I've never known a better person, never seen a more attractive man than Sanjay. We adore each other. He finds my snub nose exciting. He sings panegyrics on my good looks which you found rather plain. Sometimes I stay awake the entire night watching his sleeping face, listening to the music of his snoring."

Puja read the post-script aloud, and commented : "You see, such fairytale endings happen in real life, though they happen more frequently in films and pulp fictions. One thing is certain. You don't marry just anybody; you marry the person you're destined to. Being cleverer than men, the gods conceal their designs beneath the telltale ruses of chance."

"Excellently you've put it, Puja," exclaimed I, and added : "I completely agree with you regarding the divine origin of marriage. This doctrine has proved more enduring than the divine origin of the kings and more beneficial to boot."

"Are you sure you are not joking?," Puja asked incredulously.

"For heaven's sake no. I have both empirical and dialectical reasons to believe so."

"What're they?" Puja asked, and shouted at the servant to make coffee.

I told her about the predictions of the bearded man in the Railway station, not forgetting to mention the year and the date.

"You know that came true, don't you?"

"Of course!" she agreed broodingly. "Did you meet that man after the marriage?"

I began : "Two months after my, I mean, our marriage, it suddenly occurred to Subramaniam and he brought the house down with his announcement. You were living in the village then. Javed and Nityanand soon found their pocket diaries and compared the date with my marriage invitation card, and could not believe their eyes. One clue led to the other. Sudhakar had already left the lodge before my marriage, but we also recollected what the Sadhu said to Sudhakar. "If you trust the man," the bearded Sadhu had warned him, "who persuades you to chase a dream you are a goner. Your will power is feeble. I am afraid, you will change your profession and place shortly, may be frequently." Then he dropped a warning : "You know, young man, what's bound to happen, will happen."

We remembered how Sudhakar's cousin, a chemical Engineer, persuaded him and won him over. We advised Sudhakar against taking the risk. He wrote from his village after some time that he was trying to arrange a big bank loan to set up a plastic industry and hoping to become a millionaire in five years.

"If the first half came true, the other half will follow suit," observed Nityanand. "He may become insolvent, or worse."

We rushed to the railway station with a basket-full of choicest fruits. The soothsayer was not there. We talked with the guards, but they had no information about the peripatetic man.

I spent many afternoons brooding over the mysteries that surround us. What beat me was the Sadhu's confidence.

That, too, by reading my palm he could predict the exact date of an event!

Puja was beginning to feel queer and nervous. She sidled to me, and whispered : "He could have told my name had you insisted."

I was also getting upset and inattentive. Both of us were actually nervous as if we saw a needle standing up automatically in front of us.

"What can be your dialectical reason, dear?" Puja wanted to make me talk.

"Look, Puja," I argued, "we have heard about hundred per cent correct predictions in the Indian and Greek epics and folklores, haven't we? The oracles of Apollo and the predictions of Cassandra are common knowledge. Forget that; now this single instance of accurate prediction is a mystery which brings in its wake other mysteries."

Puja, I know, dislikes my theorizing of everything, and always finds some excuses to be somewhere else at that time. Why can't he be precise and direct, thinks she. Why can't she be patient and serious, I think. But our thoughts run parallel.

"Your Apollo and Cassandra are not common knowledge, dear," she reminded me good-humouredly. "I want to know what could be your dialectical reason for a correct prediction which could well pass off as a case of coincidence."

"Listen, Puia, I'm coming to that. You must realize patience is better than impatience. Well, you are free to ignore those countless instances of accurate prediction, or write them off as coincidences. But I consider this incident in my life to be more important and disturbing than all other cases of prediction in the lives of other people and in the epics put together. It was not a coincidence, just as the falling of the Newtonian apple was not a coincidence. It was the tip of the iceberg. Had Newton thought, like other people of his time, that God loved His children and therefore, made apples come within their easy reach instead of sending them upwards like helium-filled balloons, he couldn't have discovered the force of gravitation."

"But what are you going to prove by this incident?"

Puja enquired.

"Why, this isolated instance," I gushed, "if we take it as an irrefutable one, would supply us with a glimpse into a vital principle in nature. If what will happen tomorrow is known today, then what will happen tomorrow is bound to happen tomorrow and that won't suffer change, nor would it be altered by all other events, as well as an exercise of human will. Then everything to come is spread before us like a map, but buried under a patina of darkness or submerged under water. Those who dive deep, get a glimpse of that map."

Puja declared that she could not, nor was she willing to, make out what I so passionately elucidated, but agreed to hear me out. "There ought to be something to what you speak considering the vehemence and eloquence with which you speak it."

"To put it briefly, darling," I went on "there is a pattern, a readymade pattern in the world, which makes correct predictions possible. The lines on my plain-looking palm could reveal the exact date of my marriage almost one year before it actually took place, and I was born with my palms. And those criss-cross lines which I always thought random crinkles meant to give flexibility to the palm, suddenly became hieroglyphics, the coded chart of my destiny. My little life which believed itself to be an eagle with a will of its own became a guided, micro-chipped falcon, its every movement regulated by an unknown remote control, by an unknown falconer."

I was really puzzled. Puja only maintained her easy posture and most innocent smile. "I'd be equally puzzled," she implied through her facial expressions, "if I fail to locate one of my ear-rings while I'm titivating myself before going out."

28

A PECULIAR SICKNESS

Javed returned from home after fifteen days. He looked very pale and spoke less. When we enquired about his family, he said there was no trouble. But we all felt he was hiding something serious. He looked at the sea and sky hours together, smiled out of habit, talked when forced, avoided everyone, ate less.

After the Uri incident, we were more or less accustomed to the sea-changes of our own selves. Uri went beyond our reach, but Javed the jovial was one of us. He was every one's darling boy, the youngest and the prettiest of the group. His presence in the company worked as a catalyst, because his silence was enthusiastic, and his capacity to be surprised was unending. We all were talkative in his presence, and used to drop erotic references only to embarrass him and to see him blush. His natural passivity joined him to Subramaniam initially, but he later found his room-mate a bit too clumsy and fanatical on some important issues like religion and sleeping habits. Subramaniam used to go to bed at 10 and insist that the room should be dark at 10 P.M.. Javed didn't like it. Javed also didn't like the way Subramaniam asserted himself and insisted that what he said or did was the only correct thing. One day he complained humorously : "This Southern Brahmin my room-mate has his great grand father as the model and his horoscope tallies with Hitler's. Any one younger than him even by a day knows less than him, hence has no right to contradict him. He believes it is in bad taste to contradict any one older than you."

Javed shared the room with Subramaniam, but did not open his mouth for days together. Practical jokes could not elicit a smile from him. Nityanand narrated Andy's plight in the stinking rendezvous and the mysterious expressions which could not be located in the largest Oxford Dictionary, but Javed didn't show the slightest inclination to laugh. I had my last fling, but it ricocheted off him. I fibbed : "Javed has actually loved a cute girl. He was called by his anxious parents to sort out the matter because she has conceived and forced her way into Javed's family. Is that not so, Javed?" my joke fell flat on him. He looked on vacantly as if he didn't hear me.

When Anjan da learnt about Javed's depression, he paid us a visit. Javed greeted him with a cold hello and disappeared from his view. Andy was at the rock-bottom of his own misery at the time, but he showed great concern for Javed's plight. We all feared that such a state would certainly lead to a severe mental condition, which might lead to insanity or suicide.

Andy averred, his tongue firmly in his cheek, that it was a case of unrequited love or betrayal, or both; that our sloppy films have done this type of damage to a million blooming Romeos. "Look friends," he pontificated like a celebrity, "fall in love in good earnest, and try to earn the love of your girl, yes try your very best, be truer than all the legendary lovers, but after doing all that, if you find her as hard as the arctic ice, and as cold as cucumber, and hobnobbing with others or betraying your faith, or cold shouldering you, or trying to ignore and insult you, you should call her a hussy in a public place and be through with her. That's the only way to prove that you are not chicken soup. I tell you Javed, don't get so upset for your girl, for any girl for that matter. Do you know, boy, when you shed pots of tear for her, she must be flirting with another impressionable smart Alec to arouse his passion and break his heart."

He might have gone on talking, had not Anjan da beckoned him to stop. Other inmates of the lodge knew what inspired Andy's tirade against the female species, but no body wanted to tell him that. Anjan da turned to Javed and blessed him with a cordial, reassuring smile.

"You're avoiding me, Javed," he complained. "But why?"

"Ah no!" Javed shrivelled and fidgetted, and pleaded for mercy. "How can I avoid you, Anjan da. You know it's not true."

"Then why did you greet me formally and run to your room?"

"I am an unhappy man, dada; very unhappy. I was thinking of meeting you. I wanted to meet you alone."

"I am passing through a turbulent time, too," Anjan da said quietly. "It seems all the inimical forces were lying in wait for me, but afraid of touching me, as long as I was single. Now for mysterious reasons, they have rallied all their force against me and cornered me. Honestly, I am no less wretched than anybody I know of."

Javed caught hold of Anjan da's hand. It was as if a drowning man caught hold of a floating plank.

Anjan da marked the intensity of his grief. He took Javed's limp hand into his and suggested that Javed should be left alone in his company. "We'd take a long, long walk on the beach, and come back late at night and take dinner in the Lodge. Is that acceptable, gentlemen?"

"Most welcome idea," I said. "Are you staying here tonight, Anjan da? I am afraid, that'd be too late for you to return home."

"Don't worry, Debasis. No hour is late enough for an unhappy man to return home. The road that leads to hell is paradise." Anjan da winked meaningfully.

"You are not unhappy after marriage, Anjan da, are you?" Javed asked anxiously before they were out of the gate. We couldn't know for certain whether he spoke the truth or deliberately lied to elicit a favourable response from a truly unhappy Javed. Our gaiety repelled him, but Anjan da's admission of his unhappiness created an instant impact on him. That Anjan da could not tell a lie on any circumstance, was an acceptable fact.

"Honestly, Javed, I am more disadvantaged than unhappy. Though it would be too hasty to draw a ship-shape conclusion regarding marriage, I may say a person of my type will never make a good husband. Mind you, I blame it on nobody," Anjan da said gravely.

"Is she trying to adjust herself to your life-style, or are you changing your life-style to suit hers?" Javed felt brave enough to bring in highly personal issues.

"Look, young man," said Anjan da, "do not attach so much of importance to that aspect. Compromise is a sickening expression like the condolence messages of politicians or coded telegraph messages. The body reigns supreme during the first few months of marriage, and after that stage, other considerations take up, like the runners in a relay race, the onus of responsibility. Well, we'll talk about that later. Tell me what ails you?"

Javed and Anjan da saw me loitering alone and called me. That was what I wanted. My curiosity tempted me to follow them alone. With some pretexts, I separated myself from the uncomfortable company. Andy was trying to make others laugh most insincerely with his stale jokes and facile witticisms and he had already occupied the chair where Anjan da was sitting earlier. The pretentious clown was trying to replace the natural hero. I also wanted to know the troubles of those two unhappy friends.

"I don't know if Javed would take me into confidence," I said sulkily. "That's why I kept a distance from you. I won't mind walking alone."

"No! No!" Javed protested. "I could have asked you to accompany us, but thought others would mind such discrimination."

Anjan da nodded in agreement. "I was just asking Javed what ailed him," he said, looking at me.

"I'm fed up with asking that question," I corroborated nonchalantly. "Every one wants to know what ails Javed. He should at least tell us the nature of his sorrow. It is personal or general? Please tell us that," I added.

"Can there be two types of sorrow, think it over?" Javed charged me.

"Of course!" I contended "There can be as many types of sorrow as men who suffer them. Yes, I mean it. Each man suffers in a unique way. I dare say no man had ever suffered like you since the creation of man, and no man will suffer like you in the future. I don't mean to flatter you. That's true for every one else."

There was an uneasy pause. Then I added : "I only made two broad categories of sorrow-personal or general. You know categorizing anything is an arbitrary and subjective activity." I smiled softly.

"What other categories can you think of?", Javed asked. "Why, you can easily notice that the sick man, the man who attends the sick man, the poor man, the lover whose love is not requited, the couples who, like caged birds, flutter, and fight with each other from morning to midnight, the orphans and the victims of cyclone, do not suffer alike, do they? If you simply try to document the sorrows that afflict man, even without being emotionally involved, will you actually reach a point of closure and say finally I've done it?" I looked at Javed for an answer.

"I do say, Debasis, without contradicting you," Javed observed in a thoughtful tone, "I mean... there is only one type of suffering, only one sorrow, one explosive that breaks the heart into pieces. What you just enumerated are factors responsible, ingredients used, for that explosive."

"You one-God worshiper!" I told him, desiring to offend him; "You simplify everything. Don't forget, we Hindus have only thirty three crore gods and goddesses- each one having an indispensable cause to exist in that gigantic pantheon."

"So what?", barked Javed, furious with rage. "Either they are various manifestations of the same one God, or they are nothing."

Anjan da was listening to our arguments, speaking not a word. Now that he found we were getting worked up on totally vague issues, wide of the mark, he interfered.

"That is not our point at present, I suppose. Besides, we should not champion the cause of our respective religions. The priests and mullahs, those attorneys of the gods, can do that for their clients."

He looked at me sternly and added : "If you are not crazy, please tell me what link could be there between the sub division of human suffering and the multitude of Hindu gods. This, I think, is an outrage on sense, a non sequitur."

I pretended to be ashamed. "I only wanted to tease Javed," I muttered, "to make him talk."

Javed glared at me. "The devil take you," he cursed me with mock anger.

We walked to a remote part of the beach and sat in a triangle. Anjan da materialized a small thermos flask full of tea and paper cups. He carried the flask in his curduroy carry-bag. We were delighted to sip tea while watching the sea. The breeze was a caress of peace, and the sun was lampshaded by hovering white clouds. I remembered a stanza from the Meghaduta where the poet Kalidas describes the climate of Yakshapuri, the veritable heaven. Peacocks dance, lotuses bloom, swans swim cackling and the day time is as cool and lambent as a clear fullmoon night. Then I saw a gray hawk coming down in a rushing movement and swooping up a large fish from the waters. The fish tried to wrench itself free from the bird's talons.

I averted my eyes from the struggling fish, for it was not in harmony with my idea of a paradise. Anjan da and Javed were watching the bird and its prey. I was curious to know what the bird would do next, and looked at it again. The bird stalled in mid-air and then flapped its wings and rose almost vertically to a great height. The fish stopped struggling. It had either died, or realized the futility of its struggle.

Javed's wretchedness, I soon gathered, sprung from most unexpected sources. There was no mishap in the family, nor was there any pre-marital pregnancy.

"The ghost of Salman Rushdie is haunting me," he announced quietly. His announcement struck us like a blitzkrieg. "What do you mean, boy?" blurted out Anjan da; "I know Rushdie is still young, living and kicking in some benigh British hideout."

"I know that, I know that," Javed said.

"Then how can the ghost of a living man haunt you?" I shook him as if he was sleep-talking.

"Don't touch me, I tell you. I'm fully awake and sane, and saner than you." He told, pointing his finger at me.

"You must prove it. Haunted by a living man's ghost? What an idea!" I returned sarcastically.

"Frankly, I couldn't get you," Anjan da said in a cool tone of voice.

"He is living, no doubt," Javed said referring to Salman Rushdie, "but living posthumously. A living man forced into a coffin with an oxygen pipe stuck to his nostrils just to keep him alive, so that he would take a long time to die. Of late, I have become quite peculiar, even to my own self. The condition of that unfortunate man keeps on possessing me. When it happens, I run out of the house in terror, because the ceiling and the walls close in on me; my powers fail me; my blood boils and my body hairs stand at an end, my mind threatens to bolt out of its bony prison, shrinks and dilates in quick succession. I feel as if I shall explode like a time bomb and lose my sanity for ever. Then I almost run to the open air, to the street and feel suddenly relieved."

Anjan da put his hand on Javed's shoulder, looked kindly at him, but decided not to interrupt his talk.

"It all started in my native town. In my family, in my circle of friends, everywhere the topic of the *fatwah* ranges and brings out the best and the worst in human nature. Some contend that the *fatwa* rightly serves the blasphemer, the storm-trooper of the devil, the foster son of Satan. In the name of freedom of speech and writing, they say, one person cannot offend another person or a community of believers. Others — liberal-minded as they are — maintain that no book should be banned in a democratic society because such ban curtails individual freedom and encourages in tolerance of the clerics'. They disapprove of the fatwah on a writer who wrote some unflattering things about the Prophet. An ordinary man, they say, does not kill his son who criticises him. Then how can God the Merciful be pleased to see

His followers spilling the blood of his dissident children? But the majority of people belonging to my community and other communities do not have any opinion of their own. They have many constraints. Besides, the fact that the author of that controversial book has not yet changed his religion so far, and is still a Muslim proves that he does not question the fundamental aspects of Islam."

"That does not follow, Javed," I contradicted him. "The change of religion would have made matters worse for Rushdie. He cannot prefer one religion to the other because his sanity would not allow him to slip into any strait-jacket. He is a brave nonconformist. I wonder why he doesn't throw off his voluntary captivity and move about like anybody else. Such an action, I think, might have simplified his problems and endeared himself to millions of his admirers. He should stand on his own two feet and die the death of a martyr. A brave man should be prepared to die for the cause he espouses."

Javed's face was contorted with the purest form of anger. "You say that?" he charged me. "Is there any shortage of the hired assassins in our world? They kill people for a song, for a bottle of whisky, for a little money. There are many pathological killers who would be happy to kill a celebrity simply for notoriety. Is Rushdie a god or a superman or a celluloid hero? That would not be an act of courage but an act of bravado, of knight-errantry of sorts."

"I think Javed is right," observed Anjan da quietly. "What, after all, is Rushdie's cause? Truth, you'll say. But unfortunately it is not a conflict between Truth and Untruth. It is a case of the personal dogma pitted against a collective dogma, each side flaunting Truth as *its causa sine qua non*."

Anjan da took a brief pause, and then resumed his observation : "Celebrities, messiahs, the greats," Anjan da said placidly, "are more or less like the moon. They've their places in the sun. The moon, you know, turns and moves in such a way as to show a particular sunbathed portion of its topography to the earthlings, and to conceal the other portion permanently from our view. This is a time-honoured, hence sacred, practice. Any attempt on the part of man to subvert this arrangement and pry into the invisible and private space of those luminaries has always been considered sacrilegious."

Anjan da chuckled good-naturedly.

Javed looked thankfully at Anjan da.

"Do you remember, Anjan da," Javed resumed, "What Einstein said regarding Bertrand Russell when the learned judges and holier-than-thou priests rallied all their forces against that single free-thinker?"

"Verbatim!" Anjan da promptly replied, "Great spirits have always found violent opposition from mediocrities. The latter cannot understand it when a man does not thoughtlessly submit to hereditary prejudices but honestly and courageously used his intelligence."

"Bravo! Bravo!" I interjected. I marvelled at his memory. Javed said, "Yes that's exactly what he said. Opposition, criticism, debate are expected from sensible antagonists. But petty, cowardly people would attack their adversaries with automatic guns when they have nothing on them but pens or portable typewriters."

I told Javed bluntly that his angry rhetoric was more ridiculous than the donkey's baying at the moon, that we would certainly get into a scrape if we were carried away by our own enthusiasm. "If we have not yet known that political decisions are taken considering the points of expediency and appeasement, not of propriety and ethics, we are nincompoops. You know, Javed, to be correct is not enough; you should be politically correct." I advocated piously.

"In that case," Javed protested impatiently, "why do our political heavy weights, as soon as they see microphones in front of them, pontificate on freedom of speech, democracy, secularism and religious tolerance? And once the microphones are removed and they get down the dias, they behave like medieval inquisitors. How do these people accommodate such contradictions in their minds and still look so frighteningly sober?"

Anjan da blessed him with a special smile of appreciation, and I didn't like it. I thought Anjan da who by the long odds, was the sanest amongst us, should discourage such political sacrilege Javed was airing.

"I know, Javed, what troubles you," Anjan da said, looking at the vast blue sea. "I know it well. I also think he is helpless before his imagination. He is riding a ferocious beast and is left with no choice. Besides what else can a fibber cursed or blessed with such a brook-no-barrier flamboyance of syntax, do, but be utterly socio-centric and bend all his ideas, fantasies, fabulations, similitudes and sentences towards the deeply entrehcned, though time-honoured, illusions of society, concepts and religions. His problem is a sad one. Philosophy, or the effacement of factuality could have supplied an effective ambiguity to his narrative. You know how he tried to problematize the narrative by making his fictional protagonist Gabreel Farista dream about his ancient role as a courier between God and the Prophet. Anything can happen in a dream. He got a nightmare for giving his protagonist a dream. I hope this trauma of confinement would gravitate him towards the beyond. And instead of hurting his adversaries with deadly Tyson punches, he would vex them with kid-gloves allegories."

"You see, Anjan da," Javed said reflectively, "compulsory confinement could be more painful than a voluntary one. In his case, it is a live-in-coffin-or-die sort of choice."

"Indeed, it is so." Anjan da agreed with him.

29

WALKING IN SLEEP

Andy's misery following his disappointment at the stinking grove, which he hated to call a rendezvous, instead of dampening his spirit, made him voluble and aggressive, and he brazened it out as the general fate of lovers to which he could not possibly be an exception. He tried to ingratiate himself, though insincerely, with our company of non-lovers. But at the same time, he let go his tongue which, like a self-appointed sanctimonious scourge, lashed us for our carnal trafficking with a temptress, and went on tormenting us with his apologetic smiles. Whenever we protested and frowned at his gross insinuations, he would knit up his hairy brows and scratch his ears, and say "Oh my God, why're you overreacting? I was only joking. Why can't you guys digest a joke?" His pretentious surprise, more than his naggings, infuriated us, and we even thought of disclosing the mystery of the love letter to checkmate him. But we considered later that impulsiveness wouldn't be a good weapon for revenge; that once he began distrusting us, we would lose our power over him.

We decided to bide our time, but certain events seemed to be conspiring with us to bring about his ruin. Or that is what we persuaded ourselves to believe.

Andy got up one night, almost two hours before sunrise, looked out of the window facing the street. As he lifted the window curtains, the cool night wind brushed against his face and blew away his sleepiness. He decided to take a walk in the open; washed his face, combed his hair, drank a glass of water and went out. The sea beach on the other side of the four-foot tall boundary wall was lighted by the stars. A thin layer of mist hung over the swollen stormy sea. He closed the door behind him, and reached the gate facing the street. Freshness of the breeze made him brave. He took the short-cut route through the cremation ground to the beach. Had any one seen him at that time, leisurely walking down the forbidden ground in his white trousers and punjabi, he could have taken Andy to be a spectre or a somnambulist, for no living or conscious person dared walk that stretch of ground allotted to the dead, in the night.

Loud noise and repeated knocking awakened the inmates of the Lodge. It was full day, about seven, and the sun had risen to a considerable height in the sky. I rushed out of the room and saw Andy being carried by two bare-bodied men, and other three persons were talking loudly among themselves. As soon as they saw me, they pointed at Andy and enquired if I knew that man. "We found him lying on sand. We took him for dead. But he is not dead," said the man who carried Andy. They deposited the inert body on the verandah.

Andy opened his eyes slowly after a lot of massaging. His body was ice-cold and his pulse was feeble. The nervous Man Lion rubbed hot mustard oil on Andy's heels furiously, holding them on his lap. As soon as Andy opened his eyes, he felt ticklish and giggled. "Hey, stop it, stop it," he muttered weakly, kicking at the servant. But Man Lion didn't free Andy's legs. He sat firmly over one leg, held the other in a vice-like grip and went on rubbing the helpless heel. Andy groaned in frantic amusement, writhed like a python in captivity, and then laughed like mad. We sat on the steps and watched the show with great satisfaction.

"Believe me," one of the persons who had carried Andy said, "we thought him dead. Now see, he is laughing. Has he gone mad, or what? Some evil spirit has possessed him. You must find some one to drive out the evil spirit."

"No, he is laughing at your mistakes," Nityanand explained gravely. "You think anybody that sleeps on the beach must be dead? Why don't you go and do your work? If not you, vultures, crows and dogs could have woken him up."

"No bakshish for all that trouble, sab? He was very heavy, sab." One of them ventured at last. We gave them a ten rupee note and asked them to share it among themselves. "Two each, mind you. Don't fight over it, OK?" said Man Lion, still busy doing his piece of work with an exaggerated devotion.

Andy sat up with a jerk and pushed Man Lion with his hands. "Didn't I tell you to leave my heels alone," he said indignantly.

Within an hour, Andy was up again, loitering on the verandah, whistling a tune.

"What was the matter with you, Andy?" We surrounded him with eager enquiries. "How come, you slept on your bed and were transported to the beach?"

"The Devil took me there, the Devil!" Andy announced, without intending any pun, and added : "Who else?"

"How did he do it? I mean did he make you walk, or simply lifted you and dropped you there like the Genie of the lamp?" It was Nityanand again.

"I suppose the Devil made him walk all the way," I said, "Because the door was open when I got up."

"I thought I should take a walk and so I walked out."

But I should not have done it," Andy explained, looking down.

"Look, Andy," I told him clearly, "you knowingly or unknowingly become the centre of attraction, the apple of discord and the burning topic of all conversations wherever you go. You must make your presence felt, often with sinister frequency, in any company. Say, am I wrong? Please, tell us why did you decide to visit the beach in the midnight, why?"

Andy looked crushed, fazed. He glared at us with a wild look, the look of a persecuted criminal. "I felt a strong desire to walk in the open," he drawled; "It was as if I had an important appointment with some one, and my life depended on my meeting that some one." He stopped, rather abruptly, and kept blinking his eyes in a peculiar way.

We believed in what he said, and pitied him.

"What happened then? Did you meet any one, anything?" I asked softly.

"I'm afraid of saying it. Didn't you people ridicule me when I said the white cat was not a cat at all?"

"Was it a bandicoot, an enlarged rat?" Sudhakar snickered.

"If you make such snide comments, Sudhakar," I scolded, "you rather leave us alone. Where on earth you have seen a snow-white bandicoot?"

"I don't want to make myself the object of your jokes, nor do I try to make myself notorious in any way," Andy spoke with a ponderous drawling accent, and added, "Only thing is, many misfortunes befall me, and I'm singled out."

He took a pause, and then began :

"Had I taken the broad road, it would have been better. But I was not within my own control. I realize this only now. I wended towards the beach through that cremation ground, and I was not afraid. I saw that white creature there. It walked in front of me, I followed it trustingly. I was feeling all the time that I was surrounded by many people, I knew them, they were friendly, well-meaning, and we were going to attend a good congregation or a festival!" He quickly turned to me, "Do you remember how we felt that day at the sand ridge — that long wall of sand touching the sea — and where we had lain down panting?"

"I do remember. It was an unforgettable occasion," I said. "I felt when I was running that some one was pursuing me."

"Had I found myself in that place, I should have been dead by now. The waves must have swept me in," Andy said. "Were you thinking at that time, Andy?" Subramaniam put in.

"How can I remember all that, if I was not thinking?" Andy replied.

"The white creature suddenly vanished from my sight. I stopped short. The feeling that I was surrounded by many people, left me. I suddenly realized I was all alone. I was standing on the verge of the treacherously slippery cliff of that ridge. I could see the foamy crests of waves ten or twelve feet below. The sea was ink-black and roaring. The road lights were not visible because there was mist. I thought I was dreaming. But such thoughts only made me more wretched. I stood transfixed for a long time. Any physical activity terrified me. I took a backstep when I felt the sand under my feet was sliding. Then I ran and ran, my only aim was to move away from the sea as far as possible as soon as possible. I lost direction, but didn't slow down till I stumbled and fell on my face."

It was a close shave for poor Andy. We felt jittery and

believed whatever Andy said regarding that mysterious white creature.

"I thought it was just another white cat." I said seriously.

"A cat with a difference!", Andy corrected me.

"There can be no doubt about that," I said. It pleased Andy, and he tried desperately to smile.

Next day I called a carpenter, and told him to fix a hook and a chain to the inner part of the door of our room. Before going to bed, I used to lock the door and keep the key in my purse, and put the purse under my pillow, so that Andy could not get out of the room without waking me up.

30

A PECULIAR SICKNESS (TWO)

Javed's reaction to this episode was rather sedate. He didn't open his mouth even once. He simply watched the whole scene as if he was deaf and dumb. I thought, after his frank discussion on the beach with Anjan da and me, he would get over his trauma and be his usual self. My small knowledge of psychology convinced me that the passionate outpourings of a constipated heart could purge off excesses of emotion and sedimented delusions. But I was utterly mistaken in my optimism, for Javed showed no such sign of recovery. He shunned company and chose lonely walks holding his hands stiffly behind him.

Anjan da had told me privately after our conversation with Javed; "When a man begins to be troubled by problems which remotely concern him or do not concern him at all, his sharing of his troubles with friends does not lessen the intensity of his angst. Poor chap would be normal if the object of his concern is released from his captivity, if the fatwah is lifted, or if he is murdered by the hired assassins."

"Not likely to happen," I intoned sceptically.

Anjan da looked at me, surprised by my scepticism.

"I'll tell you why," I hastened to add. "First of all Salman is relatively young and physically robust. If diseases and hired assassins threaten him, good doctors and the adroit Scotland Yard are there to foil all attempts on their protege's life. Quarantined because of apostasy, he has no fear of catching the germs of AIDS and of faith which afflict humanity and defy cure."

Anjan da was embarrassed. He looked displeased. "By the way, Debasis," he observed, "why on earth you equate faith with AIDS? It is not faith, but the lack of it which troubles humanity. When will you understand that?"

I felt to have been possessed with the poltergeist of a free thinker, or of an iconoclast. All of a sudden I recollected all the evils the religious enthusiasts had perpetrated while spreading their respective faiths and punishing the alleged accomplices of the Devil.

"I don't know, Anjan da," I gushed, "what you think of religion, but I believe all religions are based upon superstitions and unverifiable assumptions. God only knows how religion originated and flourished, but in course of time it has become an empty slogan, a palimpsest of malafide intentions, a magic wand in the hands of the galoots and crooks to threaten and subjugate gullible men, a sort of spiritual graffiti, and what not."

"Had Andy been here," said Anjan da, "he must have throttled you."

"Oh no!", I said; "I've already said it to him."

"Really, what was his reaction?"

"He refused to take me seriously, and smiled like a saint."

"Why, so?", Anjan da wondered. "That day he attacked poor Sudhakar when he commented on his gods."

"That may be because Sudhakar made a pointed remark on his own gods, not on everybody's. Besides, Andy you know is the most unpredictable person I've ever known. There are a number of occasions when we deliberately tried to hurt and offend him, but he was vastly amused."

"Andy, I believe," observed Anjan da, "is as predictable as you all. Not a whit more. I never thought you would be so violently casual, so tongue-in-cheek while talking about serious and sacred things."

Javed was slowly slipping into an abnormal state of being. At any time of day, whether he was on bed, or in the office (he was an officer in the Syndicate Bank), he used to imagine a particular situation — a coal miner's plight, caught in a dark, shoulder-high tunnel, a thousand yards below the sun-lit surface of the earth, earth caved in blocking the exit-crawling with his oxygen mask in that tunnel, a hurricane lamp lighting up a small area, but intensifying the darkness around — his mind bolting out of his cranium-case, his body crawling helplessly like a maimed beetle but possessed with an irresistible urge to spread himself....

Once that thought occurred, he'd begin to feel queasy and look around awkwardly to ascertain if any one was peeping into his mind. Then his feelings for the trapped miner would intensify, and he'd begin to identify with that person. He would feel the ceiling slowly coming down and walls closing in on him. His body would feel the clammy walls; a clangorous din would fill his head; the top of his skull would burn as if somebody has rubbed a paste of chillies on it; his heart would beat faster and he'd feel as if he were dying of suffocation. Suddenly he would stand up and run out of that closed place like mad. Any one who'd try to block his way was pushed aside like furniture; he could not recognize any one at that time. The big halls oppressed him like claustra, but the sky gave him some comfort. Within minutes he'd recover from that trauma, and return to his seat with a shambling gait and do his bit of work as a normal employee.

Gradually the frequency increased, and it annoyed and inconvenienced other employees of the bank. On one such occasion, he violently bumped into the Assistant Manager, a large man with a chubby genial face. "What's the matter, young man? Are you in a hurry?", he enquired anxiously, holding his hand. Javed couldn't disengage his hand easily, and gave a hard push on the naval area of Mr. Rao's enormous belly and rushed out. Rao sat down on a chair, caressing his belly, completely bewildered by the behaviour of the innocent-looking young officer. Other employees told him how on several occasions they were pushed off or even knocked down by Javed. "What bothers him?" enquired the Assistant Manager. As Javed had not told any one in the bank about his problem, they gave their own interpretations of it. "He thinks a cobra is in the room, and runs away," said one. "The point is," said another, this time a middle-aged, frolicsome lady with frizzled hair, "he expects an important visitor and alas, she does not turn up on time. I know where the shoe pinches." She giggled. The Assistant Manager was slightly enthused by the lady's yarn, and quipped : "Sure, Mrs. Dey, the nails are supposed to know where they pinch." Mrs. Dey, the past mistress of coquetry, elated by the demi-boss's reference to her pinching power, opened her casket of guardedly erotic wit. Repartees and peppy retorts shuttled like shuttlecocks and merry laughter filled the place. Javed silently meandered through the crowd of boisterous customers and employees, and occupied his seat and opened a fat register to make some entries.

31

THE PRESSURE OF GUILT

Anjan da, we all knew, was no less sensitive than any of us, but unlike us, he refused to be rattled by what generally rattled others.

But why was he so steady, so rock-like when we, made though of the same ingredients, doodled, shook and dithered when the winds of change blew over us? We, the inmates of the Lodge, asked each other and our own secret selves whether Anjan da would take easy his wife's premarital sexual overtures and cheapness, and for that matter, would any husband carry on the relationship with those culprits who treated his present wife so disrespectfully before she was married. In our heart of hearts, in the innermost part of our solitary thoughts, was crouching the beast of the night, the blackness of a stacked-away guilt congealed into a question mark. We knew its surfacing would be a sort of acid test of Anjan da's composure and of our ability to stand up to what we considered our moment of reckoning. Things, we all realized, were getting curiouser and curiouser in the Lodge everyday. Countenancing the inevitable seemed to be the only way out of the situation.

One sunny afternoon, a few days before Sudhakar's resignation from his job I accompanied him to a bar. Nityanand met us on the way and told us how he was in search of ways to spend time. "Exact ways I have not found," he told in a comic vein, "but a lot of surplus time is always spent in searching for them. Work expands, as your Parkinson'd say, so as to fill the time available for its completion, ha, ha."

We, however, didn't try to understand what he said, but asked him to accompany us to some bar. The bar we chose was a less frequented one. The owner was a remarkably good-looking man, in white trousers and banian; he ushered us in and led us to a sequestered cabin. We swirled a bottle of beer each, pepping up our palates with tangy and crisp chips. Sudhakar, ebullient as usual, was in high spirits. His pent up dreams to be rich, to buy a luxury car and drive it to wherever he listed, were nearing their fruition. He had already started the process of relinquishing his job.

"Debasis," he told me, "I feel like flying to my goal instead of plodding slowly to it."

Nityanand, who sat on the other end of the table, made a lascivious grimace. He pulled his chair close to the table and leaned forward to speak something important. "You're boys before me, mere kids," he whispered hoarsely; "Imagine, I stayed single till I was as old as you are. I was not so sexy. But as soon as my marriage date was fixed and I saw the girl, I felt I couldn't wait a day longer. I grew restless as if I'd drunk gasoline. Once I attempted to enter her house through the balcony to hug and kiss that cute slip of a girl."

"Ha-ha-" laughed Sudhakar. "Don't say you were or are not sexy, Nityanandaji. You are the sexiest man I ever met, an old satyr. Your zodiac sign must be Capricorn, the Goat." Instead of being abashed, he beamed. "No, boy, I was born under Virgo, indeed," he corrected Sudhakar with a chuckle; "Do you know some of the great Virgos? Sophia Lauren, Greta Garbo and D.H. Lawrence, those Laureates of Love!"

"You're in great company, really," I joined the conversation; "I believe your fellow Virgos might have gone to their graves as virgins."

"No wonder, no wonder," corroborated Nityanand. "They knew how to stay virgin all through their lives while making love a million times; that's a secret they won't reveal to any one. That's their mystique, boy."

He suddenly became silent and sat in a posture of meditation. He was perhaps remembering the charming faces of these two actresses. He saw a hotel boy, and told him to bring a pint of rum and full plate of green peas.

We left him alone, and remembered why we had come to the hotel. We had planned to talk of something which concerned us immediately. Sudhakar cleared his throat.

"Let that vigorous man die by over-drinking, so that he'd deflower his fellow Virgos in the other world," Sudhakar said, pointing at the meditating figure, intending to be heard. Nityanand looked at us calmly as if surprised by human noise. He said "Let me alone, chaps," hardly opening his lips, and relapsed into a simulation of trance. Sudhakar took a slurping sip from the beer mug to fortify himself to broach the embarrassing topic.

"Don't you feel, Debasis," said he, "there is something wrong in the structure of our relationship with Anjan da? I don't know if you think the way I do. And I tell you I'm not leaving this place without setting it right." He paused. I knew what was he aiming at. I was no less troubled than he was, considering my intimacy with Anjan da.

"What do you suggest? What's the remedy?", I asked anxiously.

"Truth travels in a straight line, however thorny and dangerous the path may be," Sudhakar philosophized half-heartedly. "I do not understand why we weren't feeling uneasy about the whole thing before Anjan da's marriage."

"That's simple!" I promptly explained. "She was just another girl when we did it. But once she married Anjan da, the act became a secret which we took care to conceal. An act, Sudha, becomes a guilt the very moment we try to conceal it. If we had told everything to Anjan da before it was too late that could have been better for every one."

"Better late than never," Sudhakar said flamboyantly. "I am going to tell everything to Anjan da, everything I know, everything I did. What'll I do with this secret once I am gone from this place? The world, you know, is big enough to separate us for ever. I know that."

That was, too, my initial determination to come out with a confession, which seemed to me no less painful than harakiri, but it got a short shrift due to some other considerations. While granting truth its freedom of expression, I was not oblivious of the fact that such self-gratuitous truth-telling would affect Anjan da's conjugal life. While I was still uncertain about the quality and nature of good that would ensue from my frankness, I was certain about the bad blood it would generate. I debated with my own self on this theme. "Why did you decide to tell that to me now?" Anjan da would ask in a wretched tone. I couldn't find a convincing answer to that.

I tried to convince Sudhakar that such belated confessions would foul up the situation. I told him that the guilt concealed might trouble us alone, but the guilt announced would affect and trouble other people.

Sudhakar, however, didn't fully subscribe to my interpretation. "You see, my good friend," he said, "in my opinion, a truth spoken out earnestly is always less harmful than a truth unspoken."

Our debate ended inconclusively because Nityanand, after emptying the bottle of rum, asked for more and showed some symptoms of drunkenness. Sudhakar footed the bill, and we took an auto-rickshaw to reach the Wave Crest House.

The topic concerning our confession to Anjan da was broached again as soon as we reached the lodge. Andy was not present there.

Subramaniam, Javed and even Nityanand initially supported Sudhakar's arguments, and all were in favour of telling Anjan da about the whole thing and be through with it. Once the proposal was passed with a majority vote, I reluctantly agreed after pointing out my reading of the possible consequences. It was also decided that Andy should not be informed about the whole thing. The venue would be a lonely part of the beach. Each of us warned the other that we should be mentally prepared to face the worst.

Despite my apparent resistance to the move, I saw at least one good point in the absurd drama which we were all set to stage : That occasion would prove whether Anjan da really deserved the regards and love we so spontaneously lavished on him. A clever man could talk wisely and pass off as a sage.

Shrewd men galore. I have to walk ten miles to locate a fool, and a few days later I would realize he was only playing that role. The world has become a large Stock Exchange where each person I lay my hands on turns out to be more cunning than the other, where the motto is surpass as many competitors as possible in the race, not exactly to go to the forefront, but only to stay where you are. How could I be sure that Anjan da was not one of those clever people? That thought bolstered up my courage to face the horrific situation.

Javed's unusual sickness assumed a grimly pathological shape of dementia, and his colleagues had already ostracized him. Things came to such a bad pass as to force the genial Assistant Manager to advise Javed to proceed on leave for some treatment.

"It means I'm out of this job," lamented the unhappy young man. "It means you're completely mistaken," corrected the portly Assistant Manager with a friendly grin. "It beats me why you go nuts about the confined places. You should not think we conduct financial transactions under the sky, you understand me?"

When the Manager came to know of it, he called Javed to his chamber, talked kindly to him and learnt about his peculiar problem. "Believe me, young man," he observed gravely; "You see a common lizard, but think you've seen a full-grown dragon." Javed explained his position, and said that his thoughts had gone haywire, that it was not a case of deliberate exaggeration. It was true that in the initial stage he brooded deeply over the confinement of an innocent man for such a long period of time. But soon his obsessions guided his thinking process. His deluded mind conjured up many horrifying situations people could be in — in the coal mines, under the debris of a multi-storied building razed to the ground by an earthquake, in the dark, underground prison cells, in the galleys of old ships, in the deep dry desert wells, bunkers and silos, tunnels and caves. He imagined the tortuous mental state of the galley-slaves in the Roman ships. Once these horrors paraded before his mind, he sweated, shivered, clenched his fists, bit his lips and looked fazed.

He told all these things to the Manager who listened to him patiently. He advised Javed to spend one or, two weeks in some hill stations and remember some good things of life. "If it is not within your reach to think of the good side of life," the Manager advised, "you can identify with millions of people who are fortunately deprived of any enclosed space which they'd call their home, and spend their entire lifetime on the streets and open places. May be, once you think of that segment of humanity, you'd always find yourself under the vast blue sky even when you sit in the dungeon. Try this method."

Javed could clearly mark the irony in the Manager's suggestion, and that made him more nervous.

When he told that to us, we assured him that there was nothing to worry so much about. We prescribed a variety of remedies for his illness, but all agreed on one particular remedy — that universal, time-atrophied remedy : Take it easy. It hardly bothered us then, (and it hardly bothers most of us all the time), that it was an insincere piece of advice we doled out to a friend in distress.

It struck me, only after I said it to an unconvinced Javed, that three-word expression is a weapon which cuts both ways. Most of our present day ills spring from such an attitude of the doer *vis-a-vis* his better judgement; and the absence of such an attitude and our common failure to take things easy cause cataclysms, big or small, in the soul, in the family, in interpersonal and international spheres. We had not also asked our unsteady selves if taking things easy were so effective a solution, why we were so bothered about our sexual overture with a girl who accidentally became our friend's wife, Again, what good reason we had to suppose that Anjan da would take it easy when we told him our lurid stories concerning Uri?

Javed, however, didn't take our prescriptions seriously. He was feeling uneasy because he felt a great injustice had been done to some one whom he had neither met, nor did he hope of meeting him ever.

Two days following our unanimous decision to invite Anjan da and tell him everything, Javed announced in a tone of severe disagreement that he won't be a party to that most hypocritical confession. "I don't feel guilty on that account any more," he remarked irritably; "I was rather seduced by that girl. Besides did I know then that she'd marry Anjan da? My friend Subrato fell in love with a beautiful prostitute and married her in face of strong opposition. They are now the happiest couple in the world, I know it. Why on earth Anjan da should bother how many men touched Uri before he married her? We are only trying to be very clean persons, aren't we? As if that was the only stain on our immaculate outfit, and that it would be erased without any trace if we launder it with a detergent called frankness. Exclude me from your list, please."

Javed's categorical disagreement dampened the general enthusiasm. We looked askance at each other. Sudhakar made it clear that he would not leave the place with a cat in his bag, or a skeleton in his cupboard and he didn't care for other's opinions in the matter.

I was sitting on the fence; so Javed's arguments somewhat affected me, and I tilted to his side. Subramaniam and Nityanand made feeble attempts to justify truth-telling, and then chose to watch the proceedings like two outsiders. Sudhakar delivered an impassioned tirade favouring frankness with friends, but he weakened his points by repeatedly referring to his leaving his friends, particularly Anjan da, and the place in the near future. We could see the vanity and superciliousness in his references; he was talking like one who was only staying with us for the time-being, but did not belong to this fixed-income fraternity of sluggards. His yet unaquired wealth had already contaminated his thinking process. When he said he might not meet any of us in the future, he was not exactly worried or sad for such a possibility. Had any of us remembered the prophetic words of the soothsayer at the Railway Station, we could have thrown cold water on his speculations.

Javed articulated some of our sentiments. "If you have begun talking like a strange tycoon to us before applying for a bank loan to set up an industry," he told him indignantly, "I bet you won't recognize any of us when you actually become a tycoon." But a highly conceited Sudhakar refuted the allegation by maintaining that he was neither talking like a stranger, nor having great dreams. "Entrepreneurship, you know," he lectured, "is a risky thing. You rise like a rocket or fall like a shooting star. But look at the type of life we are leading. No chance to rise; nor fear to fall. Potted plants! Bonsai sort of thing. If we try to grow a little above the wonted proportion, the big scissors of the Tax Department cut us to size. Adventure suits me, so I go. Don't think I'm proud. You're mistaken. If perchance we meet in the future, I promise I shall be happier than you."

"But why you are determined to speak out everything to Anjan da?" barked Javed, exasperated by Sudhakar's pious platitudes. "It is as good as saying, I shall break up the family of my beloved friend Anjan da before I leave this place for ever."

Sudhakar's face fell. He looked at Javed flabbergasted. "You mean he'd take it so seriously?" He muttered anxiously. "You're a fool not to think that way," retorted Javed brusquely.

Not Sudhakar alone, but all of us were fools to think that way. Javed, we found, could be eloquent when he was inspired or agitated.

"There are many other things to bother about," he addressed us, looking like an unhappy child. "If we think we have committed some crime by touching a girl, we make a mountain of a mole-hill. I believe we'll do it again if a prettier wench of easy virtue were around to serve us tea and potato chips. By another stroke of bad luck, if that victim of our collective or individual lust turned out to be a cousin of one of us, we're again undone."

32

REVELATION

His talk came to a screeching halt when the familiar voice of Anjan da was heard not far from where we sat. "Hey Narasingh!" his voice rang out. "Where're your masters? I don't see any of them."

Narasingh promptly led him to the last room in the row, where we were sitting. We looked awkwardly at one another. Anjan da was in a jolly, ebullient mood. "We wanted to surprise you," he said, "and here we are. What's the matter, Nityanadaji?

When I find you five together, I suspect something must be cooking. What's it? See who is there?" We looked out and noticed Uri there. I stood up, walked out and greeted the burning topic of our conversation. She was clad in a shining white saree with embroidered borders. She looked slim and a bit fairer in her new incarnation as a Hindu orthodox house-wife, complete with a red bindi, vermilion on the parting-line of her hair and gold ornaments. She returned our greetings with a shy smile of old familiarity. Our eyes were watching and our minds were busy comparing her old self with her new one. An awkward silence continued : none of us dared break it. Finally Uri simpered and her lavishly red lips trembled to let out words. "You people sit and talk here," she addressed the gathering : "I'll prepare tea with Narasingh."

"You should," sounded Anjan da in a way of suggesting, marking our discomfort in her presence, and added : "You're the odd one out, aren't you?" Looking furtively around, she slithered into the kitchen and we could hear her chitchatting with Man Lion.

Man Lion brought us tea and informed that she had just gone out to meet her parents. "She won't stay there long, she told me that," he announced.

"A good riddance, I should say," observed Anjan da trying to humour us. We were pale in spite of ourselves. "Now that she is gone, we've some time to relax and talk something."

Sudhakar pulled the wooden stool he was sitting on close to Anjan da's chair and sat astride it facing him.

"Those filmiwallahs must have approached you with an offer had they seen you," observed Anjan da referring to the latter's tall frame and good looks.

Sudhakar was too preoccupied with his thoughts to be flattered by these compliments and react to them.

"You know, Anjan da," he said seriously, "I am leaving you very shortly. The sheer monotony of my life here has exasperated me. I want to make a break-through, somehow. It seems I've an itch for adventure."

"Yes, yes, you'd told me that sometime back," Anjan da said. "Are you serious really?"

"Why, I've already tendered my resignation," Sudhakar informed him. "I must have gone to you had not you come here today."

Anjan da suddenly grew thoughtful.

"Why this craze for the jet-set, Sudhakar? You've already given up your job? What's your problem?"

Sudhakar's problem, we all knew, was ambition aggravated by envy. He called it adventure.

"Believe me, Anjan da," he began half shyly and half proudly, "there is a spirit of adventure in me which would not let me be. I want to prove that I am not cut out for the ordinary, stagnant life I am leading at present. When I see a magnificent building with an arched portico flaunting a luxury car, surrounded with a lovely garden, when a Contessa, a Mercedes or even a Maruti Esteem glides past me tears well up in my eyes, my blood boils, heart beats faster and a hot sharp knife cuts into my flesh. A bitter feeling of deprivation makes me restless. My humble bicycle mocks at me. I have a lot of energy, resourcefulness and drive in me, which can fetch me all the state-of-the-art items that arouse my desire. I know my petty job can give me enough to survive, but not enough to get any one of my desired things. For me, frankly, life becomes worth living when I can become the source of other's envy, not an envious wretch myself."

"Cool down, young man, cool down!", blurted out Nityanand impatiently; "Learn to be simple."

"Ha!", mocked Sudhakar, "modesty was never my virtue. Simplicity was never my virtue. But believe me, Nityanandaji, I'll be modest and simple when I became rich, when I own a couple of palatial buildings and a fleet of limousines."

The oxymoronic slant in Sudhakar's statement aroused a brief spurt of giggles, but we knew he was in earnest. Though he had every reason to be proud of his handsome appearance and good height, we had never heard him alluding to his assets in his conversation, not even once. On one occasion, when he was praised effusively for his good looks and tallness, he said had he been endowed materially he would have managed comfortably with a slighter frame and less beauty. "Bill Gates, you know," he'd said, "is a plain looking man, and a junior assistant in my office looks like Sanjay Khan."

Anjan da was listening to what Sudhakar said like a psychotherapist to his patient's frank talk. "That's why I had taken this drastic step," resumed Sudhakar, and added : "tell me, Anjan da, have I not taken the right step?"

Anjan da straigtened his back up, crossed his legs and said : "Look, Sudhakar, you've already taken the step. I don't like to discourage you. But if you permit me to be straight with you, your reasons for taking that brave step sound like the symptoms of a sickness. You'll rarely meet a man who declares openly that he is suffering from venereal diseases, and there are many people around who proudly tell to the strangers about their angina pectoris and coronary thrombosis. Do you know why those sick men do that? Because certain diseases have the snob-appeal and modernity brands. People are proud of having great connections. It does not matter if they are friends or enemies. Now you're proud of having a lot of ambition and envy. But in your haste you've forgotten that envy is a cardinal sin."

"But, Anjan da," protested Sudhakar, "it is good emotion if it makes people pro-active and more adventurous. It's an incentive in a sense. It's the functional ethics of the modern consumerist society. Envy is as essential for progress, for modern society as electricity and diesel. Stop its supply, and the world will come to a grinding halt."

"Whatever you say, Sudhakar," snapped Anjan da annoyed by his adulation of envy, "sounds like a confession without repentance. Envy, I tell you, is an irrational condition of the mind; it's a masochistic suffering a person inflicts upon himself by taking a decision to be unhappy when he finds other people happier or more fortunate than him. Like a moth, he flies to a fire to get himself singed. The fire does not come to him. That's why an envious man is unfortunate, an object of pity. Keep doing what you want to do; build your empire from scratch; be affluent and brash, but please do not use envy as your driving force. When it's too late, you'll realise you have been doing everything for the wrong reason. Because, Sudhakar, envy, as a strategy, masquerades as a friend. It's a wily enemy. Its aim is to make you unhappy when you have all the reasons to be happy. In your case, poor young man, you'll be an envious wretch even after possessing half a dozen palatial buildings and a dozen luxury cars because there will always be people richer, happier and more fortunate than you."

Anjan da's sermon against envy didn't put Sudhakar off. "I've trust in me," he said gravely; "I'll never be envious when I am rich. I know where to stop."

"Then I've nothing to say," spoke Anjan da in a neutral manner; "I can only wish you luck. The ant that walks on a globe may not be aware of its roundness, and, as a result, may have erroneous ideas about it's progress. I hope you got my point?"

We looked at Sudhakar. He smiled confidently and said : "I assure you, Anjan da, I'd thought deeply over it before taking this step. I've a bird's eye view, not a worm's eye view, of the globe." Anjan da smiled and admired Sudhakar's self confidence.

Andy was conspicuous by his absence. Anjan da sat silently for sometime lost in thought. I found a shade of melancholy on his face, and it struck me as unusual.

"Is something bothering you, Anjan da?", I ventured in a personal tone. "You look a bit worried, so suddenly!"

Anjan da looked up and peered questioningly into my face.

"I look worried, don't I?" he said with a sulking irony. "But I was not worried when I entered the gate of your lodge."

"Then what happened at the gate?", Sudhakar asked. We looked anxiously at him.

"You want to hear?", he erupted abruptly. "I heard some sentences of your debate, particularly Javed's words. What were you talking about so passionately? Why you fell into uncomfortable silence when my visit was announced by Narasingh? Why did you look so abashed when Uri and I entered the room? What's galling you? That's why I am worried. By the way, I don't find Andy. Where's he?" Nityanand found the last question most answerable. "Andy has gone out to buy his cigarettes," said he, and added deliberately : "He had a quarrel with Narasingh yesterday, and vowed that he won't ask him to run his errand any more. He'll be back soon."

"That's not important," said Anjan da. "I only want to know what flummoxed you, why were you so much embarrassed when you met my wife? I know you won't tell me that. So I am broaching the topic."

Anjan da took a pause, allowing us to take the lead. But each of us was too puzzled to speak.

Then Anjan da muttered : "I might have been greatly surprised had she not told me everything."

We started as if a swarm of hornets stung us. Our hearts imploded. A sharp current of pain coursed through our spines. We felt helplessly cornered. Our heads swam. Our faces contorted with horror trying to hide our guilt, trying to brazen it out.

"What do you mean, Anjan da?" blurted out Nityanand. His was the desperate courage of a guardsman who was caught napping.

"I want to speak what precisely worried you when you saw her. For your information, chaps, she had told everything to me before we got married. When you people expressed your disapproval of our marriage, I discussed that with her, and she frankly told me everything, taking all the blame on herself. I believe that piece of frankness brought us closer. She said she had flirted with you all. And you know why she did that, don't you?"

Our faces fell. It was our hour of reckoning. Sweat drenched us and shame inundated us. I felt I had never experienced that type of mortification before.

"We've behaved abominably," muttered Javed, looking wretched like a polite guest who was caught red-handed while stealing a spoon.

"Yes, Anjan da, we've behaved most abominably," I put in slowly.

"Don't worry too much. You have not behaved admirably. That's true. The point is we are often helpless before our desires — desires for money, power, sex and revenge. Watch a drunken man lurching across a half-lit corridor, a cat licking the glass-case which contains fried fish or the crowd scrambling in a Stock Exchange — and you feel pity for them. But when we find ourselves in such desperate conditions, we refuse to look at ourselves, and still maintain a flattering attitude towards ourselves, don't we?"

"You're right, Anjan da," I said. "We never thought you know all that. Many times we have tried to tell you everything, many many times. But we could never do it. We're ashamed of what has happened."

Anjan da said : "You have reasons to feel guilty and ashamed. I was initially horrified when I heard it from Uri. It was too heavy a revelation, you know. But somehow I overcame it. I felt pity for you."

"Why?" I muttered looking at him guiltily.

"What else should I feel for you?", asked Anjan da in a casual, light tone of voice. "You see, Debasis, life had put you to a simple test; you failed in it. Temptations galore! They test our ability to defeat them, to overcome them. People glitter with virtues of all kinds : poor men glitter with simplicity, politicians glitter with concerns for the downtrodden and homilies, academics glitter with learning, writers glitter with ideas and creativity, holy men glitter with transcendence, and the righteously indignant public speakers like me glitter with erudition, non-comformity and eloquence. The world is a gigantic glass jar containing a billion fireflies, each trying to out-glow the other. But all these glitzy glitterati, these self-important people move around with un-tested virtues. Give money to the poor, power to the politician, authority to our academics, applause and éclat to our authors, pleasures of terrestrial kind to our holy men and put their respective virtues to test. Don't you think most of those glitter-bugs would come a cropper? By making the humblest pauper affluent you make him vain and arrogant; by giving power to the most obsequious and self-effacing clown you turn him into a Nero, a diabolical dictator; by putting a vulnerable young woman in the midst of some sophisticated and sexually abstemious young men you make them tipsy with desire. Mind you, I am not referring to this event alone, not to any particular event. It is a universal malady. Look at this country : geographically a mammoth, population-wise a zurassic dinosaur, politically the largest democracy of the world, and performance-wise a subaltern, a lame duck, sports-wise a circle of shame, a zero. That's because we are playthings in the hands of temptations. They overpower us so easily. That's a pity!"

Nityanand caught hold of Anjan da's hand and pressed it to his face.

I am very ashamed, Anjan da, he blubbered sentimentally. "I promise by holding your hand I'll try to fight with the temptations, I am their weakest victim. I've wronged her in the worst possible way. Please, please forgive me, Anjan da."

He started sobbing.

"Lets call it quits, and talk of something else. My wife may appear at any time. I hope you behave with her in a better, more friendly manner this time. She's after all your brother's wife. She's forgiven you. Now it's your turn to forgive her, OK?"

Andy the voyeur had followed the couple when they entered the Lodge. He was taking tea in a roadside tea-stall when he saw Anjan da and Uri on a rickshaw, and decided to follow them. On entering the gate, he paused for a while under a window opening to the road to hear what would be the nature of the absurd encounter. He heard the entire conversation standing there. He wanted to hear more.

Uri returned half an hour later. She marked a change in the atmosphere for the better as soon as she looked around. "Was the tea good?," she enquired casually, and settled herself on Javed's bed near the window. She was addicted to tobacco before marriage, but soon switched over to betel chewing. The well-made betel which looks like the horn of plenty contains aromatic spices to freshen the mouth, processed tobacco to add piquancy and some amount of catechu and lime to dye the lips red. Catechu, a type of gum rich in tennin, interacts with lime and produces a frighteningly blood-red brew which the chewer has to spout out of his or her mouth once in a while just as the whales do while foraging for food. Finding no other place to spit out half a glass of scarlet spittle which she had accumulated in her mouth, she poured it leaning over the window sill. It was a singular mishap, because Andy had posted himself just beneath that window. His head, face, shirt were dabbled and dappled by the shower. The pungent smell of chewed betel nauseated him. For a few minutes he was at his wit's end. It was not possible for him to continue standing in an unusual place in that unusual condition, nor was it possible to enter the Lodge. He chose the lesser evil and tried surreptiously to get into his room which had an attached bath, without being seen by the others.

Argus-eyed Man Lion saw him first and exclaimed loudly. He thought Andy had met an accident, and ran full speed to the corner room to announce the big event. In no time Andy found himself surrounded by a crowd of eight. Instead of hurrying, he ambled in a lurching manner, because the stink and nicotine had already affected him. I led him carefully into the room. Anjan da smelt the tacky coat of paint and declared it was not blood at all. We were relieved. He didn't listen to our pressing queries — What's happened? And how? and snatched a towel and headed towards the bath-room.

Man Lion broke into an irresistible fit of giggling. He perhaps remembered yesterday's quarrel and meant "It rightly served him." Uri the uncanny quickly guessed the possible truth and revealed her surmise. Man Lion ran to the exact spot where Uri belched out her spittle, and shouted across the window that there was not a drop of coloured spit on the ground.

We all agreed that the punishment was in character with the crime, and there was nothing to worry about. Only Anjan da was unhappy, and was full of pity for poor Andy.

"Hey, Narasingh," Anjan da called out. "Why did you quarrel with him? You have become a bit spoilt, I suppose."

"No, sir," Man Lion replied haughtily. "It was not a quarrel. He scolded me for no fault of mine, and promised not to talk to me."

"Why? He must have some good reasons?"

"I can put it rightly," I volunteered. I sternly warned Man Lion not to simper, or giggle, or guffaw when I told the story.

"Day before yesterday," I began, "Andy had some trouble in the bathroom. His ring slipped from his finger and found its way into the hole of the latrine. He retrieved the ring, but his left hand up to the arm-pit was covered with excrement."

"He had forgotten to switch on the electric motor which deposited the water in the overhead tank. I was not around.

"It was always his habit to sing in the toilet. But the foul smell and helpless condition made him unmusical. He patiently waited for some one to switch on the motor. But the reverse happened. This rogue Man Lion was loitering around, and when he found the doors of the room and the bathroom open, little comprehending that somebody could be in the latrine, or inside the bathroom, he promptly closed the bathroom door and locked up the room, and entered the kitchen. Andy, encouraged by the noise, shouted my name, and receiving no response, he came out of the latrine and found the bathroom door closed from outside. He hollered and howled and cursed, but it produced no result. He thought it was I who did it knowingly.

Andy stayed in that condition a little more than two hours. He didn't thank me when I finally opened the door and delivered him from that infernal state, but glared at me with mad, violent look of a pathological killer, walked to the motor cabin in a hurry, switched on the motor and reentered the bathroom after filling the room with the foulest reek.

"Fearing vendetta, I had already brought Narasingh to the room and made him stand there. Andy emerged from the bathroom, looking clean and smelling like a toilet soap. Instead of muttering curses, he was reciting holy mantaras to purify himself. The nervous Man Lion narrated his version of the story, though unasked, in one breath. Andy cast a nasty look at the boy, and gestured at him to go away."

"What happened then?" Anjan da showed a keen interest.

Nothing much. The divine power of the mantras had already pacified him. He didn't blame anybody, but his fate and his karma. "I am not angry with you or with Narasingh," he assured me, when I tried to plead for my innocence. I must have been a sinner in my previous lives, Debasis, a bad sinner. The baker's daughter has ditched me several times. Can you imagine she didn't turn up even once. Four days, I waited for her in that stinking place. Not even once. The ghosts also have picked me up for their target. Now, you cannot know what it means to watch excrements hardening on your own body, and you have no clothes to cover up your outraged nostrils. Do you suppose, such suffering could be inflicted by human agents without the divine sanctions?

"I don't know if you were a sinner in your previous incarnations, but I bet you are a vile sinner in this life, for which God Almighty puts you to such types of misery." I took liberties with him, smiling in mock anger, when I found him in a favourable mood. "You don't know how you torment others, do you? You chase us relentlessly, pinching our sore spots, twisting our sprained arms, infuriating us with your I-am-cruel-only-to-be-kind malevolence and, at the same time, spending four hours daily to have a tryst with a girl. Again you often forget to clean the latrine after using it, and wish that your roommate should do that for you. Have you ever bothered about your scatological habits, though I have reminded you of them several times? Now you console yourself with eschatological arguments."

Andy listened to my accusations, looked out through the open window and said nothing.

"Yesterday it was proved that he didn't forgive Narasingh as he pretended to have done. He scolded him because he detected a hair in the curry and tea-dust in the tea. Then a bitter quarrel broke out when he was preparing to leave and Man Lion sneezed thrice. He accused him of deliberate sneezing, and it piqued Narasingh to such an extent that he declared defiantly it was so. 'So what?' this giggling rogue hit back. "I'd sneeze whenever I like. What's that to you? Am I not permitted to sneeze? Do whatever you like. I shall go on sneezing like that!" His tone offended Andy. He used some animal names for the insubordinate brute, and vowed that he'd never ask him to do his work as long as he lived on this earth."

Uri and Narasingh laughed full-throatedly until Anjan da told them to stop.

"Any of you can be in a situation like that," said Anjan da, and added : "Please verify if he is not in a similar situation now. If there is no water in the overhead tank, you can switch on the motor."

Javed went into the bathroom and informed Anjan da that there was water.

"What girl he was talking about? Who's she? Why is he tormenting you?" asked Uri, nonplussed by my reference. Anjan da, also looked at me questioningly.

I was taken aback. In my enthusiasm, I spoke out certain things which would show me, as well as my accomplices, in an unfavourable light. Man Lion giggled meaningfully looking at Uri and went away. Nityanand and Subramaniam eyed me anxiously. Javed and Sudhakar pretended that they were as surprised by my revelation as Uri, and looked at me innocently.

"Andy told us that he was in love with a beautiful girl, and she wrote him a letter asking him to meet her in some place; but she did not keep her promise. We know only that much. As much as he told us. You know he has many secrets." I informed her in a casual manner.

Anjan da was much moved by Andy's misfortune. "It's sad thing," he said thoughtfully and added : "But I've a doubt the girl might not have written such letters herself. Her friends might have played that dirty trick on him."

"May be! That's also possible," I said, and added after a pause; "Anjan da, I don't know how you rate him as a person, but the fellow deserves such gulling if what you guess be true."

"You think that?", asked Anjan da fixing his gaze in mine. I averted my look, lest his eyes should get a glimpse of my hidden guilt. "Why so?"

All the conspirators eyed me with concern and disdain.

"Because the fellow preaches hate and falls in love." I adlibbed desperately.

33

CONVALESCENCE

For some strange reasons, Javed showed some positive improvements after Anian da's announcement regarding our affairs with Uri. Javed resumed his long-postponed, amicable conversation with us. He told us that he had succeeded, twice or thrice, in overpowering the demon of fear, and restraining himself from running out.

It was unanimously concluded that a heavy weight had been lifted from Javed's subconscious mind as soon as the guilt was disclosed and forgiven by the wronged party, so that his mind was liberated and strengthened to face the challenges of life. This view was also endorsed by Anjan da.

Two days before Sudhakar's departure, Anjan da invited all the inmates of the Wave Crest Lodge to dine with him at his residence. Sudhakar, who had become a bit spoilt and emboldened by prospective opulence, suggested to Anjan da when the latter invited him to the farewell party that the evening should not be a dry one; that even beer would do. Anjan da didn't like to disappoint him, and bought some bottles of beer. A glass of beer was placed before each of us. At first Javed beseeched us to spare him as he didn't like to taste that sort of thing in the presence of Anjan da. But when Anjan da assured him that he didn't mind it, provided he retained his reason and never became an addict, he drank one glass of the golden liquid and thought he was dead drunk. To our consternation, he started crying bitterly and loudly, lamenting : "How can I show my face to my mother after this? I have desecrated myself. I've lost everything; I have no right to continue living shamelessly. I'm a goner. O, Allah Almighty, O Allah the Merciful, please forgive me before I die. Tell Nagma to forgive and forget me. She is free to marry Amzad. I am dying before receiving the responses to my letters. I'll never know. I know I'm dying now — a great sinner."

Uri wept. Anjan da ran out to collect some ice. We flocked around him. Subramaniam buried his face on the table. He was perhaps weeping too. It was a trying moment for all of us, listening to the piteous cries of a perfectly healthy man predicting his imminent death repeatedly. He didn't stop talking for a moment and banged his head on the table. "What a fragile constitution!" I muttered aloud, stroking his head. "Listen Javed, it's nothing. You'll feel all right in half-an-hour, I tell you." He did not listen; he only babbled, frothing in the mouth, glaring around like mad.

Ice sobered him to some extent, but he was still tipsy. "You'll remember me," he blabbed, "when letters will come in my address and the police will come to arrest me. I've struck the hornets' nest. If you're my friends, tell every one that I died because of a cardiac arrest, not because of drinking. My parents would be ashamed of my death; their poor hearts will break. Please tell a lie for my sake. Tell them I died of snake-bite."

"You're grammatically correct, you fool," said Anjan da in a tone of controlled exasperation, "but you grossly exaggerate. You are not dying. You drank only a glass of beer. Not poison."

Javed, heedless to whatever was said, was beginning another scare story on his last wishes, when Uri, original as ever, poured a jug of cold water on his head, standing behind him.

"Where am I?" he drawled, winking his much abridged eyes.

"You're safe in my house, Javed, quite safe. Now tell me what letters you wrote and what type of fears trouble you?"

Javed confessed without much persuasion that he had sent ten letters off to ten important persons who could do something to free Salman Rushdie from his terrible confinement, to remove the sword of Democles hanging over his head. He had thrown out these feelers, he said, to six heads of the state and four leading dailies.

"The history of mankind, I wrote," said Javed "these three thousand years, is replete with totalitarian repressions of the word. The ruling class we have today is not different from, and better than, those who murdered Socrates and Jesus of Nazareth, banished Voltaire, Solzhenytsyn, burnt great libraries and galleries of artworks, cut off the hands of those who wrote, chopped off the tongues of those who spoke the truth. Rulers always feel unsafe when freedom-loving people are around. They always want that the jungle should contain only the rabbits, cows, deer and lambs, so that they would wolfishly prey on them for ever. They misrepresented the Prophet and misinterpreted his words, that too knowingly in a way that suits them down to the ground." He paused and asked for water. I offered him an empty glass and asked him to take the water from the jug. "I tell you all this" he said finally, "because I know I am going to die very shortly. Please tell the world, please tell my parents that I died in sleep. You're my only friends. I see my end is nearing...." "Shut up," shouted Anjan da indignantly; "You'll outlive most of us. Be sure of that. Now I'll tell you what a bad writer of letters you are. You have little originality in all that stuff, and I tell you it won't affect any one. There were many before you, who had scavenged the trash-lands of history to collect some faded gauzy ribbons in order to deck out facades of their ideas. Why didn't you go straight to the matter?"

I, however, did not understand the cause of Anjan da's annoyance. I looked at him vacantly. I clearly noticed a link between Socrates drinking hemlock and the modern author being sentenced to death for telling a story. Anjan da, I presumed, might have been annoyed by Javed's attempt to equate the modern victim of a medieval obscurantism with such people as Socrates and Jesus, or by citing such famous examples Javed was unwittingly glorifying what he wanted to denigrate.

Javed didn't proceed with his details as he was feeling weak and guilty as soon as he got back his composure. We also didn't force him to. We could well guess what was the content of his letters. I expressed concern regarding the reprisals of such letters which, I believed, would disturb the mega-minds.

But Anjan da smiled sceptically. "Do you suppose, Debasis" he said, "that they'd be so sensitive and impressionable and yet occupy such high positions? I'm sure these letters will never reach the dignitaries. Their secretaries will find them too trite and put them in the waste paper baskets."

34

ANJAN DA'S SECOND VISIT : A BAD JOKE

Initially, I had told Puja that there was, once upon a time, a girl called Uri who had crossed my path, or I crossed hers. I was under the impression that any frank confession of a pre-marital affair by one partner would endear him to the party only and give him an immunity against further suspicion. So, while describing my purely flirtatious affair with Uri, I presented both my own self, as well as the girl in question, in most unfavourable light. By being uncharitable to my own self and by ruling out any mental liaison whatsoever, I didn't apprehend any unpleasantness or back-wash from my legit wife. But I was cheated by my own fancy. She pretended to be unruffled but I could feel the brewing of a storm. Determined to pep up my conversation and cheer her up, I harped on the stolidness of the girl and the vulnerability of other inmates of the lodge. She listened to what I said as she would listen to a bizarre tale of prurience, but when it came to my personal involvement in it, she considered herself a permanent loser for being deprived of the first physical contacts of her husband. "It's true that girl was clever and cheap; it's true most men are like that; it's also true that the whole thing happened before we saw each other, but it's so difficult to digest the hard fact that you allowed yourself, I mean you degraded yourself to such a level. It hurts me. It still stinks." I repented for having told it; then I took a mental decision not to broach Uri-related topics to her, for that I feared, would further complicate matters. I thought time would heal her feelings of being robbed of my first contact. She was also trying in her own way to cope with her mental tension by arguing with her own disconsolate self that the alleged thief of her property was no where around to bother her again.

"I know", she told me, "a woman who has offered herself to a man once, would offer it always if she bumps into her ex-lover, provided the circumstances are favourable and safe."

I was impressed with her analysis of feminine psyche, but didn't subscribe to it.

"Not always true, Puja," I protested; "you know things change, desires wane, we're not always the same."

Puja said she knew better because she was a woman.

"But I am not apprehensive about its recurrence, in your case at least" she declared in a cruel, ironical tone. "Do you know why? Because the hussy would most probably be in a whore-house busy fleecing her customers. If not there, she may be living in a sea-side jhuggi in the fishers' village, a happy mother of six naked dirty children, drying the fish her husband caught. She must be stinking like a creel. You won't be interested in such stuff, would you?"

That wishful imaginings gave her immense satisfaction. She would be pleased to locate Uri in worst imaginable circumstances.

The matter might have closed there had I not disclosed further details regarding Uri. One afternoon, when Puja and I were taking a long walk together, I narrated the whole story inspired by the cordiality of the moment.

"Uri didn't go to a whore-house, didn't marry a fisher man," I revealed to her; "She married Anjan da. Can you believe it?"

Puja flew into a rage.

"You're lying, it cannot be true," she snapped at me.

"I am not lying," I said quietly.

"Then, why didn't you inquire about her from Anjan da? We talked on so many things, but you never asked a single question about his wife and family. You're cooking it up. You're still hooked on that woman."

"I had my own inhibitions," I said defensively. "I didn't feel like uttering her name, nor did I want to refer to his wife as bhavi. In fitness of things, I should have called her bhavi respectfully. But I was afraid any reference to her might have reminded Anjan da of something unpleasant, and even trashy."

"You mean to say Anjan da knew of it?" she asked incredulously.

"Of course!", I replied.

Puja was surprised, offended and silenced by my terse revelation. For several months following this revelation, she didn't mention the topic even once, and I thought the matter was closed.

One evening when I was reading Kafka's story "The metamorphosis" (which I had read several times before), Puja entered my study with an impish smile and sat herself on a flat wooden stool and kept gazing at my face. She used to behave like that when she had something portentous or unpredictable to reveal. As it had become her habit to return home loaded with "most unpredictable" news items every alternate day, I had cultivated the habit of showing little or no interest in them, and no surprise after hearing them, however surprising they might be.

"Anjan da and his wife are dining with us tomorrow," she announced, peering into my face to read my reactions. "Really?" I exclaimed. "Your sorority, I must admit, does two good things to me."

"What're they, please?"

"It recreates you to your fill, so that you feel no need to recreate yourself here at home by squabbling over the cabbages and the kings. Again, it has done me a favour, though inadvertently by inviting my most valued friend and bringing him to my dinner table not once, but twice."

Puja wore her mischievous smile all through, unaffected as it were, by my observations, and watched my face with absurd curiosity. "I thought, this time our sorority had done you an extra favour by bringing your Uri to the dining table which, I am afraid, is adjacent to your bed room. You should be grateful to us, to me in particular, for such a chance encounter. She's after all your first woman."

I looked belligerantly at her and asked her to stop talking that sort of thing. I told her curtly that even Anjan da knew it before marriage and it was a closed chapter now. "God bless those gullible males, I thought aloud, who, inspired by love and trust, melt like an ice-slab on the palm of women, and speak out their erotic picadillos with a view to perpetuating love through frankness. They are all fools. I, however, realize it too late." I sighed.

Puja looked or pretended to look contrite for hurting my sentiment. I resumed my tirade : "I have a friend who shunned the company of females as if they all had AIDS, until he got married to a woman three years older than he was. Her confessions were more pious than a scripture, though she was almost thirty. But my poor friend, encouraged by her purity, tried to purify himself by confessing his many onanistic orgies conjuring up some film actresses and real-life flirts. He told me that not a week passed without his virtuous wife pinching, scratching and injuring him with those confessions only to make him feel wretched by reminding him of his perversions."

Puja got riled. "You must not draw conclusions like that," she rasped "without listening to your Onan's wife. I've also heard the sad tales of women who have confessed their premarital love affairs. How broad-minded do you think you are? If I cook up a story and tell you one gentleman you know had an affair with me when my breasts were like powder puffs, and he is coming to spend a few days with us, do tell me how you'll receive him?"

"Such a topic was better left undiscussed and unelaborated, for that'd put us in our tantrums. She is capable of cooking of stories with such salacious details, which'd verge on pornography and make even Anais Nin blush," I thought angrily, and acknowledged defeat.

Puja put an invitation card on the book which I was holding. I was in the middle of "The Metamorphosis," a story which had been preoccupying me for quite some time. She had noticed my preoccupation with that story when I shared my fears with her about my possible transformation. Then her light-hearted comments had offended me, and I'd decided not to bother her about my secret fears any more.

Now when she saw me reading that story, she looked at me wonderingly.

"How many pages do you read in one hour?" she interrogated me.

"Twenty to thirty five, depending on my mood and concentration, and the contents of the book," I replied.

"How many times have you read that single story?"

"What's that to you?" I retorted impatiently. "Say, many times!"

"It must be a case of manic obsession," said she. "Out of curiosity, I read it soon after you introduced it to me. But the whole story made me feel greatly relaxed, because I laughed a lot while reading it. Charlie Chaplin stuff!"

"I don't know!" I murmured sulkily. "By the way, what're the funny things regarding that story?"

"The finest comic touches are not in the story itself, but in the high serious tone the narrative maintains throughout, I mean the way it is told. You know, Debasis, the best clowns make you laugh through their seriousness, they make the people feel that they are not there to entertain others. This story of a man's mutation into an insect, a very loathsome one indeed, though all insects are more or less loathsome, is a piece of clowning which tries to circumvent reality. It's like going down a hill or a big sloping terrace on a bicycle and furiously pedalling in the reverse gear — ridiculous in spite of itself." She laughed infectiously.

"Frankly, Madam," I bantered, "I find no such risible stuff in that story. It covers my moon like a black mass of cloud. It makes me sick in a particular way."

"So, you want to fall sick repeatedly?" She said. "I honestly do not understand why a person must read a story again and again, that makes him so indisposed and steals his sunshine or moonshine."

"I don't have any answer to that," I defended myself, "excepting, perhaps, it has an attraction for me; and that, I know, is no reason. Well, I know, what, happened to Gregor does not happen to other people generally, but the changes of shape and state do occur piecemeal in various guises. These changes which took place or are taking place around me, remind me of that single change, and *vice versa*, and each re-reading of that story is an act of re-arranging what has been ruffled by the unexpectedness of reality."

"Honestly, dear, I do not understand your problem, your moonshine, nor do I care to," she told me bluntly.

"But I do understand yours," I shot back as she was going out of the room.

The invitation card which she had placed on that much-used book was another instance of absurdity. It informed me that Uri Das Gupta would preside over a meeting in the town hall. They had decided to invite the husbands of the members of the sorority with a view to acquainting them with the changes that had taken place concerning attitude towards women.

It beat me how a woman who took great pride in her ability to sign her own name a few years ago, could consent to address a big gathering. "If Uri the tart of the Wave Crest Lodge," I drew the conclusion, "has come all the way to assume the role of a public speaker, it has to be in the fitness of things, because her husband whose sanity and good judgment I have every reason to reckon on must have consented to such an arrangement."

I decided not to break my head on an issue which didn't concern me, even remotely. I hardly realized or imagined at that moment that Puja could play such a trick on me so successfully.

The meeting was well attended. Husbands dressed in bespoke suits and wives in gorgeous sarees and I-am-all-for-you-too smiles, were flaunting their charms and busy alluring alien hearts. The first speaker, an ex-minister, spoke in a high-pitched emotional tone on corruption in high places. It was a long lament. He mentioned almost all the scandals which had rocked the country after independence, named all persons involved in them and ended with a protracted sigh of despair.

Anjan da, who followed suit, talked on the same theme, but his tone and tenor were markedly different.

"If all people who condemn corruption," he began quietly, "try to abstain themselves from corruption, there'll be no corruption in this country. But the trouble is people who cry wolf are themselves the wolves in sheep's clothing. Again, if we believe we can curb or banish corruption by flogging this poor abstract noun in public, by introducing harsh and Draconian penal laws, by erecting police outposts in every village, in every lane of the town, we are underestimating the power of the concept of corruption against which man kind has been fighting a losing battle since time immemorial. It is a folly of the short-sighted to associate corruption with modernity or the twentieth century or the twenty first century. Our scriptures and innocent people always claim and make us believe that at the end of this internecine and protracted battle the force of honesty will come out victorious. But alas, this million-faced monster has always had the last laugh. When two men are fighting, we should reasonably believe that one will kill or defeat the other, but when two souls supposed to be immortal are fighting what would be the outcome. They can get tired only."

The crowd applauded for five minutes.

"My point is," he resumed with a cool, confident tone, "let's not try to kill or exterminate corruption. All we can do is to weaken our enemy by strengthening ourselves. So the responsibility is ours. Well, it sounds simple. What should we do to strengthen ourselves? It's true most of us are good, honest and strong to a certain extent. But you know a chain is as strong as its weakest link; an embankment is as reliable as its most vulnerable point which may spring a leak. So all our goodness, honesty and strength will be of no avail if we have a weak point."

Wild desk-thumping and clapping continued for full five minutes after he concluded his speech. As I listened to him I marked an unusual persuasive force in his style of presentation. He decked out depth with commonsense and spiced and spruced up commonsense with fresh analysis. Unassuming, yet unexpected; cool, yet pointedly, unsparingly critical, he, like a laser beam, attacked the malignant core without hurting the healthy tissues surrounding it.

The president of the ladies, club, who presided over the meeting gave a vote of thanks. The meeting was over. The crowd dispersed. But I couldn't see Uri in the meeting. Though her name was printed in the invitation card, no one refered to her even once, I asked a women whom I knew as an active member of the club about the absent speaker. She was in a hurry. She slowed down when she recognized me, and enquired "What speaker? You mean some other speaker? I don't think we invited anybody else." She smiled and vanished into the crowd.

Then I began to suspect that Puja had gone to the extent of printing that single invitation card to give me some hours of uneasy speculation and embarrassment. She assiduously avoided me during the function, perhaps fearing a public scene. As soon as the function was over we escorted Anjan da to our place.

"Why didn't you bring your wife with you, Anjan da?" Puja enquired, pretending to be very anxious.

Anjan da looked at the asker with a bemused expression, said nothing. Then I produced the "special" invitation card, which I was certain, must have baffled the printers. Anjan da read the invitation card.

"It is a bitter joke, a most inappropriate joke!", he exclaimed, looking down, frowning, He was trying to recover his calm. He was visibly struggling with an overpowering emotion. A number of deep lines formed on his forehead and cheeks, and gave him an ageing appearance. Some lines, emerging at the base of his nose and straggling over his cheeks, were not noticeable when he talked and smiled, but now, as he sat brooding, sullenly they showed themselves clearly. We finished our dinner in sepulchral silence, because we noticed an unusual grief writ large on the face of our quest, and we waited for him to speak which of course he never did.

"What's the problem, Anjan da?" I finally ventured to ask, as we came to the drawing room. "Didn't the organizers inform you of that previously? I thought you are coming with your wife."

"She's no more there, Debasis! Dead more than three years!" Anjan da whispered, fixing his look on the empty wall.

"My God! I did not know that. How?"

"At child-birth!"

"You didn't tell us that last time you were here, why? Are we nothing to you, nothing?" My tone was pathetic, angry and accusatory. Puja's wretchedness was complete. She didn't know that I had already ascertained her trick, and asked Anjan da regarding Uri only to pay Puja back with her own coins. She, as a result, was tormented by her secrecy, but dared not speak it out.

"We met briefly last time, and our conversation ended rather abruptly. Maybe I didn't like to spoil the mood by breaking that news. Maybe, I didn't remember it as there was no such occasion. Now I am not so much grief-stricken for her death. It pains me to see that card. Well, dear, (he looked at Puja) how come your organizers invited a person without consulting her or her husband? I always had the feeling that I establish a relationship with people I talk to, that those who invite me have some respect for me. How grievously I am mistaken!" Anjan da was in no mood to hear any explanation from my wife who was one of those organizers.

"The weirdest of all," resumed Anjan da, "the organizers neither sent that invitation card to us, nor had they the minimum courtesy to enquire about her when they welcomed me at the bus stand. Debasis, I think I should have some time for myself, for my unhappy boy who never saw his mother, and stop being a funny peripatetic preacher of ideas. I've had enough of it, enough. Haven't I been trying to persuade the public, the politicians and the educationists about introducing philosophy and Creative Thinking in the school syllabi? What have I achieved? Precious nothing. The speakers, it seems, are invited to the meetings as a ritual. What they say, is not important." He heaved a sigh.

Puja showed a piece of courage for which I admired her and forgave her and exonerated her of her mischief. She faced Anjan da directly, caught, hold of his hand and confessed her sins with tear streaming down her delicate cheeks. "I did not want to hurt you, Anjan da," she said stifling a sob. "I was driven by jealousy. I had forgotten that the woman whom you could choose to be your wife can never be just another woman. I made you so unhappy. I never thought my prank would end like this."

It was too embarrassing a situation! Anian da, I saw, was looking aghast. He was a poor judge of women, so that little act of feminine cunning horrified him. He could not understand the real motive of that contrite trickster to humiliate her husband.

"If jealousy could make you so inventive," he observed thoughtfully, "I dare say, it is quite dangerous."

"I think Puja has to apologize to me, too," I said looking at Anjan da, "for befooling me, and insulting me."

She looked at me submissively, pleadingly.

Anjan da spoke on the harmfulness of jealousy and usefulness of mutual trust, and Puja listened attentively to every word of his talk as a mode of atonement.

"It's like administering anti-venom injections to cobras," I observed sarcastically. "You perhaps do not know, Anjan da, jealousy to a wife is poison to a snake : a part of their constitution, a source of their strength."

"A sinister comparison," scolded Anjan da, and added : "Your manhood should advise you that it's unbecoming and cowardly on your part to punish your wife when she is repentant and sad."

Normalcy returned when Anjan da suggested that he must have at least two pegs of whisky or two glasses of beer before sleeping. Puja was ecstatic. "I won't take a drop, not a drop," she announced with subdued gaiety, "but won't keep Anjan da's glass empty."

"Then I'd take three pegs," Anjan da said gravely.

We had neither whisky, nor beer, but a quart of red wine which was gifted to me by a friend a fortnight ago. Puja brought a platter full of fried cashew nuts, and we took our first sips of the nourishing, ruby-red elixir.

Anjan da narrated the harrowing details of Uri's death. Puja and I were listening with rapt attention.

"The world always binds me with a single rope," Anjan da began, chewing the cashewnuts. "Mother died soon after Uri came and the child survived its mother."

"The doctors couldn't save her?" Puja asked.

"No, they didn't know she'd die because she had no complications. She slept and never woke up. When they examined her, she was dead for three hours or more. It was mysterious, troubling — too late to try." I introduced a new topic to wean him away from that unpleasant narration. I enquired about my friends at the Wave Crest Lodge after I left them.

"What about Sudhakar the dreamer? What about Andy, Javed, Nityanand and Subramaniam, and Man Lion? Do you meet them often? Are they still there?" I was eager like a dry sponge to soak up an ink-pool of narration.

A tender, cordial feeling, slightly aggravated by red wine, surged up. I was on a sentimental binge. I was prepared to weep if any mishap befell any of them. Although Andy behaved savagely with me and showed some signs of insipient neurosis, I was prepared to hug him to my heart and call him my best friend if God Almighty brought him to me. My effusions, prodigious in quantity, incarnadined by my recollections and scarlet liquid, threatened to drown me. I desperately desired to belong to that fraternity for ever to spend my days quarreling, larking about, fighting over petty issues plotting, frolicking, watching the sea and ordering for tea and always feeling as free as a blue jay. What glorious days, indeed! My mind was all surf, a hill of bubbles, lit up by the sun, each bubble fretted with a cute rainbow.

"Gone are the days of glorious carelessness, Anjan da," I gushed lamenting like an octogenarian remembering his swaddling bands, "Gone are those days of carefree laughter and flutters of heart. Salad days! Had I the wings of a crow I could have landed slap on the terraces of the Wave Crest Lodge : 0 what warmth, what mischievous schemings, what unalloyed intimacy await me there! Do they miss me, Anjan da?"

"Hush up, please, or you'll make me sick," said Anjan da impatiently.

"Why, what's the cause? Don't I have a right to remember a beautiful past?" I pleaded.

"You babble out nonsense," said Anjan da; "Do you think time looped and warped at that Lodge-site and forgot to affect your friends there? What sort of imagining is that?" His harsh reproof sobered me and filled me with ominous thoughts. I looked stupidly at him.

"Sudhakar, for your information," continued Anjan da calmly "is in his village. He was declared insolvent, and narrowly escaped imprisonment. All his property has been attached. I heard he was betrayed by his brother-in-law and his own people. He committed a blunder by chasing a dream."

"I must see him at once," I exclaimed. "I shall help him out, I'm sure I can do that."

"That you can do if you've enough to spare. Now, would you like to hear about your other mates?"

"Of course, yes," I replied.

"Six or seven months after your leaving the Lodge, the owner turned it into a hotel. Javed and Subramaniam share a room in that hotel. Man Lion is still there. He is married with one child, a daughter. Nityanand brought his family and took a rented house. Andy stayed a month with us after the eviction and made our life hell. But fortunately he was transferred to another college."

"Is he married and settled now? You told us last time he was proposing to many girls," I enquired.

"He is unmarried and unsettled, to put it briefly," Anjan da heaved a sigh, and cleaned his glasses with his handkerchief.

"I am afraid, I may sound unsympathetic while speaking of Andy. The fellow made me feel a villain in my own house. After his frequent unsuccessful overtures with women, he seems to have developed a crush on any woman who talks to him or smiles at him."

"Then he has become a regular philanderer, or sex-maniac?" I observed recollecting his pious rage at our erotic affairs with Uri and his crush on a girl called Krishnā.

"No, just the opposite of that," Anjan da corrected me. "He disdains the act of sex, and is afraid of touching or availing himself of a woman physically. Some people, you know, have sex in their bodies and when they befriend women their only intention is to seduce them physically. But Andy has sex in his heart only and he is no less desperate than those lustful satyrs in winning the love of as many women as possible. Whenever he talks with the fair sex, he talks in cautious whispers suffused with romantic smiles giving others the impression that he is talking love, but, as Uri told me, he usually tells banal, stale jokes and the news items and politics which hardly interest his listeners and such common-place conversations wouldn't surprise people should they be blared out through a loud-speaker. The way he looks at other people, particularly males, when they interrupt his romantic conversations, the sinister scowling look he hurls at them, resemble that of a jackal guarding a carcass when its booty is threatened by another jackal — the same mean growl, baring of teeth, aggressive look. It has aroused animosity in some, mirth in others. Frankly, he tried my patience on several occasions. I am almost certain he won't marry, and even if he married, no woman born of a woman would stand him more than a year."

I was interested to know about Javed whom I liked very much.

"Javed had the feeling," Anjan da narrated slowly, "that his ardent letters would cause a lot of controversy. Some of you feared that his life was in danger. But they didn't cause a ripple, a vibration. We meet sometimes, but intentionally, or unintentionally, he doesn't broach that topic. He has overcome his claustrophobia. But he has lost the zest for life. His girl friend got married to some one named Amzad. I heard he drinks too much, too often. But I set little store by what Narasingh says."

"That means," I added, "Javed and his type have always some reason, actual, concocted or exaggerated, to be unhappy. His girl friend must have realized that. It's in his chromosomes."

"Why do you say that? Are you angry with him, or something?" Anjan da enquired, puzzled by my observations.

"Yes, I do have reasons to be angry with him, with you, with everybody, with myself. You must forgive me for saying such things, but I can't help it." I knew I'd never spoken to Anjan da like that. My heart started beating faster, and was ready to pour down all its contents.

Anjan da looked more puzzled than ever. He could not imagine what was the cause of my discontent. "Why? Why is it so?" he asked.

My bitterness caused by my frequent disillusionments made me irritable and brave. Had not the magic liquid inspired me, I might have kept my feelings to myself as I had been doing all the time. Puja had already absented herself on the usual pretext of washing herself, whereas she had actually gone to sleep. It was past midnight. The world was comatose. The alarm clock on the table was tick-ticking in a stubborn rhythm like the horse of time cantering out there. I felt the pang of telling out a secret for the first time, and it threatened to be more excruciating because the man sharing my secret would not feel flattered by it.

Anjan da repeated his question and shook my shoulder. "Hey, young man, where's the rub? Come on!"

"I must tell it, Anjan da," I began; "If not for anything, at least to purge off my constipated thoughts. I am afraid, you may not be much pleased by my effluents." I paused.

"Be sure, Debasis, nothing sincere can displease me. Come on! See, I'm cocking up my ears." Anjan da prompted me, turning the clock-face to the wall so that I won't be discouraged by the lateness of night.

"I've been carrying myself, Anjan da," I went on, like a self-appointed detective to find out a steady man — steady in evil or steady in good — who is in amity with his own self, whose public and private faces can look into each other without batting an eyelid. I wonder if there is some problem with my eyes, that makes me see that way crooked things as straight and straight things as crooked-, or there is some problem with things and other people as they are. I have come to believe, Anjan da, that modern times breed only epigons in swarms- physically fit, mentally innovative, technically perfect, but spiritually skewed and flabby. Javed is the case in point. Why didn't he go mad? I wished with all my heart that he should recover his normalcy, his health but when he got it I felt cheated. Subramaniam accepted bribe after offering six months' of stiff resistance. To pay the hotel bills of his many bosses in the commercial tax departments. These bosses paid frequent visits with their families, stayed in the air-conditioned suites, ate royal cuisine, swirled imported whisky and went away without footing their bills. Subramaniam the idealist borrowed money from eveyone he knew to finance his two brothers in their colleges, to pay the mess dues- and compared his condition with an invalid challenging Mike Tyson for a boxing match. Six months later, I saw him one afternoon weeping like a raped woman in a dark room. His pillow was wet; his eyes were swollen. As soon as I touched him softly, he grabbed my hand, looked at me wildly, muttering : "Now I'm richer than any of you, all of you put together. No one will pay mess dues. I'll run the mess. Can you believe it?" Then he produced a wad of mint-fresh notes and a carton of Dunhill cigarettes. I hesitated, and was abashed and finally said : "Now I'm beginning to lose faith in everybody. In you, too."

Anjan da, I watched, looked crest-fallen. He, perhaps, realized that I would go on without his promotings and "com'on's", and waited for me to resume my tirade.

"When I met you, and knew you well, I thought I found the right person" I said in a tone of self-absorbed eloquence. "I thanked my serendipity. I still hold you in high esteem, and I know there would never be any occasion when I'd lose that esteem for you. That's because you have your heart in the right place and you cannot deviate much from the track marked out for you by you. But when you decided to marry either from desire, or for convenience, I'd a feeling that you made a fool of yourself, you bartered away your diamond for glass. You must forgive me for telling it. You won't admit it, for you did it knowingly. Javed could say it openly, but I couldn't. Do you remember that occasion when you visited us with Uri? I know you cannot forget that. We had already planned to confess our sins to you. We might have done it had you come alone. Everybody had his own reason. Do you know what my reason was? I'd a secret desire to put you to the hardest test. You stole a march on us, on me in particular. You came through the test with flying colours. Despite all that, Anjan da, I feel let down. I've a feeling you compromised with the quality of life by entering into wedlock."

Anjan da finished his glass with one drought and said : "Look, Debasis, I do not get your point, frankly, perhaps you mean to say that you found my marriage too galling. Well, that's a tall order. I am a man, not a concept. I married... I married to please my long-suffering old mother, and soon realised that I had a lot of pent-up desires. I also discovered that the dragon I took for dead and gone was only hibernating or lying in wait for the coign of vantage. You might have realized by now that every item the department store or the shopping complex of the world displays has a price-tag. One has to pay for each item of pleasure-with ready cash or with his soul, or with his heart's blood. But why should a man be called a fool for buying what he desires? How does an outsider know what I lost was diamond and what I got was glass?"

"Though an outsider," I countered, "I shall maintain that marriage, particularly when it turns out to be a happy one, makes both the partners importunate beggars; by generating and satisfying desires, it acts as a dope and deprives the happy couples of the hope of a better alternative reality. As a result, the home becomes a similitude of the heaven, or of our idea of heaven : the compliant, coy and pretty wife, radiant with an indomitable zest for life, ready with the recipes for happiness and cuisine; the bright, fresh-faced children, the obedient servants, the steady income. What's more! Joys are worth ambition, and joys galore."

"What about the unhappy marriages, Debasis?" Anjan da asked with a cryptic smile.

"The addiction is more or less similar, but when the unhappy man is as sensitive and subtle as you are, his tribulations tell him that life is elsewhere, and he tries to find out direction through indirection, ecstasy through agony. Like Plato's cave-man he feels suffocated in the dungeony womb of the cave, and wriggles his way out and sees the sun. Once the unhappy man's thoughts and being are conflated to the other reality and welded by the miseries of the world, they behave like air encased in a wreath of bubbles on the deepest part of the Pacific ocean and rise steadily to the surface defying all the odds and the drowning....powers of the sea. You know, Anjan da, nothing elevates our souls, nothing enriches our spirits like our grief. No matter how trite the causes of our grief may be. You might have been blessed with such conjugal miseries had you married a woman high on the intellectual or culture element. A working class woman, I am sure, couldn't have made your life truly unhappy. She knew how to adjust. Your wife engaged you when she was alive; now her memory and child engage you, arouse your tender feelings. Memory of love enslaves the mind more inextricably than actual love. Its appeal is subtle. Its spell is more enduring."

Moderately intoxicated as I was, I seemed to be carried away by my eloquence. Ideas sprung up like weeds after rain. Anjan da was listening to me with his eyes half-closed, and trying to make sense of my speech.

"I must thank you for giving me such a good report. Honestly, I had never considered myself so fortunate. Any way, I am not asking you what I have done or spoken just to convince you about my excellence, because I don't like being drenched by my own water of admiration. But what could be the cause of your bitterness?" Anjan da stretched himself and yawned. "I'd rather you came to your point immediately."

"While reading that monstrous story by Kafka," I went on," I had a feeling that I was being metamorphosed into a large grasshopper and the process had already started. A pathological fear of being neglected by those I love cools down my cordial feelings and checks my spontaneous expressions. I neglect others because I hate to be neglected by others should I become an insect.

"That fear has been a guiding force in me. Like a mother who has lost her child in a fair, looks around but sees nothing and partakes nothing of the festal junketings around her, I look around to find a person whose steadiness of character would instil a hope in me that he won't neglect me in the event of such a change of my shape. I meet and make friends with a few people, but they sink or burst as a cling to them like a drowning man."

Anjan da looked up and saw tears of helplessness in my eyes. His tender look mellowed me more, and melted my resistance. Tears flowed down my cheeks. He wiped them with his fingers.

"I assure you I won't neglect you if you were transformed into symbolic or actual a grass-hopper," he said affectionately.

"No, you've failed my test. You cannot. You've become a popular public speaker. Have you marked your own degeneration? Do you remember how you began, what you were when I met you? Now if you lift a big table and frighten off a big monkey, you'll look around for approbation and kudos and clappings. Why, you may flaunt about it in public."

Anjan da spoke nothing, stared at my quivering lips wide-eyed. I remained silent. I felt I had better reason to be in the sulks, for the hurt I endured was more painful than the hurt I inflicted on him. We sat like that more than ten minutes without stirring a limb, without yawning, without opening our mouths to talk. It was the time for soul-searching for both of us. We had been left with only two harsh options : to defend ourselves, or to acknowledge defeat.

Anjan da broke the ice. "I think I'm beginning to understand you," he said in a husky whisper. "If I'm right in diagnosing your ailment, Debasis, it's a precarious mental state of a man who wishes other people to become what he himself couldn't become. It is a type of illness that makes the patient think that he is superior to others simply because he suffers from it."

"There is no denying," he resumed after a brief pause, "that our times show a strong preference for kitsch, for smallness of nature and objects. We want to confine mighty oceans in an aquarium, masterpieces of world literature in floppies, feelings on the celluloid flirts and God in the gummed stickers. I do admit, my dear friend, it is we who have entrusted our religions to the men of little faith, our morality to the harem eunuchs and our political fate to the people who love power for its own sake. But that's only the seamy side of truth.

We are purblind if we do not see that there is enough of goodness and greatness in man, in our familiar world, which keeps up the resistance and helps in maintaining the spiritual ecosystem of our times. As long as you breathe and succeed in lighting a candle in a dark dungeon, be sure there is a reasonable supply of oxygen. Do you hear me?

"I do not react, Debasis, because you found me ordinary. Without pretension, I tell you as per my abilities and consistency, they leave a lot to be desired. But your cynicism is symptomatic of the evil sickness you so passionately flout. As I said earlier, I acted and spoke without trying to model myself on your ideas of the grandiose."

"Are you annoyed, Anjan da?" I asked anxiously, "I never wanted to hurt your feelings. I spoke what I felt so painfully."

"If I'm annoyed and deeply hurt, it is not because you blamed me for not becoming what you wished me to become, but you could be so cussed, so insensitive to so many good things of life. You fear an actual or symbolic transformation of your goodly human shape into a lizard's or a leech's, or a grass-hopper's, and such a possibility terrifies you more because you think people you count on would treat you as Grete and Mr Samsa treated Gregor. I know you mean much more than that."

"Yes I mean much more than that!" I repeated his sentence. I wanted to tell what I exactly mean, lest I should be misconstrued. "By being sick, out of job, poor, paralysed and old, I'd be hamstrung, a detestable flotsam and jetsam. The people who adore me, fawn on me, love me will find pretexts to desert me, will be ashamed to be seen in my company, and wish me dead and done away with. Fear of death is nothing compared to this horror of being marooned in friendless, timeless space."

"Now I have listened to your jeremiad on human evil and ingratitude," Anjan da said. But your bitterness is caused by what is yet to come. No man is sentenced before he commits a crime. You're sitting on judgment on your fellowmen who, you fear or believe, would commit a crime against you in the future. Why you turn your back to life?

"You see, Debasis, marriage has made me more human. To be human means to feel life, not only to live it. Watch a pretty child shambling up to you, its lips blooming into a smile, feel its soft warm body with your own body; watch a pretty young widow, absorbed in the mellowness of loss, her eyes as still, blue and deep as the waters of the Ganges; watch a pair of young lovers drawn to each other at the first blush, how ecstatically they discover each other's body and soul, and the world encompassing them. If you refuse to feel life, you stand in your own light, and are darkened by your own shadow. Remember the day when I surprised you by telling the name of my would-be wife. You prated on about the advantages of marriage. Then it struck me as nonsense, but later I discovered some sense in it. In a world glutted with wild availability and guided by the pleasure principle, it is healthy and even ascetic to get married. Marriage does not make a man frivolous. I think a good marriage is a charm against many frivolities."

Anjan da turned the table clock to show me the time, and stood up. "It seems," he drawled finally, "such personal issues cannot be resolved by someone else's personal convictions, or experiences. You may find your solutions in the concluding pages of your book of life, or not at all. It's time we did justice to this sleep-causing juice." He caressed the empty wine bottle and flashed a radiant chuckle at me, which, like a ray of sunshine, shot through my dark, damp room. His cordial chuckle expressed a covenant of friendship, which would prevail upon and outlast any difference of opinion. It made me feel grateful and young. A moment later when I returned the smile, I held nothing back from him;- a true, perky jubilation the like of which I had not felt long since, made me smile like that. Perhaps, he gave what I have been desiring all that time, and that, too, in spite of himself.

Puja was sound asleep — her pretty head sunk into the soft pillow, her body covered to the chest with a velvet quilt. She, I thought, must be dreaming of clouds, flowers and babies. "How beautiful a person, I mean, an adult looks when he is sound asleep. Sleep is Nature's way of reminding man everyday that he was once a child." I didn't like to disturb her. I wanted to spend some more time with Anjan da, talking with him. There was another furnished bed in that room. I wanted to occupy that.

An inauspicious idea, like an augury, began troubling me : that I may not have another occasion to talk with Anjan da at great length. Such ideas usually trouble a soldier when he bids farewell to his parents to go to the battlefield. I, however, didn't tell my thought to Anjan da, lest he should mock at my concern by saying "O Horatio, we defy augury."

We stretched ourselves on two adjacent beds. A strong night wind clashed with the rotating ceiling fan, and produced a constant wheezing noise. "If you get up early, Debasis," Anjan da said, "do wake me up. I've to set out early."

I ignored his request, and cleared my throat to hint at a change of context.

"Well, by the way.... I mean, were you a happy married man, Anjan da?" I stammered out with great effort. And added : "Did you find in Uri an ideal wife? Whatever I yammered on your conjugal life was only speculation. I know that."

"It means you won't let me sleep!" he thought aloud, patiently-annoyed. "Why on earth you're so curious?"

"If you'd like to answer, you may, if not, don't," I put in sulkily. Anjan da remained silent for full five minutes. He was deliberating with himself whether it'd be in the fitness of things to answer such a personal question. I waited. Finally he decided in my favour.

"I married in my early forties," he began slowly; "My austere life-style, my long preoccupation with serious books, abstract ideas and social reform, and my commitment to my teaching have made me believe that I had no physical desire in me. I'd never allowed myself to think on sex. Sexual desire had never bothered me. Mother was uppermost in my mind when I proposed to Uri. But in a few days following the tying of the knot, I went the way of all flesh. It was an epiphany of desire. We were devotees. For the first time I viewed body from a different angle, and was surprised by the delight of parallax. Happiness was redefined. Previously it was marked by an absence of pain or discomfort. Now it was a boiling point of ecstasy. For a year or so, Uri had no complaints. She only wished the nights were at least twice as long. She nursed mother lovingly, and didn't give her any reason to be unhappy about till mother died peacefully. Her last words were a blessing for Uri."

"When mother left us, we spent too much of time together. Fulfilment, you know, wanes desire. Prompt availability puts paid to romance. Other matters cropped up. Instead of complaining about the shortness of night, she started complaining about her not having what other women have. The desire to keep up with the Joneses was a stink-bug in her blouse. That made her sniff and fret. I tried to train her up. I asked her to live simply and happily. But she said her happiness depended on her having minimum things. She got most of the things she wanted. But there was no end to desire. Two temperaments couldn't be more different. But our bodies were out of sync with our minds, and surprisingly in sync with each other. We felt then, and I feel now that our life was reasonably happy, relatively smooth."

"No fracas, no shouting and slanging match?" I asked inquisitively.

"Only God knows why you are interested to know all that," exclaimed Anjan da with a sigh. But he was determined not to disappoint me.

Not exactly shouting and slanging matches! There were some angry exchanges of words. I suspect, Debasis, you intend to compare. OK, then. Uri was not obstinate and nagging. I knew she'd a great weakness for gold ornaments and gorgeous sarees. I considered them utterly useless. Good sense deserted her when she saw woman glittering like Puja mandapas. One evening while we were sitting together, she remembered her miseries for not having a pearl necklace.

"A neighbour woman had shown her one such necklace and assured her that it would suit her to a tee. According to my line of reasoning wearing precious ornaments is like salting the mine; and such tawdry glitter adds nothing to the beauty of a woman. She had already been fed up with my routine excuses. That day she flew into a rage and vented her anger on me : 'You skimp on ornaments and sarees in the name of reason. I know you're poor, and poverty should be your only reason. But you'd never admit it.' She wanted to insult me. If you examine our vocabulary, you'll find most of our abuses are related to poverty. That's funny, but true."

"That was cruel of her to say that," I said sympathetically. "But how did you react? How you saved the situation?"

"I didn't lose my temper," informed Anjan da; "I was rather flattered and amused by her rebuke. Simple living, voluntary or forced, I told her, is the benchmark of Indian culture. It is scandalous to be affluent in a society where millions around you are living in abject poverty. You mock people who work gruelling hours from morning to midnight for a pittance by being simply affluent, you offend them by flaunting your opulence. I've known some moderately rich villagers who conceal their wealth and pretend to be poor like the rest. We should thank our fate for saving us from that need to pretend."

"Did she understand you?" I asked.

"I don't know how she took me," he said looking very thoughtful, and added haltingly, "But I sounded pompous, even pretentious. My guardedly violent outburst calmed her."

"I think what you said was true," I said.

"What she said was true as well," he shot back. Then he added : "You see, Debasis, simple living is noble when it is practised silently, quietly. It sounds disgustingly sanctimonious when we try to justify it. It generally happens that the people who are not poor flatter poverty and the people who are truly needy exaggerate the blessings of wealth. The best way for the likes of us, who live in the loins of fortune, is to keep off the topic."

I was going to ask him some more questions, when he announced in a tone of finality : "It's time we slept."

35

AN ACCIDENT

Two days later newspapers carried Anjan da's death news, file photographs and obituary. He died in a road accident on the spot. Puja saw it first, and burst into a sobbing fit. I walked up to her and snatched away the paper. It was a traumatic news for both of us. Puja had grown very fond of Anjan da. "He was the nicest person I've ever met," she lamented, burying her face. "His was the healthiest presence. He was the only man who made me feel that the world is beautiful and safe. I wanted to suggest he should share our house with us, but I could not say that."

I walked to my study with the newspaper. My legs were shaking. I couldn't speak anything to Puja to console her. It was too heavy for me. I had lost my only mentor, my dearest friend, and I took time to realize the bitter truth. I stared at his photograph;

recollected his inimitable smile with which he bound me in an eternal assurance of friendship. I blamed myself for my rudeness to him, though I felt the blames and praises of people made no difference to the man whose heart was as big as his head. "Why did God endow man," he told me during his last visit, "with a brain six times larger than it should be for a Primate of his size, if he had not intended to make man different, a superior creature?"

The world tried to tether him to itself through his mother, wife and son, but he found his release in death.

His obituary described Anjan da as a man of great learning and personal charm. It also mentioned that he was the most sought-after public speaker of the state for ten years or more.

I knew that such hackneyed encomiums spoke nothing of the man he was, and would make him turn in his grave. A nature such as his would like to be remembered with love, rather than with admiration, and wish to be enshrined in a solitary heart. I was filled with a sense of loss that was too heavy for tears.

Next morning we hired a taxi and drove to Anjan da's house. The house was locked, but the neighbours surrounded us curiously. They took us to the child. The three-year-old child was busy with his toys. The good neighbours who were taking care of the child during his father's absence, expressed their anxiety for the orphan's permanent upkeep.

The child, whether it was his natural tendency to cling to the strangers or he discovered a loving mother in Puja, embraced her and didn't resist when she kissed him. "He takes after his father, do you mark that," Puja observed holding him in her arms stifling a sob. I nodded quietly.

"What do you call him?" I asked a woman standing there.

"Ranju," answered she.

"We've come to take Ranju with us," Puja announced in a determined tone, and would not wait for any contradiction.

On our way back I suddenly remembered something and whispered it into her ear. We had already covered ten miles, but we decided to have a look at the Wave-Crest Lodge.

We hoped to find Javed, Subramaniam and Man Lion there. The house had been given a face-lift and was unrecognizable from a distance. Narasingh greeted us with a wild toothy smile and showed us in. He had grown in height and bulk, and the hairs beneath his heavy nose ran in all directions. He had already become a man.

"You've grown like a weed, a swamp weed," I teased him, and added, "Where are Javed and Subramaniam. I heard they are staying here." Instead of listening to my teasings and query, he dragged his wife from the shed adjacent to the kitchen. She was carrying a child in her arms. Narasingh hastily introduced his wife to us, and the nervous woman slipped into the kitchen and never showed herself again. He told us that Javed and Subramaniam had gone to the office and would not be back before evening.

I separated myself from Puja who was preoccupied with the child, and walked the familiar corridors, lost in thought. Each spot I placed my feet on reminded me of something sweet and intimate, yet for ever gone. I felt an emotional outburst building up deep inside me, pushing upwards like an emetic. Things had fallen away, and I could not have put them back on place, however, hard I tried. I looked at the immutable sea, roaring and foaming as ever. I consoled my heart : "There is only one way to recover from the trauma of change; that is, by linking your changing self to the changeless, the sea."

As I turned around, I found Narasingh following me trying, perhaps, to read my thoughts from behind. In normal circumstances, I might have been irritated by his presence and ordered him to vanish. But I was preoccupied with my halcyon past of which he was a part, an important part to boot. "Hey, Man Lion," I said warmly, "do you miss us?"

He giggled for an answer.

"How is your wife? Where did you get her?" Not that school-girl, I suppose?"

"No. No. Babu. She is a good girl. Very shy," Man Lion replied shyly.

For a minute or so, we looked at each other, trying to find out how much we have changed, for better or worse, in the meantime.

"By the way, did you actually see Uri's ghost?" I asked with casual curiosity. His facial expression changed. He became grave. He was not expecting such a question. Then I informed him about Anjan da's death. He looked vacantly at me. I noticed great grief writ large on his face. His eyes collected tears. I briefly narrated the circumstances in which Anjan da died. He listened to me, but spoke nothing. We stood silently for some time. Then he said in a feeble voice : "Come, I'll show you the spot where I saw her ghost."

I followed Narasingh downstairs to the verandah.

"Here; here!" he said pointing to the spot : "It was dark, but not very dark. I could see her face. I asked her when she came. She didn't say anything. She came to surprise my wife. They had met twice earlier in this house. They were very fond of each other."

"Did she surprise her?" I asked only to make him talk at length.

"Yes, babu. She touched my wife and vanished. The poor woman got the shock of her life. She was not afraid of the dark before. But after that incident she is afraid of her own shadow. I don't know why she visited us."

"She didn't visit you," I said quietly; "She visited the lodge as I am visiting the lodge. We've our own reasons to return to it. It means something special to each of us." Narasingh asked. Man Lion looked at me, trying to make sense of what I said so seriously. Both of us felt tense and awkward.

"Tell me about Javed and Subramaniam," I asked abruptly, to relieve the tension; "Do they quarrel often?"

"Oh, no," replied he; "They never quarrel, But ... but ...

they're drinking a lot. Come, please come with me. I'll show you something."

He led me to the kitchen, and pointed at a heap of empty bottles of various shapes, brands and sizes : a solid evidence of Hindu-Muslim amity. Javed the Delicate and Subramaniam the Southern puritan had drowned their differences in a pool of alcohol.

"They're best of friends, babu," blurted out Narasingh enthusiastically.

"Do you get your share?" I teased him. He giggled again, this time apologetically. I left him and walked fast to the parlour where Puja was waiting for me.

Puja, the child and the driver were getting impatient. I took tea in the parlour. Narasingh stood by the gate and watched us till we got into the taxi. Then he turned and walked slowly into the house. He didn't look back.

PART IV

36

A PLEASANT SURPRISE : ANDY AND HIS WIFE

I bumped into Andy in a train compartment about two years after our visit to Anjan da's old place. He was searching for some one frantically, pushing his way through the crowd in the aisle, peering into the faces of the sitters on both sides. Our eyes met accidentally as I, sitting on my berth near the window, was just looking at the jostling crowd. His gaze lingered on my face for a split second; then he jerked it free and moved on. The Calcutta bound Mail was waiting on the platform. I entrusted my luggage, an attache case, to an elderly gentleman sharing my seat, spread my handkerchief on my seat to discourage invaders, and followed him.

"Hey, Andy, what's your problem? Are you searching for some one, Andy?" I shouted above the commotion, catching hold of his arm from behind. He pretended as if he saw me for the first time and exclaimed : "Oh, Debasis, how're you? Where're you going? I am searching for my wife?"

"Your wife!" I blurted out. I restrained my surprise and followed him. I thought he was trying to dodge me, but I dogged him. After sometime he looked back. He realized that I was not going to leave him alone.

"I boarded the train in the last station," he informed me. "My wife is supposed to board it here. It's her home town. She knows the compartment number and seat number, too." He took a pause and then began : "What'll I do? The train is about to leave. The hag sneezed and a cat crossed the road in front of me as I came out of my house; then and there I knew what was in store for me."

We got down from the train, and surveyed the crowded platform. "Is she supposed to come all alone?" I enquired.

"How can I know?" Andy replied impatiently.

"Give me some hints about your wife so that my eyes can locate her."

"Well, look for the prettiest face you've ever seen and you'll make no mistakes," he suggested, beaming through his misery.

"You mean she's the prettiest woman of the world, and she's your wife. Come on, Andy, be specific."

He ignored my banter and quickened his pace. The train whistled and began to move. Confused, he got into the train, and ran to his assigned berth. I followed him. And there she was in all her glory. She greeted Andy with a sunny smile of discovery, but he was in the sulks. Necessity, however, made him talk.

"When did you come? Meet my friend Debasis. He's travelling with us."

She looked at me and greeted me with an icy hello and looked out through the window.

"Debasis, meet Krishnā!" he chortled, smiling triumphantly.

"Thank you, Andy, I'm glad to meet her. We'll meet again. We're travelling in the same compartment," I said and left them abruptly, displeased by my being brushed aside by the woman. Returning to my seat, I was horrified to find both my attache-case and the man missing. I got cold feet and stood transfixed, looking vacantly around. An elderly lady marked my wretchedness, and, without speaking anything, pointed her index finger at the upper berth above her head. I found my luggage half-buried under a heap of other passangers' luggage, and was greatly relieved.

"Where's that man?" I asked. The lady pursed up her lips and opened her palm to suggest she didn't know, nor did she care to know. Disconcerted by the bahaviour of those two women in quick succession, I headed toward the basin mirror to verify my face. I found nothing wrong on my face and my mood was restored.

Andy's wife was a pretty woman no doubt, but she didn't even remotely resemble the Krishnā I knew, the girl who like the low-pressure in the Bay of Bengal, had caused much distress in the male hearts in general and a devastating cyclone in Andy. A woman may appear, I thought, lovelier than she actually is to her lover or newly married spouse. Given the grace, accomplishments and beauty of Krishnā — a type of confluence hard to come by — , her lover or spouse induced by the fabled love-potion which activates the esemplastic imagination, may consider her to be the most beautiful woman of the world without appearing uxorious and ridiculous to the world; but in this case her name-sake's petite appearance seemed to me ordinary. Andy's compliment was unwarranted, and a bit disparaging. I decided not to meet them again even if we travelled a month together.

Andy joined me after a few stations. Now, he had all the time in the world to talk to me. I looked at him and remembered Anjan da's description of him. He looked much better than what I imagined about his âppearance. He had shed some excess flab and dyed his hair. He was fragrant like a garland of jasmine. His happy disposition which attested to a marital fulfilment had erased some of the premature wrinkles from his forehead. I was happy to mark those changes in Andy. I was happy to find him married.

Andy greeted me as if he saw me for the first time. "Hello, Debasis", he began ebulliently, "You've changed so much for the better. Honestly, I took time to recognize you. I heard about you. Let me recollect who spoke about you. Alright, I know you'll accuse me for not inviting you to my marriage. I do see it on your face. I apologize for that. Only ten days — or was it eight days — I got to inform my friends and relatives. I had to do everything myself. Well, that's not the only reason. I now recollect I could not get your address. I wrote to Subramaniam and Javed and Anjan da. None of them turned up. Anjan da's absence and silence surprised me most. I was really angry with him. Only recently I discovered the cause of his absence. Well, I'll give you an interesting piece of information later. Of all our common friends, only Sudhakar attended the function. Yes, now I remember it was Anjan da who wrote about you long ago, and Sudhakar spoke about you. By the way, how are you?"

"First tell me, Andy, who is this Krishnā? Is she the same Krishnā, the baker's daughter and danseuse?"

Andy laughed loudly. "You could not mark that, eh? I thought you knew Krishnā. This is Savitri. But you know a girl can be called by a different name after marriage. You have not changed your wife's name, I suppose? You see I had promised to marry Krishnā or not at all. Besides, it was Krishnā who pierced my poor heart like a flowery arrow and stuck there inextricably. I chased a dream. It was a long chase, a sad chase, a mad chase. But I didn't acknowledge defeat. Whatever I caught hold of I named it Dream. That's how I won what I had always wanted. You've to be a bit subtle and innovative to score a victory over your fate, your bete noir. How do you like the idea?"

"Great!" I exclaimed. I was happy to note that Andy had finally found a short-cut to victory. "Should I thank some writer or friend for giving you this idea, or it's purely your own?" I asked.

"Not entirely my own," Andy said candidly. "While reading Thoreau's *Walden* just for pleasure I hit upon this idea. Have you read it, Debasis?"

"No, but I'd like to read it. You recommend it? (Andy nodded yes). OK, then. Is it a sort of confession of a jilted lover? I'm going to read it. Is it a fat novel?"

"No, Debasis, Thoreau was not a jilted lover. He was not a novelist either. He may turn in his grave, ha, ha. He was a practical philosopher. Once he was troubled by a desire to possess property, say ranches and estates. He visited all the ranches of his area, met their owners and haggled over the price of each firm, and then he purchased all of them 'imaginatively' and entrusted these people their own ranches. I mean he asked the ex-owners to supervise the work of these ranches. He got the mental satisfaction of being one of the richest ranchers of America without spending a dollar. Like Hamlet he lived in a nut-shell and considered himself the king of infinite space."

"A quite novel idea, I bet," I exclaimed. I looked around and saw many passengers listening to our conversation with interest. Most of our co-passengers were gregarious village folks. They looked appreciatingly at our direction. Andy looked around. An elderly gentleman with a turban and thick moustaches looked askance at him. Andy addressed him, breaking the invisible wall of formal politeness which usually prevented particularly the male passengers from coming close to each other : "Do you like this line of thinking?"

The elderly gentleman smiled cordially and nodded his head. "Son, was the man who said such things a bachelor? If not a bachelor, he must have been a widower or a saint."

"Yes, yes, he was confirmed bachelor, but how did you know?"

Andy was surprised.

"Very simple, son" the elderly gentleman explained; "The man, after making these purchases, will come home and break the good news to his wife ...."

"And his wife will call him a cad," Andy snatched the sentence from him.

"Yes," agreed the elderly gentleman smiling seriously.

For that matter, anybody may call him by that name; it's so easy to write him off as mad. Andy said trying to defend Thoreau. I wanted to defend my friend.

"Of course, it depends how you look at life. If you like, you can lead a simple life even if you're very rich, can't you?" I asked gravely. "Haven't you seen some misers who dress like beggars, eat chapati and cabbage and possess big estates and tons of gold?"

Many people including the sceptical elderly gentleman exclaimed yes, yes. As such misers abound in the countryside, they might have seen them.

"Then what does it prove?" I asked and hastened to answer; "It proves that if you cut short your needs, the produce of a few acres of land would be enough for you. And the profits you get from your twenty ranches are deposited in the bank. And your money goes on increasing. You get the satisfaction that you have a lot of money, and you are the owner of twenty ranches, three big hotels and one hundred hectares of irrigated land. Then one night you feel a violent pain in the chest and kick the bucket. That's how it all ends; what's true of the misers is also true for all of us. Man wants a lot, but needs a little for his own sake."

No one refuted my argument. Andy looked pleased. He thought I would oppose him. He was at a loss for words. He spoke loudly ignoring the strangers, but those so-called strangers refused to be ignored. Now it was not possible for us to resume our intimate conversation, because all eyes had zeroed in on us. They'd already appropriated our privacy.

"Krishnā must be feeling lonely. Let's go there," suggested Andy. I entrusted my suitcase to the lady who had pointed to it a few hours ago, and followed Andy. His wife was not feeling lonely at all. She was sitting propped up against two air-pillows totally engrossed in a Hindi pulp book. She greeted me once again with a cool hello and forced smile, and made room for us.

"I thought you were getting bored, so I brought my friend here," explained Andy.

"Very nice, of you," said the grave lady formally without lifting her eyes from the book. "You know I never get bored so long as I read these books."

"What's the story? Is it very interesting? Please tell us the story," Andy said, trying to drag her into a friendly conversation. But the lady wanted to be left alone.

"Why, you can read it when I finish it," she told him icily. Her eyes, like a pair of cocker spaniels, followed the zig zag trail of a teasing climax. Nothing bothered her but the chase.

The lady whose real name was Savitri repulsed me at first sight. She had a good figure and could pass of as a good-looking woman. But she lacked sensitivity and warmth which might have shown her charms in a favourable light and made her appear attractive. Her decision to cold-shoulder living humanity (which included her husband) and get immersed in a cheap pot boiler, turned her into an anathema.

I told Andy about Anjan da. "How did you get the news of his death?"

Andy started and stared at me full in the face. "What're you saying, Debasis? When? How?"

"It's strange you have not known it yet. Almost two years ago. In a road accident. You haven't heard about it? 0 my God!" This world, I thought, is like a tropical jungle or a labyrinth. People meet, make friends with one another, part ways for a variety of reasons and keep on struggling to eke out a living and hardly get any leisure to remember their friends, let alone locating them.

My thoughts were interrupted by Andy's laughter. "You're mistaken, Debasis. Anjan da is not dead. Know it from me. He is not dead. You really frightened me."

"It is a hard truth, Andy," I said sadly, "a bitter truth. Most probably, he slept his last night on this earth in my house, can you believe it? He perhaps had a premonition that he was going to die. He spoke certain things which I interpreted later. I'll never meet another person like him. His son Ranju is with us. He is five now."

Andy closed his eyes and remained silent for some time. Then he said : "I don't know what you're talking about. His son is with you, that's alright, but why do you say he died two years ago? Then how could I have met him and talked to him last July, that is, four months ago. Ask Savitri, I mean Krishnā! She was with me. He renounced the world two years ago. "That's what he told me. That, of course, was a type of death, a symbolic death."

I was horrified. "Can it be true? You must have read the obituary? Well, you might have skipped it. That's quite possible. May be, you aren't subscribing to the newspapers in which his obituaries came out. What about the news item? What about his sad neighbours and his son? I've more reasons to believe he is dead than you have about his being alive. You might have seen his ghost."

Andy, I knew, had an incorrigible tendency to see ghosts in living creatures. He was endowed or cursed with an extra vision which enabled him to see the invisible.

Andy's raucous laughter disturbed his studious spouse who, instead of enquiring about the cause of his humour, eyed him disdainfully and gestured to him to be quiet. But he was past all caring. It was, after all, a question of life and death. He had his fill of laughter, and then asked, "You said I saw his ghost, Anjan da's ghost? Ha, Ha! I know why you said that. That cat and the French woman! You still remember that. But, Debasis, I am not mistaken now, nor was I mistaken then. The difference between these two sightings is that the cat could not be verified whereas the existence of Anjan da can still be verified."

"How?"

"You want to meet Anjan da, don't you? Then you get down at the Kelbar Station, take the first bus to Chandanpur, sixty five miles north-wards, enquire about the Mahadev mountains, and walk down these four or five miles if you do not get a vehicle on hire, climb to the summit of that fairly tall mountain, not less than five thousand feet above the ground level, and search for the cottage there. If you're lucky you'll scale the mountain in twenty minutes; if unlucky, in two hours. You may bribe one of those young acolytes roaming there near the temple of Lord Shiva at the foot of that mountain and ask him to be your guide. Now, if you don't want to meet Anjan da or his ghost, believe in my words, O.K.?"

I looked at him, speechless with bewilderment. His descriptions sounded earnest.

I asked : "How did you know he was there? You took all that trouble to meet him?"

Is the old rogue in Andy active again? I asked myself. Is he trying to avenge his humiliation at the stinking grove near the light house? It was quite possible that he had known about our trick. Sudhakar, the least secretive of all, must have let the scheme out. But I soon corrected myself. Andy was not capable of such tricks.

"It was a happy coincidence, an unexpected discovery," began Andy, smiling as he spoke. "I went there with my students for a picnic. We were forbidden by the temple priests to cook meat in that area. So with great difficulty we carried the utensils, cooking pots and fire-wood to a level clearing about thirty yards above the temple premises. There was a mountain stream nearby. It originates on the top of the mountain, the temple people told us, as the Ganges flows out of Lord Shiva's tangled hair. That bit of information fired our imagination. Four of us — three students, I mean boys, and myself — decided to go to the top of the mountain and see the source of the stream. It is a steep, densely wooded mountain. It took us almost two hours. We were sweating a profusely. The summit of the mountain was flat with long stretches of granite bed. Believe me, Debasis, once there, I felt on the top of the world. The source of the stream was a wonder of Nature. Crystal-clear water spouted from a crevice, and flowed downwards murmuring the praise of God in tiny water-falls. I almost fainted in delight. We four tired mountaineers stretched ourselves beside the brook under a large tree which was laden with small violet flowers. As we lay there, we heard some one intoning the sacred Om in the vicinity. We stood up, looked around and found a small leaf-roofed cottage.

"There he sat, cross-legged, his eyes closed in deep meditation, reciting Om at regular intervals. I could not recognize him for his face was bearded and hair was long, and, but for a white loin cloth, his body was bare. He asked me to sit near him and I recognized him as I saw his eyes and heard his voice. I didn't know about his reported death, so I was not horrified. I only enquired about his son, and he answered briefly : He is taken care of. I wanted to ask him many questions. But the atmosphere had a curious effect on me. I got answers of all these questions without asking them. His beatific smile explained all."

Still incredulous, I asked him : "You just said your wife had seen him too, didn't you?"

"I didn't say she'd seen him, did I? She didn't climb the mountain with us. She was informed by me and my students. Any way, you can go and see for yourself. I think you're not believing me!" Andy sulked and became silent.

It was true that I had not seen his dead body. So what? People who reported to the police or to the press might have seen it. Otherwise, how could they know his name. Again, if I believed Andy's version of the story, I had to disbelieve many other things, many evidences which had appeared irrefutable to me then. Besides, a person like Anjan da could not have become so cruel to his own son. On the other hand, Andy, as I knew him, was not capable of cooking up such a lengthy yarn at a short notice. Our meeting was quite unexpected. To top it all, it was I who broached Anjan da's name first, not he. I felt utterly confused, intrigued.

37

AN EXPEDITION

A week later, when I returned home, the first thing I told Puja was about my chance meeting with Andy and his incredible revelation. I knew she'd call me a fool for taking such a cock and bull story seriously. She, however, belied my apprehension and became thoughtful. "It can be true," she said after a lot of thinking. I informed her of the trick we had played on Andy long ago. "Andy could well have thought it over before he bumped into me, may be when he learnt about that plot, most probably from one of my accomplices. I, of course, do not blame the informer, for I might have confessed it to him myself. You see, Puja, time turns a trick into a joke. But Andy might have decided not to forgive me."

Puja said : "I've not met your friend called Andy. I only know him as much as you've told me about him. Had I met him and talked to him, I could have studied him correctly. Now we've one way out : To ascertain the truth. I know Anjan da. He is not the type of person who will desert his child and renounce the world. He is a kind man. His nobility of nature would have blocked his exit."

"But he brushed his son aside, or jumped over the obstacle and left!" I blurted out.

"I'm pretty certain he couldn't have done that, at least if my reading of his nature be correct. You can do one thing. You can visit the place where he was staying. Ranju shouldn't know about it. So I stay with him. You remember the house where we met Ranju for the first time? You go there and enquire about Anjan da, and come back."

The scheme appeared a bit far-fetched to me, but Puja was absolutely certain about its effectiveness. On my way to Anjan da's old place I was brooding over that clear-as-sunlight incident which suddenly became a mystery, a veritable conundrum. Andy, I thought, would score a partial victory if my journey proved a fiasco, and a total victory if our journey to the summit of the mountain proved a fiasco, too.

* * *

A middle-aged amicable lady opened the door and enquired about my identity. She was the lady who used to look after the child when its father was absent. She recognized me when I introduced myself and told her that we'd taken Anjan Das Gupta's child about two years ago.

"Where's he now? I mean your Anjan Das Gupta or something?", The lady asked me.

"Well, I don't know exactly," I said hesitantly; "Do you know anything about him? Did he come here after we took away the child?"

The elderly woman looked incredulously at me for some time.

"Believe me," she said excitedly, he frightened us really. He virtually came out of the Death's kingdom. His face was full of red scars and his head was bandaged. He looked so scary, so ghostly. He enquired about the child. We told him that a husband and wife team came in a car and took away Ranju. You had not left your name and address. He wanted to know your name. Finally, my little daughter came out with your wife's name. You were calling your wife. She had heard it. Isn't her name Puja? He looked very pleased when he heard that name. I asked him if he knew you. He said yes, and went away in a huff without opening his own house. I am surprised to know he is not with you now. His belongings have been dumped in a room of that house. She pointed at the house where Anjan da used to live.

My head swam. I thought I'd collapse. I walked away as fast as I could. The woman was still talking.

"I wish I were as resourceful as you," I complimented Puja on my return. "Anjan da is alive, and that's a good thing. I'd forgive him for everything. But how on earth you thought of such a scheme?"

"If you think you know a person, you ought to be more or less certain about what he would do under different circumstances. That's so simple." Puja said politely, humbly.

Puja, like most sensitive and clever women, is most humble when she is most flattered. I have discovered this quality in many people who think they have some admirable qualities. These people are self-conscious and fully aware of their plus points. They move about with their larger-than-life-size egos. But the moment you praise them, they become very self-effacing and even go to an extent of pointing out some of their own faults and drawbacks in order to give you the proofs of their humility. They'd make you believe that they are humble without knowing that humility is a virtue. There are, on the other hand, some unabashed egotists who have a permanently strained relationship with shame. You inadvertently drop a word of admiration for them, and you're undone. They'll not only make you feel wretched for knowing so little about them, but they would bury you alive under a mound of their excellent qualities which you have forgotten to notice before.

"The scheme was so simple!" repeated Puja with an innocent smile.

Though our agitation was great, we took all precaution to conceal the matter from the child till he grew up and acquired the much needed sense of discrimination. This ability to discriminate, to know the difference between what happened and what ought to have happened, like an advanced shock-absorbing mechanism, would enable him to drive his vehicle on uneven terrains without losing his control. Anjan da had impressed me as a man who inhabited two worlds simultaneously. The quotidian, recognizable world tried to tame him as men try to tame some wild animals by administering small doses of opium or other hallucinogenic drugs in order to weaken their tendency to protest. An inner need for freedom always pulled him by an invisible cord, and neutralized the effect of these drugs upon him. As a result, he was not addicted to this world though he nibbled at these drugs and dallied with temptations. When they worked on him, he was opinionated and affectionate, intolerant and sociable, but he was always eager to repair to the centre of his being after these momentary forays into the peripheral world. He could generate human warmth while remaining cool and detached.

* * *

Puja refused to visit him. She found no sense in such a visit. "If you like to see your friend who has chosen to be an anchorite, you may go," she told me when I requested her to accompany me. "It won't be a pleasant experience to see a friend who was as ordinary as you and I totally transformed into a world-weary, napkin-clad, holy primate. It would give me the creeps to see him in this new avatar."

I tried to be an advocate for Anjan da. "Should we fault a person for his being different from us, for having a different set of longings?" I asked her. Puja evaded my question. But I persisted. She said finally : "I do not fault him. I do not fault your Gregor Samsa for being metamorphosed into an insect. It's simply a weird situation and I don't like to get messed up with it if I could avoid it. I am happy in my imperfect world, you can tell him that. But I know he'd be glad to meet you alone and won't raise the topic of my absence at all."

So I went alone.

On getting down from the bus, I enquired about the holy shrine, and was informed that it was about six miles away. There was no vehicle to ply for hire. I walked with great difficulty carrying my heavy bag full of apples, grapes, peaches and pomegranates. I was wondering how the man survived on the top of a mountain, and what he was eating there.

The temple compound, situated on the foothills of the big mountain, was cool and compact. The ground was covered with marble stuccoes of various sizes, carrying the names of their donors. A perennial stream flowed through the compound over-flowing a fifteen by twenty feet cemented receptacle with steps. The main temple was rather small. Its sandstone walls were lined with small and big niches in which the stone images of the gods and goddesses were kept. I was thirsty and tired after my long walk in the hot sun. I asked a boy who was carrying water in a bronze pot to pour water on my palms as I held them as a funnel to my mouth. He gladly obliged me. He was a cheerful lad of fourteen or fifteen. When I told him about my plan to climb to the top of the mountain to meet the sanyasi there, he expressed his readiness to accompany me and help me in carrying my bag. "I go there often," he said, and resumed when he found me eager to know more; "I take fruit offering in the morning at ten and rice and dal offering in the afternoon before it's dark. Swamiji eats little. I bring back whatever is left uneaten."

"When did Swamiji come to this mountain?," I asked.

"That I can't say. By the time I came here he was already there. I came here about a year ago. Guruji assigned this work to me."

"Does he pay for his food?"

The boy giggled disapprovingly. People as stupid as this man, he perhaps thought, also exist. "You, see," he corrected me, "Guruji would not eat without feeding all the living creatures who spend the night here, or thereabouts. They are his guests. Can a man eat without feeding his guests? Does a man charge a fee from his guest after giving him food?"

He made me feel that I asked a mean question. He excused himself and went to the stream to refill his bronze pot. Suddenly he remembered his promise, turned round and advised me to wait. I remembered Andy's words. "You bribe one of those boys," he told me, "and he'd guide you to the summit." Andy perhaps saw them from a distance, and interpreted their nature from their dress — a loin-cloth and a sacred thread — and drew his conclusion. The boy's facial expression and mode of speaking appeared quite mature for his age.

I walked to the open and looked up at the mountain I was going to scale. It was indeed a massive mountain with steep sides densely covered with bushes and trees.

The boy returned with a piece of coir rope which, as he explained, would be used to haul an inexperienced traveller up the big boulders and steep ridges while trekking, and an extra napkin. He tied a knot on the napkin joining its four ends, put my heavy bag in its spacious middle and slung it across his shoulder. "Why did you do that?" I asked him.

"You'll know it presently," he said; "you must have your hands free when you're climbing a mountain; they're as much necessary as your feet for your movement. Why, have you never climbed a mountain before?"

I shook my head. "The mountains I've climbed are actually small hillocks. This one looks so big!"

The boy was well pleased to see my hesitation and nervousness which I tried to cover up. "Don't worry, I'll be with you. I know the right way, though it is a bit roundabout. Guruji calls me the mountain cat. Well, how long you'll stay up there? I may have to come back. I've to take *prasadam* before it's too late. It is not safe to be in the mountain when it's dark."

"Yes," I agreed with him. "We can't find our way in the dark. One false step, and we roll down to our certain death."

"Oh no, no," the young acolyte contradicted me. "I was not going to say that. It is true you cannot take a single step in the dark. You've to carry a torch. But still then you are not safe. Some animals become active in the dark. I've not yet seen a leopard, but some people say they have seen them. There are wolves and snakes. The mountain is crawling with snakes — kraits, vipers, cobras, pythons. Some of them are quite large. Only a few days ago I saw such a snake. I was climbing down in the afternoon. A snake was there in front of me. I saw only a part of its body. Round and fat like the trunk of a deodar tree. An over-grown python. It was about thirty feet long. I stood stock-still, muttering snake-exorcising mantras which Guruji taught me. That worked. That always works."

The talk about snakes and wild animals reminded me of Anjan da who had already lived defenselessly in such a hazardous place for more than two years.

"They do no harm to Swamiji?"

I asked him.

"They do no harm to any body, let alone to Swamiji," my young companion informed me smiling at my concern, as we inched our way up through the thickets of bracken and bramble. He was a picture of confidence. His composed and quiet confidence struck me as a beautiful thing, and it had come to him from his experience. He seemed to have known all possible routes to the summit. "Some routes are straight and risky, some roundabout and safe," he observed. He moved briskly, nimbly, always a few steps ahead of me, and slackened his pace when he found me lagging far behind. The boy could be correct, I thought; otherwise how could the ancient sages and their disciples have practised meditation in the forests and write the Vedas, Upanishads and Puranas in the insecure hermitages which were only small clearings in the forest. I, however, couldn't decide whether the efficacy of the mantras and the power that the human mind acquires through concentration and meditation protected them from dangers, or the animals never caused any harm to the humans unless they were provoked. But it was certain that the cottage my friend built was no protection against the snakes as long as thirty feet. The level land on the summit of the mountain was forty or fifty feet wide at certain places, and stretched lengthwise more than a furlong shaded intermittently by a canopy of leaves. The gigantic monolithic slab of beige-brown granite had no big trees on its surface save a few vestiges of green-growth spread out loosely here and there. There were open areas exposed to the sun throughout the day, and they supplied heat and light to the shaded parts. The foot-hill, the base surrounding the mountain, could not be seen from the top, because the tall tangled trees rising slightly aslant on the higher tiers had flanked the plateau, as the palms cup a precious stone, as the heart preserves a sacred mystery.

The boy romped around with the agility of a leopard as soon as he reached the summit, and beckoned me to follow him. I heard the refreshing sound of flowing water and looked around expecting to see a bearded Anjan da sitting in a lotus posture or practising austerities to tame his senses. We walked to the source of the mountain spring which was located at a slight elevation. It was shaped like an anthill, and, should I stretch my imagination a little further, it could be Lord Shiva's tangle of hair which received the torrent of the Ganges from Heaven and let it flow slowly on the plains. The mountain spring did not descend from above, but bubbled out of the ground, collected in a shallow little pool nearby, now sauntering down on the sloping terraces, now bouncing over the crags and boulders, foaming and murmuring, passing through the crevices of rocks, drowning or rolling the pebbles of various colours, shapes and sizes. A few yards from the pool, on a level clearing, stood a small cottage. Its walls were made up of upright wattles of bamboo and its roof was thatched with imbricated palm leaves.

"Some kind wood-cutters have made it for me." A strange bass voice rang our just behind me. Almost simultaneously I felt a hand on my shoulder. The boy bent down and touched the toe of the figure standing behind me. I felt a peculiar sensation the likes of which I'd never felt before. The man whom I thought dead for two years was standing behind me, with his corporeal frame. Though I began believing in his existence after my visit to his old house and took all those troubles to meet him, one part of my mind had been persistently refusing to believe in it. It was, more or less, an adventure into the unreal and the uncanny. Bright sun light negated my faith in my friend's existence. The reason of the world refused to take it seriously. A shadowy figure in a shadowy enclosure, he stood behind me. I could have just turned round and whisked away the vulture of my dualism by feeling him with my hands and seeing him with my own eyes. His light touch on my sweat-soaked shoulder sent shock waves down to my whole being like a live electric wire. Time ticked by, but I stood riveted to the ground, transfixed and traumatized.

Anjan da aka Swamiji stood in front of me with a friendly smile.

"Debasis," he said softly, "if you do not like to face a fact, the fact will face you. Here I am."

I saw him, finally. Anjan da was a tall man when he was looking healthy. Now with his fat thawed away and flesh dried up he looked slender as a stick. He wore a pair of wooden sandals and a clean white napkin as the loin-cloth. His thick beard with streaks of grey and his hair carelessly tied in a top-knot and his entire body liberally powdered with fine ash — all combined transformed him into a sage, a species of almost extinct mammals mostly seen in the illustrations, mythological films and television serials. Overcome by an inexplicable intensity of feeling, I was about to hug him, but felt a shrinkage within me and desisted. It was not a case of a man meeting his friend whom he had taken for dead and mourned; it was nothing like that.

His death to the old world was symbolic in a sense, for he didn't look like a man of the world. Or was it an instance of life imitating art?

All the questions, I wanted to ask appeared mundane, even to me, and couldn't come out. His eyes and face were illumed by a loving smile. It reminded me of his special smile which he blessed me with when he acknowledged my offer of friendship two years ago. He looked calm and self possessed. He beckoned me to follow him to the cottage. The boy followed us with his load. The cottage was clean and empty of furniture. Some fruits were kept in a wicker basket; there were a coarse hay-mattress, a deer skin, an earthern pitcher, a cheap cotton blanket and a few napkins. A wooden frame made up of dry branches served as the door. What's the use of such a door? I wondered. Big animals can push it open and small, creepy creatures can pass through it. The boy had taken me for a devotee who came to meet the holy man. But when he saw Swamiji treating me as a friend, he looked at me admiringly and felt slightly guilty for not treating me with reverence that was my due. He wanted to know if I would accompany him or I could return alone. For a moment, I wished to go with the boy. I even stood up, and bent down to touch his feet. He lifted me with his hands. He told the boy : "He will go with you in the afternoon."

Left to ourselves, the situation became less tense for both of us.

"I don't know how to begin, what to say," I found myself speaking.

"Don't bother yourself," he said. I can correctly guess your questions. You want to know how a dead man came to life, why I deserted my son, why I renounced the world and made this place my sanctuary. This is how it all happened. I was travelling in a trekker. It was night. The street was deserted, so the driver was driving very fast. He couldn't control the vehicle at a sharp bend, and it rammed into a roadside tree. I was sitting at the gate of the vehicle and the jerk threw me like a thing to a distance of about ten feet. My head struck against a hard surface and started bleeding. Nothing was visible. I heard the groans and shrieks, and it was a terrible experience. I groped my way to the road. my face was wet with blood which flowed from my fractured skull above my left ear. I pressed my handkerchief to the wound to staunch the flow of blood. Just at that moment I saw a two wheeler approaching. The young man stopped his motor-cycle when I raised my hand. I got into his pillion and the fresh night breeze revived my sagging spirit. About ten kilometres from the place of accident, on the roadside, was a small Christian dispensary. The doctor was staying in the small quarters adjacent to the dispensary. The young man requested the doctor to take care of me and rushed to the police station to inform them about the accident.

"The doctor who was staying alone in his small house took me to his house and made me sleep there. He spent a lot on me. Treated me as a brother. Six days later the doctor showed me a newspaper with a sad smile. I read my own obituary in it and learnt that all the passengers had died on the spot. Their bodies were smashed and mutilated beyond recognition. They recovered my suitcase and diary and drew the inevitable conclusion. I was on my feet within a fortnight thanks to the personal care of the kind doctor. I went to my place and learnt that you had taken the child. I was greatly relieved. The world had already gotten used to my loss. A desire which had been lying in wait in me — a desire to extricate myself from the world without causing any inconvenience to any one — bestirred itself, and made me feel the difference with a shiver. It was not a desire exactly, but it's a desire nonetheless. A desire for a change, that's all. And here I am."

"You mean you came here just for a change? Nothing else?"

I asked, bewildered by his simple justification.

"Just for a change, yes," he said. Words flowed out of his lips effortlessly as the fountain bubbled out of the earth. I scratched my head, rifled for the words to dress up my thoughts, hummed and hawed, and finally consoled myself with a tentative assurance that my questions were not worth asking.

"Debasis," he said, "I've always been a half-hearted liver of life. With an incurable Robinson Crusoe mentality! Trying my best to cope with the conditions on an island as a marooned sailor, but always hoping to see a ship which can take me home. It is a simple desire. The desire of a caged bird to be free. You might have felt such a flutter within you. That yearning to be free and to make sense of the inscrutable had long been inscribed in the heart of man, and in most cases these hieroglyphs have been discarded as old hat to make space for the new writing. A palimpsest sort of thing. All my readings and broodings have told me that I have to understand my own self in order to understand the world I inhabit, not the other way round. And this precondition is by no means easy. I, perforce have to activate all my latent possibilities if I wish to understand my own self. There is no short-cut to the self. All our intellectual and philosophical reflections, all our spiritual or religious knowledge appear as useless and unaccommodating trivia to the seeker of self, particularly at one stage of his growth, as all the technical, theoretical knowledge about the game of football to a couch potato. He can at best become a theoretical expert of sorts, a good commentator. I have realized that, and that was why I came here. I tell you all this because I know you will understand my point."

"I am trying to understand," I said thoughtfully. "Can't a person do it in the world? I mean, should a man forsake the world chasing after an abstraction, an elusive quarry called perfection? Is it not a selfish act? Besides, you're still dependent on the world which you renounced, aren't you? I am not referring to your deserting the child. You knew we have no children and Puja simply adores you, and your son is in good hands. You might have handed over the child had we asked for it. That's not the point of my reference. I only champion the world's cause. Does it deserve to be deserted?" I sounded very earnest.

"You needn't champion the world's cause," he said. It's an unnecessary self-inflicted trouble! I won't be incorrect if I say that the world loves to be deserted when such desertion ensures a nobler mobility of the quality of life, just as a good mother sends her son to the battle field with a brave smile. Besides, you are much mistaken when you equate the people you interact with, with the world; and you do not desert the world simply by choosing to keep yourself at a little remove from other people who try, consciously or unconsciously, to homogenize you and intercept you while giving you the fond illusion that they are only humanizing you. I wonder how many grave errors you commit in a row! You called perfection an elusive, abstract rabbit, and I chase it. You call it a wild goose chase? That's a pity.

A little bit of reflection may prove you wrong. Yes, try to remember the life we all led down there. A rat race, a lemming-like fertility, a hate-filled competitiveness, the seven deadly sins parading in a zany array of permutations and guises, an unconditional surrender to the baser instincts and an overweening cunning to consecrate that surrender in the name of necessity. Tell me what else does inform this system? Don't give me tongue-in-cheek sermons on love, fellow-feeling, beauty, ideology, dedication, sacrifice, higher things, aesthetic participation and what have you. People mouth these terms to constitutionalize their actions, to embarrass their adversaries and ride roughshod over the scatter-brained multitudes — and they do not believe in the truth of these terms. Do you remember the scene when Andy and Sudhakar were catching each others throat and abused each other? They were championing great causes : religion and freedom of expression, weren't they? That was symptomatic of the type of life most people lead.

"Yes, you should remember that when the human life is not redeemed by a higher aspiration and the struggle to match up to it, it's sadly sub-human, it's a backing away."

I thought my hastily formulated questions hurt him and miffed him. But he smiled benignly, amicably. For a few minutes, I could not speak. His passionate unravelling of human folly had a stunning impact on me. I silently realized that the world of man is as bad as it has always been despite a steep increase in the number of pious platitudes everywhere. "The world would not be depleted of men if one man came out of it to live a life of surcharged loneliness on the top of a mountain trying to understand the laws of chaos and order that govern the universe and the mind of man," I thought.

"Anjan da," I put in reflectively, and then hastened to correct my vocative; "I hope you don't mind to be addressed this way, do you?"

He smiled precisely and patted my back, which meant he didn't mind.

Initially I didn't think it odd to address him in my usual way. But as our conversation progressed, I felt the gap between our respective worlds widening. Most often in the past, he had surprised my humble self with his nimble strides, always leaving me far behind but very conscientiously waiting for this laggard to catch up with him. But now I realised he was teaching the techniques of flight to a pedestrian bird.

"Anjan da." I said meekly, : "I understand everything you say, but, sadly, I do not feel the truth of anything. It goes over me. It seems I lack faith. I've gathered from whatever scriptures I read that faith is the most important thing, and its presence makes all the difference. To my well-adjusted self, faith is as unimportant as a mole, and I don't mind lacking it. Great distress makes me pray, but when the going is good, I have no time to spare for prayer. However I am intelligent enough to understand why I fail utterly to comprehend the truth of your position and the meaning of your exposition."

Anjan da listened to what I said patiently.

"True," he said calmly, "faith is the most important thing. To some people it comes naturally. Such people are quite few in number. But to the likes of you and me, faith, if it come at all, comes through our senses and mind, through our uncontaminated observations of the world and life, through study and thought. Whatever we think, feel, and experience will zap to our heart if the roads are not blocked with our prejudices and pretensions. Take a pause; blank out your mind for a minute; observe how the subatomic particles behave, how a million stars, each one of them larger than our sun, twinkle at a safe distance, how the tilting placement of our planet earth supports life and causes the change of seasons, how the nanotechnology of our day compresses a library of books into a pin-head; watch how the flowers bloom, animals and plants proliferate, grow and decay. Such observations, I am sure, will instill faith in you. Faith is a visitant. It visits us when our sense of wonder touches our heart, when our will is pure."

"You mean to say," I asked, "faith will come to me without my trying to have it?"

"Yes," he replied; "It may; it may not. Try you must, but you should try with patience. The worst evil that besets mankind is impatience. Man is impatient when he is unable to wait. He is unable to wait because he believes the time spent in waiting is time wasted. What you have to do is to overcome impatience and to elevate waiting to the level of action."

Then came a damper from the laggard in me :

"Can't man be patient while still living in the world? I mean should a man quarrel with the world to make friends with faith or to come by faith?"

"Look, young man," he said in a mellifluous tone, "you commit an error of judgement by equating withdrawal with quarrel. That's not always the case. When a person is seriously preoccupied with a work, he wants to be left alone. Examples galore. Should I cite them? When he wants to withdraw from the society, when he devotes his time and energy to a cause or work, he may not be angry or antisocial or sulky. For my part, Debasis, I have not quarreled with the world. I've always been, and still is a citizen of this world."

"By the way, Anjan da," I asked, "can a person love mankind and renounce the world?"

"Yes," replied he readily : Of late, I've realized that for a man with faith, pure love and true detachment are kindred conditions of being. A plenitude of spirit is present in both of them. Both love and detachment in their pristine form fire the mind with a readiness to dare the impossible, to make great sacrifices. Man in these two conditions enjoys a calm which can flow from self-sufficiency. Temptations that torments mankind sheer away from him, because they are weaker than faith.

"One thing I tell you, Debasis, as a parting advice...."

He hesitated, looked thoughtfully into my face for several minutes. Then he decided to speak. "This piece of advice, you may call it a friendly warning, is for you, for the likes of you who are good enough to be indignant and are clever enough to be complacent. You often fritter away your energy in finding fault with people who are undoubtedly evil, in blaming it on the social system which is not the best of all systems. Finding others' faults may be good for gossip, but it cannot be a proof of, or a recipe for, your own goodness. Anger, virulence, indignation, and obsession to find skeletons in other's cupboards and the Devil smiling in the whited sepulchres all about them can be roads to hell. The enemy of the good is the greatest tempter. Good and clever people like you will not be tempted by money, sex or power. The Devil perhaps knows it. So he applies different inducements. You become evil by wasting all your energy by flouting evil. You have little energy or time left to cultivate your native virtues. Believe me, Debasis, I've made friends with many worthy people who are morally unimpeachable and admirably endowed. But as soon as they open their mouth, they come down heavily on personal, institutional, social and abstract manifestations of evil, they go on vituperating, slamming, hitting, rapping, fulminating against these evils until their tongues ache and their listeners are reduced into zombies. I do admit I also did the same thing for a long time. As a public speaker, I had nothing else to speak, but the evils besetting this country, this world. Now I realize, I was only wasting my energy, my time. I took such a long time to see through to tricks of the great tempter."

Anjan da took a pause. I kept on looking at him. Then he resumed in a changed, more relaxed tone of voice :

"You did a great favour to me by visiting me. I shall not ask you to visit me again, because in that case I'll be always, expecting you. That's not good for concentration. You may come when you feel like. You had thought me dead for two years. Let that feeling continue. May your small family be a shrine of peace! That's my blessing."

He took me round the area which I found more interesting and wonderful than Andy's description of it : a place between the earth and the heaven. I asked him how he chanced upon that piece of paradise. He first visited that spot, he told me, when he was a student in the college; he came with his parents. There were some boys of his age. They climbed up to the middle of the mountain when they sighted five of six badgers in a group, took fright and decided to return. But he was determined to climb to the top. He climbed alone, surveyed the landscape at his leisure, and returned to his parents bruised, bleeding and exhausted. He visited the spot twice, alone. A longing to return to that spot was growing in him.

"You should meet the old priest of the temple. They call him Guruji. He is about hundred years old, still going strong. He has been living there for the last fifty years. He rarely talks, spends the entire day in deep meditation." He informed me casually.

That was useless information for a practical man of the world. I was not sure if I'd ever meet that old priest, and even if I'd meet him I knew it won't make any difference. Anjan da took me to the source of the stream. We sat near the shallow pool of clear water fed by the natural spring, allowing the excess water to flow downwards. He fixed his gaze on the bubbles which surfaced in clusters, sailed a distance and then burst and vanished without a trace, making space for the new ones springing up intermittently. There was a fixed rhythm in their formation and cyclical movements, a system in their randomness. A mentality was taking shape in both of us, silently. Our thoughts were synchronized, refracted on the glassy pool and transmitted into each other's mind. I remembered the world I had just left behind me, for a few hours. I became aware of a changed reality, a new world of manifold possibilities. The cool mountain breeze coming from the vast skies blew over us. Some invisible birds chirped. Anjan da filled the space by reciting a short prayer in Sanskrit : Let noble thoughts come to us from every side.

The boy came with food. "Let's go soon," he told me politely. "The eastern side of the mountain becomes dark even when it is still day." I looked into the stream once again, then at Anjan da's calm face.

"Tell me when we'll meet again? You didn't ask me to come here again. That means we'll never meet." I was feeling a pang, an unspeakable agony for losing my friend once for all.

Anjan da walked up to me, touched me tenderly and said : "I thought the stream must have told you that. Didn't it tell you? Yes, it told you, but you couldn't catch its message."

I looked foolishly on without speaking.

He asked me to eat some fruit. I ate an apple and drank water from the stream and stood before him to bid farewell.

"My blessings for you, for your wife, for your son. We'll meet again, but I cannot tell you when. All is in His will."

38

THE WOMAN AND THE ANCHORITE

A fortnight has passed. My mind was still-befuddled by my unusual experiences. I was not able to arrange my thoughts. What exactly he meant when he referred to the stream's message? Puja interpreted it for me in her pragmatic style.

"All rivers, streams, big and small," she explained, "originate in the mountains. But do they remain confined to their sources only? They flow down, render themselves useful to plants, animals and men, and finally merge in the sea."

"That means, he'll come to us," I said.

"That of course is my reading of the hint," she said candidly. And added : "For God's sake, don't bring in this topic again. It's too much morbid, gloomy, stern and grating. It'll kill my appetite for life. My physical needs and mental needs will wither away. I'll become a slab of ice. You will become a slab of ice, too. Like the damask roses on a corpse, we'll be drenched with tears of sadness, we'll be singed by the sighs of the mourners. We'll become anorexic."

"But what do you think, Puja," I grilled her; "Isn't he great? Isn't his struggle for perfection, for realization of truth admirable, a one in a billion sort of act? Are we not bogged down to a set pattern of living? He told me he assumed a different, a higher role just for a change. What makes you think that he leads a morbid, cheerless life? It has a challenge, a thrill which our routine life cannot offer. Had you gone with me, you might have formed a different opinion of him, of his mission, of the idyllic place."

Puja laughed merrily, resonantly, sensuously. We were sitting on a cement bench in the remote north-west corner of a park, facing a tall thick fence. There was no one around. She stood up with a sudden jerk, stretched her hands gracefully as a swan stretches its wings, holding the tips of her saree in her fingers. She looked like a picture, or like a statue, of God's angel or a queen of the fairies; she could be taken for a model in a fashion show promoting sarees. She loosened her hair, and laughed merrily again.

"What does all this signify?" I was truly confused. "Others may see you. Gone crazy or what?"

"It means," she said with a humorous nasal twang, "I do not subscribe to your ascetic friend's ideas. They appear incomprehensible and sunless to me. I am a humble woman. I love life, that's all. I croon a merry tune when I cook in the kitchen, I meet my jolly friends on Saturdays and sometimes on Sundays, laugh as loudly as I can at their practical bawdy jokes, take an active part in gossiping, try to appear attractive, trip the Light Fantastic, find great pleasure in quarrels and sulks and even love-making, haggle over vegetables and sarees, and, when I get leisure read any book I catch hold of. I love spices, in curry, in life. When I am unhappy, I pray to God, request Him to redress my misery and give me all good things of life; and when happy and comfortable, I don't bother Him with my supplications or applications. The Big Boss has a right to privacy, hasn't He? My recipe is simple : be happy without making others unhappy. Rest is shit."

She spoke all these things posing like an angel. Her fair complexion, her loose flowing hair and white saree made her look like a good angel. Had she put on a colourful mantle, she might have conjured up in my mind the image of a temptress. Her unrealistic posture silhouetted against the setting sun, her hair lifted softly by the strong evening breeze, and the joyous messages which her words unmistakably conveyed — transformed Puja into an adequate adversary of Anjan da. Her uncompromising attitude to my holy friend's way of life could only be matched by his total disregard for the diluted form of hedonism which my wife championed, practised and hawked about. Poor me! I felt helpless and indecisive, tugged at the head-side by sublime renunciation while having my feet of clay firmly entrenched in the simple pleasures of the world, in the simple things of life.